K. J. DAWSON

Nylann'or
Northern Channel
TRINTH
Unaria
Carrus
Neidrei
Beggarton
Easthill
To Aggord
Blackmore
Shoals End
Ironport
Heikton
The Haunted Sea
Yllalen'al

CHARACTER LIST

Ivala "Ivy" Balrel: House of Seeds, daughter of Ialant
Lord Orion Arya: Captain of the Unarian Night Guard and Portal Keeper of the Realms
Kolvar Phiro: House of Tides, son of Councilor Phiro
Nym Phiro: House of Tides, daughter of Councilor Phiro
Lial Darcassan: House of Tides, son of Omasys
Magdud "Maggie": orc warrior residing in Carrus
Rokgut: High Commander, leader of the orc armies
Zelbim "Zel": gnome, Gathering trees scientist
Agretha: Magdud's most trusted servant
Gneiss Feldspar: House of Minerals, sister to Brecc
Wirenth Olaxisys: House of Seeds ambassador
Omasys Darcassan: the right hand of the Tides Councilors
Daecyne Obsin: House of Tides, treasury advisor
Bellas Sylceran: House of Tides, law advisor
Keyyarus Neap: House of Tides, horticulture advisor
Lyra Liamoira: House of Tides, historical advisor
Ash: a Lenonius Draco

The Elven Council:

Ialant Balrel: House of Seeds Councilor
Emmyth Phiro: House of Tides Councilor
Mormaris Roble: House of Tides Councilor
Lonsdaleite Meorise: House of Minerals Councilor
Lazuli Carfina: House of Minerals Councilor

Fae Realm Royals:

King Eldrin Cor'arya: Winter Court Ruler
Princess Selleth Zrin'arya: Winter Court
Prince Rime Zrin'arya: Winter Court
Queen Elowyn Seral'Az: Summer Court Ruler
Prince Devain Seral'Rey: Summer Court

Alysatraee, the Mother of Magic: deity creator of both realms and all creatures

I

BITTER TOWER

Ivy shifted in the Winter guard's arms, as he carried her down a drafty corridor in some dark corner of the Winter citadel. Blood slicked her back and pain bloomed with her "protector" guard's every step. The seed sat in her belly, but instead of a glorious recovery, only a dull warmth stirred.

"Where are you taking me?" Ivy rasped, attempting to distract herself. She'd overheard Rithmat mention "The Tower." And from the guard's tense reaction, it wasn't a soft recovery room full of flowers and honey.

The guard ignored her as he carried her up a circular stairwell. Great. He was as useless with giving information as he was as a protector.

She'd always been warned that consuming a seed in the fae realm was futile, but she swallowed it anyway. Why not take a chance when the alternative meant dying in some unknown corner of the fae realm with the seed in her palm? Even so, between her wasted seed and Emmyth's trouncing, she wanted to scream in frustration. But her lungs burned, and the stab wound shot lines of fire through her back.

Rithmat marched ahead of them, silent and quick. With

every step, Ivy's worry increased as she waited in a vain hope for the seed to spark to life. To fill her veins with energy. Or simply to enable her to take a single, deep breath.

Instead she struggled, throbbing pain her enduring companion.

Ahead, another Winter guard with short black hair and beady eyes stood as if awaiting their arrival; with a hand signal from Rithmat, he joined their procession. From the extra ornamentation on his uniform, Ivy guessed he was of some special importance. Could this evening get any better?

"A simple exchange of power, indeed," Ivy muttered sarcastically. She'd been a fool. Who was she to believe that she could unveil the truth of the Elven Council's lies? Not even her father, a councilor, was able to stop the deadly plans; and the powerful fae courts were complicit in reigniting the war, meaning the fair folk leaders were more corrupt than the Seed Seekers.

The stairs abruptly ended at a doorway, and the beady-eyed guard pressed something small against the center of the thick, carved wooden door. The entry transformed into swirls of shadow, then a burst of snow-like dust before falling away. The guard must've held some kind of key, meaning he was the trusted gaoler or dungeon master. When he pulled his hand away, Ivy spotted a faintly glowing marble in his fingers before he slid the object away, out of sight.

"Welcome to The Tower," her guard said quietly as he trailed Rithmat through the doorway. A gust of bitter wind ripped away what was left of Ivy's breath. She realized, too late, that her cloak still hung in the infirmary.

The cell inside—if one could call it that—was open-air and akin to a towering cliff. It might have once been a spired keep, but most of the stones had crumbled long ago. A scant portion of curved wall stood intact, nearly camouflaged against the inky night sky beyond. Without a ceiling, three columns, in varying degrees of disrepair, each held up nothing but a pile of snow. The only light radiated from four orbs bobbing in the center of The Tower, casting an eerie blue glow. Near them, two posts each held a thick, dangling chain.

As much as the sight horrified her, the waiting visitor sent a shock of dread through her entire being, leaving Ivy sick and paralyzed with fear.

The guards bowed, and one spoke, "Princess Selleth, we didn't expect you."

"I wish to question the elf." Selleth stood as a shining marble sentinel, beautiful and deadly in her lace and ice dress, utterly at home in the frigid, desolate perch. Somehow the air darkened around her, and all Ivy could see was the bright princess like a harbinger of terror.

Instinct took over, and Ivy pushed away from the guard, intending to run. But the moment her feet touched the ground, pain radiated up her right leg. Both guards grabbed under her arms, restraining her. If they hadn't seized her, Ivy wasn't sure she could have remained upright, let alone fled. With the immediacy of the earlier fight over, her body was registering every stinging wound beyond the stab wound in her back. Ivy sucked in a harsh breath at the bitter reminders that she'd wasted Brecc's seed.

The guards dragged Ivy toward the princess. She glanced back at Rithmat, near the door, long enough to see his sneer. Shifting her attention ahead again, Ivy noticed something metallic behind Selleth. The orbs lit the edges of a circular metal disk, embedded in the center of the ramshackle cell, large enough for several fae to stand on.

The guards marched Ivy past Selleth, and dread crawled up her spine as they dragged their prisoner onto the metallic disk. Selleth pivoted, but not even the tip of her shoe touched the metal. Ivy's racing heart drove away any whisper of denial about her situation; she was injured, outnumbered, and without a weapon or ally.

A surge of anger sparked inside her, hot and fierce. How had it come to this? The unfairness of her captivity stoked her fury into a flame. Every lie, every betrayal, every moment of blind helplessness fueled her rage.

The gaoler with beady eyes slid on heavy, leather gloves. He grabbed the iron chains while the other tightened his grip on Ivy, stopping her from wriggling away, even if she could have put weight on her right leg or get a decent breath of air. Her fingers tightened around the healing stone still in her hand, the only thing tethering her mind to reality. The guard brought forward an iron manacle and thunked it into place around Ivy's wrist, followed quickly by the other. She pulled her arms inward, intending to wrap them around herself and retain a bit of warmth, but the heavy chains dragged and jerked to a stop, locking into place. She couldn't bring her arms in to her chest. Nor could she drop them at her sides. Instead, her arms were spread, further exposing her torso to the wind. She glared at the guards, Rithmat, and at Selleth, who stood haughtily aside, and Ivy's mind raced with bitter, hollow thoughts of revenge.

"Level three," Selleth said to the guards.

The useless "protector" who'd carried Ivy had an almost imperceptible twitch in his cheek. He stepped back, off the disk, allowing the gaoler to use the marble-key object again. This time, he touched one of the large glowing orbs, and a glass-like ping reverberated through Ivy's body, her joints already aching with cold. Deep in the sphere, streaks of lightning sparked.

The gaoler continued, touching the marble to two more orbs, performing the simple action with reverence. Ivy's "protector" dropped his gaze to the stones at his feet, confirming what Ivy already suspected—he wasn't waiting for the right moment to help her. She was on her own.

"Leave us," Selleth demanded.

The beady-eyed guard with the small orb gave Ivy an almost pitiful glance before they both gave curt bows to Selleth. The glowing orbs started a graceful descent. When each orb dropped, kissing the edge of the metal disk, their light dimmed.

The world around Ivy grew fuzzy, darker, and quiet. Cotton had been stuffed in her ears and a veil dropped over her eyes, blurring everything beyond the tower. The flames of distant bonfires became indistinct orange fireballs. The individual stones in the partial wall became a smear of grey. The insidious spheres did not seem to cause pain, but instead felt like a heavy blanket *inside,* weighing her down, dampening her magic. The rage inside her also abated, fighting the rising fear.

Selleth spoke to the guards, her words muffled. Was she holding out her hand to them, wanting something? Ivy blinked, desperate for her vision to clear. The "protector" guard opened the door. His face turned toward Ivy before disappearing beyond, but his expression was impossible to see. What was happening?

Selleth raised her voice, flicking her wrist to wave off the king's adviser, "You, too, Rithmat."

Ivy couldn't discern his reaction, either. She couldn't tell if his gait was slightly irritated or light as he disappeared through the door. Ivy shook her head, trying to shake off the suffocating magic.

"What is your intention with Orion?" Selleth asked, cocking her head at Ivy.

Ivy's mind rung with warnings. Ivy wanted to avoid the princess's ire, but she also couldn't reveal secrets about Orion, either. She had to tread carefully. Selleth had already witnessed Ivy's confession of the elven misdeeds at the equinox ceremony. The princess also knew Ivy was a guest of Orion's and that he intended to return her to Trinth soon. So, why was Selleth bothering to question an unimportant elven guest? Swallowing, Ivy schooled her bubbling emotions and concentrated.

"What is this place?" Ivy posed a different question, avoiding any discussion of Orion. It wasn't a stretch to feign confusion. Was Selleth behind this imprisonment? What did the princess have to gain?

More importantly, what did Selleth want? Ivy was desperate for the answer. Otherwise, any response, even the wrong look, could inadvertently anger or alarm Selleth. Ivy didn't want to comply with whatever Selleth was planning, but the princess wasn't above torture. Already, Ivy's body felt brittle, down to the marrow in her bones. These orbs were sapping her strength, and quickly.

Selleth raised a brow. Ivy would have to attempt to *give* information if she expected anything in return.

"My intention was to finish my father's task," Ivy's teeth chattered. Normally, she could handle the cold. But between her injuries and whatever these magical-draining devices were, her legs wavered beneath her, threatening to buckle, and a dizziness clouded her vision even further. Her energy seeped out, as if the very essence of her being was leaking away, leaving her hollow and weak. The overwhelming fatigue weighed down her limbs; every movement required arduous effort. "Teaming up with Orion was the quickest solution."

Selleth studied her prey, every moment an agony. Finally, she gestured around her, answering Ivy's question. "This ancient cell is one of the few relics remaining from the original citadel, constructed after the fae were born of the Mother's tree. The four columns represent the powerful creatures affiliated with the winter lands."

Ivy squinted into the darkness, searching for where the fourth column had once stood. A futile effort. Her blurred vision and muffled hearing frightened her almost as much as Selleth's presence.

"You wielded an iron-tipped arrow at a sacred fae ceremony," Selleth said. "A decision beyond idiotic. I had assumed Orion had invited someone of intelligence to the realm."

"I protected your family from an attack," Ivy said, irritation flaring. "I'm trained to fight. My instincts have saved my life many times. They may have saved your brother."

Ivy wasn't sure she'd had the luxury of *not* fighting back. The Summer prince hadn't signaled for his guards to stop the warrior fae until *well* after Ivy had intervened. Devain's response was diplomacy. Words. While Ivy's windpipe was being crushed.

Cold night air gusted past, and Ivy sucked in a breath, the moisture in her nostrils freezing.

"What d-do you want?" Ivy's jaw chattered, and her left leg wobbled, struggling to hold the bulk of her weight. Her body was betraying her, failing her in her moment of dire need, and the cold grip of fear began to take hold once more.

Selleth said nothing, her gaze narrow, as if trying to read Ivy's mind.

Ivy's legs collapsed, and she slammed onto her knees; her arms stretched, threatening to pop her shoulder joints. The chains kept Ivy's torso upright at a painful cost. Even an injured elf without a seed or cloak shouldn't weaken this quickly. What was wrong with her? She shifted, trying to evaluate her pained leg, but she could barely move. At this rate, she wouldn't last the night.

She wouldn't last an hour.

The realization came slowly. Selleth didn't care if Ivy ever saw another dawn.

Ivy's mind spun with regrets. In recent years, she'd rarely had time to think. But in this lopsided fight, time seemed to slow and her odd thoughts acted like a massive shovel, digging up the truest revelations of her heart. And the whisperings of her deepest wishes all boiled down to this: she hadn't been *living*. Not for a long time. Not until Orion began hunting her, and she had been forced to learn hard lessons from Brecc.

Then the unexpected had happened. Orion had saved her life the first day they actually met, then he helped her find answers about her family. He even tried to help her correct the Council's wrongdoings. He'd stayed with her long after he could've returned home.

She might've gotten a chance at a real life, days filled with joy and fulfillment. Except she made a terrible mistake. She reported to two fae courts that she'd been taught were honorable. Yet, the Summer and Winter rulers were complicit in the very elven corruption she'd come to unmask. She'd arrived in good faith to report on her own father's mistakes and instead of a reward, she was chained and dying in the fair realm. Hot tears burned her eyes, momentarily washing away her fear and leaving nothing but fury behind. Indignation coursed through her veins; her pulse quickened and her vision narrowed. Her hands clenched into fists, nails digging into her palms. The metal chains clanked as her muscles flexed with the urge to lash out, unable to release the pent-up wrath.

What was all of this for? A chance to stop the war? How was that possible when the entire Elven Council must be united and propose peace when approaching the fae courts? Only a united Council could force the hand of the courts. Who could orchestrate such a feat when the most powerful elves were corrupt?

The rage burned out of her, and Ivy slumped, pulling against the chains. Her vision dropped to the disk under her— the iron disk. Something about this prison revolted her. Weakened her. But, iron didn't bother elves as it affected other creatures tied to the fair realm, so was it infused with another magic? She swung her attention to the orbs; they had to be connected to whatever was siphoning away her strength.

"I expected more from a Balrel," Selleth said.

"You knew my f-father?" Ivy rasped, stunned she knew any creatures in Trinth.

"I met him," Selleth said. "He was quite the negotiator. We each had something the other wanted."

Ivy's mind slowly turned, analyzing Selleth's hints. Her stomach twisted as the realization hit. "He wanted a g-glamour of Emmyth Philo. But what did you gain?"

Ivy sickened, picturing her father groveling, desperately appealing to a Winter royal.

"A risky alliance," Selleth said, though her proud tone hinted that she'd bargained for something more. "But one day I'll be queen, and it's of benefit to have loyal elven councilors on my side."

"If b-blackmail c-counts as loyalty," Ivy's accusation was barely a whisper, but Selleth's grin warped into a sinister smile.

Oh, Father, of all the Winter fae to align with, you chose Selleth? The princess of plotting?

Ialant warned her to never bargain with fae. Yet he'd not taken his own advice. Then again, what choice did he have? Sometimes desperate creatures made deals where everyone loses, only because they didn't want their opponent to win.

Ivy's strength was ebbing, replaced by a cold, creeping exhaustion. With each breath, air dragged through an unseen sieve in her chest, her collapsed lung emitting sharp, stabbing pains. The stab wound in her back throbbed with each heartbeat, a relentless reminder of her fragility. Her hands, once clenched in defiance, now trembled uncontrollably. The king who'd sworn his protection was evidently retired for the evening, and Orion was securing the Spring fae. The one creature who held Ivy's fate in her clawed hand stood three steps away.

"I can arrange for you to survive the night." A cloak suddenly appeared on Selleth's outstretched arm. "I can make sure you get back to the human realm—not unharmed, but intact."

"W-what—" Ivy's chattering jaw barely cooperated.

"What do I want in return?" Selleth correctly guessed at Ivy's stuttered question. "Your cooperation. I'm about to trade your life for something greater."

Orion.

Selleth smirked, and Ivy realized she'd uttered his name aloud.

Ivy squeezed her eyes shut. "W-wait."

Ivy's foggy head swam with a fog of despair, her earlier fury dissipating into a stark realization of her vulnerability. Though she could barely think, her mind repeated over and over, *Your life is tied to Orion's. Careful. Careful.*

Ivy needed to survive, or else Orion's magic would die along with her. But she also couldn't let Selleth claim Orion's loyalty; it would destroy his relationship with Rime, the only family member Orion cared for.

"A f-future queen has need of p-powerful allies." Ivy's tongue felt too big for her mouth as she repeated Selleth's own words.

Selleth paused, pursing her lips. As immature as Rime was, he was Orion's best ally in this wretched court.

"Yes?" Selleth impatiently prompted.

Ivy forced her mouth to form words. "I can speak on ... on your b-behalf. A-as you said, I'm a Balrel."

"Your family name is now synonymous with treachery," Selleth countered. "No elf will listen to you. But, Orion will. If you tell Orion that the right choice is to align with me, I'll spare your life."

Ivy pressed her lips together, her mind sluggish. What would Selleth want more than Orion?

Selleth held out a bundled cloth. She unwrapped it, and a metal object reflected the blue light of the orbs: Ialant's knife.

Ivy growled, loathing that Selleth's hands defiled the weapon with her glance, let alone her touch.

"Oh, you'd like this trinket?" Selleth smiled. "Orion is a fool, trusting a guard to put it into your bag." She stepped closer. "I'll give it to you at no cost—a token of my future appreciation once I have Orion's support." She wrapped up the slender dagger again, hiding the blade from sight.

The door to the cell flew open, and Rime marched in. "Why am I not surprised to see you here, sister."

A glimmer of hope dared spark despite her desperate situation. Ivy was supposedly under the protection of the king, and Rime was the least likely of all his siblings to appear disobedient. He might even demand Ivy's return to the infirmary.

The cloak on Selleth's arm disappeared, along with the knife. She gave Ivy one last meaningful look before speaking to her brother. "I won't be here for long."

"You're using three orbs?" Rime rolled his eyes. "The elf is a bit feisty, but honestly, you think she has the strength of a giant? Or do you think she's as powerful as a fae?"

Selleth ignored him and sauntered toward the door, glancing back at Ivy. "Apparently, you desire a deadly path."

"I've sent a guard with my request to move the Spring warrior's trial to the top of the docket." Rime didn't look back at Ivy before he followed his sister to the door, undoubtedly aiming to harass her the entire way down the stairs.

Were they actually planning to leave her in this state?

I'm sorry, Orion, Ivy willed him to understand what she was about to do.

"I know how to m-make Orion and Rime b-both look w-weak," Ivy shouted, though it came out as more of rough whisper.

Obviously, Rime didn't have the determination to claw after the crown. His disposition wasn't a secret, but perhaps Selleth hadn't considered an alternative consequence of her brother's loss.

Selleth paused, and Ivy wished she could tell if the princess was eager or annoyed. Or worse: bored.

"I'm listening," she said.

"Well, that's a nice way to show your gratitude," Rime folded his arms. "I should've commanded the tailor to dress you in last *season's* fashion."

"Would you like the cloak or the knife?" Selleth asked, broadcasting the fact that Ivy was selling Rime's destruction for a pittance. The princess held out each hand, holding the bundled knife and the cloak.

"D-do you hate Rime enough to r-risk elevating Orion in the eyes of the c-court?" Ivy took a shallow breath. She dimly registered that she should worry that Rime was listening to her every insulting word. Then again, he wasn't helping her. So, Ivy focused on the one thing that could save her and Orion: escape.

"I'm right here. Hello!" Rime threw up his hands before storming out, his voice carrying. "I don't know why I bother with such ungra—" the door slammed shut, cutting off the rest of his frustrated response.

The fact that Rime had physically pulled the door to leave, rather than employing one of the marble-keys to fade it away, meant that Rime didn't have one; he didn't have the ability to remove her manacles. If neither Selleth nor Rime were given a key, Orion wouldn't have one, either. Besides the dungeon master, the king certainly possessed one. But Eldrin rescuing her was as likely to happen as the moon was to fall from orbit.

"Why do I sense you don't want your knife, nor your cloak for what you're about to suggest," Selleth said, her voice menacing as she neared.

Ivy focused on the one creature who had the ability to free her.

"I'm asking f-for something small, in exchange for s-something so great that it d-didn't cross your mind as a p-possibility," Ivy stuttered and stumbled through her words.

This close, Ivy didn't miss the flicker of eagerness that crossed Selleth's face, so startling that Ivy nearly lost her nerve. She swallowed, her mouth dry and her body numb.

"With Ialant g-gone, you need a new ally in the h-human realm," Ivy said.

"Go on."

"I'll d-deliver you another elf." Ivy dug her knees into the disk and forced herself to sit-up taller, though her heart throbbed in warning. "Me."

2

CENTAUR HEALING

Orion's heart stopped as he stepped into the infirmary. A blood-soaked bed sat on the far side of the room. And it was empty.

Servants dunked sponges into a bucket of tainted water and scrubbed the floor. Orion scanned the room, checking the other beds for Ivy. But the only creatures were the servants and healers. No injured.

A centaur healer clopped over, her eyes widening. "Lord Orion, come sit down. Let us inspect your injuries."

Before she could touch his bloodied temple, he blocked her hand. "I'm fine. Where's Ivy?"

"Who?" the centaur asked.

A gnome scurried forward. "The elf."

"Oh, unfortunate situation," the centaur said, simply, "Rithmat had her moved."

"She's alive, yes?" Orion clarified.

The centaur have a hesitant nod. "Yes."

"Moved? Where?" Orion demanded.

She gestured to a stool, directing Orion. "Sit, and I'll give you information."

The healers jerked the tray that rested next to the bloodied bed over to him, and Orion noticed the elixirs had been prepared, but not administered. Before he could ask questions, the centaur held his head firmly in her hands. His skull exploded with pain. Abruptly, his knees buckled, and he collapsed onto the stool. Orion had always hated healers. Yes, the method was quick, but the cost was great. He'd stopped Alion from chasing after Ivy at the Aequus, but the warrior fought hard. The Spring attending had not only landed a kick or two, Alion had grazed his spiked club across the back of Orion's head.

A headache thundered at the injured site, thanks to the healing magic, and Orion wondered if this time a blood vessel would burst. A mortifying way to die.

The centaur said something, but the words were lost in the vibrations of pain. Boiling heat lashed above and behind his ear and radiated through every nerve, all the way down his back and through his feathers as if burning them away. His mind curled back, hiding away, as he repeated the mantra, *this will end. This will end.*

The gnome spoke, his words rattling around in Orion's mind.

"My magic will help her," the gnome said.

"What magic?" the centaur pushed up her glasses. "What did—"

"But you healed Ivy, didn't you?" Orion interjected. He'd given her the seed, but he knew it wouldn't work in the fair realm. His panic rose, making his headache bloom all the greater.

"Selleth's gone too far this time," Rime shouted from behind him.

Orion blinked, seeing double. Who needed two Rimes? No one. Certainly not right now.

"Ivy's missing," Orion croaked.

"She's not missing. Selleth has her," Rime said.

"What? Where?" Orion jumped to his feet and his vision immediately blurred. The centaur grabbed his arm, steadying him.

"You must rest," she warned.

"Take me to her," Orion said to his brother.

"Fine, but I don't trust her." Rime shrugged before turning and leading the way.

Orion threw off the centaur's hand from his shoulder and followed Rime out of the infirmary. He braced his hand along the wall as his dizziness fell away. The centaur had been aggressive in her healing, which he would probably appreciate later. But at that moment, his head throbbed with every heartbeat.

Rime circumvented the main rooms, chased only by echoes of celebrating revelers. The ball seemed like another lifetime ago. His vulnerability in the atrium and the echo of her kiss felt too far away. He longed to see her again, though they'd only been apart two hours.

A lot could go wrong in a couple of hours.

As they continued down a narrow corridor, Orion realized where they were going.

"Why are we headed toward the dungeons?" Orion grabbed Rime by the arm.

Rime checked over his shoulder. "You wish we were going to the dungeons."

"What do you mean?" Orion's insides turned to water.

"I mean, Ivy's in The Tower."

"That's not poss—" he couldn't finish the statement. With horror, he recognized the truth—Selleth could make the improbable, possible.

"This is Prince Devain's doing," Rime whispered. "I heard him speak to our sister before he left. Something about him 'looking into the matter.' The innocent Summer prince-twit never dreamed that Selleth would hold Ivy in The Tower—he seriously lacks imagination. Yes, our sister is bending the law. Of course she is. Everyone knows Ivy's family is dead, and the House of Seeds is scattered with no leader. So, if the worst should happen ..."

If Ivy doesn't survive, what elf will question her death?

The corridor seemed to spin, but Orion managed to stumble toward a small repair armory—the room with nearest window access. "I shouldn't have let her out of my sight."

"Don't do anything rash," Rime hissed, as Orion shoved the door open. The scents of linseed oil, tallow and sweat assaulted Orion, making his headache spike. Rime shouted at the servants inside the room. "Out. Get out. All of you!"

The servants jerked into action. A spear clattered to the floor, the jar of polish and a cloth teetering on the edge of the repair table. But no one retrieved it, opting to flee instead. Orion stumbled past them, wishing the room would still. Rime slammed the door shut just as Orion reached the window and punched through the clear ice-pane. The magic sensed his royal blood and shattered like glass. For other creatures, it would take a lot more than a fist to break it.

"I hope you got your frustration out," Rime mocked. "That's usually my move. I can't believe I'm saying this, but we need an actual plan. Ivy is locked to the post, so we need a key."

"We'll just break her from the posts."

Rime scoffed. "You might know more about Trinth than I do, but I know the dark corners of the palace. There are a few things Father never taught you. Those posts? They're ancient magic. Neither the posts nor the chains can be removed or broken."

"Fine. If you want to help, meet me on The Tower. Don't move against Selleth until I give the signal," Orion said. "As far as a key, because no one knows the extent of your magic, I vote *you* retrieve it."

"Are you joking? That's your plan? There's one big pr—" Rime's words were lost to the wind as Orion launched into the night.

3

SHADOWS AND ICE

"Problem ..." The rest of the words dried on Rime's tongue.

The prince stormed back through the castle, ignoring the guards when they jerked their backs straighter as he passed. Their expressions seemed a cross between concern and surprise, likely because they were unaccustomed to seeing Rime skulk near the dungeons, let alone do anything with such furious determination.

The prince fumed. The request from the Summer Prince Devain-Fluff-Brains was nothing if not predictable. Naive. Whatever he had requested opened the door to the elf's demise. Rime had known Ivy could be a problem, which is why he'd tried to dump her back in Trinth. But here she was, causing Orion to make rash decisions. Rime's one potential ally would finally reside in Winter, and now everything could fall apart.

At the Aequus, Selleth had the audacity to act as if she were doing Devain a great favor. In reality, she knew Devain had given her a loophole. The fact that she'd sent away all witnesses from The Tower meant she was in a grey area of the law, which didn't bode well for Ivy. Though, perhaps that was Selleth's mistake. If she were caught and sentenced by the court ... Rime grew giddy at the thought of his sister's potential humiliation.

But would Selleth sully her reputation over an elf? Rime bit his lip, concern growing over the princess's risks. What could the princess hope to gain?

Was she leveraging Ivy to get under Orion's skin? Or did she have something more devious in mind? Something Rime hadn't considered?

Rime slowed, an idea occurring to him. Did she care if the elf were killed? She'd allowed the Spring attendings, the prince's honorary companions, to pummel the visitor. And she'd blocked the elf's healing, too. Was Ivy a potential threat?

He neared a cross-corridor that led back toward the royal quarters. If he woke his father to alert him to Selleth's questionable actions, would the king even care? Eldrin would be irritated that his daughter hadn't obeyed his decree to protect the elf. But in the past, when his sister had bent the law, her actions endeared the king to Selleth. He admired her "daring" when she achieved some new level of success. No, Rime would suffer consequences for disturbing his father's rest, especially if Selleth demonstrated that Ivy's abuse earned some new knowledge or leverage.

Rime frowned and stormed past the cross-corridor and away from the royal wing. His father's approval was earned in a specific way—showing you could control situations by any means necessary. Though, Rime had long ago given up on trying to gain his father's approval. He did, however, care about Orion. They didn't share the same mother, but he trusted his half-brother more than anyone else in Winter. Well, he had until recently.

If Orion could shadow travel, it meant he didn't completely

trust Rime. But, even if Rime had trusted his brother too much, Orion was still more straightforward than any other noble. And, most importantly, Orion felt some loyalty to him, and not for selfish, political reasons. Deep down, buried except for in his most sober, reflective moments, part of him couldn't lose his brother.

Orion was one of the few fae who could understand him. When he had been young and training in Trinth, Orion had sought him out. He'd been a friendly face during those years. Everyone else wanted something from him, but not Orion. Orion understood his humor, knew his life, and accepted him. And now that Orion had been officially invited home, Rime finally had someone to watch his back. So, if Orion wanted to protect this elf, Rime would do it.

Rime slowed as he closed the distance to the guard's meeting room. An idea began forming in his mind; if he helped the elf, she'd help him in return. Yes, the elf had turned against him when she spoke to Selleth, but he didn't take it seriously. She was just like any other creature who groveled to Selleth, desperate to save their own skin. Such an unoriginal move. Even so, what if Rime saved her?

A hopeful warmth fluttered inside him as he mulled the possibilities. What if he gained Ivy's trust, perhaps even her loyalty? It was possible, wasn't it? He'd assisted her already, so surely if he asked her, she would be a vocal support for him in the Trials; the tournament for the winter crown was creeping closer.

Ivy's actions had reminded him that elves could fight. Rime needed a champion. He didn't even want to win—he just needed to be competitive enough to look competent. To show Winter folk that he wasn't worthless.

He knew creatures across the realm were already placing

bets on who would be the first loser. He also knew his name had come up. A lot.

His plan began taking shape. Between his contacts in the fair realm and Ivy's contacts in the human realm, he could find someone suitable. A human guard; one with fair blood would be even better. Ivy would help him. She had no reason not to.

Selleth was draining and possibly killing the one creature that might actually aid him. He and Orion could thwart Selleth's plans, but he had to get the key.

Out of sight of the guards, Rime glamoured, assuming Rithmat's appearance. Even if Rithmat or the captain figured out the duplicity later, as long as he outmaneuvered his sister, his father would let the infraction go with a slap on the wrist. If Selleth outmaneuvered him, his father may put *Rime* in The Tower. Or worse, banish him to Trinth.

Nearing the offices, the guards stood as sentinels, alert.

"I need to speak with the gaoler." Rime said, matching Rithmat's voice. "Immediately. On behalf of the king."

One guard jumped and led the way into the office, lending Rime an extra air of authority. Even if the guards didn't know about the elf in The Tower, they definitely knew about the Aequus skirmish.

Inside the office, the gaoler was already on his feet. "Rithmat, what does the king require?"

Of the several guards in the room, Rime recognized two of the guards from the Aequus ceremony. Their lips pressed together, practically wincing, expecting punishment.

"I need the key to The Tower," Rime demanded.

The gaoler paled, "The king did not lend you his?"

"Obviously not. And why would he when you're already here and have the key on your person, as always." Rime sneered just as Rithmat would. Still, the gaoler wasn't a fool, and Winter had plenty of fae who could impersonate the king's adviser, though few dared try. Still, Rime had to control the conversation before the captain did.

"How is your wife faring?" Rime asked in an oily, accusing voice. "I hope she is feeling well."

Few knew that the gaoler's wife hated large parties. Every equinox and solstice, she retreated to her chambers with contrived, overly-creative excuses. The gaoler always opted to work the entire duration of the celebrations, because his wife constantly pestered him while she practically haunted their chambers. Rime couldn't care less about most faes' private business, but when it came to the guards with powerful access, his father had taught him to know their lives inside and out.

The gaoler frowned, not answering but skipping back to the original subject. "I don't have the key."

"It was stolen?" Rime kept an accusatory tone.

"No, it was requested."

By who? The gaoler officially answered only to the captain of the guard and the king. But another fae came to his mind—someone unofficial. Everyone cowered to her, fearing she'd wear the crown one day: Selleth. Rime growled, not hiding his frustration as he stormed from the room.

Selleth controlled the orbs, and she held Ivy's life in her claws. Only two keys existed, and while the princess controlled one, the other belonged to the king. A surge of irritation washed over him. He wouldn't be able to sneak into the royal chambers, nor would the guards give him access. They'd wake the king, and that was the last thing Rime wanted. Besides, his father would take his precious time and stroll to The Tower himself; by then it could be too late.

If he couldn't get the king's key, he had to at least warn Orion. They had to tread carefully or risk Selleth deciding to engage the last orb. All four orbs would bring down even the strongest fair creatures in a matter of hours. For an elf, especially an injured one, it would kill her.

Rime sucked in a breath as he realized that Selleth would expect Orion to storm to Ivy's rescue. That's what Selleth was after all along; Ivy was the trap to capture the princess's true prey, Orion. Changing plans, Rime changed his glamour to one of a page boy and sprinted to the armory.

4

IRON MEDALLION

Orion soared up to the Tower, the cold reining back his raging headache from an inferno to a mere storm. Ash yipped at his heels, announcing her presence. The dragon had responded to Orion's mental distress, as she'd done more and more since they'd met at the Gathering, showing up when needed.

As they flew, Orion cursed his agreement to separate from Ivy in order to deliver Alion and Alyssum to the dungeon. The last exchange with the attendings flashed in his mind.

"We will be celebrated as heroes one day," Alion had said. "And your court's wickedness will be revealed. Your father doesn't care if he sullies the Winter throne. But, he never *really* earned it."

It took all Orion's restraint not to shadow travel into the cell and throttle the pompous fae for his mockery of his parents. It would've been easy. But momentary revenge against an imprisoned, impotent Spring warrior wasn't worth giving away Orion's secret.

A remnant of Ivy's voice floated through the air, whooshing past him like a feather in a storm. Hearing her, Orion flew faster, pulling the shadows around him. Ash moved to his shoulder, hiding herself as well. Between the cloudy night and the dark tower, he'd be nearly invisible. He'd be able to hold the shadow form for an hour if needed, but he figured Selleth wouldn't stay that long. She'd make her threat known and be gone, letting Ivy stew.

"I don't believe you," Selleth's voice sounded over the top of the tower, hard, like a final judgment.

Orion silently slipped over the partial wall, searching desperately for Ivy. Seeing her, his stomach lurched. On her knees, the chains forced her shoulders to take the bulk of her weight. She could barely lift her head, her skin pale and her lips blue. A drop of blood trembled on the edge of her frayed tunic before falling, the agonizing moment stretching out as crimson splattered across the iron below. The sight stole his breath, a cold, nauseating wave of horror crashing over him.

He swallowed hard, trying to quell the rising sickness. The scene before him was far worse than he had feared. Rime hadn't mentioned the three, engaged orbs, their eerie glow sapping Ivy's magic. The realization twisted his horror into helplessness; freeing her would be far more challenging than he had imagined.

The orbs sapped magic, eventually leaving the prisoner helpless.

His hands clenched into fists, the horror morphing into a searing, white-hot anger. How could Selleth do this to her? Why had the guards turned their backs on this atrocity. There had been no trial. No reason for this abuse.

"Even for an elf, you're a capable liar," Selleth sneered.

The urge to rush in, to attack the princess, surged within him, but he forced himself to stay hidden. He couldn't free Ivy with brute strength. He needed a key, which meant he needed

Rime. Of all the times to depend on his brother, of course, it would be right after they'd fought.

Unable to act, Orion stewed, his fury growing hotter with every breath. He crouched, pressing his hand to the frigid stones, reminding himself that, at the very least, Selleth had no way of engaging the fourth orb; she also needed a key. A small mercy. He put the pillar between him and Selleth's line of sight; the last thing he wanted was for her to sense someone watching.

"How can my l-loyalty be to Orion after what I've told you," Ivy said, her brows screwed up with pain or cold, probably both.

Orion's emotions brewed, but he still watched Ivy closely. Was she lying? He couldn't read her with her eyes half-closed and her body language hampered. Or perhaps his own crashing emotions hindered his objectivity. Ash nuzzled his cheek in a futile attempt to calm him.

"Besides," Ivy continued slowly, each word labored, "Orion is a bird, and I'm a s-seed. I feed him, but what can he do for me b-besides tempt me to stay in your realm and d-die an early death?"

Orion tensed, and Ash's claws dug through his formal tunic into the flesh of his shoulder. He winced, but it was nothing compared to the how his heart sunk at her words.

"So, you're willing to swear by your promise?" Selleth purred.

What promise?

Orion itched to attack, to stop whatever bargain was in the making. But he needed the key and the element of surprise. Still, if he waited too long, not even a seed in Trinth could save her. His body grew cold at the thought. Ivy whimpered and shifted her shoulders, obviously looking for relief. He wanted to scream as he stood mere steps away, unable to help.

He had to get her to Trinth, where the seed would work. He could only guess at the extent of Alysatraee's punishment in store for him, but he cared more about Ivy than he feared losing his magic. Part of him was surprised at his feelings, but that thought was smothered by the urgency to get Ivy out of The Tower by any means necessary.

He'd reveal his shadow travel magic without a second thought if it meant saving her. His action would draw Selleth's attention. And possibly her jealousy. Even his father would be in an uproar at Orion's kept secrets. But all potential punishments paled compared to watching Ivy's torture.

Ivy's gaze flicked toward Orion, a glare, practically pinning him in place. Or was he just hoping she noticed him? Between her elven sight siphoned away and his shadows, she couldn't see a trace of him. Could she?

If she did see him, her message was clear: stay put. He would obey for now. But once Rime appeared, Orion would act, even if Ivy begged him to leave her.

"Trust me." Ivy looked right at him, then she took a shaky breath and turned her full focus to Selleth. "Yes, I'm w-willing."

"Your plan has merit," Selleth spoke, almost to herself. "Let Orion and Rime tie their fates together, and their inevitable failure."

"You'll b-become the clear choice, b-beyond the outcome of the c-competition. If Orion s-supports Rime and Rime l-loses, they'll b-both look w-weak."

Orion's mouth went dry. Ivy's plan was genuinely diabolical. Rime had no desire for the crown; with Orion tied to the losing brother, they would both lose influence. Selleth would become the indisputable leader among Eldrin's children. Orion shifted and glanced at Selleth. She was studying her prey, a hand on her chin.

Was Ivy helping Selleth in order to save herself? Did she not trust Orion?

With Orion sitting in the shadows unable to help as the painful medallion drained her magic, he couldn't blame Ivy for striking a bargain. He chewed the inside of his cheek, hating that he had to wait as Ivy had signaled—or what he hoped had been a signal. He knew Selleth wouldn't seal the bargain right away. She never took the first deal offered; the princess always countered to make sure the bargain was heavily weighted in her favor.

Despite Ivy's warning, more drops of blood fell from her tunic and she sagged further, straining her limbs. Every moment felt like an eternity.

"Orion is l-loyal to this c-court." Ivy's voice cracked, her teeth chattering. "He will s-still advise and s-serve the r-ruler to the best of his ability. It's in his n-nature ... look at his w-work for the Unarian d-duke."

"Captain of the Night Guard." Selleth tapped her chin with an object wrapped in cloth. "Always dutiful, even to the lowest creatures—humans."

"D-do you hate Rime enough to r-risk elevating Orion in the eyes of the c-court?" Ivy took a shallow breath, her eyes narrowing. "If Orion sides with you, he'll rise with you, too."

"I'll let my brothers think they're aligning against my will," Selleth said, her tone softening. Ivy didn't know the princess well, but Orion did. His sister was definitely warming to Ivy's plan.

Ivy's gaze dropped to the iron, and she took a slow breath. She was hiding something, and she was calming herself before continuing the negotiation. What was she up to?

Orion stilled, realizing Ivy was manipulating Selleth. Even in Ivy's weakened state, she dangled a prize Selleth couldn't refuse. Orion glanced at the door, hoping to see it fall away to mist, proving he'd gotten the key. If his brother failed … no, Orion couldn't even think about that option.

"What do you ask in return for your loyalty to me?" Selleth asked, a grin twitching at the edge of her lips.

Orion's stomach dropped, his heart thrumming hard. Had Ivy proposed a bargain? In her state, could she process the impact of each word? By using the word "loyalty" Ivy could inadvertently bind herself to Selleth. Whether or not Ivy understood the full implications, she would be honor-bound to do whatever Selleth asked. If Selleth asked Ivy to fetch her a cloak, or follow her around the castle, or poison an enemy, Ivy would have little choice but to do it.

"Orion's freedom," Ivy responded with her request.

"A bargain?" Selleth glanced over her shoulder to check the door.

Ivy gave a shaky nod.

Orion pressed a hand to the pillar, bracing himself. He absolutely could not, would not, allow Ivy to rashly tie herself to the Winter Princess.

Ivy was dangling bait that would seal *all* their fates.

5

SELLETH'S BARGAIN

Even in her dazed state, Ivy recognized Orion's presence—merely a sensation, a flicker next to the pillar behind Selleth. She ached to hold him, but she tore her gaze away, not wanting to give away his location.

When she proposed her bargain, the hint of his shadow shot up into the sky, and Ivy's heart sunk at his abandonment. He was fleeing, understandably hurt at her negotiation with Selleth. Still, his departure stung, leaving a familiar ache of loneliness, and her earlier resolve wavered. The thought of him misconstruing her intentions gnawed inside her, a sharp contrast to the physical pain she endured. She gritted her teeth, determined. She would finish what she'd started. Hopefully, one day he'd understand that she'd done it for him.

She and Orion could never be together, but she could secure him options with his closest ally in the fair realm. Orion had always been isolated and lonely as a child, and she would keep the door open for true kinship with his brother now that he had been welcomed home.

In the air behind Selleth, Orion's figure appeared. He quickly descended, his shadows falling away. He slammed down on the ground, the blurry form of his wings stretched wide. Selleth spun, surprised. Orion ignored her, his attention pointedly on Ivy.

A spark of warmth stirred in her belly, her heart practically bursting at the sight of him. Through the dull thrum of her brain, she sensed a warning. Wasn't she supposed to stop Orion from doing something? But in that moment, all she could do was gaze, stunned, as Orion openly confronted his sister.

"You won't be making any deals with Ivy. Not tonight," Orion said.

"You can do many things, Orion, but not even you can speak on behalf of the elves," Selleth said, coolly.

"You will not manipulate her." Orion moved between Ivy and Selleth.

"What do you plan to do? Hold her upright while you stand on an active medallion?" Selleth scoffed.

Orion tensed, but stepped toward Ivy though he didn't touch the metal.

"Righteous bravado?" Selleth smirked.

"What's h-happening to me?" Ivy whispered.

"The disk and orbs work together to rob fair folk of their gifts from Alysatraee," Orion quickly explained, shifting closer, just outside the medallion. "If chained, a Winter fae would lose their ability to glamour."

"Or do shadow magic," Rime's voice announced his presence before he flew over the crumbling wall.

"Ignore these fools," Selleth said to Ivy. "What is your exact offer, elf?"

Orion's attention was on Rime, whose lips were moving, but Ivy couldn't hear the words. Wait, was he mouthing something to his brother?

"My allegiance and s-support in your b-bid for the throne," Ivy whispered.

Rime stumbled back, and she could only guess his level of offense over a real bargain negotiation. Hopefully he'd figure out she was helping him. Eventually.

Orion spun to Ivy, "No—"

"Mother moons, elf! Why would you, a peacekeeper, support Selleth?" Rime interjected in a pinched voice, his earlier, flippant tone gone. "She's so vile that even pixies obey her."

"All I ask is that you n-never align with Orion," Ivy said.

In front of her, Orion widened his stance, as if expecting a fight, Ash poised on his shoulder. The dragon slightly flared her wings, ready to leap into action. Ivy would rather any other dragon attempt to rescue her. Literally, *any* other dragon.

"Why should I care about your allegiance?" Selleth's lip curled as if offended at the paltry offer. "The Balrel name is ruined, and you're unlikely to gain the seat." Selleth's attention fell to the last orb, then to Orion, scrutinizing.

"It's a r-risk you'll have to take," Ivy said. "Either way, aligning with Orion is the w-weaker choice."

Rime stormed forward, but Orion hissed, "Rime! Focus!"

Rime's lips moved, again, but this time he jabbed his finger toward Selleth, pointing at her.

Ivy blinked, trying to clear her vision. Behind Selleth, Rime was a mere blur of pale skin against black wings, but his arms moved, signaling something to his brother. Orion's attention whipped to Selleth as his knees bent, but Selleth laughed as her dress billowed and disappeared. Flurries of snow flew from where she'd once stood.

Of course, the princess could shadow travel. Ivy crumbled inside, waiting helplessly for Selleth's next move. The world around Ivy seemed to slow, her mind unable to pick up every nuance. The air wavered around Orion. Shadows bled into his skin. He disappeared from view, something Ivy had experienced but never witnessed. Ivy gasped, stunned that he would reveal his gift, but even that emotion was swallowed by a maelstrom of fear.

Ivy felt distant from herself, as if The Tower and her surroundings weren't real. Yet at the same time, a sense of danger barreled through her veins. The royal siblings were like children tugging on two ends of a flower after it had been ripped out of the ground, cut off from what gave it life in the first place.

Selleth reappeared next to the last floating orb. A sickening ping sounded that Ivy already knew too well; the princess activated the last orb. Ivy's breathing quickened, and dread sunk her spirits as a single spark flared in the last orb. Then another, and another as it came to life.

The dragon lifted off Orion's shoulder as he disappeared from sight.

Selleth gasped, her attention lingering on where Orion had once stood. Orion's invisible force shoved Selleth to the stone floor. She cried out, sending a chill through Ivy, as the shadows writhed in a violent dance.

The orb's descent ended, hitting the metal, and cold water poured from Ivy's head down her spine, spiraling from her shoulders to her fingertips. As if she were submerged into an icy river headfirst, her torso tingled with numbness, followed by her thighs and down her calves. Soon she couldn't feel her toes. Hearing Ash's cry, Ivy forced her lids to open.

Sound barely pierced the muted air, and everything was a blur. A small form spiraled upward, and Ivy could only suppose it was Ash. The dark form dove toward the edge of the medallion.

The sound of claws scrapped across the smooth surface of the orb followed by a ferocious roar. Ash spun away, responding as if she'd been burned. Rime snapped a sarcastic remark, but Ivy couldn't make out the words.

A small object dove straight at Ivy, and she shrunk away before recognizing it was Ash again. This time, she pressed her claws to the manacles. The dragon had literally flown into the middle of dangerous magic. A heroic attempt at Ivy's freedom, but futile all the same.

Beyond the dragon, the orb shifted, and Ivy squinted, trying to see what was happening. The sphere lifted from the disc, the soft blue glow returning. Why was the orb disengaging? Ivy heard a *clink,* and she realized Ash held a marble-like object in her claw.

The key. With her remaining strength, Ivy shifted her wrists, revealing the manacle's indentation for the key.

Orion landed on the far side of the disk, reaching for Ivy, his words pinched. "Crawl!"

Selleth had rammed Orion onto the medallion and had pinned him in place. Rime was near Selleth's feet. Was he trying to grab his sister? Ivy couldn't see well enough to know, but until all the orbs were released, the medallion would drain Orion of his powers, too.

"You would rob me?" Selleth shouted, twisting Orion's arm.

"Your shoulder!" Rime warned. Had Selleth maneuvered Orion against the metal? Ivy could only see the awkward positioning of Orion's wings—trapped under his own weight. Ivy's right hand dropped and she slipped sideways as she fumbled, her shoulders aching.

"Ivy's not an object to barter and leverage," Orion shouted, breathing hard. Leaning closer to him, Ivy winced, realizing that Selleth had strategically pinned Orion, making it impossible for him to move without snapping his wing.

Selleth changed her tactic. "Taking the elf to the human realm in her condition could kill her."

The second manacle suddenly released; Ivy fell, smacking her face against the metal. Her mind struggled to figure out why she was on the ground.

Ash grazed past her as she flew toward the second orb, roaring as she dared touch the dim sphere. Ivy dragged herself closer to Orion at the edge of the medallion, her body trembling. She didn't get far, but Selleth's attention shifted to Ivy. Orion jerked out from his sister's grip and off the medallion, his wings glamouring out of sight. In a flash, Selleth held something against Orion's throat.

Instinctively, Ivy guessed it was Ialant's knife. The princess's frighteningly giddy laugh confirmed it.

The dragon moved to the third orb as the second one floated upward. Ivy strained to evaluate the bargain she'd extended. Had Selleth accepted the deal? Ivy struggled to remember the princess's exact words.

No, Selleth hadn't accepted, and Ivy hadn't confirmed. So, the bargain hadn't been struck. Had Selleth figured out Ivy's trick? As long as Ivy kept away from the fae realm, as a good elf should, Selleth would have minimal control over her. Ivy planned to hide away and never return, essentially voiding the bargain's power.

"Rime, be a good little fae and fetch the guards," Selleth demanded.

"Why? I only see a captain of the guard taking the elf into custody for trial." Rime shot back, his cool sarcasm returning.

"What?" Selleth shrieked.

"Well, he is a captain of *someone's* guard," Rime said.

"As if human realm titles mean anything," Selleth screamed. "Wait until Father hears about this."

"Go, Rime. You want no part of this," Orion said.

"Father would not want me to leave my dear sister's side during a fight for all the lands of the fair," Rime said, his voice dripping with drama. "Clearly, she needs me. And, while I'm here, I'll remind Ivy that she could consider aligning with me rather than with the vile witch who rudely imprisoned her. I mean, I'm the clear choice, right?"

Selleth cursed and pivoted her attention back to Ivy. "Of the bargain you propose—"

Orion threw Selleth off him and leapt onto the medallion. His body shuddered as he stumbled before catching himself and scooping up Ivy. The moment she felt his arms around her, a wave of overwhelming relief washed over her, almost as intense as the pain. Ivy curled into him, her body instinctively seeking the comfort and safety he provided. The numbness that had protected her from the worst of her injuries began to retreat, replaced by deep, agonizing pain that tore through her senses. Despite the searing agony and the disorienting blindness, she clung to Orion, pressing her cheek to his chest, focusing on the steady beat of his heart.

Orion gripped Ivy closer and jumped off the iron. He darted for the cliffside edge of the prison tower. The shadows wavered, moving around him, though not as strong as Ivy had witnessed before. Yet he did not slow.

Selleth leapt after Orion. His wings reappeared, extended in preparation to fly. Would he jump?

"I accept your bargain, Ivy Balrel," Selleth shouted as the last orb rose into the air.

Orion vaulted off the open Tower. Behind Selleth, Rime waved his arms, signaling for Ivy to not say a word. Not to accept the deal. Orion's wings caught the updraft.

Selleth hadn't pressed for more advantage—she'd run out of time. Ivy might have smiled if she didn't feel so hollow. She would never get this chance again.

"The bargain is struck!" Ivy called back, her voice nearly

drowned out by Orion's wings and Ash's piercing screech as she flew after them.

Only Selleth's laugh pursued them, the maniacal sound sending a shudder through Ivy's core. "I look forward to our next meeting, elf!"

I won't be returning. But Orion will, and he won't be under your thumb. Ivy closed her eyes, wondering if the bargain would still hold if she died.

Orion clutched her tight, his chest heaving. He kept his anguish to himself, and Ivy was glad for it. She didn't have the energy to explain.

"Do you still have the seed?" he asked.

Ivy couldn't lie to him. She shook her head, not daring to look at him. Returning to the Winter infirmary now would only put them both in danger. So, she needed to get to Trinth. She'd made a mistake in taking the seed. She should've trusted that Orion would find her.

With Selleth blocked from aligning with Orion, he could safely exist in his home. He could, at last, find the respect and the acceptance he'd longed for. But, for Ivy, no place was more dangerous than the Winter Court.

Beyond her oath with Selleth, if she died in the fair realm or if Orion returned her to Trinth in her current state, Alysatraee would know and *his* bargain would be broken. He'd lose his magic as a result. He'd become defenseless prey to the very creatures Ivy had just bargained for Orion to live among.

6

WINGS OF FLIGHT

Orion's wing ached as he flew away from the Winter citadel. Even a full-fae would struggle after having a wing crushed while touching an enacted medallion.

"Hold on," Orion said as they dropped closer to the ground past a group of satyrs dancing around a bonfire. Ash flew overhead, alert for any coming dangers.

Blood dripped down his arm, his forearm throbbing from Selleth's savage bite. He chastised himself for not expecting her to fight dirty, nor did he expect her strength. If the stubborn centaur healer hadn't tended to his wounds, his sister may have outmatched him.

He tightened his grip around Ivy, horrified at how close he'd come to losing her. He landed and bolted under the canopy of trees, striding out of sight of the satyrs and gnomes, then changed direction. Selleth would send guards to hunt them, but Selleth had no authority to send anyone through a portal. So once they crossed into Trinth, the only real danger was his father finding out and sending someone or some*thing* to fetch him.

With her every breath, Ivy winced. He agonized over the best way to carry her, but her comfort would be far worse if they were caught, so he didn't slow.

"Almost there," Orion assured her.

Despite blending in with the night sky, Orion called Ash closer, not wanting her to be spotted above the trees. She landed on his shoulder, and he sent her assuring thoughts, letting her know she had his blessing to remain in the fair realm. She hunkered down tighter into his neck, seemingly determined to stay with him. He was grateful, knowing he'd need help when his magic was stripped.

Ivy struggled to speak, "Orion—"

"Save your strength. We'll talk in Trinth."

What he really wanted to know was *why*? Why would Ivy tie herself to Selleth? Did she hope for Selleth's help in gaining the council seat?

No. He brushed that idea away faster than it had formed. He knew Ivy, and she wasn't prideful. She cared about doing the right thing, not about power.

He might have been able to negotiate a bargain swap when he returned to the Winter Court, trading his name for Ivy's. But Ivy's stipulation blocked him from doing *anything* with Selleth. Frustration stirred inside him, but he pushed his concerns away and jogged to the portal.

Stars still glittered through patches of clouds overhead when Orion leaned against the tree, whispering to the dryad as he clutched Ivy in his arms.

"I need to get to Nylann'or," Orion said to the listening dryad. If Nym had a seed to give Ivy, she would.

"You're hoping for respite for the elf, but Nylann'or is in conflict," her lyrical voice almost belayed the warning.

"What do you mean?"

"That's all I know. If you demand I send you to Nylann'or, I will tell you which two portals lead the way. But be warned, they are loyal to Summer ..."

"So, they may not obey my request, and we won't get to Nylann'or anyway," Orion guessed at her thoughts. *Especially if King Eldrin puts a price on my head.* "If you have a suggested destination, I'll listen to your wisdom. I'm at the mercy of the dryads."

As Orion said his last words, he realized the truth of them. In his time of desperation, he still trusted them. But should he?

The dryad quieted, then her presence vanished. She'd left the portal, leaving Orion alone. Snow clumps fell from the trees, punctuating the strained silence as the stars glinted overhead. Ivy shivered in his arms, and blood slicked his skin and clothing as he clutched her close. His stomach twisted as all his mistakes flooded his mind and guilt threatened to swallow him whole. He tapped his foot, desperate to leave the realm.

He sensed the dryad flicker back, then she was gone, again. Back and forth, flitting between portals. No dryad had ever negotiated passage on his behalf before. He'd never asked. A rush of gratitude filled his chest, followed by a sinking guilt at his long-held desire to cut himself off from them.

With a harried presence, the dryad returned in a rush. "The pathway is set, though difficult."

Orion leapt into the tree, forming a protective barrier for Ivy and Ash. As he vaulted away, he sensed more than heard the dryad's last words. "Mother awaits."

The human realm greeted Orion with darkening, midday skies, the air promising a storm. A deep breath escaped him, tension easing from his body. A weight lifted from his shoulders as Ash darted upward through the branches, stretching her wings. Yet, as Orion took a step forward, exhaustion descended like the swell of the ocean crashing down on his shoulders. His fight with the Spring warriors, the iron medallion, Selleth's attack, and his sprint to the portal seemed to catch up with him all at once.

Still, he paused and whispered his gratitude to the dryads. Then scanning the forest, he quickly recognized the land south of Easthill. Ivy's wounds seeped, but her body was still warm.

"Emmyth," Ivy muttered deliriously, her lashes fluttering.

Orion's heart raced, desperate to help Ivy, desperate to run. But his legs felt unsure, almost foreign beneath him. Instinctively, he called the shadows.

But the darkness didn't respond.

A rising panic seized him, starting as a cold knot in his stomach and spreading like wildfire through his veins. His hands—green, bark-like hands of a dryad—trembled, one splayed across Ivy's shoulder as she stirred. He tried to steady himself, but the ground seemed to tilt beneath him, his mind spinning with the terrifying realization that he was powerless.

Ivy's breathing quickened. Deepened. And her eyes flew open as she gasped. Her body tightened just before she sat up in his arms, her grip strengthening.

"Orion! I can see again. Not perfectly, but better!" She swung down her legs, one hand flying to her belly. "The seed!" One of her arms was still wrapped around his neck, forcing him to lean forward to support her. "We don't have much time. Can you run?"

"Can you?" he asked, baffled. She'd taken the seed in the fair realm, so what explained her sudden improvement?

"A remnant of the seed must still be in my belly. A particle. The healing is weaker, much weaker, but I'm grateful for it." She released him as she planted her feet wide, balancing herself.

A burst of hope wove through him at Ivy's miraculous healing. Would his magic return?

"Which way?" Ivy asked.

Orion explained their location as he stretched his wings, testing them after Selleth's ruthless maneuvers, and a sharp pain protested the movement. The stark reminder of his own magical weakness tamped down his earlier, naive hope. With a crashing admission, he realized the seed's strength would only be temporary. His heart sped, not knowing how long they had until Ivy's energy crashed.

"The sea to the west and the coast to the east." Ivy nodded, oriented.

"Do you have friends who could give you a seed?"

"Not anymore." A flash of pained emotion in her eyes.

"The dryads selected this place for a reason," Orion said, scrambling to make sense of their unknown plan.

Ash darted behind him, keeping pace, their silent companion.

"Let's get away from the portal." Ivy grabbed his hand and pulled him after her. Her first few tentative steps quickly changed into a faster, limping run. Orion pushed through his exhaustion, letting the excitement of Ivy's recovery spur his feet forward.

"Dryads are your kind," Ivy said, her breathing labored. "Who do *you* know in this area?"

"There's a Winter-friendly portal in the nor—"

"No portals," Ivy said, her words sharp. "The Council and the courts are working together."

Orion's slowed to a stop. He didn't even consciously do it. His body just couldn't move and process what Ivy was saying. "What? The court and the Council?"

Ivy grabbed his elbows and squeezed as she looked up at him with a serious tone, grounding him. "Where can we go that the Council nor the courts would suspect? Someplace near this location."

The Elven Council was one thing, but the fae court *had* to follow the law.

Orion shook his head, clearing his thoughts. "The Minerals may not have heard about the Aequus skirmish nor about your involvement with The Tree House."

"We'll have to avoid the orc towers." Ivy took a labored breath, a look of alarm crossing her face. "Actually, I'll never make it to the towers. There must be someplace closer. Someplace the dryads would think to send me."

Mother awaits.

Orion's mind caught hold of a possible meaning: the Queen of the Dryads. No one would ever guess he'd even consider turning to the dryads for help. After he'd been sent away by his mother, he'd worked to embrace his fae nature and slowly cut off the rest. But they were far more than their trees and portals. Some were healers. If the High Queen of the Dryads willed it, Ivy could be saved.

Though, would the dryad queen help them? She was beholden to the courts just as all fair folk. Even speaking to Orion without reporting his location would break the laws because she'd know, from her dryad sisters, that Orion was acting without the king's permission. But it might be worth the risk; of all the fair creatures, the dryads held more information on both realms, the courts, and the Council than any other.

More importantly, the dryad queen's territory wasn't far.

Ivy stumbled, wincing as she arched her back. Orion grabbed her arm and pulled it across his shoulders helping her stand.

"I have a plan." Orion lay a new course west, and helped Ivy limp forward. She didn't ask any questions, instead her eyes narrowed, focusing on each step. The ground squished under their feet, making little sucking noises. Each step grew more difficult, and Ivy's strength waned as quickly as it had been restored.

"My lung. It's punctured. The healer centaur warned that useless protector guard, but they moved me anyway," Ivy confessed as her grip slipped away. Orion grabbed her and swung her into his arms again, his sweat mixing with the rain.

"I should never have let you out of my sight. I don't know how you stayed conscious on The Tower." Guilt and worry churned inside him, weighing him down more than Ivy in his arms. He trudged forward, not wasting time. The medallion's damage didn't reverse when crossing realms. A full seed in Trinth might have been enough to overcome the magical draining, as well as Ivy's physical injuries, but definitely not a partial one.

"The gnome in the infirmary," Ivy said, her voice growing ragged again. "He altered the seed magic somehow. I think it kept me alive in The Tower. I don't understand how. It shouldn't have worked at all."

She stopped talking, instead taking several short breaths. Ivy's heart thrummed quicker through her clothing, and Orion hugged her closer in a vain attempt to sooth her panic. He called the shadows again, but still they did not answer. He recognized the quiet of the forest and abruptly realized he wasn't catching any whispers from the trees. He'd not noticed their presence until they'd been ripped away, taking their comfort with them.

Shoving away his growing frustration, he stared at his hand and concentrated, focusing his magic to cover his dryad skin and fae wings. Everything faded away except for wringing the magic from every molecule of his body.

His hand slowly turned from the rough green hue to softer human flesh. Orion could have cried with joy. The Mother hadn't completely abandoned him. He'd been given a thread of hope, and he clung to it. Releasing his magic, he marched forward. Pushing through the pain, he tested his wings again, flapping them once, and was met by another shooting pain. They wouldn't carry his weight, let alone a passenger.

Though he couldn't fly with wings, he wouldn't give up on his shadows. When dusk fell, he'd know the extent of his curse. He gripped Ivy tighter, furiously determined to shadow travel.

Because Ivy wouldn't survive the four-day walk to the sea.

7

ORC COMMANDS

The scent of roasting meats tempted Magdud to join the rest of the orcs in the spring equinox celebrations. The Queen, Elowyn of the Summer Court, always prepared feasts to flatter and please the orcs: rare venison, wild boar, amaranth breads, sweet melons, and strong wines. She wasn't subtle; she knew the way to an orc's heart was through their belly.

But nothing would dissuade Magdud from stationing herself outside the throne room until she was ordered away. She needed information—any snippet could be useful. Her instincts warned her something was very amiss. Well, her instincts and the suspiciously-deployed warrior ship that she'd warned Orion about. Plus the fact that the queen had left the biggest festival of the year, signaling the probability of a problem that couldn't wait until morning.

Summer fae guards flanked the main entrance into the throne room, where Prince Devain was meeting with his mother. With the celebrations in distant parts of the palace in full swing, the guards were more lax than usual; she'd already heard the gossip about the queen's summons for the orc High

Commander, Rokgut. Magdud would rather eat glass than talk to him, but real leaders had to grow a limb and get into the fight.

Besides, if the rumors of his accident were true, the sight of him might bring her a bit of vengeful joy.

Despite the fact that she would rather not see Rokgut at all, he could extend an invitation to join him in the throne room with the queen. Though she'd picked up scraps of information in the hallway, the conversation in the throne room would reveal far more.

A quarter hour later, as warned, High Commander Rokgut and two lieutenants finally marched down the gilded hallway, his usual swagger identifying him from afar. Perhaps his over-confident stride made up for *the* tusk. She chuckled to herself, seeing that the word of the loss was true. As he drew near, Magdud was almost tempted to jest about his slender, youngling-tusk. But she sobered seeing the stubble on his chin and his roughly cropped hair. He hadn't looked that ragged since the war, many years before Magdud left their home city of Aggord.

"High Commander," Magdud said with a proper salute. *No need to irritate him right away.*

He blinked, as if not sure she was an illusion, before his mouth drew into a frown, which inadvertently accentuated his lopsided lips. According to the gossip, his tusk had been broken in half during a routine spar. Healing broken tusks was tricky because they wouldn't regrow unless completely pulled out of the gums. Unfortunately, tusks took a ridiculous amount of time to regrow—an unavoidable declaration that you'd lost a fight. No one wanted that. Especially not a high commander.

"I heard about the Aequus fiasco." Rokgut looked down at her. "Why were you there?"

As if I wanted to be there. "I was summoned by King Eldrin."

"It was only a matter of time," he said, a smug sneer on his lips.

Forever would be too soon.

"Of course," Magdud said, "And I obeyed."

He paused, considering her. Would he vent about Eldrin's tasking of the orcs? Did he blame her for the Aequus? Did he have a smidgen of trust in her?

He bent his left leg, and Magdud didn't realize he was positioning himself at the perfect angle for a sweep until he dropped, his leg extended. She didn't consciously recognize the move, but her body reacted. She jerked up her closest leg, followed quickly by the other, jumping back and gaining space between her and Rokgut. Smoothly shooting back to his feet, he used his upward momentum, punching upward toward her chin. Ready for his move, Magdud shifted her body and deflected his hit with the back of her right forearm, driving through to his exposed ribs with her left fist.

Knowing he was testing her, she *didn't* pull back.

He curled under her blow, the one she landed along the stitching of the ceremonial padding. If she'd hit a little lower, she'd have dropped him thanks to a war injury; one that would always be sore unless he cut off his torso—obviously a bad idea—or lived for a few years in the fair realm—which wasn't allowed. But her goal wasn't to humiliate him.

Magdud hopped back, both fists up, ready. She could've gone for her blade, but this never was about doing real damage. Rokgut was giving her another numbskull-orc test.

But instead of pushing harder, he stayed out of her range. "You used to lean into my sweeps." He looked her up and down with a condescending curl to his bottom lip. "You had learned to stop my momentum, then spin back and put *me* on the ground."

You're slipping. He didn't say it, but Magdud could practically hear the chastisement. Instead of shrinking under his gaze, she stood taller. She wasn't totally surprised by his little test, and she refused to cower. After all, he'd not laid a finger on her, and she landed her punch.

"Walk with me, Magdud. There's much to discuss." Without waiting, he pivoted and marched forward, his two lieutenants waiting a beat, allowing Magdud the honor of walking into the room next to their leader. She matched Rokgut's stride, relieved at the invitation. Apparently, she'd performed well enough to not be dismembered right then and there.

The fae guards swung open the doors into the opulent corridor that led to the main throne. The long hallway was oddly void of spectators; with the distracting festivities, this space was the most private, secure spot in the palace. The main doors to the throne room at the end of the hallway were wide open, revealing a distant figure, Queen Elowyn, deep in conversation with her son. The queen's long, flowing hair, the color of spun gold, cascaded down her back in intricate braids interwoven with delicate flowers. She sat on her throne, leaning closer to her son, and even from a distance her eyes sparkled with the false warmth and true wisdom of countless summers. Her skin, kissed by the sun, glowed, enhancing her ethereal beauty. She wore a gown made of gossamer and sunlight, a fabric so fine it appeared almost transparent, shimmering with every movement. A crown of intertwined, green vines and motes of sunlight rested upon her head.

Her presence exuded a sense of vitality and life, but Magdud knew better. Even if she couldn't sense glamours, some were obvious. Beneath her serene exterior lay a formidable will and a fierce protector of her realm and its inhabitants.

Magdud wasn't surprised to see Elowyn had sent everyone away, including her guards, as she spoke with the prince, but the emptiness of the hall still discomforted her. If the prince was informing his mother with the shocking news from the ceremony, wouldn't the queen want her advisers to hear it also?

"What have you learned while in Eldrin's court?" Rokgut asked Magdud in a low voice before they reached the royals.

Magdud considered lying, but that wouldn't get her the information she needed. "I believe elven seeds are being misappropriated. And instead of sending me on tasks in the corners of the human realm, like to Nylann'or, I was brought to the Winter Court. If I didn't know better, I'd think someone was trying to keep me out of the human realm."

The commander huffed. "You never did know when to keep your mouth shut."

"I learned from the best."

He growled and Magdud interjected before he exploded. "Rokgut, *High* Commander," she quickly amended. "I apologize." Sometimes she forgot they were no longer friends, a fact that once brought her great sadness but now only tasted bitter in the back of her throat. "I spoke out of turn."

He stopped short and stared at her, his bloodshot eyes burrowing into her own. "While you've been sleeping on rose petals and gorging on fresh stew, we've been working. Not a moment of rest."

Paranoia. The reason I left.

"You abandoned us when you left Aggord," the commander spat. "Chose to live with our enemy. Disgusting."

"You know why—"

"Yes, the Aggord Administrator approved your leave," he interrupted, disregarding her excuse before she could give it. "Yes, I know you're supposedly a spy. But don't ever forget that I *know* you. I know you turn up your nose at the ancestor's ways. Our ways." He thumped his fist against his chest. "But, Magdud, the day is coming where you, and the orcs that followed, will have to choose between your kind and our enemy."

Magdud swallowed down the rising ball of anger, his words all but a confirmation of her worst fears. Of all the intelligence she could have gathered, Rokgut's admission thundered down, threatening to tear her apart inside. But Magdud didn't react. Didn't move a muscle.

"Choose wisely," he continued. "You think you've been protecting your unit, but we've kept tabs on every single orc. Whether or not you intended to ruin them with your cowardly beliefs, it won't matter. They must follow you into battle." Rokgut's voice turned mocking. "With your track record for collecting misfits, one would think you'd have gotten Eldrin's welp under your thumb. But apparently a bastard feels himself too good for your company."

"When?" she asked, grateful her voice didn't waver. "When will we be called home to Aggord?"

His neck twitched and he let out a breath. "Soon."

"After the next spring Centennial?" Magdud pushed her luck, but she needed to know. The others needed a warning—time to prepare. She at least owed them that much.

"Loyalty. Our ways demand it." The commander spun on his heel and marched forward again without answering her question. "I'm bound by our laws if you are slow to respond to the call."

Thanks for the warning? If her unit didn't respond, her own kind would hunt down her unit, one by one, and slaughter them. And when they did respond—and they were honor bound to do so—her unit would be the first into battle. First to die.

She would be dismembered, just not today.

The queen's posture straightened, and she signaled for the orcs to approach. In her hand, she gracefully held a heartwood scepter, topped with a glowing orb. Devain kept his back to the newcomers, his arms folded. The queen's serene expression was at odds with both her son's posture and Magdud's warring thoughts.

Magdud entered the throne room on the high commander's heels, bitterness balling in the back of her throat. Her perception of what orc *loyalty* meant was something very different than his shallow definition. Rokgut was delusional if he thought the ancestors would approve of their continued preparation for war in Trinth. Threatening to kill their fellow orcs, ignoring the Spring attack on Ivy, and allowing seeds to spread was against the ancient text of the Mother's call for cooperation and peace. Magdud didn't understand all of Alysatraee's ways, but deep in her core she felt the orc responsibilities had gotten warped. There had to be a reason the same orc injury that took a year to heal in the human realm took only weeks to mend in the fair realm.

The truth was hidden beyond Magdud's understanding, but she trusted her gut. The leaders and scholars needed to re-evaluate their stories, the lore of Alysatraee. But according to some like Rokgut, their culture and traditions were too sacred to argue. Apparently. The problem had become painfully clear years ago; the orc leaders were lazy followers. Magdud's old indignation flared.

How dare he threaten me?

Devain seemed to echo Magdud's fury, his shoulders rounded and his face pinched. He didn't meet the orcs' gazes as he stormed past them on his way out, though anyone could hear his teeth grinding from the other side of the palace. The Summer Court generally viewed this prince as soft-hearted and humorless. But Magdud saw him as a stickler for the rules— and he knew them well. Perhaps too well, as far as his mother was concerned.

The four orcs bowed before Queen Elowyn, awaiting her command. Her soft, braided hair smelled of honey blossoms and other sickly-sweet flowers. Though the Summer Court touted kindness, Magdud firmly believed the queen's veins carried more poison than blood. After hearing Rokgut's dire news, Magdud was anxious to get away from him. But she had to get through this meeting without hinting to *anyone* her distress.

The queen looked from Magdud to the commander, a brow raised.

"This is Magdud, the orc who has been stationed outside of Unari," Rokgut introduced Magdud. "A contact for King Eldrin's messenger."

The king's son. But Magdud didn't correct her superior. She hadn't spoken on Orion's behalf in all these years, and she wasn't about to start now. She kept her mouth shut while Rokgut spoke about the visit to Nylenn'or *in a warship*. Hearing that Emmyth had turned against her own advisers, her own *daughter*, sickened her.

"When should we bring Emmyth to the court for an accounting?" Rokgut asked.

"Emmyth Phiro was within her rights," the queen frowned at the advice. "No law was broken."

Magdud hid her confusion at the queen's odd response. The court should want to speak with a councilor who'd very nearly been toppled by her own advisers, yet the queen didn't allow any discussion on the matter. The queen's closure on the topic indicated that Rokgut—and all the other orcs—were unaware of the queen's broader agenda.

And Elowyn didn't elaborate.

Rokgut continued his updates, which included several ships' movements. Magdud memorized how many orc units were ready to deploy and to which locations. She realized with dawning horror that every major human city would have an orc battalion within a day's walk.

But when? The orcs would need supplies and support, especially with those numbers. Magdud ran rough calculations, remembering what she'd learned from Ivy and Orion about The Tree House during the Aequus hand-off. The orc movements could potentially coincide with the Centennial. The snippets of information started to paint a wider image in Magdud's mind.

Oh, no.

Magdud felt like she was falling, her insides churned and her mind went blank. The fair folk were planning a surprise attack next spring. Alion, that rocks-for-brains Spring fae, was right. The war was merely paused, and the humans would be caught unaware. And if Rokgut had his way, Magdud and her unit would be at the front of the line, forever haunted by unnecessary carnage.

Pushing aside her shock and frustration, she realized the commander was talking about a ruined orchard and the queen's serene expression faltered.

"You're excused," the commander suddenly said to his lieutenants and Magdud.

Magdud straightened and bowed to the queen. Apparently, they wanted privacy for the discussion on The Tree House. As relieved as Magdud was to leave, she couldn't help but wonder why she'd been sent away now? Ivy had already confessed to destroying the orchard in Neidrei—the armpit of the human realm, as far as Magdud was concerned. Of course an illicit orchard would be there, and it was obviously the topic of this particular, secret conversation.

As Magdud marched out, her mind swirled, landing on another thought; Rokgut knew Magdud well. He'd purposely let her stay for certain parts of the conversation. He knew that she'd memorize the orc locations—he'd *wanted* her to know that he was as serious as a hog hunt on mid-winter's eve about calling her unit into battle.

His tactic to make her feel inferior and helpless might have worked on her before. But the young, unsure Magdud was gone, replaced by a magistrate who'd negotiated a glamour from a merciless Winter fae so she, an orc, could pose as a human and oversee the wealthiest city in Trinth. Her temper flared. She was about to die so who cared what the queen thought of her? She spun to give Rokgut a parting gesture when movement caught her attention.

Between the open door to the throne room and the wall of the royal corridor beyond, Prince Devain had attempted to conceal himself, but he couldn't hide completely. His eyes widened, waiting to be chastised. He had disobeyed the queen, likely a decision he, prince-stick-in-the-mud, didn't take lightly. In that moment, Magdud decided to take a chance on stick-in-the-mud.

She let her gaze slide over him, as if she'd never seen him. If Rokgut didn't want her to hear this dubious discussion, then that was exactly what she'd gift to prince-of-rules-Devain. Nothing would convert Devain more to Alysatraee's cause than hearing the truth from the queen's own lips. Honorable Summer fae needed to know about this mysterious orchard and the destructive plans for the humans. And Magdud sent a quick prayer to the Mother that Devain had at least a drop of honor.

The queen paused, giving Magdud a penetrating glare over the high commander's shoulder, expectant. But Magdud just swung her attention back to the main doors and marched away, past the hiding prince, letting the Summer Queen condemn herself. Magdud needed every ally she could get if she had any chance of protecting her unit—she was desperate enough to even curry favor with an out-of-favor prince.

Magdud threw open the outer doors and stormed down the

hallway. She would drink the queen's finest wine before criss-crossing Trinth on horseback, tracking down her unit and delivering the dark news.

Her mind turned back to The Tree House and Zel, and she lit on another idea. The plans for the war; it included the seeds. No, it included *Seekers*. Her breath caught, wondering if she could get word to Orion and warn Zel. Whatever the gnome was doing for the Seekers, he needed to figure it out—and fast.

8

THE OTHER SISTER

As the sun dipped, kissing the tops of the trees, Orion itched for the shadows that teased beyond his reach. His body ached with every movement, and he desperately called to his shadows again. But only empty nothingness awaited, draining away more of his hope at the wasted effort.

Each step grew heavier than the last. The forested hills dragged on, seemingly endless. His muscles screamed for rest, and his mind clouded with fatigue and doubt. Desperation gnawed, a dark whisper that he would never reach the sea, let alone beyond. The rain finally subsided as dusk approached. Ivy's shivering hadn't stopped, though he'd draped his cloak around her long ago. He imagined she was as parched as he was, their bodies utterly dehydrated and spent.

His mistakes circled in his mind, blaring all the things he should've done differently. He never truly appreciated his abilities, all the unique parts of his magic that made him *him*, until now. But those thoughts rolled around in the recess of his mind, purposefully left too deep to examine closely.

His weakness when he'd emerged into Trinth paled in comparison to the sucking dread creeping through his bones. The hours of travel sapped his energy, leaving him empty and raw. He didn't even have the luxury of tears. He silently mourned his predicament, both for him and for Ivy. But he wouldn't let fear conquer him.

Ivy winced in her sleep, her eyes pinched shut. The look on her face drove him forward, one foot in front of the other as his thoughts flew back to The Tower. As much as he dreaded his next meeting with Selleth, she was a problem for tomorrow. Selleth was a lightning storm, chaos unleashed, but she wouldn't leave her place of power, the Winter Court.

In the human realm, Emmyth and the Council controlled Trinth. He desperately wanted to believe that Nym had successfully turned the Tides' advisers against the councilors, but it wouldn't have been easy. Definitely not guaranteed.

Nym, Ivy, and Orion had depended on the fae courts to fix the Council; but if Ivy's accusation was right, no reinforcements were coming. How Ivy had come to that conclusion, he could only guess. The accusation was so outrageous, he wished he knew the source of her information. In any case, he had to keep Ivy's location a secret as neither of them was in any condition to fight. At best, Emmyth might be too distracted by Nym to notice anything beyond Nylann'or.

As much as he wanted to aid Nym, he couldn't. His immediate concern was Ivy. Her leg had swollen, and she moaned in her troubled sleep. He'd slid her purple stone into her tunic, hoping it would help. With Ivy back in the human realm, his oath was fulfilled.

He wasn't obligated to stay, nor should he unless he wanted his father's wrath. He was required back in Winter to discuss the Spring attendings, advise his father as requested, and to attend courtly functions. Orion's speedy return would sooth his father's temper and protect his standing. But he wouldn't leave Ivy. Not like this. Even if his magic wasn't gone, he would never abandon her to die alone in the forest.

He paused, leaning against a tree to catch his breath. If he were healthy, they'd be in the dryad stronghold already, not three more days away. He sagged against the bark, admitting the truth to himself; they'd never reach the dryad queen at his pace. His body would give out long before then. He'd survive, but would Ivy?

As the first stars began to appear, Orion chewed his lip, debating. Ivy's chances for survival decreased with every passing hour. Alysatree had granted him a thread of magic, just as Ivy had clung to life as she entered Trinth. Risking everything on his shadow magic, he veered off the path.

Stumbling over roots, Orion entered a denser portion of the forest. Every step off the direct course felt like a massive gamble. But he'd never make it to the dryads without magic. He felt the shadows just beyond him. Tears welled, blurring his vision as he called to them. In Trinth, they were more difficult to access, but magic still existed; his focus was on nothing but reaching for the magical energy that existed all around him, in every particle of air, every leaf, and every stone.

And the shadows answered.

Blinking back tears, Orion sent silent thanks to Alysatraee for allowing a remnant of his magic. He swore never to take it for granted again. Though weak and slow, the shadows carried him. Carried Ivy. Ash darted behind him, keeping pace, a silent companion. Orion's feet skimmed the ferns and foliage through the darkest of the forested night, but he was unable to transport himself any higher.

Orion's magic faded even before the sun rose. The day

blurred as he trudged forward. He considered leaving his satchel behind, but Ivy would need the supplies later. Ivy barely stirred, her breathing shallow and her face pale. Utterly spent, Orion only stopped when his body demanded rest. As the stars appeared the second night, Orion determined to push himself all the way to the island in the middle of the sea; the dryad queen's home.

Orion gathered the shadows, carrying them both across the final expanse of forest. In the late hours of the third watch, before the sky lightened, Orion heard the lapping shores. He neared the Haunted Sea, or so the humans had named it, due to the many sailors and fisher folk who'd disappeared over the years. Fair folk knew the water by its true name, Siren Sea. The sailors and fisher folk weren't missing; their bones were scattered on the sea bottom, their trinkets tied in the hair of the creatures who lured them to their doom.

Without slowing, he sucked in a nervous breath and crossed the threshold between the rocks and the sea's edge. Sirens, a prideful bunch, surely sensed his presence just above the lapping waters. In the past, they would've taunted but let him cross. Now he wasn't so certain. If the king had awoken and learned his son had fled without permission, he could revoke Orion's protections.

Orion shifted his attention between the island and the stars above; when the stars faded, so did his shadows. Orion slowly dropped, his toes almost in the water. He expended more strength to reinforce his magic and rose again, but not enough. His speed waned. Panic rose within him as he raced against his depleting magic. The island wasn't far, but sirens were swift.

Orion's feet dragged across the water's surface, and he jerked his legs up. His heart thumped as the shadows weakened. Above, the stars were winking out. The island was close, but he wouldn't reach the shore. Lower, lower he dipped, as his shadows became thin bands. Orion purposely slowed and glamoured away his wings just before the shadows disappeared. He and Ivy plummeted, the water's icy fingers encircling them.

Ivy's eyes popped open, and she gasped as Orion absorbed the impact of the water and the rocks. She sucked in a ragged breath as he found purchase, the water hitting at his chest. She tightened her arms around his neck, pulling close, blinking in confusion.

"We're almost there," Orion assured her, though he fought through his exhaustion and the water. The drag seemed to suck him back as he struggled toward shore. He quickly scanned the water behind them for any signs of attack, but the water's ripples were only his.

Pink shades of dawn appeared in the sky and morning fog obscured the view of the island's shores. Orion stumbled forward, his own splashing creating too much noise. Ivy coughed, her mouth near his ear; she gurgled a warning just as Ash shot past him, shrieking.

Orion spun in time to see a siren rising from the water. With his magic stripped, she drew him toward her like a fish on a hook. Ivy pushed out of his arms, sliding into the water.

Look away! He told himself, but the siren's black hair, ghostly skin, and blood-red lips, drowned his thoughts, her every movement captivating and deadly.

Ash cried out again, her small form darting between Orion and the siren long enough for him to snap out of the trance and turn his focus to Ivy. The water hit him at his thighs, but Ivy was on her knees, her head above water, her breath coming in ragged gasps. Instead of looking at him, she was fumbling in the water.

"My knife!" Her face fell, her voice cracking with desperation. "Your sister has it."

Orion shoved his hand into his satchel, his fingers wrapping around the metal hilt of Ivy's blade. When he'd grappled with Selleth, he'd stolen the weapon back. The last thing he expected was to be using it against a siren.

Ash let out another shriek, and the siren's irritated shout turned into a coughing fit. Orion dared look up, seeing the cloud of smoke encasing the siren's head.

Jumping into action, he grabbed Ivy's upper arm, dragging her toward the shore, her feet scrambling against the slick rocks, attempting to find purchase.

Ivy cursed and jerked her attention to her left, Orion's warning that another siren had emerged. "Two more!"

"Your father is looking for you," a voice hissed with cruel sarcasm. "Now, I don't remember, but did your father specify if you should be returned dead or alive?"

"Now that you mention it, the king wasn't specific," another voice answered, dripping with venom.

"Ivy!" With that word, he begged her to crawl to shore—to safety. The sirens were after him, not her.

A wave of dread washed over Orion, but he couldn't afford to be paralyzed by fear. Ash screeched again, careening past his right shoulder. The smoke she produced this time was thin and dissipated quickly. The sirens' angry shouts turned into a chilling laugh. Orion dared look at them in his periphery, seeing the siren's eyes gleaming with malice.

Panicked energy coursed through Orion, spurring him toward the shore. But a cold, slimy hand gripped his ankle, yanking him back. He only had time to drop Ivy and spin, her knife in his hand as he swiped at the pale-faced siren. The blade sliced through the air, catching the creature across her cheek. She hissed, recoiling, but not releasing her grip.

Orion's heart pounded in his chest. He kicked at the siren, trying to break free, but her hold tightened, pulling him deeper into the water. Ivy struggled to stand, her injured leg buckling beneath her as she tried to reach him.

"Orion!" she screamed, her voice hoarse.

The initial rush of energy disappeared along with the last of his strength. An image flashed in his mind, of his body being presented to his father, seaweed still wrapped around his limbs. What would the king think?

A soft, ethereal glow appeared, coming from the shore. A melodious female voice, calm and commanding, filled the air. "Release them, or face my wrath."

The sirens hissed and turned away, their eyes averted from the light. The grip on his ankle loosened, and Orion wriggled free, scrambling back to Ivy.

"Is Lord Orion under your queen's protection?" a siren shot.

"He is under mine," the dryad said. Her voice was young, but there was a vicious protectiveness to it. Orion couldn't look directly at the source, knowing the danger, but he sensed the shift in the air.

"You rob us of our prize," the siren shouted as a slap sounded against the water.

"Leave in peace, and I will grant you that as your reward," the dryad said.

Orion didn't wait for an agreement. He grabbed Ivy and they struggled together toward the dryad beacon. Behind them, the sirens didn't pursue, their anger palpable. He dropped his glamour from his wings, groaning at the drag they created as the bottom feathers wove through the water at their shins. Overhead, Ash darted toward the island.

Reaching the rocky ground, Orion collapsed next to Ivy. The sirens hissed from the water, their pale faces contorted in anger, but they didn't dare approach the dryad's brilliant light.

Ivy's hand found his, drawing his attention away from the water. Orion pushed himself onto his knees, trembling with the effort. Knowing better than to look a dryad in the eyes or ask for a name, Orion stilled, waiting for her to come to him.

"I am Orion Ke'ayra, son of the Winter King."

"And of a dryad mother," she said a defiance in her tone. "What brings you?"

This close, Orion felt compelled to look at the dryad's face. Normally, the sensation was a mere annoyance, not this overwhelming temptation.

"This elf, Ivy Balrel, needs a healer," he said, shifting to block her line of sight to the dryad. The last thing Ivy needed was to lose her memories.

"You expect me to save her twice then," the dryad said.

"Twice?" Orion said, confused.

"At the Elven Gathering." She took a step closer, the tip of her green toes in Orion's periphery. Her voice softened. "You asked me to save her then. I saved you both. Now you wish for me to save her again?"

Orion's heart raced, remembering the boon he'd been granted. What were the chances that the same dryad who'd saved them at the Gathering then would meet him here?

"Who are you?" He fought to keep his eyes down.

The dryad's voice turned tentative, a hint of deep emotion laying just beneath her words. "I'm one who is trusted to watch out for your interests."

This dryad was not his mother, he knew that much; her apple orchard was impossibly far. The dryad stepped to the side, and Orion noticed a long staff, one end pressed into the dirt. Her weapon of choice?

"Weeks ago, you told my sister in Carrus of your plans to track this elf," she said. "To hunt her. Yet now you help her?"

"The dryad in Carrus must've reported to the Winter King,

as expected, but also to your queen," Orion said aloud, connecting the dots. The queen had known the location of Ivy's Gathering and had sent this dryad? "Why help me?"

"I do not know the queen's mind," she said, her voice becoming strained. "But, I volunteered."

"Are you here to collect a favor in return?"

The dryad chuckled softly, then took a long breath, sobering, the earlier emotion he'd sensed beginning to surface. "Orion, I can hardly believe I'm standing next to you, speaking with you. I've wanted to meet you for so long." She dug her toes into the earth, and her voice wavered with emotion. "I am grateful for our queen's kindness."

"I'm afraid I must ask another boon. Ivy needs a healer." He squeezed Ivy's hand; she squeezed back, her grip weak and her eyes closed again. "If the queen knew the situation, surely she would grant us assistance."

The dryad dug her toes deeper, ready to send a message. Unexpectedly, she jumped back. "You assume the queen doesn't already know your situation."

Orion frowned, realizing their queen probably knew all about Ivy's injury.

"Which means, our meeting is no accident," the dryad said. "She sent me."

"Are you a healer?"

She snorted. "I am a protector, a sentinel of this portion of the island. It's in my blood. My father was once a knight at Blackmore castle. I've been told I inherited his physical strength and impulsive behavior. But I also have a practical nature," she paused, "like *our* mother."

Orion's attention jerked to the dryad without thinking. She was looking down, purposefully away from him, a tight-lipped grin on her face. She looked younger than he expected. Her long, polished spear was unlike any he'd ever seen—made of four twining apple tree branches; a soft green glow emanated from the cracks, before the staff cut into a wicked point. Her deep-green skin had a bark-like texture, the apple tree texture, a match to his own. Moss, leaves, and swirls of fog formed a dress that draped across her body, similar to his mother's. Her hair was woven with willows. Like his. Though instead of a crown, she had thick horns the color of apple seeds.

"I had assumed you'd take our mother's place?" he forced himself to look at her feet, again.

"That makes two of us," she said. "But I'd *acted* at the Gathering, when I was only meant to sustain the tree."

Orion gripped Ivy tighter, realizing his sister had acted because of his request. Instead of inheriting her mother's territory, his sister had become a sentinel. Becoming a sentinel was honorable, but she wasn't connected to her own tree, nor was she granted the honor of protecting her own portion of land. What other dryad would've risked their future for him?

"Sister?" he breathed.

"Brother," she whispered back.

Orion wasn't sure what to say. Instead he tried to swallow back the disbelief and guilt. He'd always kept his distance, convinced she'd never care about him, that she saw him as unworthy of her time or love. He'd never tried to find his half-sister, assuming she'd never given him a thought.

"I'm sorry. I didn't know," his voice barely more than a whisper. His mind whirled with confusion and regret, each thought a storm of what-ifs and missed opportunities. He felt a deep ache, realizing how wrong he had been, how much he had misjudged her and their bond.

He searched for more words, but they seemed to catch in his throat, too tangled to unravel. The weight of his assumptions pressed, and he fought to make sense of the revelations crashing over him. Her presence, her sacrifices, shattered the image he'd held on to for so long, leaving him vulnerable and exposed.

"You're here now." She cleared her throat, stepping back. "The queen arranged our meeting. She relocated me to this part of the forest only two days ago. She must've known you were coming, and she sent me here to intercept you."

"And you can't announce to the dryad network that I'm here." He kept his attention on his sister's toes. "Your queen is beholden to the fae rulers. And the courts may report our location to the Elven Council. If so, they'll hunt us down."

"What have you gotten yourself into?" she asked, a youthful, almost teasing in her tone. "Actually, we don't have time. I love royal gossip, but the queen didn't send her healer, which is a warning for you to look elsewhere." The dryad rapped her fingers against her staff in a soft tap, tap, tap. "This means, she's avoiding involvement, but signaling that she's giving her blessing for *me* to assist you."

"I can't portal, or the dryads will report my location." Orion shifted Ivy into his arms, explaining their predicament. "My horse is stabled near Blackmore castle. Too far."

She took a step closer to Orion. "How long have you been gone from the Winter Court?"

"This is day three."

"Too long. You must return before the king does something rash—something that hurts more fair folk. You care for the elf, but you have a greater responsibility to all creatures. Don't be his excuse to lose his temper. You're well respected among the dryads and many fair folk. And you've put up with too much court nonsense to let yourself be robbed of your birthright." She stepped back and changed subjects. "I have a salve for Ivy. I will return shortly."

She retreated, and Orion shook his head, unable to believe she'd taken an interest in his life. He knew nothing of her or her dreams. Could that change? Or was it too late to build something from the remnants of their fractured connection?

Holding Ivy, Orion took her a few more steps to a spot with softer sand. Shifting his cloak, he covered her face so she wouldn't look upon the dryad if she awoke. Soon, his sister rushed back, shifting Ivy onto her side and lifting her tunic to reveal the wound.

"Drink this," the dryad said, handing him a wax-covered, wooden jug. She also gave him a dose of medicine wrapped in leaves, giving instructions as she packed Ivy's wound. "This salve will help stop the elf's bleeding. It might be too late to prevent infection, unfortunately. She obviously doesn't have a seed. It doesn't take a genius to figure that out. Are you taking her back to the fair realm for treatment? Spring Court would help."

He shuddered at the memory of Ivy getting dragged into the coliseum by the Spring fae. "The fair realm isn't an option. Actually, right now, I don't know who to trust."

As Orion told the dryad of the corrupted Elven Council, his sister had no shortage of pithy remarks and groans, especially when he explained the misuse of the seeds.

"Oh, that explains ... everything," his sister said. "Why the queen sent me to Ivy's Gathering. Why she sent me to intercept you now. The queen follows fair law, of course, but she also considers the deeper ethics of Alysatraee's ways." She paused for a beat before she snapped her fingers, her words coming quickly. "Oh, the feelings I had in the Gathering tree make so much more sense now. When I used my magic to transform the tree into a great Gathering tree, it felt wrong, like growing mold in full view of the sun. I told myself the process was Alysatraee's way, and I followed instruction. Why did I ignore my instincts?"

"When we follow leaders we trust, we don't always question what we should." Orion consoled himself, as well as his sister, knowing he'd made his share of mistakes, too. "Your queen is listening to her instincts, fortunately. She's fighting back by sending you and keeping my location a secret. As long as your queen only suspects, but doesn't *know* for certain, then she's keeping the Mother's law."

"Orion," his sister's voice was soft, "I understand why you don't trust the Minerals, but they're Ivy's best chance. They're the closest, and she'll die if she stays here." She stepped toward him. "I'll transport the elf to a safe human healer. Some can be trusted, and no one will find her. You must return to the king and assure him of your loyalty."

"I have faith in you, but a human healer won't suffice." Seeing Ivy trapped on the medallion with three orbs activated would be seared into his memory forever. Ivy required more than human positivity and smiles to heal her; she needed someone gifted in magical remedies.

"But your father won't just sit—" she stopped her warning short. "Wait," her voice grew excited. "Follow me."

It took all Orion's strength to keep up with the dryad as she flit through the trees.

"It will cost you another day, but I can't do this alone," she said.

"Do what alone?"

"The queen is clever," she muttered mostly to herself, ignoring his question. "The rumor must be true ... of a portal nearby that goes to the borderlands."

"Borderlands?" Orion slowed. "You can't mean Heikton."

"Past Heikton, *past* the sentinels. No one will know you're coming."

"Those portals were ..." *Destroyed.* He couldn't bear to speak their dark history aloud. His mother never did. The war took the lives of many fair folk, including dryads.

"It's a wasteland, yes. Poisoned air, yes," she said. "So, no one enters that desert. And because you've kept your dryad nature, it can work."

"You can't be serious," Orion's voice boomed louder than he'd intended. Battles had converged in Heikton, destroying the city. Desperate not to lose their stronghold, fair folk magic had cut through the land, leaving it uninhabitable. Without a dryad, the land never recovered.

Ivy stirred in his arms, her eyes fluttering. Orion swallowed, quieting. "You want me to act as a dryad and open a dead portal?"

"No, I need you to act as a dryad and open up the Heikton side of the portal."

He waited for his sister to laugh. She didn't.

"This plan is insanity," Orion growled. A portal with no dryad no longer functioned. Even younglings understood this concept.

"So, you don't have faith in our queen?"

I have faith this won't work.

The dryad continued, "Why would she put me here in this territory if not to use this portal to get Ivy to the Minerals?"

Her reasoning was flawed. Surreal. Orion countered, "Maybe because your queen knew the east side of the island was the closest to the Winter portal I journeyed through. A despoiled portal just *happened* to be in the same area."

"Alysatraee will help us. I know she will."

Orion's insides soured at her naivete. "I'll take Ivy to Carrus; surely someone there can help."

She stopped and slammed a hand to her hip. "Oh, so you think you're going to walk for over a week, *hoping* to come across a magical healer in a human city?"

Carrus was impossibly far and with magical creatures hunting him, so, yes, it was an insane plan. Yet reaching

Magdud's distant city seemed more realistic than using a broken portal.

His sister marched forward, spouting the history of the ruined portal. During the war, a sentinel warrior dryad had portaled to Heikton to help a sister in danger. They'd fought valiantly, but were both killed. Both dryads' trees began to wither soon after.

His sister's voice grew pinched, and she sniffled as she finished the tale. Moments later, they arrived at a towering cedar tree. Perhaps once it had been a magnificent sight, but now it was a merely a wide trunk, barren of needles and cones. A husk. Ash flew around the weathered pole, but didn't risk landing on any part of it.

Most of the long branches had broken off, so it looked like the Mother herself had stuck a massive, bone-dry stick into the ground. Part of Orion's heart broke at seeing the derelict tree, but the other part of him was horrified at what his sister planned to attempt.

Her back to him, his sister put her hand on the tree, her head dropping in concentration. If she couldn't enter, he certainly couldn't. She leaned into the tree, and for a moment, her hand sat against the solid bark. Then she slid inside.

Orion stepped forward, his body trembling. Was this really the best option? He pulled Ivy into an embrace, smelling sweat, linden trees, and earth, the essence of Ivy. How could he risk using a dead portal? But what other choice did they have?

He sensed his sister holding the portal open, but even so, he had to concentrate as he stepped into the tree. Without a bound dryad to ground him, he quickly became disoriented.

"Feel your way to the other side. This portal has only one exit."

"I can't feel anything." *This was a mistake.*

"I admit, this is a bit more difficult than I'd anticipated," she grunted.

"Perhaps the Mother doesn't will—"

"Find help for Ivy, then return to the Heikton portal at dusk," she blurted an interruption, her voice strained. "We'll figure this out. I trust Alysatraee. Don't be late."

And with that, she shoved him forward, sending him hurtling into the abyss.

9

POISON AND THREATS

Ivy coughed, bringing her into dull consciousness. A heavy cloak laid across her face, the awareness bringing a sense of suffocation. She jerked, but could barely move.

"Stay still, Ivy," Orion said, before a hacking cough stole his words.

An itch tickled the back of her throat, and she wheezed a cough, sending a sharp pain through her lungs. She wanted to scream, to get out all her frustrations, but she bit back tears knowing it would only make things worse. For what seemed like ages, Orion stumbled forward through an unseen landscape. Ivy could barely think past her stabbing pains and the gagging phlegm at the back of her throat.

Pinpricks of light penetrated through the dark cloak, giving her a much-needed distraction. Once the seed wore off, her field of vision had narrowed again. At least she was no longer blinded like she had been on the horrendous medallion.

When Orion finally pulled back the cloak from her face, she winced against the bright sunshine. She almost asked where they were, but the question died on her tongue. He held her near the edge of a cliff, overlooking a spoiled land. Plumes of acidic smoke rose into the air, and rotting trees dotted the rocky, burnt earth. North of the swath of ruined land, green forest blurred far into the distance. Only one place in Trinth was poisoned by blood and dark magic.

She jerked her attention up to Orion. His face was red and swollen, irritated by the toxic air. Red-tinted ash coated his hair and clothing.

"Oh, Orion ..." Pity and guilt vied inside her. He'd carried her across the desecrated land and up a narrow path to the Yllalen'al cliffs. Each step must have been agony for him, yet he'd never faltered. The land was impassable for humans, the poison an unintended barrier between humans and elves. But even fair folk rarely crossed, and in Orion's weakened state, she was shocked he'd attempted it.

Orion turned away from the destruction to face a completely different landscape. Ahead, green trees stood in welcome respite along the bluff. Beyond her sight lay the southern elven city of Yllalen'al, the House of Minerals. Awake, Ivy insisted on walking, but even the slightest pressure on her leg nearly made her crumple to the dirt.

"Medicine," Orion said, handing her a wrapped leaf.

Inside, she found a glass vial with a syrup inside and an herb bread. Taking them quickly, she tasted ginseng, rhodiola, and peppermint in the syrup. Basil, rare star milk, and something bitter she didn't recognize infused the bread.

As they dragged themselves in the general direction of the greenery ahead, Orion gagged and expelled whatever fluid was in his lungs while she used him as a crutch. They were a sorry pair. Though the medicine masked her pain and increased her energy, the remedy was much weaker than the remnant of the seed she'd had in her belly when she'd portaled home.

Exhaustion and pain lined Orion's face. He should be back in his own land, by the king's side, fulfilling his duties and ensuring his own safety. Instead, he had risked everything for her, hauling himself through perilous terrain when he could barely stand.

The realization of his sacrifice hit her like a blow. He had valued her life above his own, despite the cost to himself. She felt unworthy of such devotion, knowing that without his help, she would have perished in the forests of Easthill. Gratitude mingled with the sorrow, her heart aching over what he'd sacrificed for her.

As the sun lowered well past its zenith, towering buildings emerged from the tree line. Closer to the greenery, Ash waited, squatting in the dirt. Apparently, she didn't trust the scraggly branches. Ivy and Orion kept stumbling unsteadily, agony growing with each step. Ivy used every drop of her stubborn, diminishing strength and kept going until the trees' branches boasted deep green leaves.

Humans believed that only orcs lived south of Heikton, in the far southern, punishing desert. Nor did humans imagine anyone could cross the poisoned land, except for the narrow, orc-guarded pass. They didn't know that hidden, just past the cliffs, a patch of life still existed: Yllalen'al.

Ivy nearly asked him what had happened on the island, as her delirium only temporarily cleared as the dryad painfully shoved some kind of salve into her wounded back. But a rustling sound in the bushes caused them both to still. Hearing the movement draw closer, Orion shifted, concealing themselves by putting a tree between them and the unknown creature. Then, a gnome came skipping into the forest, passing them without notice.

"You should go before anyone sees you," Ivy whispered, her throat sore. If the courts thought Orion had abandoned her, they might go easier on him. Besides, Yllalen'al was rumored to be even bigger than Nylenn'or. The councilors might never even know she was there.

"I can't leave without knowing you have a healer."

"Worried about your magic?" she teased, pretending she wasn't afraid. Pretending her back, lungs, and leg didn't feel like they were on fire. Pretending that darkness didn't pulse at the edges of her vision.

He grinned, despite his ragged breathing. "Should I not be?"

Ivy soaked in the humor in his voice, the smile on the edge of his lips. Orion whispered to Ash, who then flew off toward the gnome.

"Ivy, can you do most of the talking?" Orion asked, a look of determination on his face.

She gave him a halting nod, unsure of his plan. Moments later, Ash returned with the smiling gnome right behind her. Though, the moment the gnome spied Ivy and Orion, her face fell.

"Are you all right?" she gasped, running forward.

"I need a healer. Can you help me?" Ivy asked.

"I can fetch help right away. Several healers live on this side of the city." She looked from Orion to Ivy. "Were you at the Battle of the Gathering?"

Ivy bit her lip, shoving away the rising memories. "Yes."

"The others arrived nearly a week ago. You poor thing! I'll be back soon. Very soon!"

As the gnome turned to rush to the city, Orion stopped the gnome, gently taking her hand. His quiet words seemed to punctuate through the air like a blade. "The dragon guided you to an elf, who is traveling *alone*. You must hurry and find a healer."

The gnome's attention seemed to fade, but she nodded and hurried to the city. As she disappeared into the bushes, Orion sighed, and his glamour fell away completely. Ivy blinked, realizing that he'd kept some of his glamour in place the entire time she'd been conscious.

"What just happened?" Ivy asked, wondering what he'd just done to deplete his magical strength.

"Memory magic," Orion said, not explaining further, but moving to kneel next to her. "When I've smoothed things over with the king, I'll return to find you."

Ivy simply nodded, knowing he would come to his senses when he spent time in the Winter Court. Besides, a few days in the fair realm equaled about a month in the human realm. Even if he did search her out, *years* might pass her by. Her heart fractured at the thought.

Ash swooped down, hopping next to Orion before moving to sit between him and Ivy. The dragon bumped his head under Orion's hand, like a cat. Because apparently she needed attention at that very moment.

"Do me one favor?" Ivy asked.

"A boon?" he scratched behind Ash's ears.

"No, just a small kindness," she grinned despite the tightness in her chest.

"Of course." Orion's eyes half-closed, exhausted.

"Enjoy the Winter Court a bit. It's your home now. I hope it's everything you hoped for." Ivy felt the air shift between them, like an unwelcome wet blanket in winter. Ivy changed the subject, not wanting to dwell on the fact that they lived in two different realms. "And find Zel. I think he really can cure the Seekers."

"That's two favors," Orion gave her a little smirk.

Ivy snorted, pressing the heel of her hand against her ribs in a vain attempt at relief. "How will you get back to the Winter Court? I heard what the sirens said, and every magical creature would love to be the one to capture you."

"Don't worry about me." He brushed off her concern, but

still Ivy's stomach coiled. He'd worked so hard to be welcomed home and she threatened everything he'd ever wanted.

She lifted her hand and gently touched the side of his face, looking past the irritated, swollen flesh. Instead, she focused on the rough dryad lines he could no longer glamour and the willow branches in his hair. The holly-crown on his brow was fully visible. He needed healing, too, but from the Winter centaur.

Orion leaned forward, and Ivy gripped the front of his tunic as he kissed her forehead. He shifted back, then searched her face. Unready to release him, Ivy tugged him closer, stealing one last kiss. Even as the dryad's medicine wore off, leaving her spent, she felt a rush of senses: the trees, the leaves, the blossoms, each one distinct in the forest. Through it all, a spike of awareness warned her that three creatures were closing in.

Soon the gnome and others would return. It wouldn't take them long to figure out his identity, and they had no allies here. No matter how much Ivy wanted him to stay, he needed to return to the fair realm, a place she could never reside. She wished she could be surrounded by the scents of berries and snow forever, to keep Orion at her side. But she couldn't. The thought of them being forever separated sent a wave of panic through her core, and her fingers gripped his tunic tighter.

Orion pulled her into an embrace, and something niggled at the back of her mind. Something important. Then, it dawned on her that she'd need to tell him that Emmyth could portal. Maybe other councilors could, too.

But if she told him now, she'd have to explain that Emmyth had gone to the effort of hunting her down. If he knew the truth of her danger, he wouldn't leave. So she would somehow get him a message later, after he had been healed in the Winter infirmary.

Shoving away all other worries, Ivy forced herself to her

knees, each movement a fresh wave of agony radiating from her wounds. But she ignored the pain, recognizing that these might be her final moments with the dryad-fae she had come to love so deeply. Face to face with Orion, she gazed into his eyes, drowning in the worry and love she saw reflected there. She kissed him gently on his rough cheek, her lips lingering, savoring the brief connection. His chest shuddered with unshed emotion, the silent tremor mirroring the turmoil in her own heart.

Hearing the gnome crashing through the underbrush, Ivy reluctantly pushed Orion away as hard as she could, which was really a pathetic nudge. She couldn't speak, her voice lost to heartbreak, so she mouthed, "Go."

Orion gave her one more kiss, this time on her lips, desperate and filled with unspoken words. The kiss was a promise, a plea, and a farewell all in one. Tears streamed down her cheeks, and she couldn't tell if they were hers or his. The salt of their sorrow stung, adding to her pain. Her heart ached, a raw wound that mirrored the one burrowed into her back. She wasn't sure which was worse, the stab wound or being ripped away from the person she'd come to care for so deeply.

"She's right up here," the gnome's voice carried through the forest. Their time was up.

Orion slipped into the forest, moving with a stealth born of necessity, but he wouldn't be far. She knew he was staying close, protecting her until he was sure she was safe—a futile act, but comforting nonetheless.

The little gnome appeared through thick ferns and patted Ivy's arm lightly. "Not to worry, you're in good hands now," he said, his voice kind but resolute.

Ivy nodded, her gaze lingering in the direction Orion had disappeared. The warmth of his kiss still lingered on her lips, a bittersweet reminder of what she was fighting for. She took a pained breath, steeling herself for what was to come.

Ivy awoke to the same healer's chamber she'd been in for the last two days. Her wounds had been cleaned, though now the sores throbbed. Yet, they were nothing compared to how raw and pained she felt inside now that Orion wasn't at her side.

Ash shifted in her sleep, her claws tickling the bottoms of Ivy's feet under the blanket before relaxing into a deeper slumber. The dragon had trailed Ivy to the Mineral's city, which Ivy had mixed feelings about. On one hand, Ivy knew the dragon was a kindness from Orion. On the other hand, Ash was a smoke-spewing nuisance.

And she was illegal.

The healer assumed Ivy had gotten lost after the Battle of the Gathering, and that she'd crossed alone at the orc pass. And Ivy let him believe his own story. Besides, she hadn't had enough strength to come up with a believable lie about her injuries or her journey south. At least she'd kept Ash hidden. And even luckier, no one recognized her as Ialant Balrel's daughter.

The elf youngling, the healer's grandson and apprentice, skipped into the room and plopped down on Ivy's mat. She'd only exchanged a few words with the lighthearted youngling since she'd arrived. "You're up! Finally. You look like you played a game with a gargoyle. And lost."

"Do I?" Ivy clutched her stone, grateful Orion had secured it. He had protected her ever since saving her life at the Gathering. The dark hole in her heart threatened to open and suck her into a downward spiral, the one she'd been fighting ever since she'd arrived. Not just because of Orion's departure, but because she missed her family. Her mother would never wrap her in her arms, she'd never hear her father's voice, nor her sister's teasing.

Ivy was on her own, with no delusions that her family lived. She'd searched for her family and found them. But now what? Refusing to feel sorry for herself, Ivy gingerly shifted onto her side, her mind still groggy after her long hours of rest.

"Why didn't they put you in the central infirmary with the rest of the injured from the Gathering?" the youngling asked, then answered himself. "Maybe because you arrived so much later. Or maybe—" he stopped short, his eyes widening with delight. "Ohhh, a dragon!" he clapped, giddy. "You have a *dragon?*"

He slid over to where Ash had kicked away the blanket. Ivy sighed, knowing she'd been lucky to keep the dragon hidden for this long.

The youngling leaned dangerously close to her smokey nostrils.

"Dragons are fickle creatures, in my experience," Ivy warned, her voice cracking with disuse. This was already the longest conversation she'd had since arriving. "So it's best to back away from their mouths."

"Papa says they're majestic. They have a sense of those destined for great things," he said in a reverent voice.

Ivy grinned, wondering what Orion would say about such folklore. What would Brecc think? Though Ash had lived with Brecc, even he'd said that the dragon barely tolerated him. Ash seemed to have a much stronger connection with Orion. She imagined Orion scoffing at the boy's prediction, but then her heart wrung, missing him even more acutely.

The healer, glided into the room, signaling for his apprentice to move away from his patient. He'd been kind and offered her privacy since she'd arrived, asking her few questions and letting her sleep. From what she'd gathered, he'd been in the war, which worried Ivy; if and when he realized she had spoken on behalf of the Seekers—humans—at the Gathering, he would undoubtedly become less friendly.

"Sorry about the ruckus outside," he said, closing the only window in the room. "I don't know why satyrs insist on harassing the centaurs. Some kind of game to them."

Ivy just smiled and nodded, but she hadn't heard the uproar. She hadn't heard anything. She kept hoping that the medallion's damage would reverse, but her sight and hearing had only marginally improved. The healer could more efficiently heal her if he knew the full spectrum of her injuries, but he hadn't earned that much trust, not yet. Ivy smoothed away her distress, but the healer raised a brow as he considered her before moving to Ivy's side, inspecting her wounds.

"Even without a seed, your wounds are healing slower than they should. You're more on the pace of a fae or a human."

Or an elf who was magically hampered by an evil iron medallion contraption in the fae realm. Ivy had hoped that the healer would procure a seed for her from *someone* in the massive city. Yes, it would've been very generous, but, apparently, no one had a single seed to spare. Though could she blame them for their caution? They'd just been attacked by Seekers, and those who'd fought had greatly depleted their stores.

Ivy wished she could talk to Orion. Or just have him nearby. If they'd had more time, he could've explained more about the medallion's power. She desperately wanted her innate magical abilities back, but even more, she longed for Orion's steady presence.

But wishes and wants would only make her miserable. Yet again, she pushed aside thoughts of Orion and focused on what she *could* do. She was curious to be among the elves in Yllalen'al and assess the mood. Maybe she just needed a distraction, but she wanted to know this unfamiliar House. Did they fear the Seekers? Was there any distrust of their councilors? Or were they as stingy about leadership change as they were with sharing seeds? Did they know they were slipping closer to war? Were they calling for it?

"At your rate of recovery, I'm rather surprised your other lung didn't collapse," the healer continued.

"The gnome who brought you claimed that you'd been touched by his kind's magic," the youngling excitedly interjected, "and that may have saved your life."

Ivy pressed a hand to her belly, remembering the gnome in the Winter infirmary who had touched Brecc's seed. She didn't know much about gnome magic, but she was grateful he'd helped her.

"Your stab wound was starting to get infected when you arrived. Another day and you'd have developed a fever." The healer paused, as he had done multiple times before, waiting for Ivy to provide insight. When she remained quiet, he continued. "You will heal, but a full recovery may take many months. You might consider laying low until the Centennial. You'll get a seed then."

Ivy had confessed that she'd lost her vial and seeds in a fight with the Seekers. It was true, but the fight had happened weeks before the Gathering.

"You know what's strange," the healer began. "It's almost like these injuries are days old, not weeks."

"Perhaps it had something to do with the gnome magic?" Ivy lied. Who would believe she had been stabbed in the back by Emmyth, one of the most respected elven leaders?

Ivy closed her eyes, her body aching with more than just her physical injuries. The healer didn't press Ivy for information as he cleaned her wounds. When he was done applying fresh bandages, he stood to leave.

"I didn't have any luck locating Wirenth, like you'd asked," he said. "Gneiss Feldspar was the last to see him. She said he fought Seekers to the bitter end. I'm so sorry, but I don't think he survived."

The edges of the rock bit into Ivy's palm. She'd clutched a wisp of a hope that Wirenth had survived. Yes, as a friend of her father's and her closest House of Seeds ally, he might have given her a seed. Even if he hadn't, she would've had a friend in this city. But, Wirenth was dead, and Gneiss, Brecc's sister who hated her, knew someone was asking about him. Not that the Mineral's elf should care about a Seeds Ambassador, but Ivy hoped Gneiss wasn't the curious sort.

"Now that you're awake, there is someone who would like to see you. They're waiting outside."

"I apologize, my exhaustion makes me terrible company. Can they return tomorrow instead?" Ivy dreaded a confrontation with Gneiss. If she confirmed Ivy's identity, things would get complicated.

"I'm afraid this person won't wait." He gave her a genuinely pitying look before he sent his grandson to fetch the visitor.

Ivy didn't have time to formulate a story about how she'd survived her travel from the Gathering before the newcomer entered.

"This is Councilor Lonsdaleite, one of our Minerals councilors," the healer said.

Lonsdale. Ivy's insides shriveled at the sight of him. He'd been at the Gathering with Ivy. She didn't know his evil intentions then. She did now.

The entrance was mere steps away, which afforded Ivy the luxury of watching the councilor's eyes widen for a fraction of a moment. Ivy saw his true emotion, his shock melting into a flash of anger. He knew *everything.* He knew Ivy was behind the destruction of the orchard in The Tree House. He knew she'd spoken against him at the Aequus. He knew she wanted to strip away his position, power, and his life's plans. And he hated her.

Then Lonsdale's face became an impenetrable mask.

"I'm sorry, but I don't even know my patient's name," the healer said, apologetically.

"Her name is Ivy." Lonsdaleite raised a lazy brow at the sight of the sleeping dragon. "This elf spoke on behalf of the Seekers at the Gathering. Judging by the injuries she sustained, I see the Seekers must've appreciated her support."

The healer stiffened at the councilor's words, staying quiet —a wise decision as Lonsdale was one of the most influential elves in both realms. But Ivy wanted to lash out at Lonsdale. Emmyth had nearly killed her. Seekers were mindless, but Emmyth had maliciously plotted to attack Ivy at the Aequus. No, the entire Council, including Lonsdale, had plotted to have her entire family murdered.

Ivy gripped the blanket in her fists, refusing to rise to his bait. Londsdale was a seasoned fighter, known for his combat skills in the Realm Wars. He would love nothing more than for Ivy to attack. Instead, Ivy braced herself. With Lonsdale aware of her presence, she had to endure whatever abuse he was about to dole. Until she healed, she was at the mercy of the Minerals.

So, she needed to recuperate quickly. She suspected that he'd waste no time in telling the rest of the Council exactly where to find her, and they'd finish the job Emmyth started.

Lonsdale continued, his voice carrying a combination of mockery and hatred, a chilling combination. "I suggest you stay well within elven protection next time, Ivy. Your father wandered too far. Remember, outside our embrace, danger lurks."

IO

BLACKENED COINS

Orion awoke, thanks to his sister shaking his shoulder. Dryads never touched anyone, but his sister seemed to make all kinds of exceptions for him. He blinked his eyes open, grateful his sister had turned away so as to not accidentally catch his eye. He sat up, ignoring his body aches, but the dryness of his throat and the tightness in his lungs refused to dissipate, even after two days of resting on the island. His time crossing the poisoned lands had forced him to seek refuge with his sister. Even she admitted he needed to rest.

Orion pushed to his feet, and they stood not far from the lake, but still hidden in the trees from siren onlookers. The sun had dropped past the trees, the sky already darkening, thanks to incoming clouds.

"It's time for me to go," Orion said.

"You've slept like the dead. But you're still not well. Between your siren-pasty skin and those bags under your eyes, you look horrible. But, yes, you must return and placate your king," she said. "I've been listening to the trees. Carrus is your safest, most welcoming portal."

"That makes sense." That dryad had been his messenger for decades. But, in his condition, the journey would take weeks. Orion resisted complaining. What good would it do?

"I might have sent you off sooner, but ... I have a surprise," she said, a hint of mischief in her voice. His sister let Orion squirm before she continued. "Your horse will await you in Beggarton."

"What? How?" Relief washed over him, but he kept his attention on her feet. His horse would cut down his travel time and preserve his energy. With rest and his sister's care, his small magical reserves had nearly replenished, but he'd worried about the travel draining his powers again. In Carrus, he'd need his glamour.

"Being the queen's warrior has its perks." She offered no more insights, and Orion hoped someone wasn't missing their memories. Though if her father had resided at Blackmore, she could have human contacts at the castle. Perhaps her father, himself, if he was alive.

"You'll need these." She grabbed Orion's hand and pressed three, wet, blackened coins into his palm, gritty sand still clinging to them. "I'll never use them. They're yours."

"Dare I ask how you got human coins?" Orion said, recognizing the symbols on the coins—images that hadn't been stamped in decades.

"Let's just say I have a few siren friends who enjoy gambling."

"So will your friends let me pass?"

"Well, calling them 'friends' might be a bit of a stretch. So, don't be an object I have to bargain to get back. Stay out of their reach, because I cannot compete with what your father offers as a reward." Her voice still held a teasing tone, but he knew she wasn't joking about the getting captured part.

"How can I repay you?" Orion asked.

"Visit me again," she said. "You know where to find me. And get your dryad senses back. Otherwise I might not know you're here."

Orion paused, surprised by her comment. "You couldn't sense me when I arrived on the island?"

"I knew there was an intruder, but I had no idea it was *you*." She grabbed his elbow, catching him off guard. "We could dally all day chatting about your magic, but you need to go. Take advantage of the extra moments of darkness."

He trusted his sister's advice, but still, it took a moment to remind himself that he could reveal his ability to gather shadows. Selleth and Rime both knew; it was only a matter of time until others did as well. A few sirens had probably figured it out, too.

As the sun dropped below the horizon and clouds blanketed the sky, Orion felt his sister's attention on his back. He summoned the shadows with a deep, weary breath. They gathered around him, thin and wispy, barely lifting him above the ground. The shadows flickered weakly, struggling with forward movement, threatening to disperse. Gritting his teeth, he pushed on, the effort draining him further, but he had no other way to cross the sea.

As the faint shadows carried him over the water, a mix of foreign emotions churned inside him. Guilt still pricked at him for not seeking his sister out, for assuming she'd reject him. He'd never given her a chance, but she had forgiven him before they'd ever met. He'd learned to spot lies, thanks to his father's training and his many years as a guard. He had quickly recognized his dryad sister's straight-forward honesty. Her loyalty to her queen and to her brother were both so pure, it forced him to evaluate his own allegiances. She held no malice, no jealousy, no care for dominion or authority. She broke so many unsaid dryad rules, yet he'd seen her do the unimaginable—open a withered portal. He didn't know quite what to make of his sister, but he found himself looking forward to visiting her again. One day.

Over the next three nights, as Orion traveled, his thoughts continually wandered to Ivy. The growing distance between them became a physical weight pressing down on his heart. Doubt became his constant companion, gnawing at the edges of his resolve. He could still feel the lingering warmth of her touch, the soft press of her lips against his cheek, and it only deepened the hollow ache inside him.

Had she been given a seed? The question haunted him, as did the image of her getting conveyed by elves toward the city. Would his magic heal along with hers? Or was his condition permanent? The uncertainty became a relentless whisper in the back of his mind.

Every passing hour, the shadows he summoned weakened, the flickering wisps barely supporting him above the ferns and shrubs as the night waned. The effort expended to stay aloft mirrored the effort spent to keep his fears for Ivy at bay.

He yearned for her presence, her strength. He missed the way she scowled at Ash. He even missed how he always had to watch whatever he ate and drank in case she decided to render him unconscious for a few hours. He chuckled, temporarily distracting himself from the fact that he didn't know when he would see her again. The uncertainty was almost unbearable.

As he neared Beggarton, his concern for Ivy's safety only grew. Was she truly safe in an unfamiliar city? Had she found shelter and a competent healer? His heart clenched at the thought of her languishing, struggling without him. Uncertainty gnawed as terrible scenarios unfolded in his mind.

Pushing his fears away, he forced himself to imagine positive experiences with the Minerals. He hoped Ivy was laughing, healing, then leaving their city before a councilor discovered her whereabouts.

He tromped through the muddy small town of Beggarton, using the last of his strength to create his Unarian guard glamour. He'd cleaned the tarnished coins from his sister to a silver-shine, and paid for his room, a hot dinner, and provisions. For the rest of the trip to Carrus, he'd sleep outside, which was his preference. But for now, he needed food and protection from the storm he could see coming.

The next morning, he rewarded the courier for delivering the horse. The young man brightened, seeing the amount, and asked if there were any other services Orion needed.

"Only your silence. I was never here," Orion said.

The courier winked and hurried away, having no idea that Orion was avoiding rumors that might reach fair folk ears. Humans were ignorant, not realizing that they teetered on the edge of war. Orion galloped toward Carrus, hoping to stop the bloody disaster before it began.

Orion considered his next steps. His sister had listened to the trees, confirming that the dryad in Carrus had communicated no distrust of Orion. She, of all dryads, would be prone to aid him. Dryads kept to themselves, but even so, they'd protected his privacy over the years—specifically the dryad in Carrus. She'd always helped him, and he'd assumed it was because she was loyal to Winter. But now he wasn't sure. Dryads always had their reasons; they just rarely revealed them.

The fact that his sister didn't sense Orion specifically, also meant he could travel without worry of discovery. A dryad would detect a presence, but they'd assume he was simply another human passing through. With his horse, Orion traveled on an animal track without glamour and without expending his magical reserves. That night, he forced himself to eat and rest, missing Ash's company, but grateful he'd been able to buy dried meat and bread in Beggarton.

Ash hadn't wanted to abandon him, but how could Orion let Ivy go without a safeguard. Besides, he would return and find them both. This trip to the fair realm was temporary. And it had to be quick. In a mere nine days within the fair domain, an entire season passed by in Trinth. Anything could happen. A sharp pang made his chest tighten knowing that Ivy was accustomed to looking out for herself. She was capable and strong, and in time her feelings for him might fade. Relationships inevitably shifted, so how soon would Ivy forget him?

Orion wished he didn't need Ivy, but he realized more and more that he hated the idea of being without her.

An unseasonably cold, desolate wind blew, cutting through Orion's tunic. Pushing himself harder, Orion stopped just outside Carrus's gates as one new moon and one crescent hung in the night sky. Thick clouds rolled in, threatening rain and blotting out the stars. He'd timed his arrival with precision. Tying up his horse in the woods, Orion wrapped shadows around himself and flew over the towering wall. Below him, the city blurred, but he saw well enough to land at the edge of the inner forest. Striding into the heart of the woods, he dropped his shadows, but moved with care. Orion quickly found his way to the dryad tree, despite the darkness.

Pressing his hand on the bark, he whispered his name.

He didn't wait long until her presence rose to meet him. Like with his sister, temptation pulled at him to look at her face. Forcing his attention down, he reminded himself that the darkness couldn't protect him from catching her eye and having his memory wiped away.

"Where have you been?" she asked before hurrying to add, "Don't tell me. It's better that I don't know."

Guilt tugged at Orion, knowing his sister hadn't revealed

his presence, not to her queen nor anyone else. Her action could land her in the middle of a fae court if the fae guards ever connected him to the dryads' island.

"Summer Court has demanded all the dryads to watch for you and Ivy."

Orion swallowed, despite the fact that he'd already suspected as much. Spies were everywhere. If Orion was carted off to Summer before he voluntarily returned to the Winter Court, the consequences would be *so* much worse when he faced his father.

With everyone hunting him, he nearly leapt into the portal to return straight to the Winter Court, but the dryad interrupted his request.

"Oddly, a gnome is looking for you. He came from Winter to Carrus."

Zel? "Is he still here?"

"He hasn't been granted permission to use another portal, but I can't say for certain where he's located."

"I don't understand how he returned to Trinth," Orion said. "Who granted permission?"

"Technically, his permission was from the Summer Queen."

Technically?

The dryad continued, "He came through with Magdud. I communicated the presence of both of them to my queen."

Of course Zel would've come through with Maggie. Otherwise, he would've had to request special permission from a royal. Clever on his part, but a risk for Maggie.

Finding no reason to hide it, Orion quickly relayed information about the illicit orchard in Neidrei. And he warned her that the one, surviving older tree now housed a dryad who might be in danger. The dryad said nothing, either already aware or processing her shock. He didn't know which, and he didn't have time to wait and find out.

"Now that I know Magdud has returned," Orion said, "I must speak with her before I return home."

He turned to leave, but paused at hearing her soft voice, "Orion. You ran from the Winter Court right after your father extended you a proper place and office. How does that reflect on him as a ruler?"

Poorly.

"I must report having seen you. King Eldrin isn't a patient fae. I don't know who or *what* he'll send after you," she paused, her voice almost pleading. "I fear for you. That isn't the path your mother wanted." Her voice dropped to barely a whisper, as if she wasn't sure she should speak her next words. "She wishes to see you."

Orion pinched the bridge of his nose and took a shuddering breath, struggling to ignore her last comment. Suppressed rage surged within him, ripping open festering old wounds. After all these years of cold, unyielding silence, his mother now wished to see him? The audacity of it made his blood boil. He batted away the surge of bitter curiosity, reminding himself that he wasn't at the beck and call of her whims. She had cast him out when he was just a child without a hint of remorse. Now, she could wait. He wasn't about to let her sudden interest dictate his actions; she had forfeited any claim to his time and attention long ago.

"Do what you must," Orion said, trying not to imagine his father's rage when he returned. But he might not get another chance to speak to Magdud or find Zel; he had to take it.

II

JUSTIFICATION

Emmyth had to handle Kolvar delicately. His tender heart would make him a good ruler during times of peace, but in times of war ... his soft nature was a liability. If Nym could falter, Kolvar could too. She vowed to do better with him. She strode to her son's office, a recent addition to his schedule since his health had begun to improve.

She greeted citizens as she walked, but her mind actively assessed her wayward daughter. Her most recent questioning in The Hand was like the others. Emmyth hated those visits. Her daughter had grown gaunt, a shell of her old self, yet she remained as stubborn as ever. Her iron will was unbending and blind. Despite Emmyth's frustration, she put on a calm demeanor to greet her son.

Entering his rooms, she was unsurprised to see him hovering over his desk, a pile of missives teetering on the side. He looked up and smiled, an expression that brought a wave of joy. Then suspicion.

"Good afternoon, Mother," he stood and gave her a respectful nod. "I'm glad you took time to visit."

Emmyth gestured to his couch, and he picked up his tea and

a missive, then moved to sit across from her. She watched him carefully for signs of the poisoning, specifically disorientation, short-term memory loss, or clumsiness. The healer had explained the symptoms; Emmyth hadn't even bothered to ask Nym about it knowing her daughter had certainly only meant to incapacitate him for the day.

Another one of Nym's many mistakes.

Her daughter's plan wasn't terrible, in theory. But the plant root caused complications when Emmyth employed the healer to render Kolvar unconscious for several days after the attempted coup. Now, he had lingering effects. Nym knew that his spotless reputation was paramount, so the least she could have done was use bitterel bark, which layered nicely with other herbs. Another rash oversight on Nym's part. Irritation flared at her daughter's blunders, but she snuffed the emotion out just as quickly.

Kolvar handed Emmyth a missive before he sat down. "Ivy is back in the realm."

Emmyth raised a brow. She'd not read her messages yet today, so this was the first she'd heard of it. Emmyth kept her thoughts hidden as she scanned the missive, feeling Kolvar watching her as he drank his tea. But annoyance flared hot and bright. Ivy still breathed.

She'd overheard the daft Summer prince ask Selleth to hold Ivy in the fair realm. And Emmyth had been delighted to see Selleth preparing The Tower. Emmyth would've happily stayed to watch Ivy's demise, but a councilor didn't have the luxury of lingering. Hearing that Ivy not only survived, but had traveled to the Minerals unaided ... it was not plausible.

"She arrived alone," she mused.

Kolvar nodded. "Lonsdale's report indicated that she trekked, injured, to the Mineral's city after the Gathering, according to the rumors. But we know Ivy and Nym journeyed up to Neidrei. Apparently, after Ivy and Nym parted, Ivy traveled south."

Not to mention a little detour to the Winter Court.

Kolvar continued, "I can't figure out what would prompt Ivy to risk traveling across the poisoned land to Yllalen'al."

Logically, she must have gotten help from the king's outcast son, Orion. But Lonsdale would've noticed the king's son skulking nearby. So, had Orion realized Ivy was nothing special?

According to the missive, Ivy's symptoms matched with a magical weakening. Had Selleth activated the orbs? A giddiness rose at the thought, and Emmyth made a mental note to apprise Lonsdale of the possibility. If Ivy had lost her abilities, it further explained why Orion had abandoned her—she'd become baggage too heavy to carry, especially after the debacle at the equinox ceremony.

"You look pleased," Kolvar said.

"It seems that the Minerals councilors see through Ivy just as you did. Their good judgment pleases me."

Emmyth couldn't be sure how much Kolvar had learned from his sister. According to Nym, she divulged to Kolvar that the Council was corrupt and that seeds were being used against the humans. No further details. Kolvar claimed to barely remember Nym's return at all, but Emmyth had her doubts.

Had Nym told her brother about the Tree House, or what she'd done to the trees? Probably not. Nym wouldn't want to explain her actions, nor had she the time that day to justify them. So, Emmyth took a breath and started weaving her side of the story.

"Ivy has twisted Nym's perceptions of the Council. I know it's hard to hear, but we can know the truth of a creature by their actions. By her own hand, Ivy killed an entire orchard of trees, the sacred Gathering trees we'd protected in Neidrei. Ivy entered in disguise, glamoured as me, and poisoned the trees.

Her duplicity was discovered, but so was Nym's. That's why your sister is in prison. Not because of her slander against me, but because Nym aided in destroying an entire orchard, gifts from Alysatraee."

Kolvar gripped his cup and glanced down, his brow furrowed. "I have a hard time imagining Ivy would do such a thing. And if she did, she must've had good reason."

"No matter what Ivy thought she knew, there was no reason for the poison. Her mindset is so repulsive, I can barely think about how much time she spent planning such an unnatural act. She should've brought the problem to the Council—a public meeting. Or spoken at the next Gathering. She should've asked questions. Instead, she made assumptions. Costly mistakes that have stained her soul. Selfishly, she only wanted to save her father's legacy and her family's reputation."

Kolvar set down his cup and stood up, pacing to his unlit fireplace. "Ivy was never reverent about our ways, but she'd never hurt a living thing without cause."

"Kolvar, read the missive again. Ivy's magic has been impacted, which indicates that the Mother herself has cast her judgment against her. She's broken the law." Yes, Ivy deserved her punishment. Didn't deserve a seed. Smugly, Emmyth noted that no Minerals elf had deigned to give her one. Ivy was without friends. Without allies. Exactly where she should be.

It wouldn't be difficult to have Ivy killed. She was weak, and it wouldn't draw attention. Who would care? She glanced up at her pacing son and realized that someone would notice. So, she wouldn't give the order. Not yet, anyway.

Emmyth couldn't give Kolvar any reason to suspect foul play. She sensed the division in him as he weighed what he knew of his childhood friend against her recent actions. The Tides needed Kolvar, a beacon of stability and calm. If Ivy died, Kolvar would grow suspicious. He might do his own digging and, from his perch inside the protective bubble he'd always known, he might go against the Council. He might make a disastrous decision, like push back against the coming war. He'd be viewed as someone who supported the loss of their fair folk ancestral lands. Unacceptable.

Emmyth moved and stood in front of her son, gripping one of his shoulders. "It's natural, compassionate even, that you should be pained over the situation. Your reaction indicates your potential to be a great leader one day. But a leader must also put their own feelings aside and consider the greater good."

"I don't know what to believe anymore." Kolvar ran a hand over his shaved head, something he'd always done when distressed. He wasn't yet convinced.

"I didn't want to tell you this. Didn't want to upset you further. But I got word that Ivy was in the fair realm. She had a dalliance with a half-fae. Then at the fair equinox ceremony, their sacred event, Ivy engaged in combat. She shot a Spring attending with an arrow, wounding the fae." Emmyth pressed her lips together, feigning inner turmoil. "I fear she was the one who drew the Seekers to the Gathering."

"Ivy? On accident? Or ..." He seemed reluctant to say the accusatory words.

"Who knows for certain. She deceived Nym into believing the sacrilege was my doing, however it was all part of Ivy's plan to redeem herself. She's fooled many fair folk. Don't be ashamed if you were taken in by her charms."

Kolvar scratched his chin, his brows drawn. "I'm glad you told me what happened. But, I'd like permission to question Ivy. I did care for her as a dear friend, and we owe her that much."

"Of course. You can return with the orcs when they travel south. I'll make the arrangements," Emmyth said, feigning gracious calm. She had anticipated his request though she would never actually allow it.

"Thank you, Mother."

Emmyth watched him carefully for any signs of duplicity. But his mind seemed to be thoughtfully considering her every word. His thinking had been a little softer after awaking from the extended, drug-induced sleep. Perhaps Alysatraee in her wisdom had slowed his healing, or perhaps he just trusted his mother. Either way, she wasn't concerned. His mind would be completely healed, even sharper, by the time he ruled. In the meantime, this was best.

"I'll leave you to rest." Emmyth squeezed his shoulder. An uncharacteristic amount of affection, but a necessity for today. She'd give Kolvar time to process her words, a few days at least, before approaching him again. He wasn't completely in her palm, but after a bit more nudging, he would be swayed. She turned to leave, but Kolvar stopped her.

"What about Nym?" Kolvar asked. "Can I see her?"

Emmyth bristled. So far, no one had seen Nym in her reduced state. However, perhaps the encounter would drive home the message that Alysatraee had abandoned Nym and Ivy. At this point, Emmyth had to consider that Nym was beyond her reach, her life a ruin.

She should have died at the Gathering. At least her honor would be intact.

Emmyth's face fell, and she didn't hide her sadness. The realization settled between her ribs, leaving her aching with loss—Nym's future was over; it was time to cut her from the branch. "Have her moved from The Hand to the dungeon with the rest of my traitorous advisers."

She sighed, disappointed in her parenting, blaming herself for the utter waste of Nym's future.

"I will go right away." Kolvar then pressed his lips into a tight line.

A knock came at the door and Kolvar answered. Adviser Bellas entered, and when she noticed Emmyth, her gait became stiff and her expression wooden. Hiding her thoughts was never her strong suit, which had contributed to Emmyth thwarting the forming coup.

"My apologies," Bellas said. "I'm interrupting. I'll leave you."

"Kolvar was just leaving on an errand." Emmyth turned to her son, wanting Bellas to hear her parting words. "Make sure no one treats Nym with a seed. The healers may attend her, but Nym must feel the consequences of disobedience."

"The laws are a sacred trust," Bellas added quietly.

Kolvar gave a solemn nod. "We leave Nym in Alysatraee's trust?"

Emmyth stiffened at his words, reminding her of his strict dedication to the old beliefs, just like his sister.

"Sometimes Alysatraee trusts us to step back and take a wider view," Emmyth instructed. "Nym's actions seemed righteous, but they weakened our kind. If we don't want a repeat of the Battle of the Gathering, we need to punish those who would rather harm us than help us."

Bellas paled at the thinly-veiled warning but said nothing. Her family reputation had saved her, but it wouldn't save her twice. Bellas and the other advisers walked a fine line.

"I understand," Kolvar said, a muscle ticking in his jaw.

He marched out his rooms with Bellas right behind him, leaving Emmyth to riffle through his missives undisturbed. Not seeing any black wax letters, Emmyth grew even more confident that Lial had been snuffed. With him and his father successfully swept aside, Emmyth had hinted at her favored replacements to her loyal advisers.

Now, she awaited their nominations within the next moon. Soon the remaining orcs would leave Nylenn'or, deployed according to the battle plans. And Ivy would die long before Kolvar left on the ship to find her, but not until after her son was fully aligned with the Council. Things were unfolding nicely.

Feeling a sense of gleeful irony, Emmyth jotted an instruction to Lonsdale with Kolvar's quill and ink:

Keep Ivy in your sights. Her fate remains sealed, but the final act must wait for my command.

—Councilor Phiro

After the Centennial, when the seeds were distributed and the Seekers scattered their human counterparts, the fair folk would prevail. Transforming humans into Seekers was the most logical strategy because, when chaos ruled, the waves of attacks would catch the humans off guard. Ivy had become an unpredictable nuisance with dangerous ideas, too much like her father. But, in the end, the Balrels wouldn't matter. Trinth had been dutifully ruled by fair folk from its inception, and it was time to take it back.

12
HOUSE OF MINERALS

Ivy stretched her legs, walking through the market as the healer had instructed. He'd told her a little exercise would be good for her. Ivy had simply nodded in agreement, hiding the fact that she had eagerly awaited another opportunity to explore.

The stitches in her back pulled if she wasn't careful, and her leg was still sore. But she limped along well enough. As she ventured out the second time in the last week, the sun shone, banishing the rain and bringing droves of fair folk outside. Ash abandoned her—typical—spying some shiny trinket in one of the stalls.

At first, Ivy worried that Ash would draw attention, but on her last excursion she'd seen another small dragon and two hellhounds. Not to mention the stone gargoyle hovering on the central spire of some grand old elven building at the end of the street. The carving sent a chill through her; a Winter King's tool, one that, strictly speaking, wasn't allowed to reside in Trinth.

Technically, the fae courts shouldn't hunt her, especially after Prince Devain relayed the truth of what Ivy had witnessed. Still, Ivy strongly suspected the Summer Queen's compliance with the Spring warriors' attack. No, the danger went far deeper; Winter was likely complicit, too. No matter the level of their involvement, neither Court had grounds to haul her in for questioning. Even so, Ivy didn't plan to stick around long enough to put her theory to the test. However, the courts were not her biggest fear; they moved slowly.

If she feared anyone, it was Emmyth.

Only two elven cities had survived the war, Nylann'or in the north and Yllalen'al in the south. Past Yllalen'al lay Aggord, the orc stronghold, at the edge of the harsh desert of scalding sands. According to the stories, the orcs had built a massive iron cube structure that dove into the sands, melding with the earth's crust deep below.

Here in Yllalen'al, orcs, gnomes, satyrs, and other creatures mingled with the throngs of elves, bartering for everything from arrow tips, to seed vials, to satin fabric, to flax. A group of satyrs played flutes, and groups of younglings of all kinds danced, at odds with Ivy's mood. Compared to her insular childhood surrounded by immediate family, spending most of her time in the woods, and the occasional trip visits to the comparatively sterile city of Nylenn'or, this place was like a town festival. But compared to her recent years fleeing from human city to city like her feet were on fire, Yllalen'al felt beyond surreal.

Yllalen'al had rebuilt, healing the land. Thousands of creatures lived in the city, more populated and sprawling than their sister city in the north. The city's original elven architecture still boasted tall, slender buildings constructed of pale stone and intricately carved wood. Living greenery adorned roofs and flowed into the canopy above the newer buildings, the structures being more rustic without the help of the dwarves, but beautiful all the same. Vibrant flowers and lush foliage lined the streets, and everyone smiled.

They might be less jolly if they knew they were hurtling toward a war.

Ivy limped through the heart of the city, the marketplace, which bustled with activity. Colorful stalls and open-air shops lined both sides of the street; Ivy pretended to be distracted by the sights, though her true goal lay beyond. Elven artisans displayed their finely crafted jewelry that caught the sun's rays and woven fabrics that felt as light as air.

Because the city resided high on a cliff, no humans had noticed its existence. And the poisoned land between Yllalen'al and the rest of Trinth protected the city from wanderers. Her heart twisted with jealousy, part of her wishing she'd grown up here. Not betrayed with Mineral magic on the back of her family drawing and hunted by Seekers. Few in her House still survived. What would they think of this thriving place?

As she passed a gap between stalls, Ivy caught a glimpse of a red tunic. The elven attire seemed familiar, but with her impeded sight, she didn't know for certain. Even after a week with the healer, she hadn't dared confess the extent of her magic depletion, fearing questions. Fearing he would reveal her weakness to Lonsdale.

Ivy's innate, elven-heightened sight and hearing hadn't returned. Her senses were improving, but by her rough calculations, she figured that her magic wouldn't return for several years. Emmyth certainly wouldn't wait that long to make Ivy "disappear."

Unable to purchase anything, Ivy gazed past the wares. But what she couldn't ignore was how everyone bristled when she neared. Fortunately, between her limp and the loose scarf over her head, not many elves, if any, should recognize her. Brushing off her paranoia, she turned her thoughts to Emmyth as she wove through the crowd.

The northern councilor could send more than messages

through dryad portals. She could *use* them, herself, by taking advantage of the wartime emergency permissions. A loophole in the Mother's law. Ivy frowned, hating the constant abuse of power.

But more immediately, Emmyth could send a directive to have Ivy dispatched at any hour. And she certainly wouldn't want Ivy to leave the city alive. The feeling of a hand closing around her throat never quite went away. Ivy would have fled already, but she wouldn't survive until the worst of her wounds had healed. So, as soon as the stitches in her back could be removed, she would have to find another place to live—someplace Emmyth wouldn't think to look.

In the meantime, Ivy followed all the healer's instructions, desperate to speed her recovery. Besides her own life, she thought of Orion. They were connected; as she healed, Orion should, too. Ivy warmed at the thought, missing him acutely and hoping he was safe.

While stuck in Yllalen'al, Ivy had time to reflect on her next steps. She'd already done everything she'd set out to do. Initially, she'd just wanted to find out what happened to her family, which led to uncovering the illicit Council's plans. She'd even gone to the effort of taking the plans to the fae courts, ruining her own family name in the process, only to be attacked by vicious Spring attendings. She'd done everything she was "supposed" to do. Exhaustion wore her down, deep in her bones, weary of fighting the Council. They weren't her responsibility. What could she actually do anyway, especially considering her physical condition?

In the short time she'd lived in a bustling city where fair folk could be themselves, she realized she would love a chance to settle into a community with no bloody attacks. A place of refuge and peace. Clearly she couldn't stay in Yllalen'al, but somewhere in Trinth, she could make a home.

But after all she'd done to uncover the truth, she owed it to herself to pass on her knowledge to a Minerals elf. Someone who wouldn't easily fall for the Council's lies.

Ivy knew of one elf who already hated the Council: Gneiss Feldspar, Brecc's obnoxious sister. After a few careful questions to the healer's apprentice, she learned the general location of the central infirmary. If Gneiss had decided to conserve her seeds and use a healer instead, she might still be there.

Determined, Ivy continued forward until the breeze carried a familiar scent. Something about the smell reminded her of her family. She paused, inspecting a table of minerals. Each stone was stored in a small draw-string bag. She lifted each one closer, far closer than an elf should need, and her cheeks heated. But her curiosity overcame her embarrassment. Inside one linen sack, vibrant blue stones immediately reminded her of Brecc. He'd shown her one just like these, but these were perfectly spherical.

"What stone is this?" Ivy asked. She already knew the answer, and she hoped they didn't notice her voice trembling.

"Azurite," the male elf said, giving his partner an odd look. Both of them had crystals jutting from the back of their hands, symbolizing their mastery.

"They're beautiful," Ivy said, picking one up, identifying the smell she'd carried on the back of her family's image for years. "I've seen this before, but it was crushed to fine powder."

The female elf shifted uncomfortably. "Oh?"

As a Seeds elf, Ivy shouldn't know they were beacons, used in wartime to track each other. She shouldn't know the powder was used to hone in on and murder her family. Brecc had broken the rules, and his knowledge had set her free. She now carried the responsibility to share the damage the Mineral's secrets had inflicted.

"I once had a drawing of my family," Ivy said. "There was a

message on the back, with bits of this stone mixed into the ink. It's hard to miss the graininess, even when finely ground, don't you think?"

The pair stared at her, and another elf standing next to Ivy turned to watch.

"And it was mixed with a crushed seed." Ivy let the accusation drop. Hard.

The woman paled, but the male elf shook his head. "Who would do such a thing?"

The disbelieving tone of his words seemed to say, *no one would be so evil.* The herbalist in the next stall rolled her eyes, and the elf at Ivy's side scoffed. Yes, Ivy's story was unbelievable, yet the fact that they were dismissing her story without question pricked a warning in the back of her mind. But she didn't have time to examine it.

"My whole family had pictures of each other," Ivy pressed.

"That's nice to have the same sort of item between you. Especially as Seeds travel so often." His placating words grated. "And I'm sure it's a comfort when you're alone."

Ivy wondered how he already knew she was a Seeds elf. And alone.

"What happened to your family, Ivy?" the female elf asked. Her timid voice signaled she knew they were dead already.

They knew her name. They knew Ivy was a Balrel.

Ivy swallowed her irritation at the impertinent question. She wanted to leave without a word, but if she didn't attempt to tell the truth of her family, no one would.

"They were murdered," Ivy said, flatly. "The midwife left messages with ink mixed with this powdered stone and seed remnants. On every single image." Ivy paused to let that information sink in. "I should have died, too. None of us had any idea that we'd been marked for Seekers to find. And kill. Can you can explain to me *why* anyone would do such a terrible thing?"

Gasps sounded from several elves nearby, and both merchants leaned back from Ivy, as if she were a contagious disease.

"That's what I thought," Ivy huffed and stormed off. Unfortunately, her slow, limping march robbed her of a dramatic exit.

It was just as well. The merchants were not the true source of her frustration: it was with the community for withholding seeds. Seeds were sacred, yes, only to be given to the recipient of the fruit. However, part of her couldn't believe that no one had even considered gifting her one of theirs. Ivy had been on death's door when she'd arrived, yet offering her a seed hadn't crossed their minds. The Council could give seeds to poison humans, but not break the rules for her.

Grinding her teeth, Ivy turned off onto a side road, grateful when the buildings muffled the cheerful music. She picked up where she'd left off last time, continuing to look for the infirmary in the western part of the city. Many elves were outside watering flowers, sweeping the porches, and replacing roof thatch. Ivy frowned at the sight—contented activities meant they were unlikely to force out their councilors.

Ivy stopped in the middle of some unknown street. No one knew her. And if they did, they only knew her as the daughter of the disgraced Seeds councilor. Her family was dead. Orion was gone. Nym had her own problems. No one would mourn her if she disappeared. No one would even notice.

She was completely and utterly alone.

The black hole she'd fought to keep at bay ripped open and sucked her inside, drowning in the abyss. Why even attempt to continue? The creatures here were happy. Sure, they were breaking a hundred rules by allowing fair creatures to live here.

But no one enforced the law. No one listened to her warning. Would Ivy be the last elf in both realms to care?

Ivy blinked back tears, letting self-pity wash over her. Her insides hollow and her body tired, she dragged her feet forward wondering if she'd wandered right by the infirmary on her last trip without knowing. The streets quieted, and Ivy came to a large building set apart from the others. Her mind half-blank, she wandered closer.

Through the cracked windows, she heard moans. The pained sounds drilled past the numbness of her mind, pulling her back to shore. Ivy hurried and glanced through an open window. Inside, rows and rows of injured elves lay on cots. What were they all doing here, instead of with individual healers? The answer came to her just as quickly: there were too many.

From the corner of her eye, she glimpsed the same red material she'd spotted earlier, darting down an alley and disappearing from sight. Wait, was that the third time she'd noticed that tunic? Yes.

She frowned. Someone was spying on her. Dread crawled up her spine, but then she reminded herself that if they wanted her dead, they could've dispatched her ten times already. And they'd run off, so they wouldn't be able to spy on her—at least not at that moment.

Ivy hurried around the building to a set of open double-doors. The interior of the facility was too dark for Ivy to pick out individual faces, and she didn't feel welcome. But, she wouldn't be cowed by the eerie place. Ivy let her eyes adjust to the dim light.

Healers quickly moved from cot to cot, attending to the injured. Ivy walked slowly down the aisle, her limp helping her blend in with the others.

"Well, well, Ivy Balrel," a female voice shouted, the hard sarcasm identifying her.

"Gneiss Feldspar." Ivy forced herself to stand tall as she moved toward the redheaded elf. On the table next to her sat several vases of fresh flowers and a pile of little gifts. A healer brought a stool next to Gneiss's cot for Ivy to sit on.

"She won't be staying long," Gneiss said, letting everyone know Ivy was no friend.

Ivy sat down on the seat anyway, already irritated. "I'd like to say it's nice to see you, but that would be a lie."

Gneiss snorted. "That might be the first truth I've heard from your lips."

"I'm not in the mood for your barbs today, Gneiss."

"Well, then, take your privileged-self right on out of the infirmary. I don't much want to see your face, either."

The elf laying on the next cot grimaced and turned away, and probably not due to her pain. Ivy glanced at the table between her and Gneiss, assuming the kind well wishes and flowers were for the other elf. Inexplicably, the closest card clearly had "Gneiss" written in shimmering ink across the front.

Ivy pulled her gaze away, remembering this meeting was an exchange of information. Anything more was a waste of breath. "Are all of these injured elves from the Gathering?"

"Give this one an award. She's a clever one," Gneiss said. Loudly.

Ivy shook her head, confused. Why had so many elves not taken their seeds received at the Gathering? After this much time under a healer's care, only the seriously injured elves would still be here. Didn't that justify a seed? Gneiss had fought off Seekers until the end, so it made sense that she wouldn't have many seeds remaining. She'd conserve. But, what about the others?

What if, like Ivy, they were out?

Ivy's attention shot to Gneiss, stunned. As if sensing her question, Gneiss dropped her gaze, her lips pressed tightly together, her cheeks flaring red.

Every elf here felt some level of humiliation; none of them had remaining seeds. No wonder no one had even mentioned sharing with Ivy; everyone was worried about depleting their supply. And running out of seeds signaled that the Mother had removed her blessing. Ivy blinked, contemplating the sheer number of impacted elves. Her stomach twisted in knots knowing they'd all felt her same pain, worried they'd been abandoned and wondering if they'd done something wrong.

Without Gneiss's penetrating glare, Ivy took a moment to evaluate the elf. She wore a simple linen tunic, and a plain blue sheet was draped from her waist to the end of the bed. Ivy could only guess at the injury, but she'd witnessed Gneiss taking a seed during the fight. How many had Brecc's sister used that day? Gneiss had fought to the bitter end before limping away.

"I don't think the Mother is punishing you for some unknown deed," Ivy said softly. "You used your seeds protecting a Gathering tree. How could you be judged for that?"

Gneiss clenched her fists around her blanket, not looking up. "I know."

Did she?

An oppressive scrutiny bore down on the infirmary, and Ivy realized why. The elves who'd stayed behind to give everyone else enough time to escape questioned their own guilt.

But Ivy realized the problem went much deeper. The fact that no one had offered Ivy a seed signaled they were *all* running thin on supplies. Yet they were blissfully dancing, shopping, and stiffly ignoring the elves in the infirmary. They were refusing to dig into the reason *why* the foundations of their culture—the seeds—were disappearing.

Ivy's mind swirled, trying to make sense of everything ...

anything. Then an answer became blaringly obvious. Every elf knew that Alysatraee gifted extended life in exchange for keeping the peace between the realms. Yet, the elves had abandoned their duty and lost their reward.

Sure, the warriors' supplies depleted first, but every elf would eventually run out of seeds. They just didn't know it yet.

Ivy dropped her voice to a whisper. "What you said to me when we met, about the seats of power?" Ivy paused, letting Gneiss recall how she'd railed about the councilors and how they needed a change. "You were right."

Gneiss looked at Ivy, her eyes narrowed. "You mock me?"

"Do I look like I'm joking?"

Gneiss's hard expression cracked, revealing hope, but only for a moment. "Do you know what they say about you, Ivy Balrel?"

Ivy winced, surprised that anyone would speak about her at all. "That I'm terrible at speeches? I don't know why anyone would even remember my remarks after the attack. We have bigger problems."

Gneiss snorted. "Well, you *should* be right, but your little speech has become the foundation for your new reputation. Everyone is whispering that you're a Seeker-lover who isn't to be trusted. They say your father broke the laws. And you burned sacred trees. Is that true?"

Ivy cocked her head, surprised. No one should have connected the attack back to her already, if ever. And her face shouldn't have been noticed, especially in a city she'd never visited before.

The councilors.

Emmyth must have used "emergency" dryad communication for gossip and political maneuvering. That's how Lonsdale found out about the orchard so quickly. And he'd spread rumors about Ivy and then announced that she was in the city. Lonsdale's rumors explained the strange interaction she'd had with the two elves in the marketplace and the cold shoulder from others. He was probably the one who'd sent a spy to trail her. She fumed, realizing he was discrediting her. She needed to fight back, but if she couldn't convince Gneiss, a feisty elf who hated the councilors, who would believe her?

"Let me guess, Lonsdale told my healer that I'm unstable," Ivy whispered, "or some such nonsense."

Gneiss nodded. "That about sums it up. Lonsdale practically put up posters around the city with your face and all your crimes. You're *the* talk of the city. But what did you expect? You *did* speak for the Seekers. They're murderers who feed on sacred seeds," she looked exasperated. "So it's not a stretch to think you guided them to the Gathering, perhaps naively. You are pretty thick-skulled, after all."

"I know you don't believe me about Brecc," Ivy spoke in barely a whisper, attempting to keep the conversation private but knowing that was nearly impossible. "But he's the one who told me the *real* truth about the Seekers."

Gneiss closed her eyes, and Ivy thought she was going to demand she leave. But instead, Gneiss grabbed Ivy's tunic and pulled her closer, whispering in her ear. "Brecc spoke to our family. He shared his *concerns.* We'd hoped he would find his way back to sanity—back to the Mother's law. But ..."

Gneiss shoved Ivy away, stewing.

"The Seekers killed my entire family," Ivy said. "I'm the last person to speak up for them after the heartache they caused me, but Brecc convinced me to try." Ivy didn't dare voice blasphemy against the Council. Not here. But there were other things she could say. "I know his ideas are wild and unpopular. But it doesn't make them wrong. I should be able to speak my thoughts without this rain of suspicion falling on me. Whoever is spreading the rumors has their own agenda. My guess is that if they want to silence a Seeds elf who was driven from place to place and isolated for over a decade, that elf must have learned something dangerously important."

Ivy wondered if the spy had returned to the building. Were they inside? It would be better if they didn't find her talking to Gneiss, so Ivy stood to leave.

Gneiss grabbed Ivy's arm and yanked her closer again. "It's not that I don't believe what you said about Brecc. It's that I do. And I wish I didn't."

Ivy wanted to talk further, but it was too risky. Instead, she gave Gneiss a wink and then ripped out of her grip.

"Believe what you want, Gneiss," Ivy spat as she limped away. "Just stay away from me!"

13
GNOMES AND ORCS

Knowing the dryad was reporting his location at that very moment, Orion rushed to the magistrate's home in the middle of the finest part of Carrus. Maggie's home was fairly modest compared to the rest, with their cupolas, arched windows, and stone chimneys. But her house had features no other did. Though it was the middle of the night, he pounded on the door. There was no sound before the door flew open, a sword tip at his throat.

"Nice to see you too?" Orion said, careful not to move.

"What in the blazing desert are you doing here?" Maggie hissed. She dropped away her blade and grabbed his collar, dragging him inside. The chandelier crystals pinged against each other when she slammed the door shut. "What's wrong with you. I shouldn't have been able to nick your throat."

Orion put a hand to his neck and then checked his fingers. Sure enough, they were bloody. Embarrassed to admit to how his magic had been hampered, he brushed it off. "A scratch."

"Princess! Back!" Maggie pivoted and yelled at the advancing cockatrice and ripped off her glamour at he same time. The vile creature slouched, and a drop of acid sizzled against the fine marble floors, adding another pockmark to the myriad of others.

"Princess is making herself at home." Orion muttered, but Magdud didn't notice. She was busy apologizing to her deadly pet for yelling, scooping Princess up at patting her head.

"Mama is under a bit of stress. I'm so sorry, Princess-poo," she cooed.

"I'm relieved you're home," Orion said. "I didn't expect you to be back so soon."

"I didn't either." Maggie's shoulders dropped. "But, perhaps it is the Mother's providence. I have news." Magdud filled Orion in on what she'd overheard at the Summer Court; the orcs were moving into battle positions, and the courts were abuzz with the events at the Tree House.

"Ivy suspects the fae courts are involved in all this." Orion half expected Magdud to laugh at the accusation, but she simply pressed her lips and nodded. "I'm not sure what we can do without a new Elven Council."

"We have a plan." Magdud led him past the foyer, rooms for entertaining, dining rooms, and then after a long passage, through an empty kitchen. In the back of the manor, she led him up a flight of stairs into the staff's quarters.

Though her house appeared like the others, the interior was far more expansive. Most of her human guests only ever visited the same few rooms, so they were none the wiser. Ivy would love exploring this place, all the rooms in the sprawling maze-like interior. The estate was far cozier than a castle, but large enough to get lost in. Orion warmed, just thinking about Ivy laughing as she roamed from room to room, reading the books and eating the cupcakes that the servants put under glass-domed stands in every room.

"I've sent the servants away, other than Agretha, and I requested that she move into the guest quarters," Magdud continued. "I won't be here long, and our friend needs his privacy. He also appreciates the light from the western windows."

She knocked and Zel, who was mid-yawn, cracked open the door.

"My lord," he exclaimed, throwing the door fully open and bowing. "Thank Alysatraee, you found me."

"I'm glad you are safe and well." A bit of pressure lifted off Orion's shoulders at seeing the gnome again. He turned to Magdud. "You said you had a plan?"

Magdud tapped the wall and a light magically illuminated the space. A bed pallet sprawled on one side of the room, and a narrow strip of material, an eye mask, sat on top of the blanket. Orion hoped the gnome's migraines were not flaring up. A table and bench sat against the wall, liquid tinctures and jars of powder carefully shelved behind them. On the tabletop, glass containers and notes waited in mid-experiment, a blue box within easy reach.

"I'm close to curing the corruption," Zel said, rubbing his temple as he glanced at the blue box. "I'm recording my findings because I work alone. To be safe, we cannot lose what I've learned. In my vision from the Mother, I didn't understand her clues at first. But when I started working with an intention to heal the Seekers rather than for destruction of the trees, my next steps became clear."

"Th-that's unbelievable." Orion stuttered. "Wonderful."

"Tell fancy-lord the downside," Maggie said.

"Once I've found the right combination, I believe I'll be able to clear the seeds from the Seeker's bodily systems," Zel began, "and they'll regain their sensibilities. However, most of the Seekers took seeds to cure illnesses, which worked well in many cases ... until the seeds corrupted their minds. So, without the seeds, their original illnesses will return. Whatever ailed them before will ail them again. I almost pity them when they come to that realization. The seeds could never truly help them."

"And tell fancy-lord your next steps," Magdud pressed.

"Well," Zel hedged, wringing his hands, "I'm testing every combination of plants I can find. Agretha has brought me samples of most every available plant in Trinth. Nothing has worked."

After Zel had his vision, Orion had hoped the pieces might fall easily into place. But, apparently, the right path didn't negate obstacles. He'd been taught the Mother's ways, but this situation was yet another reminder that just because Alysatraee guided one to a righteous endeavor didn't mean achieving it didn't come without challenges.

"I suspect I need an ingredient only found in the fair realm." Zel's expression turned serious as he gazed up at Orion. "I need help from someone who can access both realms."

"Let me get this straight. You want me to bring back plant leaves from the Winter atrium?" Orion asked, though he already knew the answer.

"And roots, fruit, and anything else you can think of," Zel said. "It's spring in the fair realm so gathering materials should be an easy task."

"Easy?" Orion shook his head, grateful they were not attempting this conversation via missives. "If Eldrin finds out I'm bringing supplies back without his permission, he won't be pleased."

Magdud set Princess on the floor with a huff, and Zel hopped up on the bench, out of the cockatrice's easy reach. Magdud put her hands on her hips and spoke to Orion, "A war will start, with my unit at the front of the bloody mess. So, forgive me if I don't care too much about Eldrin's delicate feelings. Get supplies into Zel's hands. Quickly."

Maggie was right, though he hated to admit it, and Orion had come too far to not fulfill this request.

"I'd thought the fighting wouldn't start until after the Centennial, but now I'm not so sure," Magdud continued.

"What changed?" Orion asked. "You'd said the orcs were moving battleships into position already, but the seeds won't be plucked and distributed until spring."

"Whatever you and Ivy did, it panicked the wrong fair creatures. Powerful ones. Orcs may strike and *then* distribute the seeds for all I know. Orcs don't trust me, not since I left Aggord."

"Seeds have been the center of their plans from the beginning," Zel said, rubbing his chin as he looked up at the ceiling. "Would they ...? No. No, they wouldn't. It's a travesty, against the Mother's ways. But ... would they?"

"What?" Orion asked, a coil of tension tightening in the room. Even Princess stilled.

Zel dropped his attention to Orion. "They could force the mature tree, the one you didn't poison, to bloom early."

Magdud's jaw dropped. "Is that possible?

Orion's stomach lurched, fearing if it could be done the Council would break all natural laws and do it. He imagined the strain on the dryad inside, and bile rose in the back of his throat. Would it be exhausting? Painful? Deadly?

Magdud's voice deepened. "I may not have long until I'm summoned back to Summer. While I'm here, I'll be spending missives to my unit. Warnings, really." Maggie pounded a fist into her open palm, muttering about how she'd done everything her superiors demanded. Monthly reports home, providing Orion safe access to a dryad, attending dull Aequus ceremonies ... her complaints rolled on, naming favors she'd done for everyone from the Winter royals to the Administrator. "All this. For what? I'd hoped to show the orcs I am still on their side. I played by their rules. Did never-ending military drills for *decades* after the war. We all did. And now they're mobilizing my unit and throwing us into the jaws of battle."

Though Magdud wouldn't want sympathy, pity for her predicament settled like a stone in Orion's gut. She'd straddled two worlds for decades, just as he had. She'd drawn herself into knots trying to keep the respect of the orcs, but when push came to shove, they'd found her expendable.

"I'll return to Trinth as soon as I'm able," Orion promised. He wouldn't abandon his friends. "King Eldrin will task me with embedding another fae into the Unarian duke's guard." The duke was a good man, and Orion knew the infiltration would happen no matter what, so Orion wanted to select the replacement. "I'll get Zel plants from the atrium. If we can keep the influential humans healthy, perhaps the fair leaders will rethink their plan."

"How long until you can return?" Zel asked.

He was at the mercy of his father, and they all knew it. "For now, I must return to the Winter Court. King Eldrin knows I'm in Carrus, and he's awaiting my return."

Maggie blinked and straightened. "You visited the dryad already?" Orion nodded and then quick as a viper, she grabbed his arm, dragging him back to the front door. "If your father expects you, you mustn't delay. Besides, the Summer Queen now knows your location as well. This could potentially turn into a very, very bad night."

"Best of luck," Zel called from behind them. "I'll be ready for your return!"

"I'll walk you to the portal. We can't have you getting lost. King Eldrin may send a horde of fae guards to fetch you. Or gargoyles." She grumbled about having enough trouble to deal with.

Orion shrugged out of her grip, shifting his tunic back into place. "You're welcome to join me. Not drag me, Maggie."

"Fine." She grabbed her pendant, putting on her human glamour before she opened the front door and practically shoved him outside.

As they marched to the dryad portal, Orion started rehearsing apologies for his father. Would his father threaten to take away Orion's title? Would he expect Orion to grovel? No matter what happened, he needed the king to send him back to Unaria to install a new captain of the guard.

"Oh, by the way," Orion said, "would you board my horse for a while?"

"I cannot believe you're asking me for a favor right now, young lord. You have *nerve*." She straightened as she strode next to him. "Yet another reason you're not the absolute worst."

14

NYLANN'OR PRISON

Kolvar stood across the crevasse from Nym. Dark circles bruised under her eyes and her strong body had wasted considerably since she'd been held in The Hand. His heart broke at the sight of her. A wave of anguish washed over him, his chest tightening painfully as he took in her fragile state. In the weeks since he'd seen her, she'd been reduced from a fiery warrior to a dim flicker of her former self. It tore at him to see her so weakened and vulnerable.

How could anyone, let alone their mother, be supported by Alysatraee for condemning Nym? He clenched his fists, determined to free his sister. He stepped closer to the edge of the crevasse, and his heartbeat increased, thudding in his chest. Emmyth had given her permission for him to move Nym. But if what his sister had said about their mother's lies were true, did Emmyth still hold the rights and power associated with her title?

"Kol?" Nym was on her knees, leaning against a pillar. The stone hand gripped the base of the floating prison, as if holding the little island aloft. "Are you sure it's safe?"

He peeked beyond the brink of the jagged edge and down

into the endless chasm, and his mouth dried. For anyone who crossed, their life depended on magical permission—a power that vanished if Emmyth didn't hold the authority to send one across to The Hand.

Forcing a breath, he reminded himself that if Emmyth had a glimmer of doubt, she would never have tasked her son.

Would she?

No, Kolvar reminded himself. Even if his mother didn't love them in the traditional way, she was loyal to the elves, and she saw Kolvar as their best path forward. He trusted in *that*, at least. Even so, the thought of the first step of faith, stepping on air, made him feel faint. If he was wrong, and Alysatraee's powers had abandoned Emmyth, he'd fall to his death, his bones never to be recovered.

He breathed through his nose and lifted his foot. Then he stepped off the ledge. For a moment, he dropped, and his heart jumped into his throat as he fell through the air. But he stopped short, his leg wobbling, on a solid bridge that had magically formed underfoot. With each step, more stones flew upward, *clacking* as each piece snapped together like a puzzle.

The stories described this very mechanism, but experiencing the enchantment was beyond expectation. Kolvar's body buzzed, elated that he was not just alive, but experiencing the ancient power. The magic recognized Emmyth as a leader of the Tides. If magic still responded to her authority, what did that mean?

He stepped onto The Hand, energy still thrumming through him.

Nym released the death-clutch she had on the front of her tunic, taking a gulping breath.

"Kol." She blinked and for a moment he thought his sister might burst into tears. But instead, she braced against the column to pull herself into a standing position. He jumped forward and grabbed her arm, securing it across the back of his shoulders.

"Let's get you out of here," he said gently.

"Why is Emmyth moving me now?" Nym asked as he escorted her off the dungeon island.

"Maybe she is softening?"

"She's given up on me."

"She's moving you in with the other advisers."

"That confirms it. She's definitely given up," Nym said, her voice hard.

Kolvar swallowed the lump in his throat. Even *if* Nym was right, she'd miscalculated. The Mother's magic continued responding to Emmyth, but had shrunken his sister down to a human-like state.

"Emmyth is insane," Nym fumed aloud. "Part of her died with father. Maybe part of all of us died. He survived the war in body, but not mind. Do you remember him, Kol? Do you?"

Kolvar wasn't sure what to make of Nym's rambling. He repositioned her arm, supporting her weight as she stumbled toward the door at the top of the rough stairs.

"I remember him teaching me to press flowers." As a youngling, Kolvar spent most of his time with his father. His mother had grown busier with her meetings and obligations. "I remember you bundled on his back, as a baby, while we explored the greenhouse. I was a bit jealous because I had to share him with you after you were born."

"Do you think I'll die like him? Withering away?"

Kolvar's heart jumped and cracked at the words as much as the hollowness. Had she disconnected from reality? He knew, in theory, that The Hand diminished innate magical abilities somehow, and prisoners didn't get much food, but being next to his sister filled him with a burning sense of injustice. His mind swirled with a mix of sorrow and anger, but also confusion, unsure of why Alysatraee hadn't abandoned the councilors.

He pushed open the door and wove through the caverns. Earlier, he'd redirected the guards to other parts of the dungeon, choosing to shield Nym in her weakened state.

"Where are we?" Nym asked.

"The dungeon." The lower-level cells.

"Everything is a blur. The walls are a smudge. Everything sounds muffled."

"I'll help you get better," Kol said. "You can rest in your new cell."

Nym struggled to keep up, so he stopped to let her catch her breath. An occupied cell was mere steps away, but the magic of the opaque, glass-like doors blocked all sights and sounds into the individual units. Prisoners had no idea if a guard was approaching, let alone overhear a conversation.

Several perfectly carved tunnels branched off the main corridor, quiet and dark. Nym stopped several times before they reached the mid-level cells. Kolvar took a breath of relief upon seeing them. Then guilt flooded him.

Moving past the three advisers' cells, Kolvar pressed the runes carved into their doors, enabling them to see and hear him. There was no point in not telling them all the truth. They'd waited vainly for information for too long.

"Well, well," Daecyne, the treasury adviser said in a mocking tone as Kolvar crossed in front of his cell. "No one can say that Councilor Phiro unfairly protects her own flesh and blood."

"Emmyth protected herself just fine," Keyyarus snapped. The horticultural adviser shared a cell with Daecyne, which would make anyone irritable. Lyra, the historian, had a cell to herself, as did Omasys, who was on the end.

Daecyne glared at Nym. "Did our dear councilor send a spy?"

"Be kind," Lyra said, sympathetically. "Nym was tricked just like the rest of us."

"Outmaneuvered," Daecyne grumbled.

Nym roused at the sentiment and hissed in the advisers' direction. "*I* would've secured a majority before going up against Emmyth."

Kolvar almost smiled—his sister's bite wasn't completely toothless after all. He selected the cell across from Omasys because the chamber was offset by a step and angled, offering Nym some privacy. He pressed his palm to a cell door four times. The first tap allowed him to see the interior clearly, as if the wall were made of glass. The second time allowed any prisoner to hear outside their cell. The third tap enabled the prisoner to see through the glass. With the fourth tap, the wall vanished.

Few had the permission and ability to trigger the doors, fewer still controlled the fourth tap. His ability to manipulate the cells confirmed he had authority, and his authority came from Emmyth's words and intent. She wanted Kolvar to operate on the council's behalf, so he did.

He sat his sister on the thin pallet, and she slumped down. He reached to the small table, wanting a cup of water to give her, but there was none. Stepping back, he couldn't help but feel the walls closing in on his sister. Her bones felt hollow and her senses seemed numbed. The pain of seeing his sister so broken nearly overwhelmed him. How could he leave her here? This didn't feel like justice. It felt wrong. Perhaps Nym had been right; Emmyth had dumped her own daughter here like refuse, not even caring about appearances.

That didn't bode well for Nym.

"Is Lial well?" Omasys spoke up, his voice cracking with

disuse. He stood at the invisible wall, his clothing rumpled and pieces of blond hair falling from the usually impeccable braid.

"Well enough," Kolvar lied. Embarrassed and a social outcast, Lial had become a shell of his old self. "I'm sure he'd visit if he could."

Omasys gave a slight nod, his jaw tight. Then he turned his back to Kolvar and fell into a thick silence.

"Will we receive a pardon?" Lyra asked. "Historically, a pardon can occur when—"

"No pardon, yet." Kolvar wasn't in the mood for a history lesson. "But I'll inquire about moving you to the upper level where you can have family visits."

"So, we should expect to rot in the dungeon, then," Keyyarus frowned. "Either in squalor or with a thicker mat."

"You'll each have more privacy on the upper level," Kolvar offered.

"I'll stay here, rather than insinuate I'm in good favor with the Council," Lyra said quietly. "I want history to show that I stood for Alysatraee's Law."

"Agreed," Daecyne added. "Even before Omasys and Bellas approached me, I knew the Tides' Councilors were rotten. I sensed it."

"You are full of your own manure," Keyyarus said. "Bellas ought to be sitting in a cell with Lyra, but her family is too influential to risk crossing. Bellas might have charged forward and pulled us into this mess, but when it came down to it, she hid behind her name."

On the floor of her cell, Nym scowled, likely remembering how Daecyne had been eager to rip her position away and bestow the office on his nephew. For someone who hated nepotism, Daecyne leveraged favoritism without guilt when it suited him.

"If Emmyth didn't need Bellas, she'd be down in the

dungeon, too," Lyra said. "With five advisers at her disposal, Emmyth has the votes required to make any changes she wishes. None of the five will dare oppose her. If Emmyth wasn't in complete control of the Tides before, she is now. She'll submit names for new advisers, and the remaining five will select elves from her list. Of course she'll only suggest elves with unquestionable loyalty to her, reinforcing her control for hundreds of years. The system is flawed."

"Deeply," Daecyne muttered.

Kolvar reached down and squeezed Nym's hand and then stepped from her cell. As he pressed the rune to lock the translucent wall in place, his insides felt scraped out. He loved his sister, and he believed she honestly thought the Council was planting Gathering trees. And perhaps they were. Furthermore, the three advisers also made valid points against Emmyth.

Yet, clearly the Mother respected the authority of the current Council. The moment Kol stepped over the crevasse without dying was confirmation of Emmyth's power. She was still the recognized authority—not only did her amulet glow at her touch, but the magic recognized her permission for Kolvar to release Nym. Otherwise, he would've plummeted to his death.

"I'll have a healer come check on you all," Kolvar said, preparing to leave.

"And a seed brought for your sister," Lyra said. "Surely she has a few stored in her chambers."

"I'll look," he lied. Again.

He couldn't give Nym a seed. Emmyth would know it'd come from him, and he'd lose her trust. When Nym had flown home and found him after the Gathering, she'd emphasized that someone needed to stay in Emmyth's good graces.

After gathering verbal messages from the prisoners to discreetly pass onto their families, Kolvar strode through the dungeon, torn by his thoughts. Although he didn't agree with the Elven Council's actions at The Tree House, he didn't agree with the underhanded attempt to overthrow the Tides Councilors either. They'd obviously planned the coup for months.

He wished he could talk to Nym, but she needed rest after The Hand, not a strategy session. Even though she'd allowed the mysterious Unarian guard to glamour as her brother, he still trusted her.

But should he?

Kolvar marched through the upper level of the dungeon, frustrated. The truth and the misconceptions blended like sands in the sea, impossible to pick apart. So, he flipped his analysis and looked at the fruits of each elf's labors. After all, when the best path was obscured, wasn't the next best plan to see who produced the better results? Or, in this case, did the least amount of damage.

The Council had poisoned many humans. Ivy and Nym had poisoned an entire orchard of Gathering Trees, including their sacred seeds.

The Council had lied. Ivy and Nym had broken into an elven facility using glamours, and had invited in an outsider.

Emmyth had put her daughter on The Hand. Nym had hidden the glamour of their leader, Emmmyth, potentially putting all Tides' safety at risk.

Emmyth should have told him she'd invited orcs to Nylann'or. Nym should've called a meeting with all the advisers and the councilors together instead of attempting an ambush.

No one's actions were *good*. Irritation grew within him, frustrated with everyone including Nym and Ivy. The Council wasn't upholding the Mother's will, of course, but was there a better path his sister hadn't considered?

15

A TENUOUS ALLIANCE

Like the days before, a spy trailed Ivy as she lumbered through the city. As usual, the apprentice accompanied her on the healer's errands. Ivy continued feigning that her wounds still hampered her, though the stab wound was now merely an ache. However, her senses remained dull, she was as sluggish as a human, and her body quickly wearied. Most days, she happily took a nap. If Seekers invaded the city, she'd be the first casualty.

The sun rose above the horizon, starting to warm the brisk morning air. As she moved through the market street, a satyr and an elf nodded to Ivy, but most kept their eyes lowered or their backs turned. She was like death's shadow that they wished would pass them by. She would have kept to the side streets, but now that the Council knew she was in the city, she refused to hide. Why make it easier for Lonsdale to make her "disappear" without witnesses? Besides, when Ivy wanted to slip away, she planned to use the crowd to her advantage. She had avoided the infirmary after finding it the first time, but she intended to return—today.

"What else do we need?" the youngling asked as he handed

Ivy a round of bread. She slid the loaf into the sack, careful not to drop her purple healing stone. They only had one task left that morning, and she'd purposefully saved this errand for last.

"Lettuce," Ivy said.

"Oh," he cocked his head, half hidden in the depths of his cowl. "We passed the farmers' stalls. We'll have to go back."

"I don't mind." Ivy tugged her cloak tighter, wanting to hurry before the morning warmed sufficiently for everyone to drop their hoods. The spy today was a male in a nondescript grey cloak, making him difficult to track, especially with her poor eyesight. But his fuzzy form moved in a distinct gait, which helped.

She pushed through the growing number of creatures to a farmer's table and grabbed the first head of lettuce she found, slapping a bronze coin on the table before turning to the apprentice. Eyeing the crowd, she found another elf wearing a cloak similar to her own.

"Race you home?" she asked.

"That's not fair," he said. "I'll win for sure. You run slower than a human."

"Let's even the odds, then," Ivy grinned. "First rule: you carry the bag. Second rule: travel right behind another elf for fifty paces. Then run as fast as you like."

His face lit up, but then his brow furrowed. "Grandfather said you're not to push yourself."

"If I get too winded, I will stop and rest. I promise." She would definitely stop, but it wouldn't be much of a rest. Ivy crouched down to his height, which conveniently also made her more difficult to spot. She discreetly gestured to the stranger who was now walking away. "Follow her, the elf in the dark yellow cloak. Ready?" Ivy paused and then winked. "Go!"

The young apprentice bolted from the group gathered around the farmer's table and over to the stranger, keeping one step behind. Ivy stripped her own yellow cloak, balled it up under her arm, and shoved on a cap. Then keeping her knees bent, she moved through the crowd to the alley, mere steps away—the whole reason she'd shopped at this vendor last.

Striding through the alley, she didn't stop until she was on the parallel side street. Though she hadn't run, her heart raced. After fifty paces, she darted around the nearest corner and waited to see if her spy appeared. At worst, she'd confront him. With witnesses around, few as they might be, surely one would step in if the spy decided to attack her. Wouldn't they?

Ivy hated that she would *definitely* lose any fight. Cursing her lack of magic, she waited. But the grey-clad spy didn't storm into view.

Ivy thew her cloak back on, but dropped the hood, wanting everyone to see her face. Walking in the opposite direction of the infirmary, she calculated that the spy now realized that he was following a faux-Ivy. Meaning, he'd be extra motivated to find the real one. If he happened to go this direction, she'd give him a trail to follow. After jogging past several witnesses, Ivy slipped down a narrow street, stripped off her cloak again, and hurried toward the infirmary, all the while praying that the ruse would work.

Finally, the large infirmary came into view. Ivy practically stumbled inside, sweat dripping down the sides of her face. Not wasting a moment, Ivy jogged to Gneiss's bed, where her side table was inexplicably overflowing with even more flowers and gifts.

"Thank the Mother you're still here," Ivy gasped, breathing hard.

"You're happy that I'm still *not* recovered? Typical Balrel selfishness," Gneiss snapped back.

Ivy ignored the insult and grabbed a parchment she'd kept inside her tunic, shoving it toward the elf.

"You're too kind," Gneiss's voice dripped with sarcasm. From the short distance, Ivy couldn't mistake the look of disgust as Gneiss gingerly accepted the parchment damp with sweat.

Before Gneiss cracked the seal, Ivy lifted Brecc's necklace from her pocket. It had taken some serious cajoling, and Ivy had worried the dragon left the pendant behind with his little hoard in the fae realm, but he'd eventually traded it—surprisingly— for a piece of moldy cheese.

Gneiss stared as Ivy lowered the chain and then the pendant into her open hand. A long silence followed, one not punctuated by insults so Ivy took that as a good sign. Gneiss slid out her own vial from her neck and poured her seeds inside. Even half-blind, Ivy detected only two.

Gneiss reverently put Brecc's pendant over her head, resting her hand on it for a heartbeat before tucking it out of sight under her tunic. Looking at Ivy with a new levity, she then cracked the seal on the parchment. Ivy leaned forward, wanting to study Gneiss's face as she read.

Gneiss's eyes moved faster and faster as she scanned over Ivy's accusations of the Elven Council. Of course, it was exactly what Gneiss had always believed, but what proof did she have? Now she had Ivy's word. And Ivy wasn't a random elf making wild accusations; she had occupied in the inner-circle, having access and privilege that others didn't, including Gneiss. When Ivy visited Nylann'or, which was often as a child, she'd been trained alongside Kol and Nym. She'd enjoyed dinners with the most influential elves. She learned magic at the knee of the strongest wielders. She'd learned the law from the elders and ambassadors.

Gneiss brought the parchment to her chest and leaned forward, her nose practically in Ivy's face. "Why are you giving me this testimony? Your accusations against the

Council include your own father, ruining your own reputation. Why?"

"I prefer the harsh truth over soft lies. We've been fed a steady diet of delusion for years, and it doesn't satiate. I'm done with it. I swear on Alysatraee, everything I've written is true." Ivy nodded slowly. "And I did exactly what I said to the orchard."

Gneiss stared at Ivy, seeming to consider her next words carefully. "Bold. I would have found a different way to solve the problem. But I can understand that you might have panicked."

Ivy's hand tightened around her healing stone, fighting to keep calm. She needed Gneiss to lead the charge against the Mineral councilors; this wasn't her fight. Ivy needed to find other Seeds, hopefully the other ambassadors, and influence their new councilor choice. And she didn't dare wait much longer—who knew when Lonsdale would strike to silence her. Ivy hadn't recovered, but then again, she wouldn't any time soon.

"And you reported the council to both Winter Princess Selleth and Summer Prince Devain," Gneiss more stated than questioned. "So, we should wait for the fair realm courts to intervene."

Ivy paused, not sure Gneiss would believe that the fair courts were complicit. That one allegation, she didn't write down. She couldn't absolutely prove the outlandish claim, so Ivy didn't even try.

"Why wait for the fair realm to rescue us when the Mother gave us authority over our own kind?" Ivy said.

Gneiss grinned and sat back up. But instead of getting right in Ivy's face, she threw off her blanket and swung her feet down to the ground. She tested her legs for a moment before standing, letting her long tunic fall just below her knee, covering the massive bandage on her thigh.

Gneiss narrowed her eyes. "I've never trusted those snobby fae anyway. This is an elven problem, and they can stay out of it. Let's get to work."

"What are—"

"The healers said I need to exercise my legs today," Gneiss cut her off and changed the subject. "Is that elf looking for you?"

Ivy squinted, but couldn't see anyone else standing in the room other than healers in their pristine white robes. "Grey cloak?"

"That's the one. He's outside, watching us from the alley. He's about as stealthy as a troll." Gneiss quirked a brow, a smirk on her face. In that moment, she looked just like her brother.

Ivy swallowed, ignoring the thickness in the back of her throat. "Great."

Past memories vied for her attention, but Ivy glanced at the windows on the far side of the room. She couldn't see him. A trickle of fear started forming at the base of her spine. Lonsdale didn't bother finding the best spies to track her. Did he already know Ivy's weaknesses? If so, Lonsdale already knew that subduing her would be effortless. Why hadn't he?

"How did you escape the Seekers for so long?" Gneiss teased.

Ivy lowered her voice, her thoughts swirling. "I had my magic then."

Gneiss's eyes widened, one hand clapping over her mouth. "Your *magic*?" She blinked several times before narrowing her gaze. "Follow me. Quickly." Gneiss led Ivy through a set of double doors to another area of the infirmary and approached an elf in an official uniform. "Ivy needs an escort back to the healer's home."

She gave a somber nod, looking genuinely sympathetic. "I knew your mother, and I recognized you when you first arrived.

But, I also knew the daughter of Ialant could bring trouble, which is why I didn't allow you to recover here. I'm sad to see I was correct."

Ivy shrunk under the elf's words, but couldn't disagree. Spies would have bothered all the elves here for the entirety of her stay. And now she'd involved Gneiss. And the spy had seen them talking. The trickle of fear spread from her spine to her belly, a cold pool of liquid. When would the spy report what he'd seen? Ivy chewed her lip, knowing the Council, including Lonsdale, had already killed her family. If he had an inkling that Ivy was strategizing against him, he'd cut her down.

"Send a message sent to my family. Immediately," Gneiss said. "I need them to come to the infirmary and to bring my things. They'll know what I mean. And Ivy and I need privacy."

The woman nodded and left without question. Ivy wondered how Gneiss inexplicably wielded more than a little respect. When the door clicked shut, Gneiss turned to Ivy.

"We don't have long until your spy friend will barge in here, so talk fast," Gneiss said.

"You might be in danger," Ivy squeaked.

"Don't worry about me. What do you suggest the elves do about this gigantic mess the Council caused?"

Ivy didn't miss the insinuation that it was her father's fault, but she ignored the partially true insult. "The elves need new councilors. Like you said at the Gathering, those leaders have been in their positions far too long. It's time to cut their strings of power and put in humble elves."

"Ones who truly respect Alysatree's laws."

Ivy nodded, relieved that Gneiss's first instinct was to honor the natural order of the realms.

"And I suppose you'll want the Protectors seat?" Gneiss continued.

"I'll support whoever our ambassadors choose," Ivy said

before changing the subject. "How do the Minerals select new councilors, and who would they support?"

"Our advisers elect new councilors, and the majority wins."

"Just like the Tides, then."

Gneiss shrugged, and Ivy remembered how her brother, Brecc, had stated that the Houses were too detached from each other. She was starting to agree with him more and more. But it wasn't something she could worry about now.

"Would the Minerals be willing to oust their councilors?" Ivy asked.

"My family has pushed for change, but unless corruption is proven, the advisers have no reason to carve a new path."

Ivy pointed to the parchment Gneiss still clutched in her hand. "You have my word. And the Tides have Nym's word. We have everything to lose and nothing to gain by our statements."

"But after your father disappeared for years and your embarrassing speech at the Gathering, no one will take your word."

Ivy felt like a thousand needles had been shoved into her bones, the words digging deep. What else did an elf have if not her honor and trust? "Even so, it's the truth."

"But you cannot prove it," Gneiss said with a look of pity, making Ivy squirm; Ivy didn't know that she appreciated sympathy-Gneiss any more than cruel-Gneiss. "But, if the Tides replace their councilors, it'll make huge waves—pun intended. Their uproar will sanction us to follow suit."

"What do the Tides matter to the Minerals? How can you be sure the Minerals will act at all?"

"I swear to you that if the Tides make their move, I will do everything within my power, even to the detriment of my own family reputation, to get new councilors in place."

Even if Ivy didn't know Gneiss had been waiting decades for

such an opportunity, she believed the stubborn elf would do *exactly* as she swore to do.

"But if the Tides don't make their move, I can't risk doing so either. I've been biding my time too long to fritter away my one chance." Gneiss opened the door and allowed the administrative elf back into her own office, questioning her. "Is the elf in the grey cloak still hanging out in the alley?"

"Yes, on the north side. When I sent a messenger to your home, he looked tempted to follow, but he stayed put."

"This could get interesting." The air seemed to crackle with a new tension, yet Gneiss stifled a grin forming at the corner of her lips.

The administrator turned to Ivy. "I have two escorts ready to take you to the healer's home, with instructions to stay until you can make other arrangements."

"For protection?" Ivy's voice squeaked. Still many months from recovery, Ivy was helpless, and the thought of depending on strangers made her insides turn to water. More and more it seemed securing a seed at the Centennial seemed her best chance of recovery—assuming she survived that long.

"I would suggest you go to the council for protection, but ..." Gneiss shook her head. "Your spy isn't the stealthiest. Until you're well enough to travel north, the city, both inside and out, has many holes in which to hide. Or you can always hire a personal guard."

Ivy's stomach twisted, knowing there were a dozen flaws with any of those options. Outside the open door, she noticed two elves waiting for her, neither armed, but both looked capable. Not waiting to be forced outside, she stepped back into the hallway and nodded to her escorts.

Gneiss followed her, adding a goodbye. "I sincerely hope you live long enough to witness all the trouble the Council caused put to right. Though we may not agree on many things, I wish you no withering."

The healer's home felt stuffy as he pleaded with Ivy to stay. Ash hopped from surface to surface, agitated. If the dragon was rifling for some trinket to take, she'd be disappointed; the healer lived a humble lifestyle.

"But your lung!" the healer sputtered, again. "It's not healed. You need another month of rest!"

Ivy shoved her knife into her belt, wishing, not for the first time, that she still had her satchel, bow and arrows. But, most of her things were back in the fae realm. She didn't know exactly where she was going, but it had to be away from here. She handed him the cloak, grateful that the summer air would keep her warm while she traveled.

"Keep it," he said, handing the wrap back to her. But before Ivy could argue, Lonsdale burst into the room.

"Ivy Balrel, you're under arrest!" he shouted.

"What? Why!" Ivy asked.

"For the illegal dragon you brought into the city," Lonsdale said, drawing himself taller.

The healer looked incredulous, his jaw dropping. Looking from Ivy to Lonsdale, his shoulders curled inward, and he slunk from the room, dramatically knocking over a small table on his way out.

Taking advantage of the distraction, she spun and shimmied through the small window, landing hard on the ground. She only made it a few steps before Lonsdale grabbed her wrist from behind. The two escorts meant to "protect" her, looked at each other, unsure, but didn't budge.

"Come with me to the courthouse. You've never seen the belly of that beast," Lonsdale sneered, referring to the cells below.

Ivy yanked away hard, trying to break free of his grasp, but his grip only tightened.

"Don't make a fuss and embarrass yourself," Lonsdale snapped.

If she went with Lonsdale, she knew she'd never see the sky again. Ash cried out from far overhead.

Because, of course, the dragon is helpful.

She couldn't outrun any elf, but she could try to hide in the crowded city. Ivy bent her knee and lunged toward Lonsdale, smashing her head against his nose. His grip loosened, and she spun away, ripping her wrist free. She leapt away, ready to sprint, when the healer was suddenly between them.

"Secure her," the healer said to the escorts before turning his back to Lonsdale and mouthing to Ivy, "Trust me."

What choice did she have?

Ivy let the escorts secure her by the upper arms while the healer said he'd treat Lonsdale's injury. It was only then that Ivy realized the councilor was holding his nose, blood covering his hand and chin.

"Take her to the courthouse," Lonsdale demanded before shouting at the healer to hurry. When Lonsdale disappeared inside, the healer's apprentice rushed out and handed the cloak to Ivy.

She considered refusing again, but the boy looked sweetly eager. "I appreciate the gift. And your friendship."

He hugged her around the waist and then stepped back, watching the escorts grip her arm and tug her forward.

As they walked through the street, Gneiss ran up to intercept them.

"I'll secure her," Gneiss said, taking one of the escort's places. She shooed them ahead to clear path as she and Ivy followed several steps behind. Gneiss spoke under her breath, explaining, "I'm glad that little dragon of yours announced a warning from afar. I've never run so fast, and that's saying something."

Perhaps even Ash is accidentally helpful at times.

"I asked around, and the Tides didn't vote out Emmyth." Gneiss hid her limp, but Ivy guessed her sprint to the healer cost her. "Whatever your plan was, it didn't work."

"Kolvar and the others will figure something out," Ivy said. She had to trust that they would act, to fight against the coming conflict. The stakes were too high to simply give up.

"If they don't, then I cannot risk fighting for something that failed in the north," Gneiss said, her face darkening. "The elves here are complacent and naive."

"It might be too late if you don't push the Minerals before war is upon us all."

"Well, it's too late for you, anyway. You can't stay here, obviously. I'll get you out of the city. I can't believe Lonsdaleite didn't have me arrested, too. I'm a little insulted, actually." Gneiss rolled her eyes. "But, to ensure I'm still a free elf later, we'll need to stage a fight."

"I'm in no condition to-"

"You're just going to have to look like you fought me and won," Gneiss said. "You'd better appear to play dirty because there's no possible way you'd overpower me."

Ivy barely registered the insult, her mind consumed with worry for her friends in the north. Emmyth would not hold back against her daughter. In fact, she'd punish her all the harder. And if Kolvar was caught up in the net, too, the siblings might both be in prison.

"I'll go north. Myself. I'll try to right this," Ivy said, though she had no idea how. The mere thought of traveling that far in her condition threatened to crumble her into the dirt right then and there. "You're right, the creatures here in Yllalen'al are blind, practically living in their own little realm. But a change in the north will signal that trouble looms closer than they realize."

Gneiss chewed her lip. "If anyone can figure out a way, it's you. I can't believe I'm doing this ..."

"Doing what?"

"Listen," Gneiss shook Ivy's arm, "I have one condition. And it's a small one considering what I'm doing for you."

Ivy barely stopped herself from staring at Gneiss instead of portraying herself like a dejected, arrested elf getting dragged to the local magistrate.

"Only one Phiro can serve on the Council," she said. "Preferably Kolvar. But if I find out that two Phiros have seats, I won't make a move for the Mineral seat. The last thing I want is for the Phiro family to gain more power."

"I understand."

"No, you'll swear to it."

Ivy keenly remembered the results of Orion's broken promise, so she thought through her words carefully. "I swear that if two Phiros sit on the Council, I will not have granted them permission. I will do everything I can to ensure only one Phiro sits on the Council."

She'd come here hoping to find others who could overturn the Council, and she had merely hoped to rebuild some kind of life. But now she was tasked with getting even further involved. Had she really agreed to be the spark to overturn the remaining four councilors?

How will I survive today, let alone travel across Trinth?

From the corner of her eye Ivy saw Gneiss grab the chain connected to her vial.

"I can take the prisoner from here," Lonsdale's voice called from behind them.

Gneiss grumbled something Ivy couldn't catch before she turned around to face the councilor. He looked none the worse for the headbutt to the face, except for a cotton rag peeking out from his nostril, only partially bloody.

"Prisoner?" Gneiss raised a brow and her voice. "I'm sure you mean to say that you are taking Councilor Ialant's daughter in to question her on her recent experiences. She can't be a prisoner without a trial."

"You're taking her the wrong way, youngling," Lonsdale growled. He grabbed Ivy's other arm, his fingers threatening to crack her bone. But before Lonsdale could yank Ivy away, Gneiss slipped a seed into Ivy's hand.

For a moment, Ivy felt numb. Was this really happening? She felt Lonsdale's nails digging through her sleeve, dragging her forward, but all she could focus on was the seed clutched in her palm. With another step, she realized Lonsdale was whispering insults—ones she couldn't hear. Did he not realize the extent of his prey's vulnerability? He'd obviously known her magic had been hampered, yet he still overestimated her; she half-laughed, half-cried at her wild situation.

"You are truly as insane as your father."

That insult, she heard.

Ivy pretended to scratch her nose as she slipped the seed in her mouth.

Her entire body warmed. Heat licked her back. She almost cried with joy as the throbbing pain she'd lived with for weeks suddenly abated. The warmth in her core emanated out through her extremities, making her fingers tingle. Her next footstep was lighter, her breathing now effortless. Another pulse of magic infused her every fiber with energy and strength.

It was all Ivy could do to hide the elation of her restored health and the extra vitality coursing through her.

Pushing out her sight, she saw the courthouse. But, she refused to die in some abandoned hole.

Ivy smiled, right before she spun toward Lonsdale, her right fist already raised.

16

HOT BATH AND STAR BROTH

The sun sunk lower in the western sky, a fireball about to be punctured by the jagged Winter mountains. The palace loomed ahead, gargoyles sitting between sections of crenellation, staring at him. Although silent and still, Orion *felt* their stares.

Guards practically pounced on him as he neared, each aiming to take credit for spotting him and reporting his presence to the king. Orion waved them off, grateful for his title; no one dared touch him. He entered the castle through a side entrance and skulked through the atrium—the space blissfully vacant other than a handful of human and gnome gardeners. His body ached from the arduous travel. But more so, an empty hole cut through where his magic once filled him. Maintaining his glamour sucked his last reserves of energy. Even so, he detoured past the Gathering tree, confirming its continued survival.

His vision blurred as he marched to the royal wing. Focusing on each step, Orion finally reached his rooms. With a quick request, Orion sent away his waiting servants. Stumbling to his bed, he collapsed, dropping his glamour. Hoping his wings concealed him well enough, he sank into a deep sleep. He'd just started to dream of Ivy when Rime's obnoxious voice awoke him with sharp retort.

Sluggishly awaking from slumber, Orion instinctively pulled his glamour into place before he pushed himself up.

"Argh!" Rime said, jumping back from the foot of the bed. "You need about a thousand more hours of beauty sleep."

Orion glared, "What do you want, Rime? How did you get in here?"

"That's completely your fault for not locking your door. Any murderous stranger could have danced their way in here. Or worse, our sister."

"I've had a trying few days, so if you don't mind—"

"Did an orc sit on you? Or five orcs, perhaps. Then they smacked you around? You look like a troll ... and not in a good way. It's like a centaur kicked you in—"

"Rime!"

The prince shrugged. "I just came to warn you that our father, Ruler of the Winter Court, King of the land, who can be really scary sometimes, *that* fae ... he's not pleased with you."

"I figured as much." Orion stretched and glanced out the window. It was still light, so the sun hadn't even completely set.

"You've been gone almost two days, you realize that much, don't you?"

Twenty days in Trinth. Orion just nodded. He'd hoped to return home after a handful of Trinth days, before his father even awoke, but Ivy was his priority.

Rime left the bedroom area and disappeared into the receiving room. It was just like the prince to wander off mid-conversation. The entry door to Orion's chambers creaked open, and Rime's voice echoed as he issued some commands before slamming the door and marching back to Orion's bedside. At least this time he appeared with a plate of food.

"You need to eat and bathe before you see Father." Rime pulled a letter out from a pocket in his tunic. "This was on your floor. A servant slipped it under your door while you slept."

Orion set the plate aside, but not before shoving a bite of ham and potatoes into his mouth. Orion took the missive, the royal crest impossible to ignore. Breaking the seal, Orion read the dreaded words:

Lord Orion of the Shadowmoon Bloodline and Portal Keeper of the Realms,

Your presence is required in the king's receiving room directly after the king retires from dinner.

—Rithmat

Rime grabbed the note and quickly scanned it. "This is bad. The king is dining with high-ranking fair creatures who remained behind after the equinox celebration. They're eating right now, and he won't dally. He will shout three times louder if you're not waiting for him when he returns." Rime handed back the note. "So, don't be late."

The pit in Orion's stomach grew more pronounced, and he pushed his plate away. Would King Eldrin send him back to Trinth? Possibly. Would he strip his title? Yes. Would he force him into another role in the human realm, one that kept him even more isolated than before? Definitely.

What humiliation did the king have in store?

Orion rubbed the bridge of his nose, feeling the weight of his situation. He'd finally gained a position in the Winter Court and a welcome he'd always desired. He might finally belong. Yet, his father's anger could boil over, destroying everything. Orion had to placate him. Further angering the ruler of Winter would not help Ivy. If Orion was sent back to Trinth, he would lose any influence in the fair realm, leaving Ivy without crucial support. She needed the backing of both the Winter and Summer Courts, even if she secured the Council's unanimous vote. What could Orion do to soothe the king? He needed a plan, a way to calm his father's fury and ensure he could still aid Ivy in her quest.

Rime snapped his fingers, and Orion's eyes flew open in time to see servants filling his bathtub with water. "Make the water extra hot. And leave scrubbing sponges. And extra oils. And *lots* of soap."

Orion frowned, but stayed silent as scents of eucalyptus and rosemary filled the air. He actually relished the smell, but refused to admit it. Any positive reinforcement would only encourage Rime to insert himself even more into his life.

The centaur healer entered, carrying a large bag. Orion had planned to visit the healer after he'd seen what a good night's sleep could cure. The centaur gave a slight bow to Rime and Orion, and they gestured for her to join them.

"My apologies for interrupting your evening, Orion," she said, clutching the bag, "but your elven guest left without her things." The centaur opened the bag and withdrew Ivy's bow, quiver, and her satchel.

"That thing really should be burned." Rime grimaced as Orion took the satchel. It was much heavier than he remembered. Then again, his muscles were weaker than they'd ever been.

"If you wouldn't mind setting down the bow and quiver in my office, I would appreciate it," Orion said.

"I can treat you at your convenience," the centaur said to Orion before leaving to stow Ivy's weapons in the other room.

Setting down the satchel next to his window, Orion securely shut it before remembering that Ash was still in the human realm. A sadness washed over him, but he reminded himself that Ivy needed the little dragon more than he did.

"Bring Orion a cup of star milk broth," Rime commanded the servants. "He must report to the king's chambers within the hour, so be quick about your duties."

Rime took Orion's plate and lowered his voice, ensuring his voice was muffled by the water sloshing into the tub. "I contacted the servants in the household where Father is dining. I bribed them to add an extra course, which bought you some time."

Orion raised a brow. "Bribed? Or blackmailed?"

But Rime didn't tease him back. Instead, he grew more intense. "I'm still angry with you. The secrets you kept from me … they're not small." Rime's voice tightened around the last words. He clearly had more to say, but either didn't know how or it wasn't the right time. Instead, he gave a simple reason. "But you're my brother."

My ally. My friend.

Neither of them said the words, but Orion felt a rush of gratitude for Rime. The prince was brash and ridiculous, but he'd known their father would send for him. Rime let Orion sleep as long as possible before bursting in. His brother was helping him prepare, ordering magical broth to settle Orion's nerves after seeing he couldn't eat.

Rime spun on his heel and sauntered from the room, announcing he would arrange for Orion's clothing to be delivered. The servants bustled around, placing a towel and other items next to the tub. After they rushed away, Orion placed his palm in the center of the door and locked it.

Yes, his brother was helping him, but the rest of the castle overflowed with vultures. At the moment, not even Rime knew Orion's biggest secret—the extent of his fragility. With his magic depleted and his body exhausted, forgetting even the simplest act of protection could cost him his life.

17

COMEUPPANCE

Ivy's fist connected with Lonsdale's already injured nose. Energy coursed through her as she spun in place, backward, keeping her elbow up until smashing it into his ribs. Although he hadn't fought on the battlefield for over a hundred years, he didn't cry out in pain. Instead, he jumped back and bent his knees, falling instantly into his fighting stance. The cotton in his nostril was now red, blood dripping onto his lips, but he didn't flinch.

Ivy darted down the narrowest roadway, pretending to flee. Just as she hoped, he followed. His past battle experience gave him some advantage, but Ivy's training for Seeker attacks had never stopped.

She let him get closer. Then passing several crates, she spotted the perfect setup ahead. Bursting forward, she leapt onto a box with her right foot, pushing herself across the street, her left leg extended. Her foot found purchase on a window's lip, which she used as a springboard. Then, tucking her knees for momentum, she somersaulted while midair. Coming down, she landed on Lonsdale's back, and he crashed to the ground.

As his knees crumpled, she jabbed her elbow into the crook

of his neck. She landed only one punch before he rolled out from under her. His hand moved to his waist, not to his neck for a seed, as she'd expected. Ivy stepped on his wrist, stopping him from grabbing his knife but not crushing the bones.

"I don't want to hurt you, Ivy," he said loudly, purely for the benefit of the other elves and fair folk nearby. Most of the onlookers were either rushing off, or at least taking a healthy step back.

"When I was a youngling, I might have believed you," Ivy replied. "But not anymore." Today he had treated her like a prisoner, foregoing a trial, intending to imprison her in the cells below the courthouse. But years ago, he'd done so much worse. "You drove Seekers to kill my parents. My sister and her husband. And their *daughter*—defenseless, innocent Calla. Did you think I'd so easily forget?"

"I only want to protect you from yourself. You don't know what you're doing." He tried to wriggle his wrist free, but Ivy pressed her foot down harder. He stilled, signaling his compliance, but he caught her gaze, pleading with her. "You're threatening to unleash a battle within my House. A fight within the Minerals you couldn't possibly understand."

Ivy didn't need the seed's power to notice the twitch near his eye. It was Lonsdale's *tell*, an indicator her father had taught her. Lonsdale was lying through his teeth. He'd lied to his fellow elves for decades with success, so why wouldn't he at least attempt to manipulate her?

"Of course you don't want any arguments ... right before a war with the humans is about to break out," Ivy spat.

Ivy chanced a look at her surroundings. Near the entrance of the street, the two elves with Gneiss were positioned, steering curious elves away from the fight. In the opposite direction, Ivy expected Gneiss would appear soon, all bluster and not much else.

Lonsdale shifted, his legs wrapping around hers and vaulting her forward. She twisted just in time to avoid slamming her head into a wall, bracing her arms to break her fall as she rolled. Before she could recover from the awkward fall, Lonsdale's fists pummeled her ribs, and a swift kick knocked her down as she attempted to find her feet.

She didn't see Ash, but she recognized her cry. Black smoke filled the air above Lonsdale's head. Ash flew through the black cloud like an arrow, her wings then expanding. Several onlookers gasped at the sight.

Show off.

With Lonsdale momentarily confused, Ivy rolled backward, over her shoulder, keeping low and away from the falling debris. Lonsdale coughed and stumbled forward. Ivy kicked up, snapping his knee. She quickly followed with a leg sweep, knocking him onto his back.

"You only want to protect yourself. And I'm here to warn everyone about *you*," Ivy retorted.

"Don't be shortsighted like your father," he said, his voice low.

Her fingers itched to grab her father's knife and end him. She'd never been the primary target of the Council's deadly plot, but he'd actively schemed to murder her family, exploiting Seekers. Yet she had gotten ensnared in the net all the same. How many other elves were imperiled, too? Did he really deserve to live?

She heard someone whimper, a high timber signaling the sound was from a youngling. Someone caught off guard and too afraid to run. Part of her wanted to use the blade and end her tormentor. He was on his back, vulnerable and breathing hard, with her crouched just a step away. It would be so easy to bring justice right now on the narrow street.

Instead, Ivy shifted back, away from temptation. The decision of what to do with him couldn't be hers alone; it wasn't right, and it certainly wasn't the law.

Gneiss jogged toward her with a limping gait through the alleyway, her head held high. Ivy wasn't sure if the elf would pretend to side with Lonsdale and arrest her.

"Orcs make excellent trackers," Lonsdale spat.

Ivy frowned, realizing he didn't intend to leave the south. He'd simply employ an orc to track her down and kill her.

Just fantastic.

Lonsdale twisted and grabbed her tunic, and she let him. He wasn't dead, but he'd been defeated in front of plenty of witnesses. Besides, she wanted to hear whatever he had to say.

"You must have figured it out by now," Lonsdale whispered. "Your House Ambassadors are dead. The Council will be selecting the next Seeds Councilor. And you will be rotting in a hole long before the votes are cast at the Centennial. Enjoy the next few days, Ivy Balrel. They'll be your last."

Ivy shoved Lonsdale back and rose to face Gneiss; they'd have to make their brawl look real. Or perhaps Gneiss really intended to make it genuine. Gneiss eyes widened, and Ivy didn't register that Lonsdale had shifted until she was propelled sideways, a pain in her thigh. He'd rolled and kicked her with his good leg, sending her flying into a heavy refuse bin.

Too late, she realized that he'd been stalling, waiting for the seed's initial burst of strength to wane. But Ivy had operated without any magic for weeks. So even after the initial burst, she still felt exhilarated enough to bound over a mountain.

Using the momentum, she spun off the bin, spotting him in an awkward crouch. She whipped her leg up and slammed her foot across the side of his head. His body crumpled, unmoving, knocked out cold. Not missing a beat, Ivy spun to face Gneiss, her arms up and ready.

"What are you doing?" Gneiss hissed as she closed the gap.

"This is *my* area of the city. Why do you think I brought you here?" She started pointing out creatures in the street. "That's the gnome who helps my family in the summer. And that's my cousin right over there, standing next to his wife. I promise they are much more clever than they look right now with their jaws agape and whatnot."

"Well, you didn't warn us that you were going to bring a fight through the city," her cousin griped. "Just that we should be out and about."

"It was entertaining." His wife grinned. "I've been wanting to see someone put Lonsdaleite in his place for a long time."

"So no staged fight?" Ivy asked.

Gneiss looked from Ivy to Lonsdale and back again. "I think we're past that point. We need to get you out of here. The city guards will hear about this all too soon. Follow me."

Gneiss hobbled back through the narrow street, not disguising her pain, but not shying away from issuing orders along the way, either. One elf was dispatched to fetch the healer. Another to officially make a report to the captain of the guard. When Lonsdale awoke, he couldn't complain that Gneiss hadn't followed the law, or had even bent any ethical boundaries.

As Gneiss guided Ivy through the city, she explained what would happen next. "Lonsdale arrested you on ridiculous charges. If he publicly voices his reasoning, he will only appear small and foolish. He won't press the issue, at least not in the courthouse."

"He threatened to send an orc after me," Ivy said. She'd only get a few days head start, at best.

"Well, perhaps congratulations are in store." Gneiss's words dripped with sarcasm. "You've embarrassed the *esteemed* councilor. Now he'll use a favor—or ten—to send an orc after you. Be proud because you've made yourself worth the effort."

Ivy wanted to laugh, but her mouth had dried at the thought of evading an orc. She had caused too much trouble for Lonsdale to let her go without punishment.

Gneiss stopped at the edge of a building, only a few streets over from the main marketplace. From here, Ivy could find her way out of the city without further assistance.

"My leg is on fire, but skies above, that was the most fun I've had in a very long time." Gneiss grinned.

"I hope overthrowing the councilors is equally as entertaining," Ivy replied.

Gneiss' grin turned into one of her usual smirks. "Tides first."

"Send the new councilors to Carrus in three weeks," Ivy instructed, picking a city between the two elven strongholds. She didn't know exactly how they'd all get to the fae realm, but they'd figure it out in Carrus, together.

"Are you sure that's enough time?" Gneiss asked.

Ivy nodded, but didn't dare voice her true opinion. She'd only have a small window before Emmyth discovered her, just as Lonsdale had. So, if Ivy didn't fix whatever went wrong in Nylann'or before then, Ivy had no doubt that Emmyth would finish what she'd started in Winter. The councilor had already stabbed her in the back, literally. What *wouldn't* she do when she found Ivy plotting right under her nose?

"It's most logical to escape on the boats," Gneiss said as she fiddled with both the vials around her neck, one empty and Brecc's had one seed remaining. "If you travel northeast, to the shore, you'll find boats headed to Easthill for trading. They're just big enough for you to buy passage and hide amongst the crew for a few days."

"Good tip," Ivy said.

"But you'll definitely *not* get on the boats. And you'll avoid Easthill like it carries a plague." Gneiss rolled her eyes. "I'll *acci-*

dentally mention the boats to Lonsdalelite's associates. Let's lead the orc tracker on a wild goose chase."

Ivy scrunched her face, knowing that left only two really bad options for traveling north.

Gneiss removed her old pendant and shoved it into Ivy's hands. Without seeds, it wasn't worth much, but Ivy appreciated the gesture. Before she could express thanks at the surprise gift, Gneiss interrupted her.

"Don't get caught." She slapped Ivy on the back, shoving her into the road and toward the main city gate.

18

ORION AND THE KING

Scented, combed, and buttoned, Orion ignored how his collar chaffed as he strode to his father's chambers. His pounding heart chased away his earlier sleepiness. The guard opened the door to the king's informal receiving room, and thankfully, it was empty. One of many reserved for the king, this chilly space connected to the queen's private chambers. Fiercely private, she rarely engaged in public affairs, but she was the king's closest confidant. Her family was known for their impressive magical abilities, and she was recognized as the most clever of her generation ... undoubtedly both reasons why the king married her. King Eldrin put practicality above all else; love never entered into the equation. At least not as far as Orion could tell.

Orion inspected the room, noting a new painting on the wall between bookshelves. The idyllic scene of a mystical forest shifted in his periphery, the trees darkening. But when Orion focused directly on the artwork, the lush forest returned. Well-crafted cloth and gold bindings covered the books, generations old, with some floating just above the shelves, their pages turning by themselves as if searching for secrets. Two couches faced each other, rounded tables flanking their ends with stately blue and white vases, wedding gifts. A small fireplace squatted on the far wall, its hearth filled with rune-enchanted stones, ready to warm guests from other courts with a touch. Orion couldn't help but note a fire hadn't been lit for him.

Would his father put all the blame for the Aequus ceremony's hostility onto Orion? He had, after all, portaled the elf that the Spring warriors blamed for all their past, present, and future problems. Or would his father be angry that he'd liberated Ivy from her prison without entreating the king first? How angry would he be that two injured Spring fae resided in his dungeon awaiting a trial after decades of peace?

Two guards burst into the room, followed by King Eldrin. Glancing in Orion's direction, he dismissed the guards with a wave. The doors closed with a resounding thud, the echo hanging in the air like a death knell. Then the king lifted his gaze to meet Orion's, and his insides turned to water. The king's jaw tightened, clenching down, his facial expressions all biting, cold anger.

A chill ran down Orion's spine. His father's eyes, usually as cold as ice, now burned with a fierce, controlled fury. A tempest raged behind those eyes, barely contained. The air in the room grew heavy and oppressive. His heart pounded in his chest, the gravity of his delayed return sinking in deeper with each passing moment. The silence stretched, thick and suffocating, as the king's stare bore into him, unyielding and merciless.

King Eldrin took a step forward, his movements deliberate and measured. His next words would determine Orion's fate, and the uncertainty gnawed at him, each heartbeat a drumbeat of impending doom.

"I have given you every opportunity and, yet, you disrespect me. Keep secrets from me." A vengeful ferocity filled King Eldrin's voice. Orion braced himself to listen to his father's every complaint, swallowing a dozen different responses. The corners of the king's lips turned downward. "You have shadow magic."

Orion paused, his mind spinning. Of all the things his father was angry about, Eldrin fixated on Orion's shadow magic. Not the diplomacy fiasco. Not the two fae that Eldrin would need to put on trial—likely quietly. Not the fact that Orion had vanished with an injured elf, who was imprisoned under unethical circumstances, *at best*.

His shadow magic.

Part of him cracked, his soul fracturing in a thousand different directions as he remembered his place. Or did he still have one? Did he ever? Orion shook off his shock, reminding himself that he was a tool ... that's all he was in the eyes of the king. For Orion, secreting his magic was a matter of safety. To his father, the gift was a matter of leverage.

What can I do for you?

"I trained you, gave you every chance at success." The king's hands clenched into fists, knuckles white with suppressed rage. "And you hide an ability that can potentially blindside me. Why? Why!" He slammed his fist onto a nearby table, the impact reverberating through the room, causing even the books to rattle.

The king's eyes blazed with a fire that seemed to burn straight through Orion, each word dripping with venom. "Do you have any idea what you've done? What you've risked? You, who I've molded, who I've trusted—how dare you deceive me?" His voice rose to a roar, echoing off the stone walls, the sheer force of his anger palpable. King Eldrin took a step forward, then another, each deliberate movement closing the distance between them. But Orion didn't move. Didn't breathe. The king's face twisted with a mixture of betrayal and mania, veins bulging at his temples. "You are a means to an end, my ears among the humans, and yet you dare to keep secrets from me?"

The king seized one of the vases from an end table and hurled it across the room. The vessel shattered against the wall; porcelain echoed like thunder, spraying shards of blue and white across the room. He overturned the other table with a furious swipe, sending the second vase crashing to the floor.

Orion's heart pounded in his chest as he fought to remain still. Though his father rarely lost his temper, Orion had learned long ago not to fidget. Not to show fear, even when its grip tightened around him.

"Aren't you proud I kept a secret for so long? Wasn't that what you taught me above all else?" Orion's siblings had no chance to hide their shadow magic; the entire kingdom expected their bloodline would carry some level of their parent's ability. But no one considered that Orion could do much of anything.

"You are a true fae," the king snarled, his rumbling voice pounding like a hail storm, relentless and unyielding. "Your talent with twisting words is ever improving."

Orion's earlier rush of energy began to fade, the toll on his body taking a new, stronger grip. He'd held his glamour for months at a time, but not anymore. He needed far more rest than the nap he'd gotten. He needed a healer.

No, deep down he knew sleep and healers would only scratch the surface. His body demanded a more lasting cure.

Even if Ivy received a seed, would the Mother see fit to heal all his magical wounds? Or was he beyond repair?

"I never meant to hurt you with my secret. It wasn't my intention. I appreciate all your training and assistance," Orion soothed. If he didn't placate the king, and soon, his energy would completely fade. "I thought perhaps my greatest skill was my ability to glamour."

At his words, his energy slipped, his fae glamour dropping. Glancing down, he noticed his rough, bark-like skin, and the king's attention flew to the top of his head where a crown of holly lay.

His father's face reddened, his hands curling into fists at his sides, and the room chilled further, sending goosebumps up Orion's arms. The weight of his father's disappointment and indignation pressed down, seeming to suck the air from the room. Concentrating, Orion pulled his glamour back into place. Instead of admitting his weakness, which his father would despise, Orion acted as if he'd dropped his glamour on purpose to make a point.

"I will bear whatever punishment you designate, even if it means sending me back to the human realm," Orion said.

Surprisingly, his body didn't cringe at the thought of returning to Trinth. In fact, when he said the words, he thought of Ivy and some of his worry uncoiled. He almost felt a ghost of a touch of her fingers running over his skin, and a sense of calm washed over him. Still, he dreaded leaving Winter in disgrace.

The king stroked his chin, appraising Orion. "You will return to Trinth."

A bead of sweat rolled down Orion's back, and he hid his spike of elation at the order. "Whatever you would have me do."

"You will return to Unaria and speak with the duke, himself. Make a recommendation for another Unarian Night Guard Captain, and you will retire. And you will not be returning to Trinth again, until I require it."

Orion grasped his hands together behind his back, his mind reeling. The words felt like a dagger to his heart. Yes, he'd expected to retire, but to be banned from Trinth entirely? Orion had always been free to pass between realms as he deemed fit, but not anymore. Panic clawed at his chest, threatening to consume him. Ivy was in Trinth. The thought of being kept away from her twisted the dagger deeper, each turn sending fresh waves of anguish. His knees felt weak, and he fought to keep his composure, the horror of the king's decree settling into his bones.

"You will have three human days to incorporate the change. Then you will return here and attend to your duties at the portals and other royal necessities."

"I will still be the Portal Keeper?" Orion asked, confused. A Portal Keeper traveled often, per the nature of their duties. Was his father trying to keep him close to home? If so, why?

"Yes, you will retain your title, but you will primarily track travel into the fae realm."

Orion pressed his lips together; his father was fundamentally cutting him off at the knees. Logically, Orion knew he should feel fortunate that he retained his title, his position, and his standing in the court. It's what Ivy needed him to do. Yet, inside he railed against remaining in the fair realm indefinitely.

"What royal necessities will I attend to?" Orion asked, keeping his voice steady.

"Dinners and other social functions."

Orion clasped his hands together tighter, struggling to look calm though his energy was fading.

"Starting tonight," the king continued. He walked around the room, his attention on his books. "I've been invited to a Frostbourn dinner tonight, and you will join us afterward for poetry reading."

Orion swallowed, not sure if he could trek back to his rooms, let alone endure a night of poetry. If his glamour fell in public, even for a moment, his father would never forgive him. Today's fury would be a spring picnic compared to the king's wrath if Orion humiliated him.

So, to avoid inevitable failure tonight, he had to confess the truth now. Admit his weakness. Admit that he'd made a mistake in his bargain. Even if he lost his father's respect, at least he wouldn't degrade his family tonight.

"King Eldrin," what little pride Orion had crumbled away, but he steeled himself for what was to come, "there's something you should know. About Ivy."

"Ivy?" Eldrin turned his attention back to Orion. "The elf?"

Orion nodded and opened his mouth, but before he confessed, a flood of magic washed through his body. He gasped as vitality flowed through his veins. Suddenly, the burden of his glamour lightened, barely a feather's weight. His sleepiness vanished, replaced by an alertness he'd missed. He shifted his wings, the pain gone. His heart swelled, emotion filling him.

"Orion?" the king asked, his voice hard. "What about the elf?"

Orion choked back tears. Ivy had gotten a seed, surely. She was going to survive. He would see her again; he must before becoming chained to his father's side.

"I returned her to Trinth." Orion added a detail the king didn't know, as a peace offering. "She plans to inform her kindred of the crimes of the Elven Council."

The king nodded casually, but there was a tightness around his eyes. "I appreciate the information. I will alert the Summer Queen."

Orion hoped he'd revealed enough to show the king he could still depend on him, but not enough to hurt Ivy's chances of success.

"I hope you like poetry," the king said, heading for the door.

Orion pulled the shadows around him, the darkness concealing him. Dropping the shadows, he opened the door for his father and bowed. The display not only reassured Orion that, indeed, his magic was back, but illustrated his loyalty to the king.

The king gave Orion a calculating stare, but left without berating him in front of the guards. The lack of reprimand gave Orion a sliver of hope. He didn't know Ivy's exact plan, but he wouldn't fail her in the fair realm. In the end, she would need Eldrin's compliance, which meant Orion must make amends with him. Proving his commitment to the crown meant performing even in the smallest ways, like attending mind-numbing, political social functions.

However, he still needed to access the atrium and secretly obtain all the plant samples he could gather. Zel insisted there was no other option, but if Orion was caught, he'd have to answer uncomfortable questions and shatter any thread of trust between himself and the king. Schooling his face into a mask, one he was well practiced with but loathed more than ever, Orion marched away from his father's wing.

19

THE ORC TOWERS

Keeping hidden in the eaves underneath the platform of the south-western orc tower, Ivy was grateful for the wind sweeping through the short pass. A half moon and a gibbous shed too much light on the night, but they also created wonderful shadows. Stars glinted through the scant clouds as Ivy readied to perform her next move.

She'd run north from the Yllalen'al for a half-day until reaching the desired crossing location. Like anyone wishing to travel between the remote fair folk areas in the south and the rest of Trinth, she could either travel by the sea to the east, the poisoned lands to the west, or what the fair folk called "The Orc Pass." The humans had other colorful names for it, but few traveled the pass because they appreciated keeping their limbs attached to their bodies.

Ivy, too, wanted to escape unscathed.

She'd already tainted the food of the orc in the far tower, but the timing between poisoning both orcs had to be just right. Both sentinels needed to vacate their towers at the same time, which meant she needed to treat the second orc's food soon. She needed a window to sprint north without them spotting her in their telescopes. Not that they used them all the time, but she needed a distraction.

Ivy gripped the edge of the platform and lifted herself up ever so slowly, hoping the orc wouldn't spot her. If she had the luxury of spying on the orcs for a few days, she wouldn't have to take such a risk. But Lonsdale wouldn't wait to dispatch an orc to hunt her. With any luck, Lonsdale was disoriented and busy after his fight with Ivy, and an orc tracker would be at least a few hours behind.

The orc had rotated to the far side of the platform, as his footfalls had indicated; the desk-like wooden cube in the middle of the tower blocked the orc's view of Ivy as she crawled onto the platform. Her heart pounded, and she crawled next to the desk.

Then the wind died down.

Ivy slowed her breathing as she reached into her satchel. Next to the blissfully sleeping dragon, Ivy grabbed the herbs she'd gathered just outside Yllalen'al, still wrapped in linen.

"What did you think about the two orcs that returned yesterday?" The orc on the platform shouted across the expanse to the other sentinel. He was large, even for an orc, and he was bored. Whenever the wind quieted, he was quick to strike up conversations across the pass.

"I ignore baseless gossip," the other orc shouted back from afar. "And you should, too." The orc on the other tower was leaner than most of his kind, and his white hair was cropped where others had flowing locks. And he generally tried to shut down the conversation whenever possible, but the orc near Ivy never seemed to take the hint.

"I heard orcs that left Aggord are getting called back," the orc shouted, and Ivy was glad for his talkative nature. She slid her hand over the lip of the desk, finding his bowl of food. This was the most dangerous part of her plan.

She slipped the bowl off the desk and held it in her lap, her hands shaking. For a moment, the guards were silent. Her heart thumped. Did they spot her? She fought the urge to slide down the tower and bolt, but she forced herself to still, waiting. Listening. Her father had taught her much about the fair folk, but there were still holes in her knowledge, especially relating to orcs and their capabilities.

Finally, the orc spoke again, still from the same spot on the tower. "I guess it makes sense after the Seeker attack on the elves. Has it already been four weeks since the battle? How many units were called from Aggord to go to Neidrei afterward? I never thought I'd see the day when orcs entered the human-held lands. Plus, what happened in Nylenn'or? I heard a boat was deployed and then returned. What do you think it means?"

Nylenn'or? What did Nym do?

"I don't think. My job is to watch from the tower." The lean orc shouted across the expanse, irritation lacing his words. She'd already visited his tower. Had he eaten his food? Was that why he was grumpy?

She dumped the ripped up pieces of a leaf onto the gruel and stirred the mixture with the wooden spoon.

The wind picked back up just as the far orc spoke again. The orc near her probably couldn't hear the words, but Ivy did. "I won't make any assumptions until we hear directly from High Commander Rokgut, himself."

Ivy snuck the bowl back onto the desk and crawled on her belly back to the lip of the tower. Dangling her legs off the side, her feet danced in the air, seeking purchase when the top of the orc's head came into view. She sucked in a breath and dropped, hanging onto the edge by her fingertips.

Over the wind, Ivy couldn't hear if he gasped at seeing her, if he was eating, or if he paused, possibly sensing her presence. She swung her legs wildly, finally finding a support post. Wrapping her legs around it, she released her hold and swung upside down. Spotting a crossbeam—the one her bag was on a collision course with—she yanked her satchel to her chest saving the rat-dragon from slamming into it. Maneuvering back into the shadows, Ivy waited.

She steadied her breathing, listening for an alarm. Had she been spotted? Had the orc felt any odd vibrations underfoot from her sudden movements? Or would their renewed vigilance keep them rooted in the tower; after all, they were aware of the unusual orc deployments. Even if they didn't know for certain that war was coming, they suspected it.

Ivy chewed her lip, wondering how to evade a skilled orc tracker. They were obviously strong and could re-grow limbs. But unless they were in the fair realm, their re-growth was slow. Their speed was the bigger problem; though not as fast as elves, orcs were faster than humans. But how well could they see and smell? Ivy had no idea.

The orc in the far tower abruptly bounded down the stairs. From this angle, Ivy noticed the myriad of scars that crisscrossed his arms and face, undoubtedly earned in the Realms War.

Overhead, the orc shouted, "Hey! You're breaking protocol! You can't leave your station until relieved!"

Ivy smiled.

As long as the orc overhead swallowed a few bites of his food, he wouldn't be far behind. It would be a long night for all of them. But while the orcs cursed their bellies, Ivy would safely trek through the woods.

But then where would she go? She needed information about the orcs and how to evade them. Did Ivy dare approach Magdud? The orc hated the war, and she was some kind of ally to Orion. But would Magdud risk teaching Ivy tricks to avoid getting caught? Or would she tie Ivy up and hand her over to the tracker herself?

The orc overhead groaned, then cursed. A moment later, his feet thundered down the stairs to the ground. Ivy was already silently moving behind him, descending, too.

The moment Ivy's feet hit the dirt, she sprinted north across the pass toward the safety of the human's forest. How far could she get before the tracking orc figured out she hadn't gone to the boats? Debating between taking her chances alone or stopping to study her pursuer, Ivy set her course. Her next move was her best idea yet, or by far the worst.

Ivy dug her fingers into the stone wall surrounding Carrus. The sun set low in the sky, and Ivy had already timed the guards' shifts around the perimeter. She didn't know where Magdud lived, but she'd find out soon enough. How hard would it be to find an orc in a human city? More accurately, how difficult would it be for an orc to find Ivy?

Climbing higher, it wasn't long until she heard footfalls running in her direction. Ivy pressed her head against the wall, ignoring the way her blood pumped harder. Instead, she patiently waited for the inevitable. Without a word, two hands grabbed the back of Ivy's tunic, yanking her down to the ground.

"An elf?" the guard said, her brows shooting high before she whistled an alert and grabbed Ivy's arm.

"Really? You need reinforcements?" Ivy said, hiding her smirk.

The guard gripped her arm tighter, a show of strength, but the guard's palm sweat revealed her nervousness.

"Come with me," she said, as two more guards skidded around the bend of the wall.

One of the guards, a tall gangly man, grabbed Ivy's other arm without question. The other, a portly man with a grey-streaked beard, looked Ivy up and down before falling in next to the female guard as they marched Ivy to a side gate.

"I thought elves were supposed to be stealthy," he muttered to the guard who had captured Ivy. "She didn't even cover her ears. And *you* caught her, so she must be a slow climber. No wonder our ancestors kicked their kind completely out of the realm."

His comments were no more pesky than a single mosquito in summer. She had far more important things to do than verbally spar with a random human guard. Besides, she'd intended to get caught. The fastest way to connect with Magdud was to snag the orc's attention. What would draw more attention than rumors of an elf climbing the outer wall?

The bearded guard harrumphed and signaled to the gate guards up ahead.

"Don't get any funny ideas," he said. "You'll go straight to a cell for questioning."

Ivy swallowed, hoping Magdud was actually in Carrus. Yes, Ivy expected to get held for questioning, but she'd not let herself dwell on where she'd be held.

"You don't happen to have any orcs in the prison, do you?" Ivy asked, hating the way her voice pinched.

Both the guards tightened their grip at her question—which was a good sign. Ivy wanted to blanket the town with news of a suspicious elf asking about dangerous orcs. With even one question, news would filter back to Magdud, wherever she was hiding in Carrus.

"I mean, there can't be any orcs living in the city, can there?"

Ivy asked the second question, hoping rumors would reach Magdud, even if she lived in the forest.

Though Ivy didn't like it, she let herself get dragged past the city square and around the edge of the inner forest. Seeing those trees again brought back memories, even in the daylight. Ivy's mouth dried, and her head felt light. Yet she couldn't keep herself from staring at the woods where she'd witnessed so much destruction. She couldn't help but glare at the skies, wondering if Ash might deign to come to her rescue.

As they entered an official-looking part of the town, Ivy was taken to heavily guarded double doors of what appeared to be a fancy courthouse.

"This is a dungeon?" Ivy asked.

"It was converted to a dungeon after the new courthouse was built down the street," the female guard replied. "Don't think about escaping. It's designed to imprison humans, Seekers, and fair folk alike. It can definitely hold you."

Ivy felt like her head was floating, as if she were observing herself and the guards from afar. Her plan had seemed reasonable: spread the gossip that an elf had tried to infiltrate Carrus. If Magdud were reasonably well connected, she'd find out soon. But could Magdud even access a dungeon? What if Ivy was stuck there, indefinitely? Her heart thumped harder, and she flexed her fingers, considering a fight. She could still break free.

I must talk to Magdud, especially now. Even if an orc tracker didn't know she was in Carrus before, rumors would spread after this. An orc *would* be coming for her, but not a friendly one.

The double doors opened, and Ivy couldn't make her feet move. The guards dragged her forward, the bearded one discussing the security. Inside, white stone walls loomed overhead with ornate, masterful carvings at odds with the oppressive feeling. Ivy sensed suffocating magic of some kind over the expansive space. Several guards were stationed near arched doorways on either side. One of the doors opened, and Ivy spotted a uniformed figure at a desk, pouring over a parchment with inky fingers. Perhaps a clerk or record keeper? Ivy could only guess as the guard slammed the door shut, cutting off her prying.

In the back of the room was another set of double doors, painted a glossy black.

Ivy's body sagged. She was surrounded by guards, dozens of them. An attempt at escape would result in severely injuring a few humans and then a precarious sprint back through the doors. And even then, with so many blades in a confined space, she'd be wounded. Had she risked Carrus just to turn around and race back to the forest without contacting Magdud? And worse, nursing an injury and having announced her location to any halfway intelligent, hunting orc?

The black doors drew closer. Her heart pounded wildly, each beat echoing her rising panic. The flanking door guards grabbed the handles and pulled, revealing a rough, darkened tunnel, a maw ready to consume an unwelcome elf.

"Wait!" a familiar voice sounded from behind them.

Ivy straightened and twisted around, her heart leaping at a whisper of hope. Had her imagination conjured his voice? Could it really be him? Her breath caught in her throat as she turned, the world slowing for a moment.

Behind her, Orion stood in his Unarian guard uniform. She stared at him, dumbfounded, a wave of relief washing over her so intensely it almost brought her to her knees. His dark hair was pulled back, though a few strands had come loose, and his green eyes flashed. It was definitely him. She'd seen the look of anger on his face before, and she almost pitied the guards.

"Release her," Orion demanded, his voice steady and commanding.

The guards hesitated, their grips loosening slightly. Ivy's

gaze remained locked on Orion, her beacon in the darkness. The fury in his eyes only intensified as the guards stood, transfixed and unsure.

"And who are …" the lanky guard's question died on his tongue as Orion marched forward and several of the other guards nodded in deference.

"Captain Orion of Unaria," the bearded guard said. "Why do we have the pleasure of your—"

"Release. Her." Orion narrowed his gaze. "She is my guest."

Ivy held her breath, and the guards next to her stiffened. Every pair of eyes in the room turned to watch the confrontation between a visiting captain, the city guards, and the elf caught between them.

20

CONNECTION IN CARRUS

Orion gripped the pommel of his sheathed sword, *mostly* to remind them that he wore the duke's crest. Whether or not they feared he'd draw his sword was up to them. Both the guards released Ivy and took a half step away.

"W-we caught her climbing the outer wall," the older guard said, daring to look at Orion, though not in the eye.

"She is an elf." Orion didn't bother to explain further. "And you're taking her straight to the dungeon? Are you *trying* to pick a fight with the fair folk?"

It was all he could do to keep his composure. An invisible tether bound him to Ivy, all but drawing him closer. His hands twitched with the desire to reach out, to feel her warmth and confirm she was truly healed. He had so many questions, but he had to stay focused to deal with the guards first. The humans had to see him as unwavering, in control. So he clenched his fists, forcing himself to remain composed, even as the sight of her standing just outside his reach tore at him. The longing was almost unbearable, a physical ache.

"It was just until the elf could be questioned." The older

guard puffed out his chest, but a pink tinge colored his face. "The fair folk sightings have increased of late. We can't be too careful."

"I believe this is exactly why the magistrate will want to speak with the elf," Orion kept his voice measured, though his raw instinct was to cut off anyone's hands who dared mishandle Ivy. "Perhaps you are ignorant of the laws of the realms, but the elves are the peacekeepers."

Ivy's jaw dropped, her surprise reflecting his own. He'd spoken before thinking it through. Yes, elves supposedly kept the peace, but they had neglected their duties for over a hundred years. Even so, he trusted that Ivy could influence all of elvenkind for the better, and save them all.

Orion itched to pull her close. She stood only ten steps away, and every part of him screamed to bridge the gap between them. His heart pounded with the urge to protect her, to reassure her.

"If you wouldn't mind," Ivy interjected, "I'm rather tired from my journey, and I must speak with the magistrate."

"Of course," Orion held his hand next to him, gesturing for her move to his side. "The magistrate, Magdud, is traveling, but should be back any day."

Ivy blinked, but otherwise didn't reveal her shock at hearing an orc was the magistrate of Carrus. With Maggie gone, Ivy could have been trapped in the dungeon for several weeks before the orc even knew of an elf's presence.

As Ivy took each step toward him, his anxiety decreased. At his side, he felt the warmth emanating from her. Keeping her focus down, she whispered as they turned to leave, "Thank Alysatree you were here."

"I had hoped to find you," Orion said, escorting her out of the building and down the street. The sun shone, reflecting off the white stone of the buildings, and few young servants laughed as they carried large baskets through a side street. His anger at the guards melted a bit now that Ivy was at his side. "When I healed in—"

Ivy turned and grabbed his forearm, heat running through him at the mere touch of her fingertips. "You're magic returned?"

Orion nodded, barely suppressing a smile. He could hardly believe he'd found Ivy again, relieved that his calculations had been correct. "When I suddenly healed, I knew you'd taken a seed. And I guessed that you'd leave the Minerals shortly thereafter. I calculated how long your travel would take and, well, here I am. Though I honestly didn't know where you'd go." His joy faded as he remembered what his father had demanded. "I'm afraid it's not all good news, though."

Ivy shook her head, seeing his dour expression. "I don't want to hear it. Not yet. Give me this moment."

Though they kept a professional distance, Orion still gazed on her face, framed by the dark strands falling from her braid. Her freckles had multiplied across her nose, and a healthy flush rose to her cheeks. Her cloak clasped at her neck, a pulse in her neck feathering just above. His gaze lifted to her lips and Ivy seemed to lean closer. Then she cleared her throat and stepped back, glancing at the humans milling nearby.

Orion guided her to Magdud's home in a nearby area of the city. After knocking, a servant, Agretha, answered. He'd already stopped by and dropped off his bag of samples for Zel.

"Come in, come in." The servant swung the door wide, letting them inside. Agretha had deep wrinkles around the eyes and age spots on her cheeks and hands. "How long will you be staying?"

Ivy shrugged. "Perhaps a night? I was hoping Magdud could advise me on something."

"Perhaps we can help until she returns," the servant said,

ushering them along pock-marked tiles and expensive furniture with extensive bite marks from tiny, poisoned teeth near the bottom.

"Agretha was a servant in the fae realm," Orion explained, assuring Ivy that she could speak openly if she wished.

"A slave, more like it," Agretha said bitterly. "The Autumn fae are harsh, and I was once a young fool. Thank the Mother that Magdud offered me a job here when I was released from my servitude. I'm the only servant on staff right now, a wise decision considering, well, *everything*. But, I'm happy to help you, if I can."

"If you wouldn't mind bringing Ivy food and drink, I think that would be the most helpful," Orion said.

"Yes, of course. Would you take her to the sitting room?" Agretha hurried away. Her limp always became more pronounced when she rushed, but she never complained of pain.

Orion took Ivy's hand in his own, running his thumb across her knuckles as he led her through the wide hallway. Thoughts and emotions tumbled through his mind, fighting for attention. Every moment with her felt precious, the impending separation already seemed to loom. He wanted to memorize every detail, every touch, knowing that soon he would be torn away from her.

He led her into the sitting room, past the wall of books, paintings, and tapestries, mostly of human lore. The private library held Maggie's extensive collection of fair realm lore, except for the stand covered by a glass dome, perched on the far side of the room. Passing couches and chairs set up for conversation, he guided Ivy to the corner near the unlit fireplace.

Ivy pulled him into a tight hug, resting her head on his chest. Orion wrapped his arms around her, closing his eyes and breathing in the scent of her hair, imprinting the moment in his memory. He squeezed Ivy tighter to him, confirming the reality of her, here and now. But his feelings quickly turned to guilt, a heavy weight settling in his chest. He had abandoned her when she needed him the most.

"I was so worried," Orion said, his voice thick with all the emotion he'd held. He'd left her injured and alone, dependent on the Minerals for help. The image haunted him. How could he have done that to her? The guilt gnawed, burrowing deep, her each breath a bitter reminder of his failure to protect her. "I don't think I could ever leave you again. Especially not like that."

"You trusted me. You know, I don't always need you to save me. I mean, today I did," Ivy chuckled as she absently ran her fingers across his shoulder. "You knew I could figure things out in Yllalen'al. And I did. Though, I had some help. There is far more good in our kindred than evil. I saw it."

Her words assuaged his guilt, but only a little. The logical move had been for him to leave Ivy; his withdrawal was meant to protect all the humans from his father's wrath. But the memory of watching her get carted away by strangers still pained him deeply.

"Ivy," he whispered, his voice breaking.

Ivy held him tightly in response. He ran his hands under her cloak, still gingerly skimming his fingers over her old wounds. Ivy just relaxed into him, clearly not pained. Orion swallowed a lump in his throat, and he leaned back, brushing Ivy's hair away from her face.

"What happened?" he dared ask.

She stepped back and showed him the empty vial at her neck. "Gneiss gave me a seed, and her vial."

Orion raised a brow. "That's ... unexpected."

He unclasped the cloak at her neck, his fingers brushing her collarbone, before tossing it on a nearby chair. Ivy pulled him to the couch, and they sank into the cushions together. She updated him on what had happened, her words a comforting melody. Their closeness felt natural, his arm around her and their legs touching. Ivy animatedly explained the infirmary, Lonsdale, and her plans to meet two Mineral elves in Carrus in two and a half weeks.

Orion grinned at the thought of defying his father and staying in Carrus with Ivy until the Mineral Councilors arrived. But the grin quickly faded as reality crashed back in. He would have to leave, and she didn't know. The thought twisted like a knife in his gut, the impending farewell a dark cloud over their brief reunion.

"I have to go north, to Nylenn'or. I need to find out what happened to Nym." Ivy dropped her chin. "But, I might have one problem. Lonsdaleite may have sent an orc to track me."

"That is a problem," Agretha said as she entered the room, holding a large tray.

"Seekers are dangerous, but I know how to avoid them," Ivy said. "I don't know enough about orcs. I don't know if Magdud will help me."

"There must be a book or two in her library that we can read?" Orion suggested, ignoring Agretha's perplexed expression.

Agretha set down the tray on a little table next to Ivy with a plate of bread, a cheese spread, strawberries, and a small container of honey. Then she paced, fiddling with her apron as Ivy ate.

"Seekers can't cross the northern channel; they don't have the intelligence, but an orc can," Orion said. "They're very clever. And some don't need much sleep. Going through official channels would take weeks for an elven councilor to get an orc appointed as a scout."

"Unofficially?" Ivy asked.

Orion thought back to his father's lessons. "It depends on if a commander owes Lonsdaleite a favor. My guess is the scout was dispatched a day or two after you left. With the right combination of abilities, they're gaining on you. Though, most of their senses only are slightly better than humans, except for their olfactory senses."

"Yes, that's correct," Agretha said. "Magdud is *very* particular about her food. And she can smell what herbs the cook is chopping, even from this room. She can sniff out an apple in someone's apron or ants underground."

"They're also trained from birth to follow orders," Orion said, a protectiveness rising inside him. "If they're commanded to find you, they won't stop."

Agretha shuddered and wrapped her arms around herself, lost in a memory.

"We can attend to ourselves, now, Agretha," Orion said, releasing her from having to stand at the ready. These types of conversations often brought back difficult memories for her. "I'll take Ivy to see Zel."

"Zel?" Ivy jumped to her feet. "He's here?"

Agretha brightened, hearing the excitement in Ivy's voice. "The gnome? Yes! A studious little creature." She gave a little curtsy. "I'll be in the kitchen if you need me."

Orion put his hand on Ivy's back and guided her forward, heat radiating through her tunic. Every time they touched, the connection chased away the shadows of his own mind, and he calmed. With Ivy close, she was a balm to his soul, and his burdens seemed to lift. With her, overcoming any obstacle felt possible.

At the top of the stairs, Orion knocked and announced himself. After a moment, Zel called out, his voice groggy. It was the midmorning, but Zel had an erratic sleep schedule. Finally, Zel cracked the door open, rubbing his eyes. An eye mask had been pushed up to his forehead, and Orion hoped he didn't have another headache. Zel blinked several times and finally seemed to notice the elf next to Orion.

"Ivy!" he gasped. "How did you … Where did …" He looked over his shoulder and then back at Ivy. "Actually, this makes sense."

Zel threw the door wide and revealed Ash sitting on the chair. She spread her wings and flew to Orion, circling around him before settling on his shoulder, a familiar weight he'd missed. She rubbed the top of her head against his chin, hitting him a little harder than usual, but a content rumble sounded from her throat.

"She missed you." Ivy grinned. "She's still obnoxious, but I was grateful for her companionship. She brought me food multiple times on our trip. And she might have saved my life when I fought Lonsdale."

Orion sent thankful thoughts to Ash, and she rumbled louder in response.

Zel whistled. "You've been busy."

"So have you." Ivy walked around Zel's desk. She clasped her hands behind her back as she looked at his experiments. Then she sat on a stool, facing the gnome. "Did you know a gnome in the Winter infirmary?"

"There aren't many gnomes on staff in the citadel, and I dared approach them." He glanced at Orion before turning back to Ivy. "They helped me escape with Magdud."

"The gnome who worked as a healer, he touched the Gathering seed in my hand, and his eyes dimmed. And he said something about you, but was interrupted."

"His eyes dimmed?" Zel swallowed and pressed his lips together.

"I ate the seed shortly after. But then hours later, when I

was in the human realm, the seed still worked. Not fully, but enough for me to survive."

Orion's stomach twisted, remembering The Tower. Ivy had only been away from him for a total of two hours, but every moment for her had probably stretched indefinitely.

"He transferred a large portion of his magic into the seed, a preservation magic," Zel said, and Ivy's face fell. He leaned forward, quickly reassuring her. "Don't worry too much. He'll recover in a few days in the fair realm. If he were here in Trinth, it would be much, much longer. Years."

"Any progress on healing the Seekers?" Orion asked, changing the subject. Ivy had gotten her answer and he hated seeing her distressed.

"The good news is, Orion brought back several specimens from the Winter atrium. I know the base ingredient necessary for the medicine," Zel said to Ivy. "The bad news is, it's quite rare."

"How rare?" Orion asked.

He'd visited Zel last night, shortly after arriving in Carrus. The gnome had been enthralled with his work and had barely spared Orion a "hello" before snatching the supplies and sending him away. So, this was the first Orion was hearing about the results.

"I need the bark of a Gathering Tree," Zel said.

Silence hung, the irony like a noose. They'd just attempted to kill every Gathering tree, only to find out they held a critical ingredient. Other than the dryad-housed tree, well protected in Neidrei, only one other Gathering Tree existed in all of Trinth, the official Centennial Tree. And none of them knew the location.

Ivy stiffened, her hands grasping each other behind her back. "We can't go back to Neidrei. I'm sure they've increased their security."

"I could get in," Orion said.

"I've heard they have someone checking for glamours now," Zel said. "You'd be caught, dragged home, and thrown into a hole ... by your father."

"That only leaves the real Centennial Tree." Ivy tapped a finger against the stool. "The location will be revealed to me in the spring. All the elves attend, but I can harvest some bark in secret."

"The Seekers have suffered for over a hundred years. They can survive a couple more seasons," Zel said sadly.

"But next spring may be too late. The war might have started before the Centennial," Ivy said. "A massive number of seeds might be distributed months before I discover the Centennial Tree's location."

"There's one other option," Zel said. "The tree I brought to the Winter Court. The entire tree."

Orion ran a hand down his face. He'd have to steal the sapling and transport it to Carrus ... without anyone noticing or reporting the tree. Which meant, he was obliged to return to the Winter Court.

He didn't know why the idea bothered him so deeply, especially as he'd always planned to return. Perhaps because, for a moment, he'd envisioned staying in the human realm with Ivy even for a few extra days. Being with her was like finding a part of himself that he didn't know was lost. He didn't know if he should curse having met her or relish it, but she had changed him.

"King Eldrin will definitely notice the sapling went missing." Ivy fiddled with her fingers, like she sometimes did when she was nervous.

"It holds an essential element in the cure," Zel pressed. "Orion brought me a leaf and a scraping of bark. The bark is the most promising, but I need to test the roots, too."

"But what will that mean for you, Orion?" Ivy asked, her brow scrunched.

He'd always thought the elves were selfish for allowing so many humans to get corrupted by the seeds, and now he had a chance to potentially save those that remained. Would he gamble his position after a lifetime of work for distant humans who would never know or appreciate his risk?

"I'll do it, but I don't know how soon I'll be able to deliver the tree," Orion confessed. "I've been tasked by the king to resign from my position with the Unarian Guard."

Ivy paled and turned away. He was officially leaving Unaria, but she didn't yet know the full extend of what that meant. She'd be alone for far longer stretches than he would experience in the fair realm. Closing the distance between them, he grabbed her hand in both of his.

"I'll find every excuse to return to your side," Orion said. "I'm still the Portal Keeper, after all."

Ivy flashed him a strained smile. "Depending on what Magdud advises, I might not be able to stay in Carrus for long."

Which meant they only had a sliver of time together before they both had to go their separate ways.

Agretha knocked on the door before opening it. "I just received word that the magistrate returns within a few hours. I'll prepare dinner. Brace yourselves, the messenger said Magdud isn't her usual, cheerful self."

Orion squeezed Ivy's hand, letting her know she shouldn't worry. Maggie would be amiable after a good meal. Hopefully. But if not, he would help Ivy. There was no way he'd leave her vulnerable with an unknown orc possibly tracking her.

21

ALL THE ORC SECRETS

In the dining hall, Magdud forced another bite of mince pie. Despite the dish being one of her favorites, she could barely stomach food tonight. Too much weighed on her mind, too many dark memories threatened.

"You've outdone yourself, Agretha," Magdud said, pretending that her life wasn't imploding.

"I'm happy to do it." Agretha set a plate of sliced apples on the table for dessert, then she moved to stand near the wall where she could observe the room.

Agretha, alone, had handled the cooking and cleaning for weeks. Magdud appreciated her help, though allowing even one servant to return was a risk—a single, careless tongue could reveal that a gnome worked right in the heart of Carrus. But Agretha's friends and two generations of her family had passed away while she had been trapped in the Autumn Court. After all she'd lost, the aging human had few resources when she returned to Trinth; so Magdud had hired her. Had five years gone by already? Now Agretha was part of Magdud's eclectic family, and turning her out indefinitely was hardly appropriate.

Magdud distracted herself by watching Ash, who hopped

around on the table, nipping meat off Ivy's plate and eyeing the silverware. Princess rested at Magdud's feet, a comforting weight. Zel and Ivy discussed the Seekers and a possible cure. Orion was quiet, his attention rapt on the elf. The poor sod was going to fall apart when he had to return to the fair realm.

Magdud knew how he felt. She tapped her finger against the folded missive next to her plate, still unopened. But she knew what the notification contained: a summons.

"Ivy, we need to talk about your orc problem," Magdud said, interjecting herself into the conversation for the first time that evening.

Her three guests fell silent, and Orion's gaze slid to Agretha who was standing near the door.

"Of course Agretha told me all the juicy gossip the moment I returned." Magdud leaned back in her chair. She had little patience for tiptoeing around the important conversations that needed having—it only delayed her retreat to her bedchamber where she could finally, hopefully, get a good night's sleep.

"I wasn't sure you'd want to divulge secrets to evading your own kind," Ivy said. "I was saving the request for ... a better time."

Until after you'd eaten. Magdud could practically hear the elf thinking it, and she barked a laugh and slammed her hand on the table, making Princess jump. "Well, perhaps you don't have straw for brains. There's hope for you yet!"

She pushed back from the table and stood tall, ignoring her exhaustion. She could either make this night drag on with her bad attitude, or she could choose to enjoy the company. Orion rarely took the opportunity to stay for a proper meal, and Ivy's escape had intrigued her, so she chose the latter.

"I'm sorry I've been poor company tonight. I've spent over a week traveling Trinth, delivering bad news to my old unit." She paused, hating to say the words one more time. "We're getting called back."

Zel paled, and Orion rubbed his chin. Ivy stood, taking a step toward her. "Magdud, I'm so sorry. When do you have to report to Aggord?"

Let's find out.

Magdud snapped the wax on the missive, reading the dreaded words. Her assumption had been correct. Rokgut had done her one small mercy—given her a warning. At least she'd been able to alert her unit, giving them precious extra hours to prepare. But the gathering location was unexpected.

"We are to meet on the double new moon." Magdud calculated how much time she needed to write the letters; they must be dispatched with riders at dawn to her unit. Sleep would have to wait. "Warriors must report to the Realm of the Accords."

"The Realm of the what?" Ivy asked.

"Accords," Zel answered. "Been there a few times."

"I've only read about it," Orion said. "There are two access points within Trinth."

"Oh, I remember learning about that place," Ivy said, straightening. "Only the elven leaders go when needed."

"The fair realm isn't as strict," Zel shrugged.

Not by a long shot.

Magdud read the letter again, surprised her unit wasn't posted to Aggord for training first. Her stomach soured, considering what that meant. Were the fair folk rushing too quickly into battle? Did they not care if her unit lived or died? Did the high commander even have good contingency plans? She noticed her guests had finished eating, so she tucked the summons into her pocket, along with her questions, and picked up Princess.

Magdud stood at the head of the table. "Will you join me in the library?" It was more of a demand than a request. Not wasting any time, she began teaching as they walked through the hallways. "Four access portals were originally built by the ancients, but half were destroyed in the war."

When they approached the glass case with the book about the fair folk history, she set down Princess and lifted the protective glass and set it aside. Zel pushed a stool closer and stood next to her as she flipped through the pages of the book. Magdud pointed to the passage about the Accords, and Zel read aloud.

The Realm of the Accords appears with every double new moon in Trinth. Access points form across the land: Nylenn'or, Ne'edrei, Kailela, and Yallen'al.

As long as the two moons are shadowed, even during the daylight hours, the access remains open. The Accords, a mirror world and neutral ground for humans and fair creatures alike, is only available to Alysatraee's children for this short period of time.

A sacred land, a reflection of the attitudes and the laws of both realms, the Accords are a place of beauty. One can joyfully embrace the sanctuary without fear, as long as one never forgets to respect the rules.

As soon as the moons emerge from shadow, the Realm of the Accords will steadily shrink. The palace, in the heart of the Accords, is the first to appear and the last to fade. Those who overstay their welcome will be called home to Alysatraee.

"Kailela was once favored by the fae, but the city was completely destroyed. The humans now call the area Easthill," Magdud explained. "And Ne'edrei is now Neidrei and the rubble that was once a palace was repurposed into roads. My unit will be taking the Nylenn'or access point."

"I'm headed to Nylenn'or, too," Ivy said, tilting her head.

"But, I will return to Carrus in a little more than two weeks to meet two Minerals representatives. We'll miss each other."

"Or cross paths on the road," Magdud said. "My unit won't bother you. I swear to that. But I cannot protect you from any others, especially if outstanding orders have been issued to apprehend you."

"Hopefully I won't be stuck in the dungeon in Nylenn'or when you arrive, or worse." Ivy frowned, and Orion shifted closer, a hand resting on her waist. Yes, he was definitely going to fall apart when he had to return home.

Magdud wanted nothing more than to change into her satin pajamas and curl up with a book. Alone. But she'd be lucky to do that at *all* before she left Carrus for the war.

War. She hated that word.

In her mind, metal clashed. A phantom pain shot down her arm. Screams echoed.

She released a breath and pumped her fist, reminding herself that she'd healed. She'd lost her arm long ago. She was fine. *Fine.*

Her injury wouldn't have been so serious if she'd portaled back to the fair realm quickly. But only the very lucky avoided extended suffering as scant opportunities to jump to the magical realm existed. If they did, all orcs would portal constantly for blissful relief and regeneration. Magdud shook off the memories and focused on the present.

"There are so many rumors swirling about Emmyth, I'm not sure where to begin," Magdud said, changing to another less-than-enjoyable subject. "More than one orc is complaining that Emmyth called them up on a pretense of an inspection, when really she wanted to use us to put down an insurrection. I know others will be disgusted when they see the Tree House—orcs are at that location, and many will figure out the purpose; they will not approve, though they will follow orders. I also heard from other fair folk, too, right here in Carrus. Some think Emmyth has ruled with an iron fist for far too long, and they're hoping she'll be replaced. They just need a reason to support a change. They want it, but orcs are loyal to the law."

Ivy nodded, understanding. The orcs would follow the court's rules. And the courts would follow the Elven Council. Ivy could change the Council; their fate rested on her shoulders.

Magdud continued. "If a war begins, some may think Emmyth's strong hand is what we need, especially since hearing the rumor that Nym sided with insurgents."

"Insurgents?" Zel asked. "Who?"

"I think I'm looking at them." Magdud smirked. "I don't know where Nym is now, but the situation doesn't bode well for her. Or you."

Ivy groaned and rubbed her forehead. "I definitely need to go to Nylenn'or. I'm sure Kolvar sides with Nym."

Magdud turned to Ivy, ready to tell her what Zel already knew. After Ivy had survived the incident in Carrus's forest, how did she feel about Seekers? No matter her opinion, the elf needed to know the truth.

"After your incident in our woods, when dozens of seeds were scattered, some of the healed Seekers remained in Carrus. Plus, we took in several more recovered Seekers after the Battle of the Gathering. Most have already reverted to their corrupted state, but others are still alert. They know they'll corrupt again soon, so they're making the best of their remaining time. When Zel gets a cure, they'll be the first ones healed."

Ivy and Orion shared a meaningful look, his hand pressing her closer. Ivy gave him a little nod before turning to Magdud. "I cannot hate Seekers any more than I can hate a dagger or any weapon. But, even so, I must admit that my feelings about them are complicated. Despite that, I will work to cure every Seeker as soon as Zel has a remedy."

Magdud trusted the three of them had a plan for reaching every Seeker in Trinth. She didn't need to know the logistical details. What she yearned for more than anything was a chance at stalling or, by some miracle, stopping the war. But even if that couldn't be accomplished, reversing the travesty against the humans was also a worthy cause. Ivy could help with both. Which meant she needed to keep the elf alive.

Forget her allegiance to the fair courts, Rokgut, and her fellow orcs. As much as it pained her, she had to listen to her instincts. And they told her that Alysatraee would approve if she helped Ivy.

Magdud turned the pages again, this time landing on one titled "orcs."

"We're starting your lesson on avoiding an orc once they've got your scent, and they're commanded to locate you." Magdud pushed aside her own desires, the looming task of writing the dreaded missives and thinking about the consequences of her new loyalties. "Your speed has helped you, but it won't save you. Sit up and pay attention, Ivy, this lesson is one you won't forget. Even if you wanted to."

22

PANCAKES AND ORCS

The cool morning air wrapped around Ivy as she awoke the morning after arriving in Carrus. The scent of night jasmine and beeswax candles still lingered. Any other day, she would have burrowed deeper into the blankets, relishing the soft sheets. But she had more training with Magdud. Plus, she didn't want to waste a moment away from Orion.

Jumping up, she hurried through her morning ablutions, then threw off her nightshift and put on borrowed clothing because her own were being repaired by a local tailor. The full, linen skirt fell to her shins, and the loose tunic conveniently hid her knife when tucked into the leather belt.

Holding her shoes, she practically flew down the stairs, following the scent of breakfast. In the kitchen, Orion's back was turned as he poured batter onto a pan. On the counter next to him, Ash casually nibbled one side of the pancakes stacked high on a platter.

"I wondered when you'd show up," Orion said, smirking at her over his shoulder.

Ivy grinned. "Where's Agretha? And how many pancakes do we need?"

"She's letting the local leaders know that their magistrate is back and available for meetings, so I said I'd take over the cooking. Can I help it if she left a *lot* of batter?"

Ivy laughed and dropped her shoes by the narrow servant's dining table. "Have you seen Magdud yet?"

"No, but I imagine she'll be down shortly."

Ivy helped by slicing the strawberries, enjoying the ease of working in tandem with Orion. As she brought the fruit to the table, she noticed an opened note with Zel's scrawled signature.

"Zel has a headache and has requested an herb from the market," Orion explained.

Ivy scanned the note. "Golden bain? I've never heard of it. Perhaps gnomes have a different name for some plants."

"Perhaps. Are you up for a visit to the market?" Orion brought over the tall stack of pancakes and then handed over another note: Agretha's long list of needed items.

"Apparently, you've been assigned work." Ivy chuckled, wondering if Orion had ever been tasked like a servant.

"I will do as I've been commanded." Orion lifted the spatula in the air like a rallying cry and turned back to the last pancake in the pan.

"Magdud promised to work with me today," Ivy said, her words bringing back the orc's warnings from the night before, trickling like ice water back into her mind. Her heart dropped, her mood suddenly tempered. As the sun rose, Ivy had shut away the difficult task before her, but she had to face the reality of her situation soon.

Putting down the trembling note, Ivy pressed her palms to the tabletop and took a steadying breath. She didn't have long with Orion in Carrus. Apparently, orcs had varied abilities, and because neither Ivy nor Magdud knew who Lonsdale had hired, they had to play it safe, meaning Ivy couldn't stay in any one location on the mainland for longer than three days. Even that was a risk. Evading Seekers who'd caught her scent took all her wit and skill, and orcs were far more clever.

Magdud tromped into the kitchen, still wearing the travel-worn clothing from the day before. The stack of missives tucked into her arms threatened to spill onto the floor.

"Magdud?" Ivy looked up at the magistrate's drawn face. She'd learned that most orcs needed less sleep than humans and many fair folk, but after Magdud's travels through both realms, she looked exhausted.

"I need to get these to the messengers near the southern gate," Magdud said gruffly.

"I can deliver those for you," Orion offered.

"Don't you need to get to Unaria?" Magdud scowled as she dumped the letters into a basket.

"I promise, an extra day won't matter." A sadness flashed across his face; but Ivy blinked, and the expression was gone.

"Fine, then while you're dallying, I have a few other tasks for you," Magdud said, rubbing her red eyes. "You might as well make yourself useful."

"You're commanding the son of the Winter King to fetch things for you?" Orion teased.

"Don't be a pompous, lazy royal," Magdud scolded. "That's Prince Rime's role."

Ivy laughed before choking it back. Rime would definitely turn her into a toad if he found out they were mocking him.

Magdud grabbed a plain pancake, giving Orion orders and quizzing Ivy between bites.

"Play to your strengths," Magdud said as she chewed her food. "What are they?"

"My increased speed, ability to jump, hearing, and sight," Ivy responded.

"What are you disadvantages?"

"Everything else," Ivy muttered.

"If the orc tracking you is skilled and needs less sleep, they could catch up to you tomorrow," Magdud said, reminding them all of Ivy's deadline. "I need a few hours of sleep. Then we work. By my calculations, your tracker could enter Carrus by tomorrow night."

"Or sooner." Agretha clicked her tongue.

"My guards are on alert," Magdud assured them all, though her expression was tight. "Just make sure you're back before dark." With that, she shuffled out of the kitchen with Agretha close behind.

"So," Orion pivoted and slid closer to Ivy, "you're off the hook until dark. We can do errands together."

Ivy pushed aside her future worries as she and Orion ate. Ivy constantly leaned into him, assuring herself that he was near, and he did the same. She tried to ignore the tension just under his skin, as if he were holding himself together with a wish.

After they placed food on trays outside Magdud's and Zel's rooms, as Agretha had instructed, they gathered up the list of errands and the missives. Orion glamoured enough that no one would recognize the Captain of the Unarian Night Guard, and Ivy wore a summer scarf over her head and ears.

"Ready?" Orion said, taking her hand. The warmth resonated up her arm, warming her. She squeezed his hand in return. Tomorrow morning, she would have to run north, keeping out of reach of the orcs. She didn't know when she'd see Orion again after she left.

"Orion," she said, remembering the day before when he had mentioned he had bad news, "I'm ready to hear anything you need to tell me."

He paused, gripping her hand tighter. He opened his mouth,

but paused, blinking several times. Then his old, stoic mask returned to his features as he pulled her hand to his chest. "Later. Just give me this moment."

Then, he swept her outside and held her hand as they walked to the far side of the town. After handing over the missives to the riders, they strolled through the parks and bargained with vendors, just like everyone else. Pots of vibrant flowers graced many doorsteps, the scent of baking bread wafted down the street, and a group of children giggled as they ran by. Ivy thought she'd be tormented by memories of the Seekers hunting her in the streets. But with Orion at her side, the sharp edges of the past softened every time Orion ran his thumb across her knuckles, smiled, or pointed out another feature of the city.

Guiding her to yet another vendor, Ivy asked for the golden bain.

"You're in luck," the man said, pointing to a tall stalk with small, dark yellow leaves. "Just got these this mornin'."

Orion paid, and Ivy picked up the stalks, startled to sense a slight vibration of magic. Ivy carefully stowed the herb, and they turned back for Magdud's estate. Orion wrapped his arm around her shoulders, pulling her close.

"What's bothering you?" he asked.

"Just musing. I'd never heard of golden bain because this plant only grows in the fair realm."

"Well, that's ... interesting. Anyone might have picked it near a portal." Orion raised a brow. "A little magic slips out near the junctions in the ley lines. And some fair folk reside in Carrus, but I haven't seen any. Maggie mentioned that others, like her, had sought refuge in this city. And, apparently, a lot of the humans know, but they don't care as long as peace remains."

"Yllalen'al is crowded with magical creatures of all kinds.

They live and work in the open. I'm not even sure a human could survive there." The southern elven stronghold was unlike the more subdued Carrus. Fair folk could have easily manipulated the humans here, but they had joined their "enemies" and allowed the human culture to thrive. She'd been taught that elves should live among humans in order to understand them and speak for them in the fae courts. But she hadn't really understood how that could happen, not in any practical way, until now. "I wouldn't mind living here, with fair folk hidden in plain sight. There is a certain comfort in it."

"That's why I wanted an invitation home, to be around other fair creatures in Winter," Orion said. His lips parted, as if he had more to share on the subject, but then he pressed his lips together in a thin line, holding back. Ivy was curious to know if it had to do with his "bad news," but she didn't press. Besides, the last thing she wanted to talk about was Winter Court—it would only force her to think about the inevitable separation from Orion.

"Carrus has grown on me," Ivy said. Something about the atmosphere welcomed her like a warm blanket. "Last time, I felt like an awkward outsider."

"This time?" Orion asked.

Ivy slipped her arm around Orion's waist in response. The sun shone on her back, a pleasant breeze fanning past, and Ivy felt something she hadn't in a very long time—contentment. Everything felt right. If she let herself think, she'd drown in worry and strategy and plans, so she refused to live beyond each exhale.

They returned to Magdud's home to deliver the supplies and Zel's herb. In the kitchen, Agretha examined their purchases as she spoke. "Magdud is meeting with a stable master from an influential inn. She is up to her eyeballs in administrative duties so she will meet with you tonight."

Ivy and Orion helped around the mansion, their busy activity keeping Ivy from thinking too much, before Agretha shooed them back outside. The sun had dropped near the distant mountains, and the air was pleasantly cooling. Ivy's worries melted at the scent of sugared candy and string music playing near the park. Ivy noticed subtle touches of magic: motes of light dancing above the manicured flower beds, how the music carried unnaturally far across the park, and a masterfully carved stone fountain where water emanated with an ethereal glow.

Ivy and Orion had an unspoken agreement that they wouldn't discuss anything real, including how Ivy would continue to Nylenn'or tomorrow, and Orion had to resign from his post in Unaria. Instead, they clung to each other, seeking solace in the fleeting moments of normalcy. Ivy tucked herself into Orion's side, feeling his warmth and strength, a fragile comfort against the impending separation.

They listened to the music, each note a bittersweet reminder of their limited time together. The musicians played as the vibrant colors began splaying across the sky behind the mountain. Couples danced, including Orion and Ivy. The evening couldn't be more different than the equinox celebrations in Winter. Here, no one scrutinized their every move, stars replaced crystal chandeliers, and linen dresses swished instead of silk. Orion ran a comforting hand across her back, bringing her even closer.

"I need to get you back to the estate," Orion said at the end of the dance.

"I know," Ivy said simply, letting him guide her along the street. "What do you think Magdud would do if we didn't return before dark?"

"Send her guards to hunt us down. I'd hope one of them would find us before Maggie."

Ivy laughed as she and Orion hurried through a different part of the city, winding their way back to Magdud's home. "Do you think she'd send a note to your father, telling him that you stayed out past curfew?"

Orion snorted, and Ivy laughed harder. Suddenly, a loud clatter sounded from a nearby alley, and a cat hissed in response. An unseen metal container dropped to the stones, sliding across the ground before suddenly stopping.

Ivy and Orion jerked to a halt, the jovial mood instantly turning to alarm. Ivy's heart raced, though she told herself she was overreacting. It wasn't dark, yet.

From the alley, a woman stumbled into the open. Ivy nearly relaxed, realizing it wasn't an orc. But something deeper, an instinct born of death and shadows sent a warning shivering down her spine. The hair on her arms rose, despite the woman's weak appearance. Her torn clothing hung on her thin frame, and her dark blonde hair hung limp around her face, held back from her eyes by a dirty strip of material. She limped forward, and the slight jerkiness to her gait made Ivy's heart thump wildly in her chest.

Ivy looked straight at the woman, her hazel eyes and sharp cheekbones, and was hit with a sense of vertigo. But the woman only stared back with a vacant expression. Ivy gasped, and Orion stepped forward, putting himself between Ivy and the woman. The Seeker.

Ivy stepped back. Then stepped back again, nearly running from the woman as fast as her feet could carry her.

Never fight a Seeker.

Instead of fleeing, Ivy gripped Orion's tunic, remembering his sheltering presence and that she wasn't carrying any trace of a seed. Even so, her muscles seemed to coil in on themselves, an energy screaming through her veins. From that angle, she could see the Seeker wandering away, her attention not on Orion or Ivy. Was this how others perceived Seekers?

"Most Seekers are harmless," Orion said softly, pivoting to rest his hand on Ivy's shoulder. "That one is still somewhat aware. For now. Her family must have lost track of her at some point."

Or left her.

Ivy inspected the Seeker from the safe distance, her palms sweating and body shaking. From afar, Ivy noticed the Seeker's bare feet and the cuts along the bottom. A gash along the side of her foot oozed puss. Red lines emanated from the wound and shot up past her ankle, disappearing under her frayed skirt. Even if the Seeker had the funds for a healer, she didn't have the awareness to find one. The cut in her foot would only get worse.

Ivy shut her eyes and pressed her forehead against Orion's chest, her heart tearing. How could she feel sympathy for the creatures who killed her family? Or who had chased her and Brecc in this very city? Her mind flashed, danger and fear flooding her senses. Orion pulled her closer, running a hand along her hair.

"Let's go," he whispered.

They could just leave and never look back. That's what Ivy had done for years, ever since separating from her family. But the council had deceived her into accusing the wrong enemy. Even though she'd learned the truth and knew Seekers were merely an abused weapon, facing one was harder than she'd imagined. Would Ivy run? Or stay and help?

"Wait here," Ivy said, fiddling with her pouch of stones at her side.

Taking tentative steps, the road seemed to stretch before her, yet she reached the woman too soon.

"Hello," Ivy said, keeping out of the Seeker's reach.

The woman cocked her head, her eyes slowly coming into focus, along with a new wariness as she took a step back.

Ivy slowly reached into her pouch and pulled out the purple healing stone. Holding it up in her open palm, the woman's eyes widened.

"You know what this is?" Ivy asked, surprised.

"An elven stone," the woman whispered, not taking her eyes off of it.

"Do you know how to use it?" Ivy said.

The woman gave a halting nod, but otherwise didn't move.

Other than the knife, the stone was Ivy's most precious possession. Without it or a seed, she was vulnerable. But this woman would lose the ability to walk soon, and her mind not long after. Ivy couldn't leave the Seeker when she could actually help her. Besides, Ivy had a sinking feeling that the stone wouldn't help her if she faced Emmyth again. So, Ivy stretched out her arm further.

"It's yours."

"I'll have to bind the rock around my chest so I don't lose it when I ... forget." The woman spoke more to herself than to Ivy.

From the corner of her eye, she noticed Orion watching, his body tense, though he didn't move closer. In her moment of distraction, the woman snatched the stone and hopped back, clutching the gift in both hands.

Ivy sucked in a breath, feeling the stone's absence keenly. But, she had no regrets. In fact, her heart lightened a bit.

"Remember, the stone must touch your skin," Ivy said.

The woman simply backed away, not taking her eyes off of Ivy, before turning and limping down the nearest alley. Ivy stood as the shadows darkened, watching the woman disappear.

Orion drew closer, his warmth at Ivy's back. As always, he was her silent companion, her protector.

"I'm with you," Orion said. Whatever her decisions, he supported her. He would wait for her to think through what she'd just done all night, if she had the need.

"We should go before Magdud sends out the guards." Ivy forced a grin.

Together, they jogged the rest of the way to Magdud's estate, but the mood had shifted. Each step was one closer to their inevitable parting, the weight of unspoken words and swirling emotions pressing down on her. Entering through the front doors, Agretha met them and ushered them straight to the library.

Agretha pointed at a stack of bookmarked texts on the table, explaining that Magdud would join them later. Ivy half-expected Orion to leave, but he was the first one to pull a book off the table and start reading. Sitting across from each other, his long legs stretched under the table, touching the toe of his boots to hers as they studied.

"It makes sense that Lonsdaleite would prefer speed over strength, when selecting an orc," Orion said, thumbing through the last book.

"I agree, it's the most logical move. I'm two feet shorter than the average orc, and even an inexperienced orc will have better reach and more combat skills."

"That's correct," Magdud said, entering the library. For the next hour, Magdud taught Ivy more details about the orcs.

"Basically, I can outrun an orc, but they have better endurance and will eventually catch me," Ivy said. "So I cannot escape them."

"They won't cross the channel into Emmyth's territory," Magdud assured her. "Based on what you said, I highly doubt Lonsdaleite took the time to get permission from Emmyth or the fae courts. Orcs are trained from birth to follow protocol, so they won't cross to the north. You just have to beat them to the channel."

"I'll leave at dawn," Ivy said, standing.

"Everything you need is almost ready," Magdud said.

Orion escorted Ivy to the guest wing. Ivy stepped into her room, and Orion paused at the door. Ivy's heart ached with the knowledge of what was to come. A deep sadness furrowed across his brow. He opened his mouth as if to say something, but Agretha appeared.

"We're engaging wards tonight," Agretha said, closing Ivy's window, "just to be safe. Can you help, Orion?"

Orion raised a brow, reflecting Ivy's skepticism that they really needed his help. More likely, they wanted Ivy to sleep so she would actually leave in the morning, as promised.

"Go," Ivy said, smirking. "I'll see you in the morning."

Orion stepped closer to Ivy and gave her a kiss on the forehead before slipping out as quiet as an elf. Ivy didn't bother changing her clothes before she collapsed on the bed, exhaustion claiming her. She was glad for the energy-sapping heat and the never-ending tasks, otherwise, the tightness in her chest might have kept her awake until the wee hours of the morning.

The next morning, Ivy changed back into her clean and repaired clothing. With the fine stitching, Ivy suspected the tailor was at least half-elf. A new pack leaned against the desk and on the top sat a set of Nylenn'or palace servant's clothing— the perfect disguise. Magdud was nothing if not resourceful. Ivy finished filling the pack and shrugged it on.

Her hand lingered on the door latch as she peered into the well-appointed room. Would she ever see this place again? Yesterday had been a dream, filled with intertwined fingers and sweet dances with Orion. But now, the weight of reality settled heavily on her shoulders with a mix of fear and sadness, knowing this might be the last time she experienced such peace and normalcy. The thought of leaving Orion behind, of not feeling his comforting presence, made her chest ache. She took a deep breath, trying to steady herself. With a final, wistful glance, she shut the door, feeling as if she were closing off a part of her heart. Though her eyes stung, she squared her shoulders and marched forward.

At the top of the landing, sounds of Magdud and Orion's heated conversation carried up the stairs. Though Ivy calculated they were a few rooms away, she could hear every word.

"After I resign, I won't return to Carrus," Orion insisted. "At least not right away."

"Don't delay the inevitable. You'll only serve to anger your father. Again."

"You want to deliver me—"

"Escort," Magdud interrupted.

"*Escort* me to the Winter Court so you'll look competent in the eyes of the king. But trust me, Selleth is growing suspicious of our connection. That will make you a target. And she's an excellent shot."

"King Eldrin may suspect our alliance as well," Magdud conceded. "Kings don't win crowns by being stupid. With that in mind, if you delay even a few hours, the king will notice."

The conversation paused, and Princess's claws clacked against the polished floor. Ivy walked down the stairs, intending to reveal herself. The conversation wasn't sensitive, but she wasn't comfortable eavesdropping.

"I just need to get Ivy safely out of Unaria, without an orc right on her tail."

Hearing her name, Ivy froze. *Unaria?*

"I say this as a friend, Orion. Say your goodbyes here. Don't bring her to Unaria with you."

Ivy's heart thundered in her chest, her breath catching.

"I just found Ivy. I won't part with her until I must."

"*You must!*" Magdud said, exasperation in her voice. "Apparently someone needs to hit you in the head with a few painfully obvious things. Remember the Aequus debacle? Do you realize we are headed for a war? You are in no position to irritate your father. May I remind you that we need his cooperation, not his ire? He is the most powerful creature in the fair realm."

"That's debatable."

"I'm not here to argue with you, Orion. The actions we take impact others. We can only control our actions, not the consequences. Do you really want to test the king?"

"If it means protecting Ivy, yes," Orion said without hesitation.

Ivy moved down the steps, barely feeling the stairs beneath her feet as Magdud's angry words rolled off her tongue. "Ivy needs the king to agree with the new Elven Council. Not stall. Not ignore. We need the rulers of both courts to make a statement of peace. And if he's angry with you, your father might be vindictive. Do you dare take the chance? Your father has the power to ruin Ivy's plans!"

"Taking Ivy to Unaria is the better strategic move," Orion insisted. "I haven't asked her if she'll accompany me, but—"

"Yes!" Ivy shouted her interruption as she bounded across the massive hall and found the sitting room. A surge of happiness and anticipation swelled within her as she laid eyes on Orion. Being with him just a little longer brought the reprieve she desperately wanted. The prospect of their extended time together swallowed any of her worries. "Yes. I'd love to join you. You can speak with the duke while I move throughout the city, leaving my scent in difficult patterns to track. Unaria is right on the way to Nylenn'or."

"Hardly," Magdud interjected. "It will be faster to head straight north."

"But, an orc will have to wait until dark and wear a disguise to track me through a city like Unaria," Ivy countered. "You said you doubt they have glamours."

Magdud just huffed, but didn't argue, so Ivy knew she'd won on that point. "With the right clothing, orcs can blend in if they keep to the evening shadows," Ivy continued. "But by the time they follow my scent and realize I'm no longer in Unaria, I'll be long gone. My scent will disappear if Orion flies me over the Unarian wall."

"Orcs can't fly, but I can," Orion added. "You told Ivy to play to her strengths."

"It's the most logical move." Ivy didn't need Magdud's permission, but she did want her opinion.

"A Seeker wouldn't know what to do if they lost your scent," Magdud said, folding her arms across her chest. "Orcs will calculate that you're headed to Nylenn'or. They'll try to catch you before you reach the channel."

"But they won't," Ivy said. "You said yourself, I'm faster."

"I guess you won't stop to sleep." Magdud frowned.

"I'll help her conserve her strength," Orion said.

Magdud raised her brow. "I very much doubt that."

Heat crawled up Ivy's neck, but Orion only moved closer to her side.

"Well, your plan isn't horrible." Magdud sighed, more resigned than convinced. "Get going. You both have a long day ahead of you. Orion, you'll leave an hour before Ivy. When the orcs question the guards or witnesses in the area, they will report that you were alone."

"I'll catch up to you on the road," Ivy said to Orion.

"I promise I'll make it easy." Orion gave her half-smile, his eyes alight.

Magdud slapped her forehead, muttering about ridiculousness and straw-brained fair folk. But Ivy couldn't help but grin.

Ivy beamed at Orion as the duke's stable hands took their horses, feeling very much like a youngling getting away with sneaking an extra dessert after dinner. Orion gave instructions to one of the Unarian guards, informing him that he would ride back with his belongings and horse tomorrow.

Tonight, he'd help Ivy leave the city without a trace.

When the stable hands led the horses away, leaving them alone, Orion wrapped his arms around Ivy's shoulders, pulling her into an embrace. "I've been wanting to do this all day."

Ivy glanced around expecting a farrier or another servant to appear at any moment. "What about your cold, unfeeling reputation?"

"I'm retiring." Orion kissed her on the forehead, and Ivy closed her eyes, relishing the moment. "I'll meet you at midnight."

Ivy nodded, begrudgingly pulling away. They'd agreed to meet just over the first ridge above the Blue Mountain Guild's lodge. Last time she'd been in this city, she'd avoided the frightful Captain of the Night Guard, and she'd fled Unaria to escape him. Now, she was depending on him to help her. She waved and then turned and hurried out of the stable. The sun was already well past its zenith, and she had a lot of ground to cover.

After winding through the streets for hours, Ivy's stomach growled. Unaria didn't have parks like Carrus, so Ivy moved off the main roads, staying away from the residential houses, and found a relatively clean alley. Sitting on a crate, Ivy pulled food from her pack and glanced up at the darkening sky. She wondered if Ash was circling somewhere in the distance, or if she was hunting for food in the forest outside the city walls. The dragon had been so excited to be reunited with Orion, she'd barely left his shoulder during the entire horse ride.

As the sun dropped behind the mountains, Ivy slipped out of the alley and past revelers at the restaurants. Unlike Seekers, orcs wouldn't make their presence known. If Lonsdale had spoken to the orc supervising the towers, they'd probably tied the two orc sentinels' strange illnesses coinciding with Ivy's escape north. If Lonsdale dispatched a fast, expert tracker, the orc had followed her scent to Carrus. She would've picked an orc with those skills, even if they were physically weak compared to their kindred; Ivy would be no match for them.

If the orc lost her scent in the small city of Carrus, they'd definitely go to Magdud. And they'd obviously catch Ivy's scent there. Magdud would act surprised that the Minerals were hunting Ivy, and she'd tell the orc that Ivy had left. If Magdud lied, the orcs would eventually figure that out, too, and reveal her as a traitor—landing her only orc ally in prison.

Ivy had to assume the orc was closing in. With the stars coming out, the tracker would begin their hunt in Unaria for the elf that had eluded them for the last week. But Ivy knew the city well and hadn't made trailing her easy. Jumping across rooftops, creating scent-loops, and weaving through restaurants, Ivy used what Magdud had taught her. Orcs couldn't jump as far as elves, and they could be tricked by retracing one's steps, and their olfactory senses got overwhelmed with too many scents. With any luck, the orc would waste several night-time trips to Unaria before realizing their prey had escaped.

Hiking up the mountainside, Ivy neared the Blue Mountain Guild lodge. Lights still glowed in a few windows, but most of the staff had gone for the evening. Hikers departed early in the morning, but Ivy intended to lead the orc in another direction anyway, avoiding the humans' usual trail. Ivy checked over her shoulder, down at the road below. A few people walked along the streets, one singing a bawdy tune. But from that distance, they wouldn't notice her, especially as Ivy moved with the shadows as the clouds slid across the moonlit sky.

Not leaving any footprints, Ivy hiked the first ridge. She was an hour early, but she was anxious to see Orion. As she dropped down on the other side, she let out a sigh of relief. Glancing up at the moons, she allowed herself a few relaxing breaths.

Snow crunched on the other side of the ridge as someone moved toward her. Orion was early, too.

Yet, the hairs on the back of her neck prickled.

The heavy gait wasn't Orion.

She leapt back, spinning just in time to see a figure appear over the ridge.

Overhead, an orc loomed, his form lit by the partial moons. His cropped hair and lean form were familiar. The memory snapped into place; she'd seen him at the sentinel towers at the pass. The short-tempered, sharp orc had been selected to hunt her. Her breath caught in her throat, the icy grip of fear encasing her heart.

And Ivy had probably gotten him in trouble after she'd caused his stomach contents to turn to water, and he'd allowed her to slip past his post. She could only guess at the simmering anger rising each day he traipsed across Trinth to find her. This was not good.

Ivy's heart pounded a warning, breaking her frozen stupor. She spun on her heel and ran. The snowy landscape blurred as she pushed herself to move faster, her mind a whirl of terror. She knew the mountain trails well, but off path, with uneven terrain while speeding forward, was risky. Each step felt like a gamble.

Concentrating on the landscape, she jumped and dodged dips in the snow and boulders jutting out of the ground. Even over her footfalls and the wind in her ears, she could hear the orc running along the ridge above, keeping a terrifying pace. He jumped off the ridge and landed, the thud reverberating through her bones.

Ivy sped ahead knowing Orion would find her; orcs left footprints in the snow. She pressed harder up the mountain, but the orc was faster than she'd expected and relentless in his pursuit.

He had moved to her left, and Ivy pivoted right, not letting him flank her. She sprinted straight up the mountain and glanced overhead, calculating the risk of avalanche. Fear prickled at the edges of her mind, coupled with a sharp irritation at her predicament; she wouldn't trigger one, but the oaf below might. And she had no desire to suffocate. Putting on a burst of speed, she hiked faster. For the first time, she wished for spiked shoes.

It wasn't long until she crested the next mini ridge. Glancing back down, the orc was moving up the mountain, his speed horrifyingly steady. He'd moved to her left again. Ivy pivoted right. She cut across the mountain, raced up another snowdrift, then back down. Sweat dripped down her back, despite the cold. She couldn't slow down. She refused to be captured.

Orion.

How much longer until he found her?

Would she have to return to the city? Could she lose the tracker there? She'd have to use her riskiest Seeker-evasion tricks. But would they even work? How had he tracked her so quickly? It didn't make sense.

Her heart raced, unsure about this orc's abilities. He obviously had skills—he'd found her in the middle of the mountain. Ivy wished she knew his weaknesses.

Concentrating, Ivy glanced back again. He'd moved to her right. So, Ivy pivoted left. Ahead, she spotted a large boulder.

She'd climbed that very rock before. From the top she could see the entire area, which could help her quickly come up with a new plan. And if Orion were flying, she might spot him.

It wouldn't take her long to scramble up. She could wait for the orc to climb up behind her before she leapt off and ran. Most orcs were excellent climbers, but elves were better jumpers.

As Ivy neared, the hair on the back of her neck rose again. She glanced back over her shoulder to see she was out-pacing the orc, and he tracked directly behind her. An odd move, considering he'd attempted to flank her several times.

Wait.

Had he been manipulating her movements? Driving her to this location? Ivy's heart jumped into her throat. Despite all reason, she skidded to a stop.

From behind the boulder stepped another orc. A towering female with muscled arms, her white hair pulled back tight from her severe face.

Ivy jumped back, panic surging. Making a quick decision, she dropped her pack and bolted up the mountain, straining her reserves of strength. Behind her, on her right, the female orc pursued, her legs fresh and quick. On her left, the lean orc had closed the distance she'd gained when she'd hesitated.

Her mind spun, frantically assessing. The orcs had worked together to track her movements. They must have figured out her escape route. Had they deduced that she'd worked at the Blue Mountain? Or had they just guessed—correctly—that she'd leverage the most dangerous, natural formation in the area. These orcs were clever, far more challenging to evade than mindless Seekers.

The orcs would capture her, it was only a matter of time.

They would bring her back to Lonsdale. Or send her to the courthouse for trial. But they wouldn't kill her.

Would they?

Emmyth had already tried. Would Lonsdale? She didn't want to wait and find out. Changing tactics, Ivy charged forward, a new location in mind, her lungs starting to burn.

Ivy dropped down over another drift. Landing awkwardly in a sunken part of the snow, Ivy fell to her knees. Energy thrummed through her, and she jumped back to her feet, sprinting forward. The female orc grunted behind her, landing in the same spot. Ivy didn't look back. She just ran harder.

Clouds choked the moons, cutting off the light. Ivy blinked, her eyes adjusting. At this pace, she would be at her new target destination in no time. But she needed Orion.

She could distract the orcs, keep running, but for how long? Without help, she was outmatched. With the two orcs, clearly selected for their speed, Ivy would tire before they did. She was only buying herself time.

Leaping down the mountain like an antelope, a green glow sparked to life. Ivy could have cried in relief. Behind her, the footsteps of the orcs slowed, but only slightly. They had no idea a dwarven cave was mere steps away. The cave glowed, warning elves away, yet Ivy feared the orcs far more than superstition.

Apparently, dwarves were territorial. And they didn't appreciate elves. Even generations after the dwarves had abandoned their home in the mountain, the magic still worked—triggered by the presence of elves. As Ivy neared the entrance, the glow grew brighter. Much brighter.

"What is that?" the female orc hissed.

"Elven magic?" the male orc guessed.

"I know you can hear us," the female orc said, barely raising her voice. "The fair courts will not be pleased to hear you have magical artifacts stored in Trinth."

"Or magical weapons," the male orc growled under his breath.

They only saw the eerie, glowing snow, not the carved stones underneath that Ivy had once unearthed. The area was overgrown with trees, too, further obscuring the caved-in entrance. Ivy planted herself at the base of the dwelling and looked up at the orcs as they cautiously maneuvered forward.

"I don't want to hurt you," Ivy bluffed.

"We've been ordered to apprehend you," the female orc replied, "and return you to the House of Minerals."

"But if you resist, we must stop you from escaping," the male orc added. "The Council doesn't want you causing more problems."

"The only problem is Lonsdaleite using orcs as tools to hunt down an elf who revealed his corruption," Ivy said, lifting her chin.

"Lies, of course." The male orc put a hand on his stomach, his face twisting as if feeling phantom pains. He had definitely figured out that Ivy had poisoned him.

But the female orc paused, doubt flicking across her face.

"Did Lonsdaleite tell you who I am?" Ivy asked. Seeing their faces shift to confusion, she knew he hadn't. "I'm Ivy Balrel, daughter of the now-deceased House of Seeds Councilor. The councilors didn't appreciate my father. Now he's dead. Along with the rest of my family. You'll excuse me for not going with you. I *will* fight you if I must."

The female orc paused, her brows furrowed. But the sentinel-orc jumped down in one graceful arc, much further and landing more smoothly than Ivy anticipated.

Leaping back and grabbing her knife in one quick motion, Ivy readied herself. She'd never fought an orc before, and she knew she'd lose. Lonsdale had chosen well. As much as Ivy wanted Orion to find her, she couldn't fight the sentinel-orc in the open. Waiting until the orc closed the distance, only three steps from her, she dove to the side, rolled and sprinted toward the cave.

Squeezing between the patch of trees, Ivy raced through the entrance; the green stones glowed brighter, but they shone now as a beacon, a welcome. Outside, she caught a few syllables of a whispered argument, too muffled to decipher.

Sliding into the room on a layer of dust-covered marble, she quickly scanned the area. She had explored this place before, but portions frequently crumbled. The remaining, majestic ceiling soared more than five stories tall over the one still-standing room, the entrance hall to the city beyond. The expansive chamber stretched out before her, echoing with the whispers of long, forgotten memories.

The stone walls, once meticulously carved and polished, now bore scars; cracks snaked their way across the surface, dotted with patches of lichen. Portions had fallen away, leaving carved pockets of jagged rocks. The choking scents of mustiness, decay, and animal droppings permeated. Moonlight filtered through cracks in the ceiling near the entrance, the feeble beams twisting the cavern in eerie shapes.

Several tunnels once branched from the entrance, but only one was still accessible. On the far side, deeper within the cave where the light could not reach, a large tunnel bored about a hundred steps deeper into the mountain until blocked by a massive collapse of rock and debris. On her right, the wall had partially crumbled, leaving a jumbled mass of stone and earth.

Not waiting for the orc, Ivy sprinted into the dead-end tunnel. Though the passage darkened around her, Ivy analyzed every loose rock, making a note of their size and placement. She could see, but the orc would be plunged into darkness. Ivy ran over loose scree, navigating to a sturdy ledge near the ceiling.

Only hearing her rasping breaths and distant, irregular

drips of water, Ivy waited. Every muscle screamed for her to run, but she fought to stay calm. Soon enough, the orc tiptoed deeper into the cave. Moments later, he appeared below. Holding her breath, she waited for him to pass. She wished she had her bow and arrow to even the fight.

He hadn't noticed the collapsed end of the tunnel, but he would soon. Once he had passed beyond her, Ivy carefully, silently, made her way back down. Each heartbeat thrummed in her ears and a cold sweat broke out on her forehead.

"I know you're in here, elf." Though he didn't raise his voice, the words chilled Ivy all the same. "You act without honor so I will not feel guilty for whatever you make me do tonight."

Ivy's muscles stiffened, icy tendrils trickling down her spine, but she forced herself to maneuver back toward the entrance. Stopping several steps from the tunnel entrance where darkness still shrouded, Ivy climbed the small, steep mound made from a collapsed portion of the tunnel wall. Not disturbing the loose stones, she positioned herself behind a boulder. She just hoped she had enough strength to get the huge rock rolling.

"The Mineral Councilors say you are a threat to the security of the realm," the orc continued. "But I could not care less about the Elven Council concerns. You are all so high and mighty in your towers of self-righteousness."

Ivy stilled, feeling the malice in his words more than hearing them.

"Few elves got their hands dirty in the war, while orcs drown in the blood of our kin," he said. "I'll let you be a sacrifice for their egotistical mistakes."

Ivy held her breath, realizing that he wasn't hiding his location. He wanted her to know. Her head spun to the side, piercing the darkness, searching for the female orc. But she was nowhere to be seen. Ivy had hoped the cave's magical warning at the entrance would frighten the orcs away; perhaps the sickly light had successfully kept one at bay.

So why was he talking?

The truth hit her. He knew he couldn't hide from an elf, but he could taunt. Frighten. Unburden himself by spewing his hatred. He could force Ivy to listen to his wicked excuses and plans, sow fear into her heart and distract her mind. And it worked.

Ivy scowled and touched her fingertips to the large boulder in front of her, readying herself. She would not be verbally whipped by an orc who did not know a drop about her.

The orc kept talking, but Ivy let the terrifying words wash past her, never touching. As he neared, she steeled herself. The orc kept a relatively steady pace, aiding her calculations in springing her trap. Ivy leaned forward, ready, hoping he wouldn't hear her heart thrumming in her chest.

The orc drew closer on the path below, and at the opportune moment, she pressed forward, using all her weight to dislodge the boulder. The huge mass tumbled down, crushing smaller stones in its path. Even if the boulder missed the orc, it would serve as a critical distraction. Ivy stayed low, using the rolling boulder as cover to keep out of the orc's line of sight.

Just before the boulder crossed the main path, she leapt over it, soaring through the air well beyond the orc's last location. Before she landed, she spotted the orc below. He turned just in time to see the boulder barreling toward him.

Ivy's heart pounded as he somersaulted backward, trying to avoid the rolling stone. She landed closer to him than she had planned, her feet touching the ground with a soft thud. Taking advantage of his proximity, she slashed at the back of his thighs with her knife.

The orc's boiled leather armor, designed for speed, provided little resistance. Her blade sliced through the material and into his flesh. He roared in pain, stumbling, but not collapsing. Ivy darted to the side, shooting out of his immediate reach. He struggled to regain his footing, the cut on his thigh slowing him down.

The orc spun, his eyes narrowed in fury as he scanned the dark cave, attempting to locate her. But Ivy had already shifted. With his arm outstretched, his nails reflected a hint of moonlight. He had sharpened his thick nails into weapons, set to slash whoever stood in his way. Ivy pressed her back against the cool, damp wall, her breathing controlled and quiet. Leveraging her speed and agility, she had to stay one step ahead.

The high ceilings of the cave echoed with the orc's frustrated grunts, triggering her heart to beat against her ribs like a bird trapped in a cage. As the orc limped back into the main room of the cave, she silently climbed the wall. Now behind him, as he made his way to the entrance, she watched his every step. Assuming Ivy had fled, he limped outside and shouted at the female orc.

"Where is she?" Anger laced his every syllable.

"I haven't seen her," a female voice responded, her voice deeper than Ivy had expected. Expecting the female orc to appear, a spike of fear spurred Ivy to move.

Digging her fingers into the cracks of the stone and finding toe-holds, Ivy climbed. She rose higher and higher until she reached where the crumbling wall and fallen ceiling met. Glancing down, she spotted the male orc moving back into the cave. From this height, she'd need a seed if she fell. But with luck, the orc wouldn't spot her.

The orc hobbled back into the main entrance room, his growl turning Ivy's insides to water. The rock under her right hand crumbled. She felt the give in the stone, but didn't have time to react. Her hand fell away, and her stomach dropped. Her other hand and feet held her steady, but the bits of rock smacked against floor, announcing her general location. The orc's attention snapped to the wall, his eyes raking across the face until he found her, his acid glare practically burning.

He bounded toward Ivy, reaching for something in his belt. The orc couldn't climb, but he could throw. And Ivy had a sickening feeling he had deadly skill with multiple weapons.

Shadows shifted at the entrance behind him. Ivy blinked and realized the female orc was in the cave and also sprinting in Ivy's direction. Wings appeared at her back. With a flap of feather and sinew, she vaulted straight for the orc. Shadows curved around her, swallowing her form.

"Orion!" Ivy called, realizing it wasn't the female orc who had entered; Orion had glamoured. She moved her stiff body, climbing down the crumbled wall. A surge of elation flooded her, dispensing a burst of energy. She hurried to descend as the orc growled in frustration below. Ivy checked over her shoulder in time to see the orc unsheathe a sword from his back, the blade gleaming ominously in the dim light of the cave. Orion, armed with his own sword, squared off against him.

Orion took to the air, his wings spreading wide as he flew upward. The orc swung his sword in a wide arc, missing Orion by a hand's width. Using the shadows to his advantage, Orion vanished, reappearing behind the orc in a blur of movement. He slashed at the orc, but the orc whirled his sword behind him, blocking the blow with a clash of steel.

The orc spun and lunged, aiming a powerful strike at Orion's midsection. Orion dodged, his wings beating rapidly as he ascended just out of reach.

"Is there still a price on your head?" the orc sneered. "I wouldn't mind getting a bounty."

"I'm sorry to disappoint you," Orion replied coolly. "But you must not have received word that I'm in the king's good graces once again." Then Orion dove down, using his momentum to deliver a fierce strike. The orc parried, pushing Orion back.

Orion seemed to vanish, and Ivy frantically searched for him as she continued her descent. With a whoosh of air, Orion reappeared next to her, bouncing up and down with each flap of his wings. Her heart swelled, his presence instantly comforting.

"Is this really the best strategy for fighting an orc?" he teased.

"I'd like to see you come up with something better," Ivy shot back before lowering her voice. "Can you disarm him?"

"Can you draw him outside?"

Without waiting for a response, Orion wrapped the shadows around him again and then reappeared at the orc's side. He aimed a quick, precise thrust at the orc's injured leg, but the orc anticipated the move, swinging his sword horizontally. Orion barely managed to spin out of the way, the blade brushing dangerously close to his ribs.

Ripping her gaze away, Ivy scrambled further down the wall. Behind her, the orc bellowed in frustration. Finally reaching the steep rocks, she practically slid down on her side, maintaining her attention on the fight below.

The orc's purple-tinted skin glistened with sweat. He attempted a desperate lunge, but Orion vanished just before the orc reached him, reappearing directly behind. Once Ivy's feet hit the cave floor, Orion launched himself into the air with a powerful beat of his wings. He feigned as if he was about to strike the orc, but instead he darted to Ivy.

Orion wrapped his arms around her and darkness swirled. Even so, she didn't miss his mischievous grin. Her heart fluttered, the sight of his smile left her lightheaded. She would chastise herself for the poor timing of her ridiculous swooning later. For now, she just breathed in the combination of steel and holly.

They landed at the mouth of the cave, and she bolted through the narrow spaces between the trees. Branches scratched and pulled as they pushed through the foliage. Behind her, Orion cursed and glamoured away his wings as the sounds of pursuit grew louder.

They emerged into the open, but the orc, relentless in his chase, burst from the underbrush right behind them. Orion squared off with him, his sword at the ready. The orc, brandishing his own blade, charged forward with a roar.

Ivy's attention shifted between the fight and the expanse around them, watching for the female or any other visitors. Orion danced with fluid grace, sidestepping the orc's initial swing and countering with a swift strike; the orc barely managed to parry. The two engaged in a fierce exchange of blows, the clash of steel ringing through the night. Orion dodged and weaved, staying just out of the orc's deadly reach.

With a sudden burst of speed, Orion shadow-traveled behind the orc, aiming a strike at his unprotected back. The orc spun away, narrowly avoiding a fatal blow, but leaving himself open. Orion delivered a precise cut to the orc's sword hand, causing him to drop his weapon with a howl.

Disarmed and realizing the fight was lost, the orc attempted to run. But Orion intercepted him in an instant, pinning him to the ground with his knee and twisting the orc's arm behind his back.

Orion growled, and the orc grunted in pain but ceased his struggling. Throwing his pack to Ivy, she quickly found some sturdy rope. Together, they tied the orc to one of the nearby trees, securing the knots tightly. The orc glared at them with defiant eyes, but he was well and truly subdued.

Breathing heavily, Orion and Ivy stepped back. Pulling Ivy close, Orion extended his wings, and they were airborne in a blink. Below, Ivy spotted the female orc. She was conscious and tied to a tree, looking furious enough to eat through the bark.

"She was much easier to subdue," Orion confessed.

"Did you attack her from behind?" Ivy rolled her eyes, tightening her grip around his neck.

"I was in a hurry!"

"How long do you think they'll be stuck here?"

"A few hours at least."

Orion flew higher, and soon the orcs were smaller than ants below.

"Oh, my pack!" Ivy said, remembering, and she guided Orion back to where she'd dropped it.

As they flew, Orion continued. "I interrogated the orc and got a bit more information on how they found you. Lonsdaleite requested her, specifically, and her captain approved the mission. Apparently, the other one insisted he join her, but he was sick the first day, which slowed them. By her tone, she doesn't respect her companion nor Lonsdaleite."

"She isn't fond of us either. How did they find me?"

"They questioned a Carrus guard who told them you went to Unaria. Fortunately, they thought you were alone."

I will be, too soon.

Wrapping them both in darkness again, Orion flew over the city of Unaria. For a moment, he dropped the shadow magic, allowing Ivy to see the entire city. Lights shone in windows, torches burned, and the buildings looked like toys.

For a moment, the realm seemed small. A profound new perspective settled over her, and Ivy felt her own insignificance. Even the Council shrunk in importance. Yet, a flicker of resolve burned within her. Even a small elf had a role to play.

Ash swooped closer, landing on Orion's shoulder before he wrapped them all in shadow again, heading for the northern forest beyond the wall.

"Took you long enough to find me." Ivy poked his chest.

"The orcs left tracks all over the mountain; they led *me* on a chase. But I spotted the green glow from the cave and rushed to investigate. I wasn't sure if it was a trap. I wasn't finished tying up the orc when her companion emerged, shouting questions. Thankfully, we were out of sight, as I held a blade to her throat and told her to stay silent."

"It was you that I heard respond?" Ivy chuckled.

"I can't believe he didn't notice her voice was different. I didn't match the tone quite right. Anyway, I hurried and finished tying her up and entered the cave."

Ivy buried her head into his neck, expecting him to land just beyond the city. But he dropped his shadows in the night sky and kept flying north.

"Where are you dropping me?" Ivy asked, confused.

"Just a little further. There are things I need to tell you before we part."

The bad news.

Ivy took a deep breath, holding tight. Her body began to shake, which often happened after a confrontation with Seekers.

"The night didn't go as I'd anticipated," Ivy admitted.

"Do your plans *ever* go as you'd imagined?" Orion teased as he lowered to the ground.

Ivy couldn't help but smile. Orion seemed more and more relaxed around her, and now they had to part ways again.

"Will you leave for Carrus in the morning?" Ivy asked.

"I'll be wrapping up business in Unaria for the next two days. My father won't mind." Orion rubbed her arms, waiting for her anxious tremors to pass.

"What aren't you telling me?"

"I've arranged for my things to be sent to Carrus in two days. But I'll portal to the fair realm via a dryad in the north."

"How far north?" Ivy asked, trying and failing not to grin.

"All the way to the northern channel," he said, his arms tightening around her. "I mean, with *two* orcs hunting you, I can't let the daughter of the former Seeds Councilor travel without assistance. After all, she was my guest in the Winter court. She uncovered the illicit Tree House in the middle of the human realm. It's my duty to see her safely to her next destination."

Relief and happiness washed over her, easily pushing aside the nagging fear about the bad news Orion *wasn't* telling her.

"That's what I'll tell my father, anyway. And it *is* the truth."

"Of course it is," Ivy said, tucking closer.

23

STRATEGIES AND WYVERNS

Though Orion longed to slow his pace so he could spend more time with Ivy, neither of them could afford this option. After delaying the orcs, he flew fast toward the north. Using his shadow magic, they traveled just above the trees unseen, and Ivy slept for a couple of hours in his arms just before dawn.

As the sky lightened, he dropped his shadows and flew higher. Though he wasn't following any roads, he didn't want to chance any travelers spotting him. By the time the sun rose, he arms and wings ached. He glided down, landing in a small meadow. As they descended, Ash dismounted from his shoulder, already starting her hunt for breakfast.

"We're more than halfway to the wyvern stables," Orion said as he put Ivy down.

They'd briefly debated going to the small human village on the northern coast and procuring passage on a boat. But wyverns were faster, and very few humans dared cross a cold channel that ended in the last known elven stronghold. They didn't have a death wish.

"I could run from here and arrive by the end of the day," Ivy said, debating her next move aloud. "But then I'd be exhausted before I even mount the wyvern."

"If you wait for me to rest, I can take you north and arrange for the wyvern," Orion said. "No one at the stables will know you're in the area. I'll request a wyvern that will stay put for several days. That way you have an escape route from Nylenn'or."

"I didn't know that was an option. But I like it. I'd prefer not to be stuck in the north until their boats leave for the Centennial next spring." Ivy looked past him at the forest surrounding the meadow. "Rest while I find something for us to eat. Agretha packed me two days' worth of rations, but I'll hunt for edible plants nearby, too."

Orion didn't even bother making a proper bed. He just dragged himself to the edge of the meadow and laid down in the crook of two tree roots. It felt like he'd just closed his eyes when discomforting heat awoke him. The sun was at its peak and part of his leg was directly in the light, practically cooking in the sun. Jerking back, he rubbed his eyes, blinking away his drowsiness. Next to him, Ash slept, her body coiled with her tail pulled up to her chest. On the other side of a root, Ivy was also asleep, as the drool on the side of her lip attested.

"Fine sentinels you both are," Orion sighed, grateful they were away from any populated areas. Absently, Orion dug his fingers into the earth, feeling the trees pulse with energy. With his magic returned, he relished the little whispers, knowing many of the dryads would communicate with him if he asked. Some dryads he avoided more than others, one being his mother. Irritation at her request flared. Her audacity amazed him. Yet curiosity nagged at him. Why had she reached out to him? She'd cruelly cast him aside and then expected him to spend his precious little time in Trinth with her?

A box at his feet caught his attention, and he shoved aside

thoughts of his mother. He wouldn't waste what precious time he had in Trinth even thinking about her.

Carefully, he inspected the box made of folded leaves. Orion smiled at Ivy's handiwork. Removing the lid, he found foraged berries and roots along with a roll, half an apple, and dried cheese. He smiled at not just her thoughtfulness, but her resourcefulness. But then, his mood tempered remembering *why* she'd become so resourceful. He put his head in his hands, wondering if he could leave her again when they reached the channel.

Ivy stirred, and Orion straightened, hiding his distress. Then he jumped to his feet and held out his hand, helping her up. Refreshed, they walked north while Orion ate. Ash sometimes flew overhead, but mostly she stayed on Orion's shoulder, her body like a fireball nuzzling into his neck.

"This heat," Orion groused. "I'm glad I opted to travel light." He'd only brought a pack and sword for the trip. His things would wait at Magdud's estate until his return. Unless, the war started, and Magdud was killed, in which case he really didn't care what happened to his belongings. The thought of her invading Trinth at the court's command sickened him.

"Orion," Ivy said, her words tentative as if she were walking on glass, "you arranged to have your things sent to Carrus before you ever saw the orcs on the Blue Mountain. Why did you change your mind about traveling with me?"

"You know why," Orion whispered, his heart jumping into his throat.

Would he have the strength to part with her once she had a wyvern? The thought frayed the edges of the pretend life they'd woven the last two days, a bubble with them inside and keeping their real obligations blurred beyond. He didn't want to be without her in the fair realm, but he had his brother. Who did Ivy have? Now that he knew her better, he understood why she'd come with him blindly to the fair realm. She hadn't wanted to be alone.

But he wasn't staying with her out of pity. He cared for her deeply, more than he'd ever admitted to himself. His feelings had only become more apparent in his days apart from her, each moment away sharpening the ache in his heart. The thought of her navigating the dangers of Nylenn'or without him filled him with dread.

Ivy reached out and took his hand, interlocking their fingers. The simple touch sent a jolt through him, bringing him back to her in the moment. The whispers of the trees spoke clearer, the distant birds' songs more distinct, and every leaf on the trees sharpened. He gazed at her, his heart growing heavy. He had to confess his father's demand; he had to burst the bubble and allow the ugliness of reality back in.

It wasn't fair not to tell her the truth—that he was leaving with no plans of returning. How could he tell her that he'd joined her and not just to protect her, but because of his own fears. The fear of losing her. The fear of living his life surrounded by galas and wine and shallow fae.

He wouldn't lay his fears on her. She had enough of her own. And if he wanted to stay in Trinth, Ivy would let him. But he was the only fae who would speak to the king on the elves behalf. Was it fair to ask her to choose between him and her own kind? No. And in the end, it wasn't just about what he wanted—the war would impact so many more creatures. If he had the slightest chance of swaying his father, to influence him to do the right thing, Orion had to be responsible and try.

Orion squeezed her hand, readying himself to tell her that his father had banned him from returning. But before he could, Ivy spoke first.

"I've been thinking about my vision," Ivy said as she

absently scanned their surroundings. "The one sent through the dryad tree to me as I reentered the fair realm."

Orion's mind snapped back to his argument with Rime in the forest when Ivy appeared through the tree. She'd fallen to the ground, clutching her head as if in pain. She'd said it was the same vision she'd received from the Gathering tree that spring, except the second vision had more.

"Remember how I was chased by fair creatures?" Ivy asked.

Orion nodded. That had been in both visions. "Like the orcs hunting you?"

Ivy nodded. "While I was gathering the berries this morning, it occurred to me that I didn't feel like I was running away. I was running toward something."

"So you were not being chased?"

Ivy shrugged. "In the last part of the second dream, the new part, *elves* were behind me."

"But maybe they were following you? Following your lead?"

"All I know is that I wasn't afraid during the vision. Only after I emerged from the tree and processed what I'd seen did I worry."

"Do you feel more secure in your decision to go to Nylenn'or? Nym might be in trouble, but with your help, Kolvar will fix things. You'll convince other elves to make leadership changes. Just like you convinced Gneiss in the south."

Ivy just bit her lip and fell into her own thoughts. And as the sun descended toward the mountains in the west, they picked up their pace.

"Dusk is a great time to fly. Shall we?" Orion said, holding out his hand to Ivy.

But Ivy shook her head. "We're too close to the elven outpost, and I'll tire you. Besides, I need to run. I have too much on my mind."

Her refusal stung, but he accepted her logic. Still, as he took to the sky, he missed having her at his side. Suddenly, the hours were too short, and he dreaded his return to the fair realm. Below him, he couldn't see Ivy but he trusted she was there, keeping pace with him.

After the sun fell, Orion turned and flew toward the northernmost mountain in the range, to the wyverns' housing. He landed in the forest a good distance away, too far for elven eyes. Moments later, Ivy was at his side. She smiled, though she was breathing hard.

"I haven't ridden a wyvern in many years, but I remember the stables," Ivy said. "I was enamored with them as a youngling. They're the one creature I actually relished more than Nym did."

"What's the layout?"

"There's a sprawling estate not visible to humans unless they climb past the tree line. The strong dissuasion spells keep the property hidden. When you fly there, you'll see several buildings dotting the mountain, but the wyverns are held deep inside the caves. You'll talk with the elf in the easternmost structure, the second lowest building on the mountain."

"You think I should glamour as a fae creature?"

"Yes, just hide the fact that you're Winter. They'll be more likely to trust you."

Orion glamoured to look like Prince Devain, the Summer Prince, and Ivy snorted. "It's not that I don't like Devain's dragon wings, it's just that he doesn't have *any* wings."

"But do they know that?"

"Do you want to chance it?" Ivy nudged him with her shoulder.

"It might make for a good story later."

"I don't think we're short on interesting tales."

Orion chuckled and glamoured into a lower noble Summer fae that he'd seen on occasion.

"You might as well make the arrangements tonight," Ivy said as she riffled through her pack. "They have elves stationed at the entrance at all times. Travelers tend to show up here at odd hours. And it's usually an 'emergency.' Bring the wyvern back here, and I'll leave when I'm rested."

Orion kissed her on the cheek and flew into the sky. Procuring the wyvern was a relatively simple task, especially when helped along by gold coin from the fair realm. It wasn't long until the elves escorted Orion to the landing and brought out a dark wyvern. Like humans used horses in Trinth, fair folk used wyverns for travel. The stable hands promised the creature had mellowed with age, and though she wasn't their fastest beast, she would wait patiently until commanded to leave. She'd even hunt for her own food, not needing any care for up to a week. She could go even longer, but they liked to check their paws for thorns and give them regular magic-infused feed from the fair realm to keep them in peak health.

Mounting the beast, Orion flew back down to the forest where Ivy waited. The creature easily responded to the slightest nudge, reassuring him that Ivy would be safe on the journey. Ash shot over, flying next to the wyvern, hurling little screeching noises at the creature. Then she flew circles around her head, trying to pick a fight.

"Calm down," Orion chuckled and tapped his shoulder. But instead of perching, Ash snorted, and a bit of smoke unfurled from her nostrils. Then she tucked in her wings and darted down to the ground, not far from Ivy.

Landing, Orion dismounted and started looking for a place for them to rest that night. The moons' light filtered through the evergreens, and the air had finally cooled. Ash sat on Ivy's pack, crouched down like she was ready to pounce on the wyvern.

"Someone's jealous," Ivy teased.

"I don't know why." Orion shrugged.

"I could've seen that coming. Have you *met* Ash?"

Ivy moved past Orion and started to secure her pack to the wyvern's saddle. A bolt of energy went through Orion, followed by a sinking feeling in his gut. He'd assumed that Ivy would leave in the morning at dawn. Not *now*.

Ivy stood back up, but her shoulders sagged. Mere steps apart, they didn't move. Ivy lifted her gaze to meet Orion's, and a vice tightened around his heart. She closed the distance and put a hand on his cheek. "You're not coming back."

Orion's heart cracked, hearing the words said aloud, shattering the glass in a way he'd refused to do. "How did you know?"

She rubbed her thumb across his lips, searching him. "I knew from the moment you tried to tell me, after you'd rescued me from my fate in the Carrus dungeon." She paused, letting her words sink in. "The truth is, I always knew we would go our separate ways. You did, too. My life is meant for Trinth. Your family wants you in Winter."

Orion put his hand over hers, knowing their duties would always keep them apart. He'd been conceived, always destined, for Winter. Still, he was the portal keeper. "I'm part dryad. I'm meant to live in both realms. Some part of me always hoped it could work. Somehow."

Ivy blinked up at him, the moons revealing the tears in her eyes. "For a grumpy pixie, you have a lot of hope."

"I don't know when I'll return. It could be years. Do you … do you want me to find you?" Orion felt as if his insides had shattered, and her hand on his cheek was the only thing holding him together.

"And I'll take whatever snippet of time you give me. Days with you are enough to fill me for a lifetime. But, when we're together, I want to see *you*."

In an instant, he let all his glamours fall, revealing his dryad-fae nature. Ivy blinked, tears welling. Orion pulled her hand to his chest, and she moved closer.

"What if we meet in the Accords?" Orion whispered. The idea was a little insane, yet it blossomed within his mind as he spoke. "It won't be difficult to convince the Summer Queen to be there to oversee the orc movements. I'll tell her we want to meet on neutral ground to return the Spring attendings." His father would be tougher to convince. But Orion didn't want to dig into the politics. That was for him to worry about, not Ivy. "I'll remain in the Accord's realm as long as I can."

"Knowing you're nearby will lend me courage." Excitement infused her words.

"If you can arrive before us, the queen is less likely to leave. She won't want to go without her Spring attendings. I'll wait until the fourth hour after the moons shift into full shadow." Orion spun through scenarios, analyzing their best options.

"I need your help with something." Ivy squeezed Orion's forearms, her brows raised. "Send word to Carrus that the Mineral Councilors must meet us in Nylenn'or for the Accords."

Orion nodded, understanding her plan. If the entire Council entered the Accords together, it would catch the queen off guard. "The queen won't have any good excuse *not* to see you. And with a united front, she'll be forced to agree. As will my father." If Orion could get him there. "The war will end before the Realm of the Accords even closes."

The Accords also afforded Orion an opportunity to deliver the Gathering sapling in the neutral territory. Before he could think about contacting Zel, Ivy wrapped her arms around his waist, squeezing tight.

"This could work," she breathed a smile then rested her head on his shoulder.

Neither of them discussed what would happen if Emmyth

were still in power. Gneiss wouldn't overthrow the leadership in the south, and no one would confront the Summer queen. So if Ivy didn't appear at the Accords castle, she was imprisoned in Nylenn'or. Orion wasn't sure what he'd do in that scenario, but he certainly wouldn't sit back and hope elven laws would protect her.

"The realm is vast, so I'll tell the queen to meet us in the heart of the land, in the castle. Look for her there."

Ivy nodded, understanding the gravity of the situation. Her eyes held a mix of determination and fear, mirroring his own feelings. He reached out, cupping her face gently, his thumb brushing against her cheek. The touch was meant to reassure her, but it also grounded him, anchoring him in the moment.

Their lips met in a kiss, tempered but filled with pain. The uncertainty of their future loomed over them, making every moment felt precious. The kiss deepened, a desperate attempt to cling to each other, to hold on to the broken bits of the world they'd just shattered.

They'd be in the same Realm of the Accords soon, but whether they'd be able to be alone or even talk was another matter. At least they'd see each other, but beyond that, the future was a terrifying unknown.

Orion pulled back slightly, his forehead resting against hers. "We'll find a way," he said, his voice raw with emotion.

Ivy's fingers tightened around his, her eyes searching his. "I'll be here."

He nodded, though doubt gnawed. His father would be watching him closely, especially in the coming days. If the new Elven Council forced the courts into a peace agreement, the fae rulers would be salivating at the thought of regaining their land. They wouldn't be happy when that dream was snatched away.

Orion kissed her again, and when they finally broke apart, he held her gaze, trying to memorize every detail of her face.

"Stay safe," he murmured, his voice barely above a whisper as Ivy mounted the wyvern.

"You too," Ivy replied, her eyes glistening with unshed tears.

As the wyvern lifted Ivy into the air, a sense of foreboding settled over him. He knew this wasn't the end, but a beginning of another challenging chapter. The uncertainty and the looming threats cast a long shadow. But he clung to the belief that Ivy would overturn the Council, and he'd convince his father to side with the elves.

He watched Ivy, leaning forward and resolute, as she flew north, he imprinted the image in his mind. In that moment, she was his beacon amid the coming storm.

24

ICY GREENHOUSE

Through an underground tunnel, Kolvar made his way to the greenhouses, a thin mat tucked under his arm. Before he even ascended to the entrance, the aroma of ripening apricots, pungent basil and thyme, and rich soil beckoned. As he climbed the stone steps, the muscles in his back began to uncoil. He emerged into the sunlight, the morning sun rising higher in the sky.

The glass walls of the atrium allowed for breathtaking views of the surrounding forest, the birch leaves swaying gently in the breeze. Inside, the ceiling beams arched overhead like the branches of ancient trees, and vines twined their way around the supports. Polished granite crunched underfoot as Kolvar strode past servants picking greens, carrots, and peas. Bees flitted from blossom to blossom, working as well.

Snow still lingered at higher elevations, but the atrium was already warming. This time of year, panes of glass in the ceiling would be raised in the afternoon, releasing the excess heat. But now, the atrium was the perfect temperature, and Kolvar intended to meditate before he returned to aiding the councilors in their duties.

Nym never left the back of his mind. Even when he meditated, worry nagged from the corners of his consciousness. His mother had rewarded his loyalty by allowing him to move Nym from The Hand. If he continued to prove himself, his mother would release Nym to his care. Eventually. She was a shrewd negotiator, but she did negotiate, especially when she desired something in return. And Kolvar knew that she wanted his trust, especially after losing Nym's.

The apple orchards this time of year were vacant as the trees wouldn't be ready to pick for several more months. Kolvar headed to the center of the orchard where he rolled out his mat and pondered on the Elven Council.

Everyone had made mistakes, including him. But what did the law dictate? The fuzzy gray lines seemed to crystallize as he thought through what Alysatraee had gifted the councilors, and the power his mother still wielded. Was that a sign Emmyth was in the right?

Glancing up, he noticed another servant checking the limbs. Kolvar stood and grabbed his mat, irritation flashing. Servants knew to give him space this time of day, and generally respected his preferred locations. Intending to find a quiet corner, Kolvar nearly turned to leave when the elf walked around the trunk, revealing herself.

"Ivy?" The mat slipped from Kolvar's grasp, tumbling to the ground.

"I'm sorry to startle you," Ivy whispered. "I didn't know what else to do. I remembered your habits of visiting the atriums before lunch."

Kolvar let out a long breath and lifted his attention to the glass ceiling, relief washing over him. All the accusations about her receded, and all he could see was the innocent youngling he'd once played with. He hadn't heard any updates on Ivy since the report of her presence with the Minerals, and part of him feared she'd been killed.

"Did anyone see you?" Kolvar stepped closer, leaving his mat behind. As the daughter of the infamous Seeds Councilor, more than one elf would recognize her face.

"I joined a group of elves this morning after they foraged for mushrooms in the forest. I kept my head down, and the servants' attention was on the mushrooms, anyway. I was sent to wash carrots, but it was easy enough to slip away and find the atrium." Ivy stepped closer. "What happened with Nym?"

Kolvar checked over his shoulder, the atrium suddenly feeling too small. He quickly explained to Ivy about Nym's involvement with the coup, and getting thrown in The Hand. Ivy recoiled, her hands shooting to her lips at the news.

"She's since been moved to the dungeon," Kolvar said. Not sugar-coating the trouble Ivy had pulled his sister into, he continued. "Her mind is sharp, but her body has taken a beating. Even with a healing stone, she confessed that her magical abilities are not returning."

Ivy paled, and she stumbled closer to the nearest tree. Gripping a sturdy branch, Ivy steadied. In the past, Kol would've comforted her. They'd been friends since before he could remember, and she'd always held a special place in his heart. What would have happened if she'd accepted his invitation and escaped to the north with him? She'd shaken his trust that day. If she'd not abandoned the Tides, would things be different between them? If she'd stayed on the ship, she never would've gone to Neidrei and been complicit in allowing an outsider to glamour as him. Her actions brought him under scrutiny, tarnishing his reputation.

Seeing Ivy now, he realized his feelings for her had shifted. He didn't know when they'd dulled, but they had. This meeting was a blessing, in a way. He didn't feel obligated to help her—

not like he had before. In a way, Nym had brought her punishment on herself, as harsh as it was, but Ivy was partly responsible, too.

"So, you've seen Nym," Ivy confirmed. "But you weren't able to get her a seed. Are you searched by guards before you enter the dungeon?"

"If I give Nym a seed, the councilors will know it was me, and I'll lose their trust." Kolvar shifted his weight, ignoring Ivy's incredulous expression.

If Ivy or Nym had been more methodical, they might have avoided all the trouble they'd caused. "Look, I know the Council needs to correct course, but Nym's plan landed herself and half the advisers in the dungeon. All the elves are unsettled, especially after The Battle of the Gathering. We need stability. Then changes."

Ivy shook her head. "I would feel the same way if I hadn't seen the orchard of Gathering Trees in Neidrei myself. I don't even know that I'd believe anyone who claimed that they'd revealed corruption to the Winter King himself, and it was ignored. The stories are unbelievable."

Ivy was in the fair realm? Kolvar's mother had said as much, but he hadn't really believed her. He ignored the thought, not having time to discuss it. Not when another servant could appear at any moment and reveal Ivy's identity to the rest of the palace.

"Can you take me to see Nym?" Ivy asked. It was a bold request, one Kolvar couldn't even begin to respond to in that moment.

"Stay hidden the best you can," Kolvar instructed. "I'd take you to see my sister myself, but I'll only draw attention to you, and you'll be identified." Did she not know that the Council wanted to question her? That they'd likely arrest her if found? "I'll send someone else to help you get whatever you need. But you won't be able to stay in Nylenn'or long. The sooner you get out of here, the less likely you are to get yourself into deeper trouble.

Ivy gave him a tentative nod, her eyes wide. She was nervous, that was certain. But he realized his instinct to hide her was more than just keeping her out of the dungeon. He needed distance from Ivy. Getting caught in her net would only hurt his chances of freeing his sister.

Picking up his mat, Kolvar strode out of the greenhouses. Instead of taking the tunnel, Kolvar pushed through a side door. The crisp air cleared his head as he hurried toward the palace to find Lial. Lial knew firsthand what it meant to be punished for choosing the losing side of a coup. He'd become all but invisible—the perfect person to assist Ivy in getting whatever closure she needed. Then Lial would escort her from the city, letting her know she wasn't welcome back.

More and more, Kolvar realized the Balrel's caused trouble wherever they went, and they didn't need it in the North.

Passing two young guards, Kolvar entered the western wing of the palace. Striding toward Lial's quarters, Kolvar rushed through the marble hallways. Several servants and other elves scurried through the hallways, all attending to their duties. Through the throng, Kolvar spotted his mother headed his direction. Deep in conversation with one of her remaining advisers, she hadn't noticed her son. If Emmyth spoke with him, she'd know he was hiding something—he'd never been good at keeping secrets from her, especially with his emotions high. And he didn't want Ivy to end up next to Nym in a dungeon cell.

Kolvar continued onward, intending to find his friend, but he paused. Though he didn't want to condemn Ivy, he would trade her freedom for his sister's. But the law didn't transfer responsibility of punishment from one elf to another. Nor did it allow for a trade. If only there was something Ivy could do for his sister. She could at *least* try.

Kolvar squeezed the mat in his hand, frustrated, his mind spinning. Perhaps he could get his sister out of the dungeon sooner than he'd anticipated. Making a plan, Kolvar hurried on, looking for Lial.

25

NYLENN'OR DUNGEON

I vy hesitated just outside the crowded kitchen. During the busy dinner prep, Ivy was less noticeable with all the distractions, or so Lial had claimed.

"Hurry," Lial said, not stopping. He pointed to a wooded tray with a rune carved into one side and five bowls nestled on top. Ivy snatched it and followed him out of the room. So far, everything was going to plan.

Lial was nothing like she remembered. Before, he'd been a string of never-ending teasing and jokes. Now, between his fidgeting, subdued instructions, and somber expression, Ivy suspected his fall from grace had changed him.

In the halls, Lial led her past a series of guards on their way to the dungeon. She clutched the tray tighter with her clammy hands. As much as they'd explored as younglings, they'd never even attempted to enter this area of the palace. As they continued down a vacant hall, Ivy's thoughts slipped to Orion. Had he returned to the fair realm? Every hour he was there, time sped by in Trinth. For her, years could pass before he might be allowed to return.

Ivy ached to be with him, but she couldn't waste her time pining. She would see him in the Accords, and that would have to be enough until he could return to Trinth. She'd already spent years alone, even then knowing in her heart that her family was gone. Orion still lived, and he would find her.

Choosing Orion meant taking everything that came with him, which meant they'd be spending long periods apart. She didn't know what their future held, but she owed it to herself to find out what might be possible.

"I can take you through the first chamber of the dungeons, but no further. It won't be difficult to direct you from that point," Lial continued explaining his plan as they walked.

As the hallway curved, a stately elf appeared, and Lial clamped his mouth shut. The elf looked vaguely familiar. Ivy dropped her face down and away, hoping not to be noticed.

"Bellas," Lial said, brightly. "It's good to see you."

Ivy's stomach dropped, recognizing the name. Tides' advisers definitely knew the Balrels.

"I didn't expect to see you in this part of the palace," Bellas said in a flat, even tone.

"I was just helping a new trainee." Lial turned to Ivy, blocking Bellas's view of the tray. "Simply continue down this curved passage, and you'll see two guards. You can't miss them." He slipped a seed on to the tray and under a napkin—a seed from a Gathering Tree. Ivy sucked in a breath, keenly aware of her empty vial.

But it wasn't for her. It was intended for Nym.

His back was only turned to Bellas for a moment, before he turned to face the adviser. "It's been weeks since I've seen you."

"Excuse me," a female elf's voice commanded their attention as she stormed toward them. She wasn't dressed as a guard, but she must've held some official position.

"This area is off limits. Lial, you're not allowed here. And, you," she spat at Ivy. "Who are you?"

"She's new," Lial offered. "She was hopelessly turned around. But, you make a good point. I probably shouldn't be here. Bellas, would you like to accompany her to the doors?"

Ivy stiffened, horrified.

"I have a schedule to keep, Lial," Bellas said, a note of annoyance in her voice. "I'm sure she can find the entrance from here." Ivy felt the adviser's attention on her, and she kept her focus on the tray. "You're new, clearly, so let me remind you that back in your village, one's appearance doesn't matter as much as your work ethic. Here at the palace, both matter."

Ivy swallowed back a laugh. If Bellas only knew that Ivy had basically jumped off a wyvern and ran to the atrium, she might think Ivy looked pretty decent, considering.

"Also, just because you're serving in the dungeon doesn't mean you can be late," Bellas droned. "They dine earlier than the rest of us, and their stomachs are used to the schedule. We don't let prisoners go hungry. A lesson you should learn now: treat everyone with respect. The rule book for servants states that you show respect by having your hair braided neatly and your face washed."

"Thank you," Lial interjected with a nervous chuckle. With a hand on Bellas's elbow, he guided the adviser away, back down the hall. While Ivy was grateful that Lial had *finally* distracted Bellas, he hadn't prepared Ivy to enter the dungeon alone. As the two elves disappeared around the curve in the wall, Ivy's mouth dried.

Her guide was gone, and surely guards stood watch ahead. She was infiltrating the dungeon as a hunted elf. A nervous energy coursed through her, but she forced herself to think. Shifting the tray to one arm, Ivy grabbed the seed and slid it into the vial at her neck. The last thing she needed was to lose the tiny, precious resource. Forcing her feet to move, she soon came upon two guards, as expected. They flanked massive, black double doors.

The guards inspected Ivy's tray, and she breathed a sigh of relief, grateful that she'd removed the seed. Still, had trainees seen the inside of the dungeon before they started their first shift? Should she know the interior layout? Could she ask for directions without looking completely suspicious?

Fearing any questions from her would only prompt more from them, she stayed silent as they pushed open the doors with a grunt. At just the right angle, deep, purple orc-styled painted runes appeared and disappeared just as quickly. Ivy chewed her lip and stepped inside, hoping the guards didn't notice how her hands trembled.

The doors slammed behind her, leaving her blinking, willing her eyes to adjust to the darkness.

The scents of putrid water and must hit Ivy first, well before her eyes adjusted to the pinkish light of the underground tunnels. The walls were roughly carved rocks typical of human caves, nothing like the dwarven home she'd seen, and decidedly more cramped.

Standing taller than most elves, massive crystals dominated the far right side of the cave. The long, vertical crystals glowed pink with a golden glow deep inside, casting the room in dim light. Directly in front of Ivy, a wide stone walkway, about ten steps long, was flanked on either side by a sharp drop off.

The stone path ran into a perpendicular, narrow walkway that extended through carved doorways beyond the cave entrance in either direction. Lial had intended to give her further instructions at this point, but now she had to wander around and hope she didn't get lost in, as Lial put it, the "beastly labyrinth of tunnels." Though Ivy's curiosity piqued at this unknown place, her task pressed heavily on her shoulders.

Ivy gripped the tray and strode across the bridge. On either side, the drop-off ended in brackish water, far below. Where the initial walkway met the perpendicular path, looking right and then left, Ivy selected the brighter direction. Moving into the next cavern, Ivy quickly realized there was more water than walkway.

Ahead, an elven guard marched in her direction. Ivy forced herself to relax and drop her shoulders, feigning a calm attitude. The guard glanced at her uniform and tray, and moved past her without a word. Ivy paused and glanced over her shoulder, wondering if she should stop him and ask for directions. The guard continued marching around the bend and out of sight; Ivy wondered how many guards monitored the dungeon. Lial had failed to mention that information.

The tunnel descended deeper. She trudged passed more crystals, wider around than she could even reach, lighting the paths. Several stone support posts and beams lined portions of the path, with elegantly carved arches at the apex. The supports framed the ponds of water beyond, some of which were littered with fallen metal structures, almost whimsical in their design. Was the debris remnants of ancient magic, broken and no longer in use? Glancing up at the lofty ceiling, soaring high through this section of the dungeon, she noticed strange carvings—stone jutting down, broken on the ends. A dull buzz of magic permeated the space, but Ivy couldn't pinpoint why.

Remembering the ancient ruins of The Tower, Ivy shuddered. Her gaze dropped to the metal-barred structures half hidden in the water. Then the reality of their use snapped into place in her mind; cages, and they'd once dangled above the water. Her stomach churned, and she gagged. Forcing her feet to move faster, Ivy tracked her every turn, determined to remember the puzzling exit from this dismal place. Had Kolvar ever been in the dungeon? Surely he and Nym had been here many times as adults, as part of their training.

Ivy hated how things had shifted between Kolvar and her. The wall he'd put up was a stark contrast to how he'd openly shared his thoughts and feelings with her in the past. She understood why, though. He'd generously offered to bring her to the safety of this very palace, and she'd accepted just long enough to steal her father's glamour amulet back from Emmyth.

Naturally, Kol would feel hurt by her easy dismissal of him. Though, surely he knew, deep down, that she had to discover what had happened to her family. She never could've unearthed the truth while stuck here. She hoped to explain everything to Kol before the Mineral advisers showed up for the Accords. But judging from his reserved demeanor, he needed more time.

Coming to a fork in the passage, Ivy noticed one path continued through a rune-covered archway. Definitely a more recent addition—sometime in the last ten thousand years. An orc had either had a lot of fun accessing their artistic-side, or the runes were for practical use. Probably a means to secure the prisoners. But were the advisers and Nym down that passage? Would Ivy set off a silent, magical alarm if she passed under the runes?

Her stomach rumbled. It was only a matter of time until the guards at the door decided she'd been gone too long and came looking for her. If she wasn't where she was supposed to be ... she didn't even want to imagine what alarms they would raise. And Emmyth would surely find out about the servant-that-no-one-knew wandering around in the dungeon. Ivy did not go to the fair realm, almost die, then flee across Trinth with orcs tracking her just to get caught in the Nylenn'or dungeon.

She sucked in a deep breath and listened. Asking for directions would draw less attention at this point. Rhythmic footfalls sounded down the not-rune path, far heavier than a typical elf. Who was it? Her stomach twisted knowing, logically, the creature was an orc. Why were orcs still in Nylenn'or?

Ivy squeezed her eyes shut, guessing some remained behind after the supposed insurrection. Had the orc been assigned to watch the advisers? Regardless, she had to find the orc. And as long as she didn't act like the suspicious spy that she was, the orc shouldn't have any problem with her. Opening her eyes, and slinking forward like a frightened, new servant, she kept walking until she neared the orc. With his dark purple skin and boiled leather clothing he might have blended in with the cave except for his long, white hair and gleaming tusks.

"Can you help me?" Ivy asked before the orc could question her. "I'm hopelessly lost. I'm newly appointed to the dungeon and assigned to bring food to some prisoners. It's my first day."

He scowled, and Ivy realized that he must've arrived on the boat recently deployed north. By now, he should know the dungeons well enough. And, even better, few orcs knew her family, let along Ivy, which meant she'd keep her identity hidden. Emmyth had kept this orc for extra protection, but she'd unwittingly aided Ivy in the process.

"What sector?" he asked.

"Sector?" Ivy bit her lip, keeping her eyes wide. "Oh, no, I hope I don't get into trouble for not remembering!"

He frowned, and Ivy could practically sense him internally groaning at the elven incompetence. *Perfect.*

"I was given these five bowls," Ivy said, innocently. "I know three are for the advisers, but I don't know about the other two."

"I can guess." He shifted and gestured for her to pass him.

Ivy walked ahead as he gave curt instructions. She stepped down uneven stairs, a little unnerved, calculating that she was now below the water table. They crossed under another runed archway; ahead several cells came into view, though she couldn't see who was inside.

The orc's hand gripped her shoulder, just tight enough to stop her. "Cells are grouped into sections. The runes on the archway keep the prisoners from hearing anything outside their section of the dungeon. Just put the bowls on the floor and push them through the semi-translucent doors."

Ivy just nodded, looking confused, which wasn't difficult.

"If you need assistance, you must be outside of the runed tunnel. Shout, and your words will echo loud enough for someone to hear you." The orc spun on his heel, slightly shaking his head, as he left the area.

"I guess I don't need any more training, thank you very much," Ivy muttered under her breath.

The first cell door looked like a sheet of fogged ice with a rune about the size of her palm chiseled into the center. Light shone through revealing two obscured figures inside, but the cell door was nearly opaque. Lial had given her a brief overview of the runes and how to use them, though the lesson had been rushed, and she hoped she remembered correctly.

Ivy lifted the tray, facing its carved rune to the sister rune on the cell door. When she felt a slight vibration, the wall turned clear, enabling Ivy to see the two elven males inside. The tray quickly vibrated again, which allowed the prisoners to hear outside their cell.

Ivy announced her presence. "I'm a new servant. I have your food."

"About time," the slender, male elf said, his face pinched. "I'm starved."

"Send the bowls through, please," the second male said, his voice tired. "We're ready for tonight's slop."

Ivy removed Lial's seed before pressing the tray to the ice-like wall, where it slid through as if the wall was nothing but air. A moment later, the prisoners sent the tray back with their empty bowls from the previous day. Ivy didn't reactivate their cell and instead quickly moved to the second cell. This cell held a female prisoner, but not Nym. Hearing her voice, the male advisers started talking to her, their questions mundane, not knowing who was watching.

The next person was Lial's father, a voice she vaguely recognized. The rest of the cells in the section appeared vacant, except one singular cell across from the others.

Lial's information said that Nym was held near the advisers, but was she in the same section? When he fell from his short-lived pedestal, his usual channels for information disappeared. Ivy braced herself for the worst, but was interrupted before she could activate the rune.

"Next time, give us napkins," the slender male adviser complained.

Pushing the councilors chatter out of her mind, Ivy lifted the tray, activating the rune twice, desperate to see who was inside. A lone figure was curled on the bed, her back to Ivy. The thin and frail body scarcely resembled her friend. Then Ivy recognized the short, black hair barely reaching into a ponytail, and braids splayed across the side of her face.

"Nym?" Ivy activated the rune a third time. "Nym!"

Ivy's heart pounded faster. Her friend wasn't moving. Was she breathing? Ivy lifted the tray again, but the rune didn't respond. Ivy slammed her hand on the invisible wall.

"My dear," the female adviser said in a calm tone, "do not worry. Just slide the bowl along the floor, and she will eat it later. I assure you, Nym is fine."

She's anything but *fine*. White knuckled and furious, Ivy put the tray on the ground and slipped the seed from the vial and dropped it carefully onto the napkin. Placing the napkin on top of the gruel, the seed prominently in the middle, Ivy paused, her finger still on the lip of the bowl.

Once Nym healed, the advisers would notice. The other servants or guards might notice, too. If word got back to Emmyth, she'd know that someone had given Nym a seed. With a little interrogation, she'd narrow the culprit down to a servant. The orc would *definitely* remember her, and they'd trace the seed back to the "new, unknown servant" in a snap. Nym wouldn't want Ivy to get caught; she'd want her to be wise.

Ivy bit the inside of her cheek and shoved the tray and bowl with the napkin and seed through to Nym. The smartest strategic move meant healing her best ally in all of Trinth.

Turning back to Lial's father's cell, she activated his rune again, revealing herself. He was slowly eating at the edge of his thin mat on the floor. He looked up at Ivy, no hint of recognition in his eyes, but forgotten childhood memories flooded her mind. "Omasys. Your son helped me find you."

He shot to his feet, his food spilling. He rushed forward, the flesh of his palms pressed against the barrier between them. "How is he? We have no real news here."

"Lial?" the female adviser sounded skeptical. "Lial brought you? Why?"

"Who are you?" one of male voices shouted as if warning Omasys not to trust anyone.

Omasys's attention moved past Ivy, and his jaw dropped. A crash of splintering wood sounded from Nym's cell. Ivy spun to see her friend upending the mat on the floor, the little table already smashed.

Nym curled her hands into fists, her chest lifted as she tilted her head back and released a feral cry. The other advisers started shouting, confused, but Omasys just stared, stunned.

Ivy ignored the advisers and folded her arms across her chest, a smile forming. "Well, welcome back, Nym."

Hearing her voice, Nym jerked her attention to the tunnel. "Ivy?"

Ivy's smile widened, studying Nym as she took several deep breaths, her usual determination lining every part of her stance.

"You better be here to rescue me." Nym's hands clenched.

"With your help," Ivy wished she had a plan. But she needed Nym for that.

"Ivy *Balrel*?" Omasys said, finally remembering her.

The other advisers erupted with questions. Ivy activated all their runes until everyone could see her. Their questions came fast, clamoring to know everything going on in Nylenn'or.

"I don't have much time, and I don't know your local gossip," Ivy held up a hand for them to stop, "but I'll tell you what I learned in the fair realm." As Ivy explained the equinox ceremony events and the lack of action after, even Nym was shocked to hear that the fae courts and the Elven Council were united in efforts to re-engage in war. The female adviser, who Ivy learned was named Lyra, paled at the news.

"Your grumpy-pixie messenger is the son of the Winter King?" Nym shouted, unnecessarily loud.

Later, Ivy mouthed to her friend. She would rather face a Seeker than discuss Orion with a bunch of Tides advisers.

"And the Minerals are willing to act if we overthrow our Council?" Lyra said, ignoring Nym's comment.

Ivy nodded.

"Then we must escape," Nym said, pounding her fist into her open palm.

Ivy tapped her foot, each moment spinning past. The cook would notice if the tray wasn't returned soon.

"Actually," Lyra said, "we don't need to get out of the prison to overthrow the councilors."

Omasys frowned and stepped back, shaking his head.

"But we need your help," Lyra said to Ivy.

"Whatever I can do." Ivy nodded.

The adviser continued, "Two things are vital: the official voting bowl and another adviser to side with us."

Ivy didn't know anything about some special bowl, but she had an idea of which adviser they meant. "You want me to approach Bellas?"

That particular adviser was always strict about following every tiny rule, which she'd found annoying as a youngling. But her rigid ways might help them now.

"She won't turn on Emmyth again," Daecyne said. "Not even her family name can save her again if she willingly goes against a councilor and fails. Plus, she's not one to even appear unethical. She's the reason we openly voted with the councilor *and* witnesses present last time."

"We have to try," Lyra said. "She's still our best chance."

"To what end?" Omasys said. "The war is coming, and we cannot stop it unless we have a—"

"Unanimous agreement," Nym finished for him. "We know." She shoveled her gruel into her mouth, threw the bowl on the tray and sent it back through her door.

Omasys continued, "You might get the Minerals to bring willing, new councilors, but what about the Seeds?"

"In the House of Seeds, we don't have advisers. Our ambassadors choose our next representative councilor. I'm sure they have someone in mind," Ivy interrupted. "And we can discuss it later. For now, I must go before someone notices I'm delayed."

"But—"

"I'll return as soon as I can." Ivy cut off Omasys, anxious to get back. She reactivated his rune first before hurrying to Lyra.

"You must get Bellas to join us," Lyra urged as Ivy arranged the empty bowls on the tray.

"And steal the bowl," Keyyarus added. "We can secretly vote in two new Tides' Councilors before Emmyth or Mormaris even realize what's happening."

So four adviser votes, plus Omasys's tie-breaker vote, meant the plan remained the same as the last attempt to change the Tides Councilors. Of course, last time they'd failed. But last time they didn't have Nym or Ivy.

"The problem is, if my mother notices her medallion dimming, she'll know exactly where to find us," Nym said, scowling. "Trapped in the dungeon. So we can't make any mistakes."

The dungeon fell silent for a moment, everyone knowing that Emmyth had put her own daughter in The Hand. Next time, only shallow graves awaited for anyone who crossed her.

"I must go," Ivy said. "Even the guards will be suspicious if I don't return soon."

Ivy reactivated the rest of the runes, turning to Nym last. "Guards and dungeon servants can activate your rune so they can see and hear you, but keep themselves concealed. Meaning, you don't know when someone is watching. But the longer you hide the fact that your magic is back, the longer I can keep my presence a secret from Emmyth. If anyone finds out, it won't take them long to figure out that a servant delivered the seed."

"I'll fake like I'm as weak as a human. Don't worry. Honestly, Kol should've sent me a seed sooner," Nym said. "I'm sure he had his reasons, though."

Ivy opened her mouth to clarify that Kol hadn't sent the seed. But Nym looked so eager, so *hopeful*. After everything she'd been through, could Ivy rip that away without explanation? Ivy wasn't ready to tell her the crushing truth. Ivy didn't know Kol's reasoning, but he hadn't been willing to risk giving his sister a seed. Then again, he had more to lose than Lial.

"Councilors don't need their medallions to use their magic, but the pendant is a clear, visual reminder of who has Alysatraee's authority," Nym said. "Do you have your father's medallion?"

"I found his Seeds medallion in my father's lab in Neidrei," Ivy said. "But I don't know where the pendant is now. Maybe Zel has it."

"I doubt he found it in your satchel where I stitched it into the lining," Nym grinned.

"What?!"

"How did you not notice the extra weight?"

"Well, I was carrying Ash half the time ... and I didn't really think about it," Ivy said, exasperated.

"Apparently you had a certain grumpy fae on your mind," Nym muttered with a raised brow.

"Why didn't you tell me?" Ivy said, throwing her arms in the air.

"I was in the middle of preparing to storm the palace and unseat my mother. So, forgive me if I forgot!"

"Well, I left everything in the fair realm when I fled to save my life."

They both paused and looked at each other. Nym blurted a laugh. Her giggles grew to an almost hysterical mania, a few tears streaking her cheeks. Ivy just shook her head and leaned her forehead against the barrier, feeling lighter.

Nym wiped her tears, but kept the grin. "When all this is over, I'm sure Orion will help you find the medallion. Don't worry."

Ivy warmed, knowing her friend understood its importance, beyond what the pendant represented to elves. It was something her father had cherished, and something Ivy would hate to lose.

Ivy squared her shoulders. Omasys and the advisers had attempted a coup and failed. The Mother didn't always give her children second chances, but Ivy knew one when she saw it. They would not waste this opportunity. "I'll return soon ... with that fancy voting bowl."

"And Bellas," Nym reminded as her cell wall fogged back, hiding her from sight.

26

THE QUEEN'S COURT

When Orion's possessions arrived in the afternoon *without* him, Magdud cursed at herself for not sending someone with him. Rushing to her office, she inked a missive ... pretending she'd written the letter an hour earlier.

> *Winter King Eldrin Cor'arya of Shadowmoon,*
>
> *Orion has gone to Unaria, per your instructions.*
>
> *Loyally,*
> *Captain Magdud*

Hiding her irritation that Orion had put her in such a position, she instructed Agretha to immediately take the message to the forest—their usual drop off spot for the dryad. If Orion didn't return to his father's side quickly, Eldrin would extend Orion's "imprisonment" in the fair realm.

Part of Magdud had pitied Orion, always having to prove himself. Running off with Ivy would only make his life exponentially more difficult when he returned home. Magdud rolled her shoulders and put on her amulet, reminding herself that Orion was no longer a youngling and could make his own decisions. All she could do was support him. And hope he didn't get thrown in the dungeon for impudence.

Besides she had bigger problems. Magdud's unit was returning, and she needed to help them prepare for the worst: battle.

Carrying two heavy bags outside, she tied them to her pack horse. Stepping back, she surveyed her home, perhaps for the last time. Brushing off any wistful emotions, Magdud tugged the ropes of her horse, and they quietly left the city of Carrus.

Not long after exiting the gates, she arrived at the ancient grove, her destination secreted by layers of spells. The fae were particular when it came to keeping their training ground, "The Forge of Dawn," well hidden from humans. Because glamours were rare and costly, Magdud's unit planned to gather at The Forge. Young fae and other creatures were assigned to train here for a few years and then return home—only months later in the fair realm—and they'd be much older, educated, and deadly.

As she continued forward, careful to avoid activating the dissuasion spell in that area, her mind shifted to another prince: Devain of Summer. What had he learned about the corruption of the fair courts? He hadn't contacted her, but she hadn't expected him to. She hadn't earned his trust as she had with Orion or even with Rime. But even if Devain had learned the truth, what could he do? He was a prince, but he held little of his own power. His mother only delegated tasks to him because he took responsibility seriously, as opposed to most of his siblings. But had he ever acted on his own, without royal command?

Magdud understood why Devain had requested the Winter

Court hold Ivy in the fair realm and question her. Though Magdud was sure that Devain never intended for Ivy to be tortured in The Tower, his actions reflected that he trusted others to too easily. Not to mention he was a blind numskull to propose anything to the Winter Princess; Selleth, who of all fae, did *not* weigh ethics when making decisions.

Yet, he *hadn't* trusted Ivy. After all, he'd arranged for her detainment. Obviously, he hadn't been sure of what to think of her outlandish stories, warranting an investigation. Still, Magdud wished she could shake some sense into that prince. Truths had been laid before him, but some portions had been twisted into lies. The reality of the situation seemed so clear to Magdud, how could he not see it? With any luck, he'd figured it out—though only days had passed in his realm.

"Magdud," Gralk, one of her soldiers, came into view in the woods. A smile spread across his face, and he dropped his pack, lifting both his arms high in greeting. "Alysatraee is good! I'm glad to see you!"

Magdud dismounted with a thud and lifted her arms in kind. "You got my letter!"

"Unfortunately," he joked before turning more serious. "How sick is it that I'm grateful we're not training in Aggord with the others. Still, it's a bit like I've been thrown from the back of a dragon into the icy northern channel."

"That's why we're meeting here first," Magdud assured him. "We'll train together. Get our minds right."

"So, we're getting battle orders in the Accords?" He shook his head.

The Accords were meant to be a place of negotiation. But for the entirety of the war, the Accords had been used as a staging ground to deploy vast battalions of fair soldiers. With a distance from the war, the recollection sickened her. Every time she portaled through the realm, the central tree edged a little closer to death.

It didn't sit right with her, but she wouldn't burden her soldiers. "Let's see who else is here. Who beat us to The Forge."

With their rejoining those who'd remained in Aggord, pressure mounted to prove their skills as warriors. But part of the reason Magdud had left Aggord in the first place was because the bloodlust had burned out of her system. Revolted her. So while in the human territory, her unit hadn't trained like the others. Would that mean they would be sent as helpless lambs to the slaughter?

No, she would do everything she could to prepare them. Their old training and instincts ran deep. They just had to revive their ancestral impulses.

Before they got far, a fae servant burst into the room, his delicate wings fluttering in a panic.

"Magdud!" he called, holding out a sealed letter. "Agretha said to give this to you immediately."

Magdud took the letter, her heart pounding as she recognized the seal of the Summer Court. She broke the seal and unfolded the parchment, her eyes scanning the elegant script.

"I've been requested at the Summer Court." Magdud folded the note and tucked it away, though burning the document would be much more cathartic.

"We were already requested—" Gralk paused, a frown pulling at his tusks. "You mean, you're requested to go alone."

"Immediately." What could the queen want that couldn't wait? "Inform my lieutenant. I'll return as soon as I can."

The timing couldn't be worse; Magdud *would* go to the Accords with her unit. Nothing, not even the Summer Queen, would stop her.

~

Magdud and two other orc captains stood outside the doors of the throne room in the Summer palace. If she were an elf, she might've understood the muffled words inside.

"What's the fuss about this time?" one of the captains grumbled. Magdud didn't know him well, but after waiting for an hour, they were both more than a little short-tempered.

The other captain, a young orc Magdud had never met, responded. "There was some uproar at the Aequus, and Devain is making a fuss. Apparently, the elf who caused the trouble is the daughter of the Seeds Councilor—"

"I thought he died," the elder captain interjected.

"Yes, well, she's still his daughter," the younger captain continued, annoyed at the interruption. "Anyway, apparently the princess took it upon herself to put the elf in The Tower—"

"Daring and—"

"Stupid royals," Magdud muttered.

They both pivoted to look at her as if they'd forgotten she was there. She bristled, hating her situation. Normally she didn't mind her demotion, even though it decimated the influence and respect she'd once enjoyed. Now, she had all the influence she wanted as a magistrate, but among her own kind, she had become all but invisible.

"The elf was under Winter protection," Magdud said with a shrug. If the argument inside centered on Ivy, the crux of the issue was obvious. "By putting the elf in The Tower, Selleth may have acted outside the king's command. And Selleth, the conniving fae that she is, probably blamed Devain for everything. So the queen is debating his punishment."

Magdud avoided the bickering of the courts. She'd done well to keep out of the cross-fire, but Orion had dragged her closer by *not* quickly returning from Unaria to his father's side.

"Devain was a fool to ask any favors of Selleth," the elder orc mumbled.

More blaringly, Devain had asked Selleth to question Ivy, which meant he trusted Ivy *less* than the Winter princess. He believed Ivy was the instigator of the fight at the Aequus, and he didn't trust what she said about the Elven Council.

That, or Devain didn't *want* to believe Ivy.

If his opinion had changed, Magdud wished she knew. The prince was straighter than a dwarven sword when it came to the laws. Would he help Ivy's cause in the end?

Either way, Magdud's hopes hung on the success of Ivy's wildly implausible plan.

The younger orc fidgeted, probably anxious to get back to his unit as well. After what seemed like an eternity, the Summer guards opened the doors, releasing an insufferable wave of heat. As they traversed the hallway, Devain stormed past them, thankfully not acknowledging Magdud. The orc captains entered the throne room, and the queen and her adviser came into view. Magdud itched her throat, already sweating.

A servant rushed to the adviser, whispering in his ear. When finished, the adviser spoke quietly to the queen, and she nodded at the servant. The queen held her head high and her back straight, as she normally did, but her cheeks were flushed with anger. Whether her frustration was due to her conversation with Devain, Magdud could only guess.

"I appreciate you three responding to my summons," the queen said, though they hadn't been given a choice. "You're units will be the first into the Accords, first to be positioned in the human realm, and the first to attack your assigned cities."

Magdud's stomach dropped. Though she'd already been warned by Rokgut, hearing the official command by the mouth of the queen herself reverberated through her entire being. Phantom screams echoed in Magdud's ears, a metallic tang coating the back of her throat. By the expressions on the other two captain's faces, this news was a surprise. And not a welcome one at that.

"An honor to lead the fight," the younger orc choked out the words.

"High Commander Rokgut will enter the portal the moment the two moons of Trinth are darkened," the queen said. "He and his leaders will be prepared to guide you from the center castle of the Accords." The queen paused her instructions and gestured for someone behind them to enter the room.

Magdud swallowed back her memories, letting her anger flare. *Was this not information that could have been sent in a missive?*

"Emmyth Phiro," the queen said, an edge to her voice. "I received your letter, announcing your visit."

Magdud stiffened, shifting to watch the commanding elf stride into the room. Emmyth wore official robes and her medallion at her neck. Unusual. Emmyth's robes shifted and the medallion touched her flesh, and glowed, signaling her authority.

And the reasoning becomes clear. The queen wanted the captains to witness something, Magdud just didn't know what … yet. Magdud drew a long breath, already dreading the coming staged, ridiculous conversation.

"I heard what happened at the Aequus," Emmyth said with a bow. "Our children seem to think they know more than their elders."

The queen gripped the arms of her throne tighter. "Indeed."

"My primary reason for coming all this way is to report that I've sent most of the orcs back to Aggord after their routine check-in," Emmyth said.

"We know that's not true," the queen said, her voice flat. "The orcs put down an insurrection."

Magdud barely choked back a laugh. Perhaps this conversation wouldn't be as dull as Magdud had anticipated. The queen had good reason to be annoyed with Emmyth. And Emmyth had moved orcs right before they were to be deployed. They'd been selfishly dispatched from Aggord to protect Emmyth's title. With a snap of her fingers, the Summer Queen could burn the elf to ash.

Magdud really hoped for a fight—the queen might not kill the elf, but she certainly wouldn't leave her unscathed. But, of course, Magdud didn't expect her day to be that good.

Emmyth shifted. "Without the orcs, our ... standing orders ... might have been altered."

Meaning, the war threatened to end.

"It's a good thing the orcs were there to do your job for you," the queen said.

Ouch. Magdud coughed, covering her threatening grin.

"I'm here to assure you that the Elven Council cannot be united in presenting any other plan than what was previously agreed," Emmyth said.

That's strange wording. Magdud's glee faded.

"But to protect our plans, just in case of emergency," Emmyth continued, "it would be best for the two ruling thrones to keep distance between each other."

The queen paused, clearly giving Emmyth new consideration. "You're suggesting I keep *any* potential Elven Council members away from the Winter King?"

"I would never suggest such a thing," Emmyth said, drawing out her words. "The Elven Council must be allowed to see the courts."

The queen's attention shifted back to the throne room doors, and she slightly raised her chin.

"But as a precaution," Emmyth continued, "perhaps do not

invite the Winter King, or an official representative, to visit until after certain events have commenced."

Even if Ivy gets the Council replaced, the Summer Queen will never let them present to both courts.

Why the elf was using cryptic language about the war they all knew was coming was beyond Magdud. Pivoting, she noticed several other fae representatives joining them through the main hallway. Ah, the staged, ridiculous conversation was about to begin. Magdud slid her gaze to the other two orcs, wondering if they realized what was about to happen.

As Magdud suspected, Emmyth loudly started sharing her story, her twisted narrative, of events in the human realm. Of Seekers out of control. Of their increasingly deadly disruption.

"The humans are increasingly dangerous," Emmyth claimed.

Loud whispers sounded from around the room.

"... they're eradicating the elves!"

"The audacity ..."

Disgusted, Magdud wished she could speak up, to rail against Emmyth's exaggerations. But, the fae hadn't even believed Ivy, the daughter of a councilor, not to mention that her kind was assigned by Alysatraee to monitor the humans. Magdud was an orc, marred by distrust for her decision to leave her homeland of Aggord. She no longer had her title nor fair folk respect. Speaking up would only get her banned from similar, important conversations—conversations she's worked hard to listen in on, though she could never be a part of them.

Orion, on the other hand, had just been invited to sit next to his father, the most powerful Winter fae. He'd gained more influence than Magdud ever had to lose. There was a chance his word would be taken more seriously than an elf's. But he was flitting around Trinth, possibly throwing away his opportunities.

Then again, the Summer Queen never would've allowed a Winter prince into this meeting. But Magdud hadn't been barred. Not yet. And she'd take careful notes. She wasn't sure who this information would help or if it would change anything. All Magdud knew was that the queen fully intended to manipulate her own court—to make them angry enough to welcome open conflict.

27

A DRYAD MOTHER

The sun shone high overhead, and Orion's stomach grumbled as he rode for Blackmore. Yet he couldn't stop wondering what Ivy was doing at that moment. He'd flown over Stormbringer Mountains with Ash during the day and shadow traveled by night, arriving in Neidrei long enough to eat, sleep, and secure a horse. Unlike the mountains, the land between Neidrei and Blackmore was well populated, meaning he couldn't fly without notice. Refusing to wait until dark to shadow travel, Orion rode a horse. Without the duke's ring, he was akin to any other traveler, which he didn't mind.

Surrounding Blackmore, the capital where the human king and his castle resided, the city flowed into the surrounding land. Before the castle walls stretched into view, Orion handed off the horse to a stable hand at a local inn with instructions to return the mare home.

Orion would be traveling home a different way.

Gripping his hands behind his back as he moved through the city outskirts, he wondered if he'd made a mistake. What would he even say to his mother? The dryad in Carrus had stated that his mother had requested him, which he'd ignored the first time. After all, why would he respond to a creature who had ignored him for over a hundred years?

In the end, his curiosity won out. That, or he was delaying his return to the Winter Court. Nearing the castle walls, he approached the old, royal orchard. A low wall protected it, along with a few guards, but Orion easily avoided them. Inside the orchard, servants tended the trees. They were easy enough to evade as well, thanks to the bright, afternoon sun casting plenty of dappled shadows. On the other side of these acres of tended trees, the vegetation turned wild, blending in with the forest beyond. Orion remembered all of it as if he'd just been here yesterday, though after the day his father fetched him, he'd never returned.

Orion paused at the edge of the pear trees, at the dirt path that separated these from the apples just beyond. He wasn't sure how long he stood there, staring. The entire area, including the forest beyond, was his mother's territory. Why could he not seem to move his feet?

"Orion?" an elderly man's voice called.

From the apple trees, an old man, a gardener from the looks of him, moved through the trees.

"Who are you?" Orion asked as he scanned the area for others, finding none.

"Your mother said you were coming," he said.

Orion scrutinized him, not sensing a glamour. The stranger clutched a hat in his hands, and his short, grey hair revealed only human features. If he were human, as he appeared, and his mother had spoken with him, it meant this man was his mother's chosen mate.

His half-sister's father.

Orion stepped back, instinctively closing himself off. But stopped himself. He didn't turn away; he'd done that to his dryad sister already. His heart cracked, and his throat thickened. Doing his best to allow for a sliver of his heart, he stayed. He studied the man, the faded brown of his eyes and the curve of his nose, knowing he'd never be able to study his sister. What features might she have inherited from him? Had this human helped arrange delivery of Orion's horse to Beggarton at his sister's request? If he'd once been a knight, he had plenty of contacts.

"Do you remember the way?" he asked, kindly.

"Yes." Orion could only find one word, though more questions stuck in the back of his throat.

The man nodded, the wrinkles around his eyes crinkling as he smiled. He walked past Orion several steps, his back stooped with age. He paused, looking back at Orion. "You're just as she described."

Orion looked down at himself, both his fae and dryad features hidden away, like they always were in Trinth. "How do you mean?"

"Confident. Commanding. Maybe a little frightening," he said, thoughtfully. "But also ... a little lost."

The old man put on his hat, giving Orion one last glance before walking through the pear trees.

I'm not lost.

Orion marched forward, wanting to get this visit with his mother over with. He was tempted to just leave and find the nearest dryad tree and portal wherever she took him. But he hadn't come this far to walk away. Ash darted down from the sky and landed on his shoulder.

As he neared his mother's tree, he hoped she would appear quickly. She obviously knew he was near. Her tree was unusually large, of course, with branches that extended above and beyond the others. A dissuasion spell kept humans away from this corner of the orchard, except, apparently, for one. During his childhood, Orion had rarely spied humans. Only after his father began his training did Orion interact with others.

As he neared the unusually large apple tree at the heart of the orchard, a dryad walked around the weathered trunk. Orion practically jumped as he jerked his gaze away. His heart pounded and his hands began to sweat, and suddenly he felt very, very small.

"Mother," he said, surprised. Dryads waited to be approached, not the other way around. "You wanted to see me?"

"This way." Her voice was like a lullaby, tugging at his heartstrings. His heart had grown so cold, he hadn't expected to feel anything while in her presence, but this place, her voice ... his happy childhood rushed back to him. His life had been encased in a warm bubble—just him, his mother, and the chatter of the trees.

Until she sent him away.

He followed the dryad, through the orchard to the edge of the forest. They'd played here hundreds of times, but he'd forgotten about this place until now. Ash leaned against his check and flared her wing as if protecting the back of his neck. The movement was almost like a hug and Orion wondered how much the dragon sensed his emotions.

"How is your father?" the dryad asked.

"Still the king," Orion replied, thinking of the deal struck before his birth. A business contract. Nothing more. She didn't care about Eldrin any more than she cared about her son.

"I enjoyed his visits when you were younger. I wish him well."

Obligations and opportunities. The dryad queen had put forth a request, and his mother had answered. That was all. He sucked in a breath, her words circling in his mind.

Was their relationship more complicated?

Perhaps they had cared about each other, at least for a time. Long ago, before Orion's memories formed. He'd never know for certain. His heart twisted, and he determined to have a different relationship with his own children. To always, no matter what came, openly care for each of them. He wasn't sure what that entailed, or how that worked, but he would learn.

His mother paused, her back to him. Her black hair looped down, cascading over the shallow ridges of her silvery-brown skin. Moss and mist formed her dress, which stopped at her ankles, revealing her always-bare feet. "I hope you're happy. Or at least, fulfilled."

Orion choked back his bitterness, swallowing. His stomach churned with it, turning to acid. She continued onward, thankfully not expecting a response. She paused again near a crooked tree. A memory surfaced of long, exposed roots cascading down one side of this embankment.

"I hear you are the Portal Keeper." She put a hand on the tree, this time, waiting for a response.

"Yes, I'm an invited member of the court."

"Is that what you want?" She rarely treated any situation with gravity, and he had no reason to believe this was any different.

"I've wanted a place at my father's side."

At anyone's side who actually wanted me. His thought caught him off guard, but he contained the notion before spewing his frustration. Why hadn't she ever tried to contact him? She could have sent a message to Carrus a hundred times, yet she never had. How could anyone birth a child and then throw them away?

"If that is your truest desire, I am glad for you." His mother glided down the embankment, her green, bare feet nimble and sure, and her mossy dress trailing behind.

He railed against himself for coming at all. He wanted

nothing more than to leave. Reaching out for a portal mid-conversation was rude, but Orion was beyond caring. Still, he sensed his mother had more to say. He owed it to himself not to leave prematurely; that way, he could close this chapter of his life when he left. Never return.

At the bottom of the little hill, the tree with its exposed roots hid a shallow, earthen cave. One of his favorite hideaways appeared much smaller than he remembered. Despite how he'd aged and his bitterness had hardened, returning here brought a sweet sense of nostalgia. This place—and his mother—were part of him, whether he wanted to admit it or not. In his mother's presence, he could easily stir the embers of his anger into full flames. But, why would he carry a bitter fire with other, better things in his life to nurture? Besides, Magdud was right all those months ago; dryads were relatively aloof creatures, especially with their male offspring, a defense mechanism buried inside their core nature.

"Inside," she pointed at the cave, keeping her back to Orion.

Orion stepped closer, and heard something breathing beyond the roots. "Who—or what—is in there?"

"A creature your sister sent me," she said. "From the elven Gathering."

Orion sucked in a breath, realizing it might not be his fault that his sister had lost her chance at her own territory and tree. He'd assumed that when his sister saved Ivy, at his request, that she'd been punished. But had she done more to earn her queen's ire?

"Did my sister *portal* a creature to you?" Orion clarified.

"He's not doing well," his mother said, her head tilting to the side.

Orion touched his hand to his lips, stunned that his sister had been able to portal anything at all. The Gathering trees were unsanctioned by Alysatraee, and were never meant to connect to the ley lines. Then again, his sister had created a portal between two dead trees. Despite her jovial youth, her dryad abilities were beyond impressive. Though she'd acted brashly on multiple occasions, he was forever grateful for her help. But apparently she'd sent an unknown creature to Blackmore. Had his sister sent a volatile Seeker? Why would she do that? Or had she sent an elf?

"I thought he might be important," his mother said.

At her words, his irritation flared into hot fury. His mother didn't even know the creature's identity. Yet, she had called him across the kingdom of Trinth to check on a complete stranger. She hadn't so much as offered him a "hello" for a hundred years, yet she snapped her fingers and pressed Orion to help a random creature?

His mother continued, "He might be important to Ivy."

Orion blinked, his anger suspended. Had he heard his mother correctly? "What do you know of Ivy?"

"Very little." She shifted so Orion could see part of her profile, keeping her gaze averted. "The world beyond my trees and my queen are of little consequence."

Orion sighed and turned his attention to the small cave. He shrugged off Ash, knowing the space beyond would be cramped. Moving through the branches, ready to pull his sword if a feral Seeker attacked, Orion's eyes quickly adjusted to the darkness within. A form lay on the ground, tattered and bloody, his ears marking him as elven. Not a Seeker. The gray hair, wrinkles, and thin frame indicated he was an elder elf, probably someone of prominence, based on the formal clothing. Fortunately, he still had color in his cheeks, despite his lack of response to Orion's presence.

Checking the elf, Orion noticed rapid, shallow breathing and burning fever. How had the elf survived this long? Knowing his mother, the only care she'd given him was carrying him here and never returning.

Tugging at the chain around the elf's neck, Orion found a vial with five seeds. His hand trembled, but the pity was quickly consumed with his ready anger.

"Why didn't you give him a seed?" he shouted out at his mother.

"Who am I to interfere with his choices or Alysatraee's will?" she said, her voice unnervingly calm.

Orion muttered a curse, ripping the lid off the vial. More than likely, his mother's mate had regularly brought water to this elf, not realizing the power of the seeds right around his neck. Orion lifted the elf a bit before shoving the seed down the elf's throat, massaging his neck to help him swallow.

The elf coughed, and for a terrifying moment, he didn't react to the seed. Then, the elf's muscles tensed, and his eyes flew open. He pushed away from Orion and jumped to his feet. Crouched, the elf's attention darted around the space, his stance wide, ready to fight.

"I'm a friend," Orion said, holding up his empty hands.

"A human?" the elf said, not relaxing. In fact, his shoulders seemed to tense even more.

Orion dropped part of his glamour, revealing his fae wings and truer appearance. "I'm the son of King Eldrin of the Winter Court."

The elf's nostril's flared. Making a split decision, Orion glamoured away his wings and dove through the roots. Outside, near his mother, Orion somersaulted and rolled to his feet, getting into a ready stance. The elf charged out after him, his face lined with fury.

"What happened to Ivy," the elf demanded. "Last I saw her, she was carried away by a massive tree cage along with you."

"Ivy survived!" Orion blinked, trying to place the elf. If he saw Ivy's rescue, he was one of the last elves fighting to protect the seeds of the Gathering Tree. Orion had been far more focused on Ivy than those around her. "She's fine. She's in Nylenn'or."

"Deceiver!" The elf threw a punch, and Orion dodged. Followed by another fist, and Orion barely pivoted away in time. "I sense your glamour."

Orion unglamoured his wings and maneuvered away from the infuriated elf. Though, with the dense trees, they were little help. Ash hissed from a tree, her wings flared, but Orion signaled her not to attack.

"This is why I don't interfere," his mother said, her tone as if she were commenting on dull weather.

"You're still glamoured," the elf said, his eyes narrowed.

Annoyed, Orion darted forward, provoking the elf. As the stranger kicked, Orion flew over the elf's head and grabbed him from behind. Using his leg to bring them both to the ground, Orion pinned the elf to the dirt. Even with the seed's strength, Orion leveraged his weight and the elf's arm to hold him in place.

"You're safe here, outside of Blackmore," Orion grunted between gritted teeth, hoping to calm him.

The elf stopped bucking, but his breathing was still uneven. "The last thing I remember is Seekers crushing me. How am I alive?"

"The dryad in the Gathering tree portaled you here," Orion said. "Do I need to point out that this conversation would go a lot easier if you would stop trying to hurt me?"

After a long pause, the elf relaxed a bit. "You make a good point."

Orion slowly released the elf and stood. The elf rolled to the side and looked up at Orion before rubbing the arm Orion had yanked back.

"You could go easy on an old elf," he said.

Orion took a deep breath and held out a hand, helping the elf to his feet. His sister must have conveyed this elf's importance, and his mother had protected him. In his mother's fuzzy logic, was the elf some kind of gift? A peace offering? Orion glanced around, realizing his mother had slipped away. He was surprised the recluse had stayed as long as she had, though disappointment still pricked that she had left without a goodbye.

The elf stretched his limbs, relief written all over his face as he looked up beyond the branches at the blue sky overhead. "Who can I thank for saving me?"

Orion rubbed his forehead, avoiding the complicated answer. "There's a stream not far from here. I'll take you there, but I cannot stay. I am expected in the Winter Court."

"My name is Wirenth," the elf offered, "a Seeds Ambassador. I must find others from my House. Do you know what happened after the Gathering?"

As they walked the short distance to the stream, Wirenth's eyes grew wider with Orion's every sentence. He explained what he and Ivy had learned, but with the pressure to return mounting, Orion kept the information succinct.

"You could wait here until the Centennial," Orion said. "Humans avoid this dryad's domain. I must return and coordinate the return of the Spring fae at the Accords. With the Mother's help, we'll stop the fair realm from invading Trinth."

Orion wished the ambassador well and strode deeper into the forest, Ash darting back and forth between the trees around him. His mother had few ley line connections, and none to the fair realm. Once he found a clearing, he'd fly to the nearest Winter portal.

"Orion," Wirenth called out, running up behind him. "The fair folk are invading the human realm."

"Invading Trinth, yes," Orion said.

Wirenth looked past Orion, lost in thought for a moment. "I'm afraid the truth of our realms has gotten lost to remembrance."

"What truth?"

"I think you'll trust the ancient records more than my words."

"Records?" Orion struggled to be patient. "Few places house ancient text."

"There's one place you can go that few others dare," Wirenth said, raising a brow. "Certainly not an elf."

"The Winter Court archives?"

"The very same."

Orion shook his head. He'd die of old age in that crypt, buried in a mountain of scrolls before he found whatever secret the ambassador hinted at. He didn't have time for the elf's lesson.

"I see you're reticent," the elf said. "Don't worry. I'll come with you. I know what to look for."

Orion ran his thumb and index finger across his eyes. He'd just told the old elf about Ivy's torture. Had he not been listening? "It's too dangerous."

"Trust me, there is information you need. Proof for your father that could convince him to side with you. I can help you find it."

Did the elf really know of documents that might help their cause? In order to stop the war, Winter Court had to support the new Elven Council. Orion hadn't been sure how to get his father's cooperation, and this could the answer.

Though, taking another elf to Winter would not please

Eldrin. This was such a bad idea. "Fine," Orion said. "But I'm not guaranteeing you safety."

"Fair enough. I've already cheated death once—why not tempt it again?"

28

THE FANCY BOWL

Near the rooms where advisers met with citizens and held public meetings, Ivy followed Bellas and Lial to a nondescript door. This area was generally busy with elves discussing trade, details of the law, greenhouse issues, and the hundred other concerns that made Nylenn'or palace the beating heart of the elves in the north. In the hallway, Ivy spotted two guards, and though they didn't stand next to the door, they definitely watched as the three of them entered.

But with Lial wearing Emmyth's glamour and Bellas at his side, no one questioned them as they entered an area that most Tides didn't realize even existed. The trio passed an open door to a well-appointed meeting room with eleven mahogany chairs around a sturdy table.

"This is such a bad idea," Bellas whispered, not for the first time, as they continued down the hall.

"I told you," Lial hissed, "you didn't need to come for this part. We have it handled."

"That's what I'm afraid of—your handling of the bowl," Bellas grumbled. "It's a sacred piece. I don't trust you."

"If you can't trust me, we're all in trouble," Lial whispered back.

"This, coming from an elf glamouring as a respected councilor?" Bellas snapped back.

"Stop it, both of you!" Ivy whispered harshly. Their bickering hadn't stopped ever since Lial had convinced Bellas to help them. They continued, wary of more guards—ones inevitably stationed near the bowl by Emmyth.

When Bellas had agreed to fetch the voting vessel, she quickly discovered it had been moved. This corridor was the most likely new location. And they were betting that the guards would not be privy to Emmyth's daily schedule, so they had no reason to suspect their subterfuge.

"Would the bowl be in the library?" Lial asked as they approached another set of doors.

"How did you know there is a library here?" Bellas whispered. "Wait, did your father tell you about this place?"

"Do you want to know?" Lial-Emmyth smirked.

"To see Emmyth speak, but with Lial's voice and mannerisms, is quite disconcerting," Bellas whispered to Ivy.

"I'm just glad he figured out how to get past Nym's security so he could hide the glamour in her chambers," Ivy said.

Apparently, decades ago, he'd learned to trick the spell Nym had placed on her doorway, just for a prank. He'd intended to make her break out in a mild rash when he'd swapped her soap, but it had given her hives. She'd made him do all her chores as a punishment. For a year.

She'd never changed her security rune, but Lial had never dared enter without permission again; not until he'd needed to hide the glamour. Though her rooms had been locked for months, Emmyth gave the guards access to search her quarters. Thankfully, Lial knew Nym's best hiding spots, and the guards hadn't located the amulet.

Nym's supposedly rune-locked room provided the perfect place for Ivy to hide while she'd waited for the pieces of their plan to come together. She clutched her knife to her chest at night, but at least she slept.

"The councilors' two secret offices aren't far," Bellas said. "But I suspect the councilors secured the bowl in a neutral location. There's a storage room, quiet large, at the end of the hall. If I were Emmyth, that's where I'd put it."

Once they secured the bowl, Ivy would transport it to the dungeon in a laundry basket. The elves only had their laundry done once every two weeks, and fortunately, the next laundry cleaning was scheduled for later that day.

"You know the fae rulers must *agree* to see you," Bellas said, trying to find flaws in Ivy's plan. "They can delay or use other tactics to avoid listening to you."

"They can't avoid the entire Council," Lial said. "Can they?"

Ivy whispered for them to silence. Besides, she'd already planned on the fae courts' "hesitancy."

The Summer Queen would be stuck in the Accords until her Spring attendings were delivered. Ivy wasn't worried about cornering her, but could Orion manipulate his father into bringing the Spring? Orion knew his father better than most, and Ivy trusted him to get The Council an audience with the Winter ruler.

Lial-Emmyth strode past two doors, one on either side of the hallway. Each bore intricate carvings, not unlike the ones Ivy had seen in the dwarven stronghold in the Blue Mountain. Though instead of dwarven motifs, masterfully created branches and leaves framed ocean scenes. Ahead, the hallway split, taking sharp turns in opposite directions. Bellas's gait grew stiffer, if that were possible, and she tapped Lial-Emmyth, tilting her head to the right. Lial-Emmyth stood taller and proceeded to lead, Ivy and Bellas hurrying right behind him as they turned down the hall. Two fae guards appeared, the storage room doorway just beyond.

"Emmyth," the guards gave her nods. "We didn't expect to see you."

"The councilor's schedule isn't your concern," Bellas said, signaling for the sentries to stand aside.

"We have very specific instructions," one guard said. They waited for a moment, expectant.

Then one swung into a fighting stance, the other quickly following, hands on the hilt of their short swords. Ivy's stomach dropped. Obviously, they suspected a ruse. Bellas had neglected to use some code word or signal. That, or Emmyth had commanded them to fight her—and trusting her strength, she knew she'd win.

At least the hallway was too narrow for both guards to fight at once.

Bellas folded her arms across her chest. "How dare you—"

The guards didn't wait for her to finish before one of them lunged. Ivy yanked up her dress and grabbed her knife from her thigh sheath. Pushing Bellas aside before the guard tackled her, Ivy slammed the butt of her knife into his ribs. Before he could draw his sword, Lial punched him in the gut.

The guard barely flinched, and from behind him, metal sang as the other guard unsheathed his short sword.

"Get back," Ivy growled at Lial just before she elbowed the first guard's nose. Then she stepped to the side and wrapped her arm around the guard's neck. She kicked against the wall, using the momentum to push the guard's body back. He fell, slamming into the ground.

"Take him!" Ivy yelled. Lial and Bellas yanked the semiconscious guard out of her space.

"Emmyth? I don't think so," the guard said to glamoured-

Lial before narrowing his eyes on Ivy. "You're no lowly servant, either. Who are you?"

Lial argued with Bellas behind her, but Ivy focused on the second guard mere steps away. His sword was at the ready. He spun it around, directly in front of him, showing his comfort with the blade.

But, in the hallway, he couldn't do a wide swing, even with a short sword. Ivy raised a brow. Not only did this guard have no idea who she was, he was a bit of a dunce for pulling his sword out at all; he was far larger than she was and could beat her on strength alone.

"Did you think this through at all?" Bellas snapped at Lial, exasperated. "Fortunately, *I* brought ties. Could you *at least* hold him still?"

Ivy stepped toward the second guard, and then spun to the side. As she'd hoped, he lunged, thrusting his sword forward, missing her completely. But before Ivy could land a punch, he slammed her with the side of his blade, batting her back against the wall. He moved to trap her throat with his elbow, but Ivy dropped to the ground and rolled toward the storage room. Scrambling to her feet, her back to the door, Ivy readied. Determination filled the guard's eyes as he advanced. Ivy glanced at Bellas and Lial, ensuring they had the first guard securely tied before refocusing on the immediate threat.

The second guard swung his sword in a controlled arc, aiming to corner her. Ivy parried with her knife, deflecting the blade just enough to avoid a fatal strike. The force of the clash reverberated through her arm, but she stayed light on her feet, darting out of the guard's range.

The guard alternated his sword in powerful strikes, attempting to overpower her, but Ivy anticipated his predictable strikes. Exploiting the narrow hallway to limit his movements, Ivy danced and wove, wearing him down. She ducked under a wide swing, stepping in close to deliver a quick slash to his side. The guard grunted, more in annoyance than pain, but it was a start.

He retaliated with a backhand swipe, the blade whistling past her face as she leaned back just in time. Ivy seized the moment, kicking the guard's knee with all her strength. He staggered, losing his balance for a moment. That was all she needed.

Ivy launched herself at him, her knife aimed at his sword arm. She didn't want to kill him, only subdue. The guard managed to block her attack with his forearm, the blade slicing into his flesh but not deeply enough to incapacitate him. He shoved her away, slamming Ivy into the wall, leaving her gasping for breath.

The guard charged, fury in his eyes. Ivy rolled to the side, barely avoiding the blade as it embedded in the wall where she had been standing. The guard yanked his sword free, but Ivy was already moving. She kicked at his wrist, disarming him.

The sword clattered to the ground, and Ivy sprang up, driving her knee into the guard's midsection. He doubled over in pain, giving her the opportunity to twist his arm behind his back and push him to the ground. The guard struggled, but Ivy's grip was firm, and she quickly pressed her knife to his throat.

"Know when you've lost," she warned, her voice low and steady.

The guard glared at her but ceased his resistance. Bellas bound forward with a rope, expertly tying it, even with her withered hand. Ivy jumped up and turned to the storage chamber.

Throwing the door open, she viewed three rows of shelves filled with boxes and crates, all neatly labeled. Directing Bellas to find the bowl, Ivy and Lial then dragged the guards to the small conference room, securing them to legs on opposite ends of the table. Thanks to the soundproofing, they would be hidden until the next guard rotation that evening. By nightfall, Emmyth's loyal advisers would know the bowl was missing.

Leaving the guards inside and slamming the door, Ivy leaned against the wall and wiped sweat from her brow. Bellas ran toward them, the bowl under her arm and a grin on her face.

"Let's move," Lial-Emmyth said, breathing hard as he melodramatically smoothed the wrinkles in his glamoured dress. "We don't have much time before the next guard rotation."

Even as they moved through the palace back to the dungeon, Ivy couldn't shake the feeling that their troubles were far from over. The guards had been a challenge, but Emmyth wouldn't go down so easily.

29

FATEFUL DRYAD DECISION

Floor to ceiling shelves loomed over Orion and Wirenth as they searched the archives. Ash flew from ledge to ledge, growing more impatient over the last hour.

Wirenth had skipped over the books, focusing on the dusty scrolls. He'd only put one on the table in the center of that wing of the archives. When he finally added a second, he motioned for Orion to open one parchment while he unfurled the other.

"You refer to the realm where the humans reside as 'Trinth.'" Wirenth pointed at the maps inside the scrolls. One showed Trinth, though the map extended further south than Orion had ever traveled. The second showed the expanded map of Trinth plus a map of the fair realm. "Look at the script of the ancients and how they label the realms."

The writing was a version of the fair language preferred by centaurs, but Orion deciphered the tongue well enough. Neither map referenced Trinth, but instead said, "The Human Realm." The map with both lands labeled the areas as "The Human Realm" and "Fairalyse," the latter being an ancient term for the fair realm. Along the bottom was written "Alysatraee's Love."

"Is that a title of a poem?" Orion asked.

"A title for a story of lore," Wirenth said, "which should be housed in this archive … somewhere. I'll find it. The lore expands on what these maps show."

Orion lifted a brow. "That the ancients distinguished the realms, one labeled as human and the other as fair folk?"

"It's more than that," Wirenth said. "The fair folk were to support the humans, allowing humans to rule their own realm. Predictably, the fair folk grew greedy, craving control over both. Alysatraee, in her wisdom, knew the natural inclination of our kind, and she dulled our powers in the human realm."

"That explains why fae gifts are stronger in this realm," Orion said, thinking aloud.

"The Mother foresaw the fair folk deluding ourselves into believing we could rule humans better. She's made her wishes plainly known, if we only stop to listen. So, if we invade, we are doomed. Perhaps we will win the war, but Alysatraee will turn her back on us. In the end, the fair folk will suffer for disobedience."

Ash glided from her perch and landed on Orion's shoulder, digging her claws into his shoulder. Not painfully so, but just enough to let him know she wanted to leave. Even without her prodding, Orion didn't have long until he needed to report.

Orion had made an effort to engage with servants upon his arrival, knowing word would get back to his father. A few extra days in the human realm was only a few hours in the fair realm, even so, he wanted rumors of his return to reassure Eldrin of his compliance. His father wouldn't begrudge him the scant hours, especially as Orion had departed at his father's command. Still, his father would expect an official report in a timely manner, and he undoubtedly had another assignment for Orion.

"I see you are anxious to be about your business," Wirenth said, "Do you mind if I search the rest of the scrolls? I specifically want to review anything written by centaurs. Their records appear the most detailed."

"I could send guards to protect you, but that approach was not as effective with Ivy as I'd hoped," Orion confessed. Because he hadn't resided in Winter, he hadn't built enough alliances, that much had become clear. But did he want to live here, just so he could foster relationships with the few ethical fae that wouldn't stab in him the back?

"This place is like a tomb. We've only had to avoid one apprenticed scribe, so I'm sure I'll be fine. I'm more worried about leaving. When I've found what I'm looking for, where can I safely wait for you?"

"My rooms are secure. I give you permission to enter." His words would be enough for Wirenth to open the doors. "Just ask for directions from any servant who isn't fae."

Wirenth nodded and continued his search, his elven feet moving swift and silent. Orion didn't waste time and hurried out of the archives. Just outside the door, he practically rammed into Selleth, her usual fae companions at her side.

A venomous anger flared at the sight of his sister. How dare she approach him so casually after what she'd done to Ivy? Then again, she'd probably brought her two friends as protection as much as for entertainment.

"Selleth," Orion said, knowing Wirenth would hear, and he'd disappear deeper into the archives. The room was an expansive maze.

"What are you doing here?" Selleth eyed the scroll and held out her hand. "May I?"

Orion realized he was still holding one of the scrolls. He pulled it closer, instinctively keeping anything that his sister might possibly be interested in concealed. But at the same time, he wanted Selleth to believe she knew what he'd come for.

Otherwise, she might be tempted to search the archives for clues.

Orion handed over the map, adopting a frown. Selleth plucked the scroll and unrolled it, tilting her head as she inspected the map. No sounds emanated from the archives. Between Wirenth's elven hearing and his innate stealth, his sister would never detect him, as long as Orion kept her out.

"What about this map interests you?" Selleth asked. One of Selleth's friends snickered, and Ash's body tensed on Orion's shoulder.

"If we're going to invade Trinth, we might as well have an idea of the entirety of the land mass," Orion snapped.

The giggling friend next to Selleth sucked in a breath, her eyes wide. Apparently, the coming war still wasn't common knowledge. Well, gossip was going to spread soon enough, and Orion might as well break the news.

"Well, if you're worried about your safety," Selleth grinned, rolling back up the scroll, "at least you have a lap dog in the human realm."

Heat erupted under Orion's skin, and he yanked the scroll from Selleth's hands.

"How is your elf, anyway?" Selleth said, testing Orion's patience.

He'd dearly revel in teaching his sister a lesson, but he wouldn't fall into her trap. She had two "witnesses" who would swear that Orion had attacked Selleth, leaving him at a further disadvantage for helping Ivy.

"I'm so glad Ivy saw reason and decided to align with me," Selleth continued. "I do hope she returns after the Centennial so I can put her to good use."

"Will we still have the Hundred Years Trial if we go to war?" one of her friends asked.

Selleth's face hardened, her hands clenching at her sides. "We'd better."

His father wasn't obsessed with keeping the throne, but the war would be an easy excuse to delay giving up his power.

"That's a good question for Rithmat," Orion said, referring to the king's adviser. "I must make a report. If you'll excuse me." With his suggestion and his leaving, he was confident Selleth would go running to Rithmat with her questions of legality on the competition. The perfect distraction until Orion could get Wirenth out of Winter.

Striding to his room, Orion's thoughts spun. Selleth's appearance only served to remind him that even in the Accords, Ivy was in danger. He had to keep his sister from joining the procession, which meant he needed his brother's help. Orion shook his head, hating that he needed Rime's complete compliance. He loved his brother, but following a plan did not play to Rime's strengths.

When Orion entered his room, Ash flew off his shoulder and around the space, as if reacquainting herself, before settling on her perch. Orion could only guess what the little dragon had stowed away, beyond prying eyes, high on the wall. Orion locked his door, dropped the map on his desk, and went to his bedchambers to change, but Ivy's bag grabbed his attention. He shouldn't look through her things; he didn't have time, nor her permission, and he would only miss her more. Still, he found himself holding the bag, clutching it to his chest.

It was heavier than he thought it would be, and he wondered if Ash had stowed a stolen treasure inside. But before he could look, his door opened. Surprised, Orion dropped her bag, and it clanked on the floor. No one could enter his rooms except for him and …

Orion darted into his receiving room, where his father and

two guards awaited. Orion bowed and with a flick of his hand, King Eldrin sent the guards away, leaving him and Orion alone.

"I was on my way to see you," Orion said, apologetically.

"Can a father not visit his son?" the king asked.

You never have before. Orion wasn't sure what to make of his father's visit, especially because he wasn't holding back thinly veiled anger.

"I recommended one of the fae from Winter to be promoted as the next Captain of the Night Guard," Orion reported. The fae he'd recommended had always been responsible under Orion's command, but how would he react when invaded by fair folk? That is why Orion had also recommended two other humans and strenuously pointed out their positive attributes as well.

Orion kept his voice neutral, knowing he needed to sway his father on a very important next step. The Accords. "Though we did everything according to the rules, the Aequus ceremony didn't go as planned." Orion spoke carefully, not wanting to inflame his father by blaming anyone. "I propose we mitigate the queen's ire by having a private trial and returning the Spring attendings at the Accords."

"A neutral location," the king nodded—a positive sign.

Orion had calculated that the king would prefer returning the Spring far away from prying eyes of either court. Neither court wanted the Spring accusations to be heard by the broader fair folk population. The Spring attendings were fools, yet they knew something that few others did: that the war never ended.

The warriors were rightfully angry, but they'd taken it out on Ivy, which Orion couldn't forgive.

"After the last Aequus, it might be best for you, personally, to return the warriors as a show of trust between courts." Orion held his breath, his heart thrumming. If his father agreed, he would be in proximity to the Summer Queen when the new Elven Council recommended peace. With both courts and a unified Council together, they would be bound to end the war.

"That's precisely why I must keep my distance," the king said. Orion's lungs deflated, though his father's response wasn't unexpected. "This is my children's mess, and they must clean it up. I sent a representative to the Aequus, and Selleth can act in the same capacity in the Accords."

Except Orion would never allow Selleth in the Accords. Ever.

"I found something you might find interesting." Something Orion hoped would sway his father to change his mind. Orion unfurled the map on his desk, pointing out how Trinth was originally referred to as "The Human Realm." He also explained the lore.

"So, based on a map that mislabeled Trinth and rumored lore, what are you suggesting?" The king's terse tone was a warning.

Orion realized that his father would ignore anything but a confrontation with the Council. Nothing would qualify as proof of the courts' error. His plan failing, Orion redirected his panic by releasing the map on his desk and stepping back. If Eldrin wouldn't risk going to the Accords, Orion needed an official Winter representative. Which meant, Rime had to cooperate— had to take a risk.

They had to trick Selleth out of her position.

Orion stopped himself from chewing the inside of his cheek, an old habit. "I'll send a message to the Summer Court and make the arrangements to receive their Spring attendings in the Accords."

A hint of a smile showed on his father's face before it disappeared. Was that pride in his son? Orion should've savored his father's approval, but all he felt was relief. Instead of leaving, the king looked up at Ash on the ledge overhead. The little dragon was peeking down at the scene, feeling Orion's discomfort.

"I hear you went to see your mother," the king said.

Ah, the real reason you came to see me.

"I did," Orion said, simply. What did it matter to the king? "As a new member of the court, I wanted to contact her before residing in Winter."

"You've decided to let go of your dryad nature at this juncture, then," Eldrin said, this time with the corners of his lips actually upturned.

For a moment, Orion almost agreed. Isn't it what he'd always wanted?

Or was it simply the pressure from his father, insisting his son blend in?

When stripped of his magic, Orion became keenly aware of the abilities the Mother had granted him. And while he loved shadow travel and glamours, he longed for the connection to the trees just as much.

Not hiding the turmoil inside, Orion spoke the truth his father would most appreciate, "I should keep a bit of my dryad nature. My unique abilities are of practical benefit to our family."

The king's pleased expression vanished. "You'll always be different."

"As the Portal Keeper to the human realm, retaining my remaining dryad abilities makes more sense."

"Your decision may bar you from progressing in the court to more prestigious positions."

"I'm happy with any place in your court, Father."

Accepting his true self was better than living a lie for those who would never really love him anyway. Even if only he respected himself, that was enough.

His father became silent for an excruciatingly long pause.

Instead of further pressure, he gave Orion a pitying look and put a hand on his shoulder, the most affection Orion had ever received from him. Only a fool would expect more, but Orion had planned on far less.

"I'll need you back in Unaria to keep your relationship with the duke strong," the king said, and Orion dared hope for another mission. "But not until the duke's son inherits the position. For now, stay by my side. Let Winter see our unity. Our family strength. After the Aequus ceremony, our court must trust that all my children are strong, competent leaders."

Orion straightened though inside he withered. His father hadn't revoked his title, but he wasn't officially sending him to Trinth until the next generation of Unarian leaders were in place. He felt Ivy's hand in his, slipping past his palm until he reached to brush her fingertips.

"Tonight," his father continued, "you'll visit a Sereveil household. You'll allow the tailor to dress you. You'll be on time. And you will be charming."

30
NOT TWO PHIROS

With the bowl hidden in her basket underneath clean clothing for the prisoners, Ivy made her way through the dungeon. Before the waterline dropped too far, Ivy knelt and filled the bowl. Behind her, Bellas winced, and Ivy could see why. The brackish water wasn't exactly up to the elven usual standards of cleanliness, let alone for use in a ceremony.

Hearing heavy footsteps, Ivy glanced back at Lial-Emmyth and Bellas. Not even the most uncoordinated elf *lumbered*. Ivy jumped to her feet, shoved the liquid-filled bowl into the basket, placed the thin board on top, and dumped the clothing over the board which kept the material from soaking up the fluid. Soon, an orc guard appeared ahead, wearing a flat, bored expression. Still, his presence chilled Ivy. Bellas had confessed that all orcs should have returned to Aggord, but Emmyth retained a handful, out of the view of the Nylenn'or residents.

Ivy avoided eye contact as she passed, keeping her head low. But the orc stopped Lial-Emmyth and Bellas behind him.

"I heard you'd left the palace," the orc said to Lial-Emmyth.

"Obviously not," Bellas snapped. "The councilor wishes to visit her daughter before departing."

Sweat beaded along Ivy's hairline as she slowed her pace, scanning the path for a safe place to hide the bowl. Had all the guards been warned of an Emmyth impersonator? Fighting orc trackers in a dark cave was one thing. On a narrow path where an orc warrior could see just fine was quite another. Even with Lial and Bellas's help, Ivy wasn't sure she could subdue him.

Ivy checked over her shoulder in time to see the orc give Lial-Emmyth a respectful elven nod and continue on. The color drained from Bellas face as she moved forward, her hands beginning to shake. Not able to console her in the open, Ivy quickly strode to the section of the dungeon holding the advisers.

Outside of Daecyne and Keyyarus's cell, Ivy lifted the basket to the opaque door, activating the rune three times. Then Ivy knelt and slid the clothing basket through, leaving the special-voting-bowl inside. As she suspected, anything inside the basket slid smoothly past the cell door.

"Where's my father?" Lial demanded as he ripped off the amulet. Ivy pointed at Omasys's cell as Keyyarus passed back through the basket. Lial grabbed the runed container and darted to his father, activating the door. He pressed his hand to the invisible barrier. "Father!"

Lial choked up, assuring his father he was fine as Omasys sputtered question after question. Bellas and Ivy activated the rest of the runes, allowing all the advisers and Nym to hear and see each other.

"I suggest you vote for Kolvar to replace Emmyth," Lial said. "He's been raised to take over one day. And the Tides will follow his lead."

"I agree," Nym quickly agreed.

"But Kolvar hasn't proven himself," Keyyarus said. "Has he been faithful to Emmyth or to Alysatraee?"

Bellas opened her mouth and then snapped it shut, an awkward silence following. Hearing movement right outside the archway, Ivy's heart jumped and she spun, expecting to see an angry orc. Instead, Kolvar descended the stairs into the muted area.

"Your silence tells us everything we need to know," Daecyne sneered, not yet seeing the new arrival.

"If it's not clear, blame me," Nym said, also unable to see Kol from her vantage point. "I begged my brother to keep our mother's trust so he could be in a position to stop the madness of the seed distribution. If he showed any hint of disloyalty, he'd be sidelined, just like Lial."

Kolvar lifted his gaze to meet Ivy's. Anger flashed behind his eyes, there then gone as he stepped into the tunnel, revealing himself.

Nym's jaw dropped. "Kol?"

He rubbed the top of his shorn head, dropping his attention lower. Ivy wrapped her arms around herself, discomforted by the argument he'd just walked into—centering on *him*.

"Kolvar is not his mother," Bellas said. "And he's the only one truly prepared to lead. The question is, who will be the second councilor?"

"If you'd been in a cell next to us, we might take your opinion seriously," Daecyne snapped.

"Lial," Omasys interjected. "We'd already agreed it would be him."

"I agree that Lial is a good choice," Kolvar said. Ivy and Nym both exchanged a glance, not totally surprised at how quickly Kol forgave his best friend for his part in the attempted coup. Lial hadn't told any Phiros about his father's plans, not even his best friends.

"We could vote an adviser to be the councilor," Lial said slowly, not jumping to any agreement.

Bellas shook her head. "You'll need all our votes for a majority rule. And I, personally, have no desire to be a councilor."

"Your father is right. We'd already settled on you becoming a councilor once before." Keyyarus forcibly pressed his lips together and glanced at Kolvar, then quickly away. "And it seems fitting that Kolvar should take his mother's seat."

"Fine," Lial said. "I agree. But I'm also open to your voting in someone else when this is all over."

"We must finish this quickly," Nym said. "My mother rarely wears her medallion, but last time you tried to vote her out, she had it stowed up her sleeve. She was watching it for changes. There's a chance she's still carrying it around her neck, as a precaution. The moment the medallion's light wavers, she'll know. And she'll be in the dungeon—with weapons and reinforcements."

Keyyarus picked up the bowl, dipping his fingers inside, and voted for Kolvar to replace Emmyth. Ivy found herself bouncing up and down on her heels. But Keyyarus didn't hand over the bowl when he finished.

"Something is wrong," Daecyne said. "The water didn't ripple. So, the vote wasn't cast."

"Is it because of the crystals in the dungeon?" Nym asked. "Is there magical interference down here?"

"No," Omasys said, pacing. "Magic works in the dungeon just fine."

"The guard we passed said something about Emmyth leaving the palace," Ivy said.

Bellas gasped, her eyes widening. "That's it. She's not in Trinth at all. She's in the fae realm. We can't vote out someone who isn't in the same realm with the bowl. Ethically, councilors should be informed they're getting replaced."

"Because righteous ethics helped us so much last time," Daecyne muttered.

Bellas looked down for a moment biting her lip. Then she shot her attention to Kolvar, her eyes bright. "Try replacing Mormaris with Kolvar. Let's see if that works."

"We can't" Ivy interjected, remembering her promise to Gneiss. "If we cannot replace Emmyth before the Minerals find out the Tides have two Phiros on the council, they won't work with us."

And Gneiss might hunt me down in anger. Ivy would prefer to face orc trackers than an irate-Gneiss.

Without arguing, Keyyarus changed his vote, this time voting in Lial to replace Mormaris. Daecyne quickly followed. They shoved the basket and bowl through and Bellas grabbed it, though her brow furrowed. But she tucked her hair behind her ear, seeming to brush off her thoughts, and moved the items to Lyra in the next cell.

Lyra sat on the floor next to the bowl and voted. Bellas leaned closer, her eyes trained on the bowl and the ripples. The law adviser pressed a hand to her chest as Lyra passed the bowl back through. Was Bellas having second thoughts?

On her knees, Bellas gripped the bowl, staring at it for several breaths. She looked so fragile in that moment, Ivy wasn't sure if she was about to crack. But then Bellas put her hands in the water and said, "Lial."

Passing the bowl to Omasys, he quickly voted in his son, his face beaming with price.

"Open the cells," Kolvar said softly to Lial, though his attention was still on the ground. "You have the authority."

Without delay, Lial touched the rune on his father's cell three times. Ivy held her breath, knowing the next tap should lower the barriers. With Lial's fourth touch, time stilled as the barrier held firm. Then, with a pop, the invisible wall vanished.

Lial freed all the advisers, all of them anxious to bathe and change into their usual clothing. Bellas led them out of the silent area where they'd been held for months. She gripped the bowl, her delicate face drawn in consternation. Ivy would definitely seek her out later and ensure that the law adviser would stick to the plan.

Lial moved to the last cell, pressing the rune four times. "Come now, Nym, we have much to do before the sun sets."

Stepping out of her cell, she punched Lial in the arm. Then she pulled Kol into an embrace.

"Thank you for the seed," Nym said to her brother as she released him.

Ivy waited for Kol to confess it hadn't been him. Instead, Lial glanced between the two siblings and then to Ivy. Then he simply rubbed his hands together, like a mischievous pixie. "While Emmyth is away, this cat is going to play."

"After what my mother has done," Nym said, "this cat is going to turn this place upside down."

31

THE AMBASSADOR PROBLEM

Back in his rooms, Orion had planned to prepare for an annoying visit from the tailor. Instead, Rime awaited him just outside his door. With a flick of his wrist, Orion dismissed the guards before he approached.

"Did you know there's an old elf wandering around here?" Rime asked. "I thought *surely* you wouldn't keep any more secrets from me, but then when I tracked his whereabouts, I ended up here. At your rooms. Very suspicious, wouldn't you say?"

"Good to see you, too, Rime," Orion said, pressing his hand to his door and pushing it open.

Inside, Wirenth was hunched over Orion's desk, studying the small scroll. It stretched out below his fingertips, though reading it must've been a challenge with Ash walking across it.

"So, you *do* have a secret old elf hiding out in your rooms," Rime said, following him inside. He folded his arms across his chest. Rime sounded more amused than anything, but Orion sensed his brother's quiet irritation. Orion had lost his brother's trust, and he wanted to earn it back.

"This is Wirenth, one of the Seeds Ambassadors," Orion

said, introducing the elf before turning to the visitor. "This is my brother, Prince Rime. Don't enter bargains with him or believe half the things he says."

"How very magnanimous of you to say," Rime said.

"You shouldn't use words you can't spell," Orion shrugged.

"Oh, I like that one. I'll make a note of that retort. Maybe I can use it on Selleth tonight."

"Wirenth," Orion said, changing the subject, "did you find the lore you spoke of?"

"I did, indeed," Wirenth spun the scroll around so the brothers could read it.

Alysatraee, the Mother of Magic, longed to create. So she touched the ground, and there a tree grew. One root was the sylph, another the mermaid, and many other fair creatures who took to the sea. Branches reached forth. One was the centaur, another the fae, and many more which were all the creatures of the land and air. Many children did she create, all with magic gifts imbued. She molded a realm for them, which was vast, ethereal, and as diverse as her mind could conjure, which was great.

As the eons passed, Alysatraee's creative spirit yearned for more. Once again, she reached out and touched the ground, and a new, cousin tree sprang forth. This tree was smaller but no less beautiful. Its roots and branches were all called humankind. The Mother fashioned another realm, a softer, fertile land, punctuated by a majestic range of mountains that cut to its heart.

Alysatraee cherished both her creations and desired cooperation and peace between the cousin realms. She charged the fair ones to assist their younger cousins.

And the elves she entrusted with a unique responsibility: to be the keepers of peace and live apart from their own kind. But the elves were sad to reside apart from their fae siblings. Alysatraee recognized their sacrifice, and she gifted them a reward; in exchange for watching over the humans and representing their needs to the fair ones, the Mother bestowed special gifts upon the elves—seeds.

The elves now gather at sacred trees, in special events set aside for the purpose of collecting the magical seeds. For they live a hundred years in the fae realm, but with the seeds, a thousand in the human realm. Elven longevity enables them to stabilize both realms through generational relationships and hard-won wisdom.

But as Alysatraee does, if her rules are corrupted, so too are her rewards.

"Are they talking about the humans? That we are to help those useless creatures?" Rime grimaced.

"This specifies that elves must watch over the humans and represent their needs to the fair folk in this realm," Wirenth explained. "While most fair folk are merely to stay away, the elves were charged with much more. According to this record, we have failed a number of tasks."

Everything about the realms started to make more sense. "This is why orcs can quickly grow limbs in this realm."

Wirenth nodded quickly. "Yes, because they're meant to reside with the fair folk, as defenders."

"And why our fae magic is so pathetic in the human realm," Rime added.

"The only fair folk appointed to live outside the fair realm are the elves," Wirenth added. "And we're rewarded with seeds for the sacrifice. But we're to help the humans, not conspire against them."

"And dryads," Rime added. "They can reside in either realm, can't they?"

"Yes." Orion rubbed his chin. "They can." Though, strictly speaking, they lived in ley lines between realms.

"You can take these scrolls when you meet with the

Summer Queen," Wirenth said, gesturing to the written lore and the two maps, the second one he'd brought with him. "It'll remind her majesty of Alysatraee's will. Even if Ivy is successful with the Elven Council, the queen may try to wriggle out of the law. These will serve as a stark reminder of her duty."

The proof hadn't worked with King Eldrin, but if the documents were shared publicly, they would be much more difficult to ignore.

"Too much hinges on the Elven Council." Rime folded his arms. "I don't like their odds."

"It's even more complicated than you realize." Wirenth's face saddened. "They'll need bark from a Gathering tree when they vote. And, more unfortunate, as long as I'm alive, the council cannot vote in any new members."

"But you can vote Ivy in, right?" Rime's voice caught in his throat as he realized what Orion already had.

When they escorted the Spring attendings, they would need the Winter King's permission to bring along an elf to visit the queen. Logically, he had no reason to bar a visitor, Ivy, from speaking within his domain. But it was quite a different situation to bring a surprise elven visitor in their procession when approaching the ruler of an opposing court in the Accords. The small delegation from Winter would be expected, but any extra elf would need to be approved and negotiated in advance. Otherwise, they risked not getting into the room with the queen at all.

"Can you vote Ivy in now?" Orion asked, pressing his knuckles to the desk. "I can get you bark from a Gathering Tree."

"We must be in the same realm," Wirenth said. "And ethically, she should agree to the position."

"But it's not against the rules to put her in power without her permission, right?" Rime asked.

"I don't know," Wirenth confessed. "It's never been done. I could vote her in while we are both at the Accords. But, what are the chances your father figures out who I am, and I 'disappear' to some unknown location until the war is underway?"

"The dryads know you're here," Orion said, admitting the elf had a good point. "They undoubtedly know your identity, too." But would they tell the king? Could he risk it?

"And any Winter from the war might have recognized me, too. Ialant already dedicated and lost his life trying to stop this war," Wirenth said, resigned. "We can't risk me getting caught. You both seem nice enough, but can you really protect me? No, I've thought this through, and the Council cannot vote Ivy in if I still live. This is the best solution."

A heavy silence fell on them as they all stared down at the scrolls. There had to be some other way.

Wirenth put a hand on Orion's shoulder. "Your family has already done so much for me. I'm so sorry."

"This is messy business," Rime grumbled. "But leave it to me. I have a plan. I'll take care of everything."

32

WYVERNS AND MINERALS

Ivy slipped away before dawn, desperate to be away from the bustle of the castle and the constant pressure to make their plan work. She stood alone on the cliffs overlooking the northern channel. The grey, choppy water extended beyond Ivy's sight line. Despite the summer season, cold wind gusted up from the water and up the rocky cliffs. Ivy shuddered, pulling her cloak tighter.

At sunrise, she heard Nym approach.

"I can't believe we're trusting Lial's plan," Ivy said to Nym.

"The only upside to this *not* working is an opportunity to rub it in his face," Nym said, moving to stand at her side.

"A poor consolation if we're all sitting in the dungeon."

"Trust me, the crystal dungeon will be a holiday compared to whatever my mother would have in store for us."

Ivy shuddered, and not because of the cold breeze coming off the water. As the sun rose, they searched across the waves, hoping to see the Minerals.

"I can't stay long," Nym said, slipping on the glamour and lowering her voice to match her mother's tone. "Emmyth has meetings she cannot miss."

"Your impersonation is uncanny."

"I'll take that as a compliment."

Ivy smirked and continued scanning the water. She chewed her lip, calculating, again, how long traveling from Carrus to Nylenn'or would take. "The Minerals advisers should arrive any day."

Nym didn't know where the local dryad portal was located. Yet. But even if she did, it'd be too late for Lial to travel and prod Gneiss to overthrow their councilors. They were relying on Lial and Nym-Emmyth and their massive changes to cause enough uproar for gossip to spread from Mormaris or another elf, alerting all the elves in Trinth, including Gneiss.

"There's no way for Gneiss to know that it's not my mother making all these changes," Nym said. "She may not come at all."

"We can't think that way," Ivy said. "Gneiss must know that our situation is suspicious, at the very least. Plus, she's been wanting an authority change for decades. I don't think it would take much to push her into taking the leap."

"So, we're trying on our positivity caps. Good to know." Nym gave her a half-grin. "Maybe they'll arrive via the dryad portal?"

"Perhaps, but I don't think the dryad in Carrus has direct access to Nylenn'or."

Orion hadn't suggested the Carrus dryad as an option when traveling to meet with Nym, so the local Nylenn'or dryad didn't connect with Carrus ... at least not directly. With Orion, the dryads did whatever was necessary, even if it meant multiple portal jumps. For councilors, she wasn't sure they would be so accommodating.

Lial jogged out to meet them, his face flushed, "Emmyth is sleeping in today? No one has seen her in the castle this morning. Perhaps she's ill? Because she *never* sleeps past sunrise."

"Emmyth is feeling rather sick." Nym fake-coughed into her hand. "Leave me alone."

Lial lifted his hands. "Don't be angry with the messenger."

"He's right," Ivy said, elbowing her friend. "The servants will inform us when wyverns arrive. We don't have to watch the waters all day." But she would return after lunch, just in case.

"Wait," Lial said, pointing out across the channel. "Is that two riders?"

Nym spun and narrowed her gaze, as did Ivy. Not seeing anything, they both scanned the waters again. When Lial laughed, Nym punched him in the arm.

"You are ridiculous, you know that, right?" Nym threw her arms in the air and marched toward the palace.

"This will get her into the proper mood for acting like Emmyth in the meetings today, don't you think?" Lial wagged his eyebrows at Ivy.

Ivy made a face at him and shooed him away. Nym was halfway up the rock embankment, muttering about how he should be more worried about mastering his magical authority.

"Have you figured out how to unlock Emmyth's secret office?" Ivy asked.

"Some of the magic is a little tricky. I'll see if Kolvar can go with me next time and give me some tips." Lial winked, and then did an exaggerated double-take out at the water, pointing. "They're arriving!"

Ivy smacked his hand away, weary of his constant teasing. Even so, she looked across the channel. She didn't spot anything in the air, but she did spy a boat in the water.

"Nym!" Ivy shouted. "Nyyyyym!"

It wasn't long until the boat came close enough for the elves to identify the passengers—orcs. The first unit was arriving.

"Do you recognize their captain?" Nym asked.

"It's not Magdud, unfortunately," Ivy said, hoping she

would arrive soon. "Are you ready to trick them all into thinking you're Emmyth?"

Nym shifted her voice again, sounding exactly like her mother. "But of course, peasant. Now, go fetch the venison."

Lial snorted, but before he could add a snarky comment, Ivy spotted three wyverns, mere specks in the distance.

"It's our lucky day, councilors," Ivy said, pushing her sight and seeing the red-headed elf. "The wyverns will be here much sooner than the orcs, so that gives us time to plan."

A half-hour later, Nym and Lial met Gneiss and an older elf in the wyvern stables. The third wyvern held Zel, who had ridden in a special sling contraption underneath the wyvern's belly. Ivy scurried to help the sleepy gnome from his bed-like sling, the mask still resting across his eyes. Gneiss jumped off her wyvern, a smug expression of superiority in the quirk of her brow.

"The gnome insisted on coming," Gneiss said, annoyance lacing every syllable. "He's not fast on his feet or comfortable on a horse. So traveling was a real treat. And then he took an herb that knocked him out for the ride here. So I'm glad one of us is well rested."

The other elf, someone Ivy had never met, slid off, his face a little green.

"I know how you feel," Nym said, locking her arm through his. "I'll walk with you to the palace."

"Bless you," he said, but he waited for Gneiss.

"You're looking at the new Minerals Councilors," Gneiss announced, strutting around her wyvern.

I'm not surprised, Ivy thought, keeping her sarcasm to herself. Though Ivy found Gneiss abrasive, she was well liked among her House, and they needed the Minerals' cooperation.

"Congratulations," Ivy said to them both as stable hands took the reins of the beasts.

Gneiss bowed with a flourish. She straightened, giving them both serious looks. "So, we came here hoping the rumors of Emmyth still sitting on her throne of power were a lie. Please tell me she's been relegated to some dark hole." She turned to Nym. "No offense."

"Only a little taken," Nym said, her tone a bit irritated. "She's in the fair realm, hiding. Which means we need to draw her out. Don't worry, the plan is already in place."

"I look forward to hearing every detail," Gneiss said.

Nym turned, still keeping a solid grip on the elder Mineral as they walked out of the stable. "Of course."

Ivy suppressed a grin as she guided disoriented-Zel toward the palace. Gneiss wanted to know every detail of the plan, yet she would only get a few. The less she knew, the better. And if Gneiss figured out their ruse, there would be hell to pay.

33

KOLVAR'S FIGHT

Kolvar paced in his office, the room feeling more like a prison than his protected, quiet space. After a restless night, Kolvar waited for Nym to visit that morning with an update to her plan. But he waited in vain, his only company the swirl of his own thoughts.

Bellas had suggested that Kolvar spend time in his chambers when he wasn't with guards. Now that Mormaris had lost his councilor seat, he would be seeking revenge. And Kolvar could be his first target. Mormaris sometimes acted without thinking and then scrambled to avoid consequences later.

Kolvar's office balcony, which was barely more than a ledge, had been installed with magicked spikes. The sickly green sheen warned off anyone who wished him harm. The only outside access to his rooms was a window, too narrow for even a youngling to squeeze through.

Kolvar's stomach twisted with worry. What if the plan didn't work? Perhaps Nym had leapt into trouble not fully aware of the consequences. But he'd seen The Hand up close, its devastating effects to Nym. Shoving away his dark thoughts, he focused on what he knew for certain. With Omasys, the advisers had a majority. Though, he assumed the captain of the guard was still loyal to Emmyth.

Rock debris cascaded past his narrow window, catching his attention. Startled, he spun in time to see two legs drop into view. Then a body, followed by Mormaris's face.

"Councilor," Kolvar gasped as Mormaris pushed open the window. The councilor had made himself scarce over the last two days, and Nym had wondered if he'd fled. Kolvar had known he wouldn't be that lucky.

"Thank the Mother you're here," Mormaris said, "The captain informed me of your situation. What a disaster! Why did your mother replace me with idiot youngling Lial? And why put the advisers who supported her into the dungeon, all except for Bellas."

Mormaris's words indicated that their ruse had worked, and he believed Kolvar to be as much of an outcast as himself. It had been a risk for Kolvar to be at Lial's side, but Nym-Emmyth had publicly ordered the guards to keep her brother from flee-ing. For all Mormaris knew, the spikes trapped the occupant inside rather than protecting him.

Kolvar took a step closer, playing along. "The person on the throne isn't the real Emmyth. Last I saw her, she was leaving the realm."

"I knew it! I tried to tell the guards, but they wouldn't listen."

"My sister has a glamour. She's the impostor." Kolvar had dreaded facing Mormaris, but perhaps this situation would work to his advantage.

"Lial stole my councilor seat," Mormaris growled.

"Did you see the medallion glow in his hand?" Kolvar asked, curious if anyone had caught on to his mother's ruse. The one he'd gone along with.

"Apparently, he doesn't need to prove anything," Mormaris

spat. "With your pseudo-mother, four advisers, and Omasys backing his claim, no one dares question Lial's authority."

Horror and pride vied inside him. Horrified at how easily an impostor could take control and pride in that everything was unfolding exactly as his mother had predicted.

"The palace is in chaos," Mormaris said. "Without the Steward Adviser, the basic functions of this place are in disarray."

"Don't worry too much," Kolvar assured him. "Both Tides councilors must agree to vote in new advisers. Without Emmyth, they cannot make any changes."

Mormaris shook his head. "There is more than one loop-hole, which Bellas has pointed out. They're actively planning to replace the two longest acting advisers. Not the eldest elves, but the ones who have been advisers for over two hundred years. Technically, no one is supposed to be an adviser that long, but during the war ..."

Kolvar frowned. His sister hadn't mentioned the plan. It was a good one. Nym was implementing their mother's strategy: to give "suggested names" to the advisers for consideration —all whom disliked Emmyth. Soon, two of Emmyth's remaining three loyal advisers would be gone, replaced by elves loyal to ... anyone else. She'd lose control of the advisers. Which meant, Emmyth's plan would fall apart.

Emmyth had planned for Kolvar and her to rule the Tides. Ever since his childhood, she'd prepared him to become a leader. But, if she only had one loyal adviser remaining, she'd lose her position. In fact, the new advisers would be waiting for her, like snow cats ready to pounce on their prey.

"Can you reach Emmyth?" Kolvar took another step toward Mormaris. From this angle, he noticed the rope at his waist. How far had he dropped?

"In the fair realm?" Mormaris's nostrils flared, and his jaw flexed. A trained warrior with a large build, Mormaris would be a formidable foe. Kolvar felt selfish relief that his sister hadn't found the disgraced councilor and revealed that Kolvar had conspired to steal his position, too. Mormaris faced Kolvar, frowning. "The dryads won't respond to me now that I no longer carry the magical authority."

"We must send a message to Emmyth before my sister controls the advisers. If Emmyth returns too late, the new advisers will vote to remove her. She'll lose her seat the moment she returns to our realm." Kolvar took another step closer. "It's now or never."

Mormaris's hand shot through the narrow window, wrapping his fingers around Kolvar's throat. "Very convenient of Emmyth to flee the realm without me. If this is a trick, Kolvar, you will not live long enough to regret it."

Kolvar strained to suck in a breath, but couldn't. Panic spiked, and he struggled to shake his head. Mormaris squeezed a bit harder, and Kolvar struck Mormaris's elbow attempting to break it. But his arm didn't budge.

Mormaris released Kolvar, and he stumbled back, gasping for breath.

"No trick," Kolvar more mouthed the words than spoke them, his throat refusing to comply.

An object—about the size of his palm—flew toward Kolvar's chest. Reacting, he knocked it out of the way, and the curved metal smacked against Kolvar's hand.

And the object glowed. Just for a moment, lighting brighter, before it diminished as it clattered on the ground.

Mormaris's medallion. All the councilors had one. Of course, the Mormaris had hidden his. Emmyth unsuccessfully schemed to find it before she left.

"No tricks?" Mormaris's chest heaved, his teeth bared through the slit window. Kolvar's heart thumped, and he feared

Mormaris would risk the poisoned spikes and burst into his chambers. "Neither of the elf leaders have any real authority. So how did they release the advisers? How do they do *anything* unless you're aligned with them?"

Kolvar swallowed, his throat burning. With his windpipe spasming, he was unable to explain how he'd reported Ivy's presence to his mother. And Emmyth had thought through every conceivable plan Ivy might conjure. Instead of guessing which adviser might turn on her, Emmyth employed an orc to rune the bowl. The orc had little knowledge of the sacrilege, and had even less difficulty scratching the symbol on the bottom of the voting apparatus. Any vote cast in the bowl changed to Kolvar's name. If anyone had been paying close attention to the ripples, they would've noticed the inconsistency. All Tides children were taught to read the ripples in the water, but they were all too anxious to escape to notice.

What else did they miss in their duties? They all needed to be replaced when the time came.

"Nym and Lial don't know." Kolvar touched his throat, the skin hot. He'd have bruises tomorrow. "When I *advise* Lial what to do, I word it carefully to give him permissions, which lends him the authority to perform the action." Kolvar's words mattered, but so did the intention. Just like his mother's word allowing him to cross the abyss of The Hand, Kolvar's words enabled Lial to access prison doors, locked cabinets, and anything else necessary. So far, his old friend hadn't noticed anything amiss. "All three of us, including you, will land in the dungeon once the deception is uncovered. We need Emmyth."

"You stole my power!" Mormaris grabbed the edges of the window, jutting his face forward. Kolvar stumbled back, startled.

"Surely you realize that under the law, you will earn a harsh sentence for your part in colluding to continue the war," Kolvar said, attempting to reason with Mormaris. The advisers would take revenge for being thrown into the dungeon by demanding the fullest punishment for the councilors. "All your friends," Kolvar tried to steady his words, "they'll distance themselves from you and Emmyth. Even the captain of the guard."

Mormaris growled, his teeth bared again. Then he pursed his lips and turned his face away, squinting out at the mountains. Kolvar wanted to assure him that he'd only taken his power to safeguard it from Lial, but would the words taste like a lie? Mormaris could always spot a liar. Finally, Mormaris faced Kolvar, his eyes narrowed.

"I'll get a message to the Summer Court. A letter is all I can manage, and I don't know how long it will take until the dryad accepts it. But I'll do it." Mormaris gripped the ledge, his muscles flexing as he prepared to climb. "The three of us are in this together. For now. But watch your back, youngling. This isn't over."

"There's a wyvern somewhere in the woods," Kolvar said. "If the beast is still here, and you are compelled to leave the north, the beast is your escape." If Kolvar was trapped in Nylenn'or, Ivy would be, too. "Ivy Balrel used it as transportation to get here. She's the reason Nylenn'or is in an uproar."

"A troublemaker, like her father." Mormaris's face darkened, "If I find her, I'll end her myself."

34
NOT EXACTLY A LIE

Orion half-heartedly played a game in a field surrounded by a manicured garden at the latest festivity, this one honoring some Witherthorn family. Someone hit a ball, spiraling it in his direction. Orion flew up and caught it, barely feeling it in his fingers, his entire body still numb after his conversation with Wirenth. Across the field, Rime gave him an extra big smile, attempting to remind him to not resemble, what he called, "an angry dwarf."

From the air, Orion forced what he thought was a pleasant expression, but by Rime's grimace, he'd clearly failed. Glancing around the garden, Orion counted the number of guards stationed between the perfectly appointed garden and the wild forest. Thirty. Too many guards for a casual party. Orion threw the ball back to the pitcher at the center of the field, more than ready to leave.

When the game finally ended, Rime showed up in record time with two wine glasses in hand.

"I appreciate the drink," Orion said.

"What?" Rime smirked. "These are both for me. I'm just pretending to share. Obviously."

"I need you to keep your wits about you," Orion snapped.

"I've been thinking about tonight," Rime said. "I don't think I'm the best choice to replace King Eldrin. I'm not Winter Court Representative material."

Orion nearly barked at Rime and punched him in the face, but instead he forced his fury down and kept his voice steady. "With any luck, Ivy will be at the Accords. Would you condemn her by allowing Selleth to find her?"

"I know you care about Ivy, but she's not who you imagine. Love has blinded you to her true nature." Rime gulped down one of the goblets. "I don't think we should help her."

"Ivy sacrificed herself to protect my relationship with *you*," Orion said to defend her, but Rime's eyes glazed over.

"Or is that what she wants you to *think*?" Rime asked.

Orion shook his head, reminding himself of all the reasons he should not pummel his brother. Ivy had sacrificed herself to help Rime, but he couldn't recognize it for his pride. And Orion's avoidance of officially aligning with his brother for the competition for the crown hadn't helped. As with all fair creatures, Orion had the option of not publicly aligning with any of the competitors. And if Orion threw his support behind Rime, who was extremely clear about not wanting to win anyway, he'd become Selleth's next target. More and more, Orion simply wanted peace within his own family.

Changing tactics, Orion appealed to the greater good. "When you act as the Winter representative, you'll be helping the realms avoid bloodshed. Isn't that reason enough?"

"Selleth will follow the law. She won't even know she's stopping a war when she returns the attendings. If she thinks I've tricked her out of 'her place of honor,' she might focus her icy claws in my direction. Why would I do that? Besides, I've already helped you out with one elf today."

"It's done then," Orion asked, thinking of Wirenth. His heart twisted, thinking of the selfless elf. He'd suffered terribly since the Gathering and healed only long enough dive into the fair realm, aid with their cause, and offer himself up as a martyr.

Rime nodded. "It wasn't pleasant. You owe me. Oh, and the old elf reminded me to tell you to fetch that tree before you go to the Accords." Rime flashed a fake smile at someone behind Orion and lifted his glass as he muttered under his breath. "You should mingle. If Eldrin finds out how sullen and reclusive you've been, you'll never hear the end of it."

"Rime," Orion said, ignoring his brother's comment, "you must stand up to Selleth or forever be subservient. You plan to allow her to beat you at the Trials, which I understand. But if you never push her at all, she'll walk all over you. Do you really want to be crushed under her heel with her every step once she's queen? Or do you want to be her respected ally in the court?"

Rime slammed his empty glass on a tray as a brownie passed by. Then, spinning to face his brother, he spoke through gritted teeth. "Fine. I'll go. But we're inviting Selleth into *your* chambers. Mine are a mess, and she's been anxious to get another look inside your rooms. She'll definitely come, if only to analyze your surroundings for weaknesses."

Great. He'd have to let the conniving snake into his rooms. But Ivy was worth the risk.

After suffering through small talk and gossip from a couple of fae, Rime finally agreed to leave. The moment they were back in the Winter citadel, Orion sent word with a servant for Selleth to meet with him in his rooms.

He shut the door to his bedchamber, closed every cabinet, and slid all the items off his desk into a drawer; no reason for her to see anything more than necessary. The princess arrived in his study in record time, the guards announcing her presence.

When Selleth entered, a wave of bitter anger washed over him. Clutching his hands behind his back, he dug his fingernails into his palm, focusing on the pain rather than on how much he wanted to punish his sister. He doubted his reaction to her would ever change. The memory of Selleth taunting Ivy on the medallion was forever seared in his memory.

"I did the boring work you dislike and arranged to meet the Summer Queen at the Accords and deliver her attendings," Rime said. "Their trial is done—if one could call it that. King Eldrin barely questioned them."

Selleth's attention roamed across the room, skimming past his clean, over-sized desk and the double doors to his balcony. Above the empty fireplace, her attention traveled up the stone wall to the little, cushioned perch. When her gaze met with Ash's above, the dragon glided down, landing on Orion's shoulder, in a defensive position. Selleth scoffed, but ignored the little creature. "Why am I here? The attendings don't deserve a royal escort."

"I could go as the representative," Orion offered, pretending he didn't want to punch her. "I'm barely a royal."

"Sorry, brother," Rime said, rejecting his offer. "It must be Selleth. She was the representative before, and she needs to smooth things over with the queen and her golden child, Devain."

Selleth's frown echoed Orion's reaction. Why was Rime pushing for Selleth? That's not what they'd planned.

"I'll do no such thing," Selleth snapped. "You'll go, Rime. And I'll owe you no favor for it." She flicked her hands in the air as if the room itself disgusted her. Turning on her heel, she sauntered out without another word.

When the guards shut the doors behind her, Orion spun on his brother, furious. "What was that?"

"It doesn't feel good, does it," Rime said, sarcastically. "Being left in the dark while your brother strategizes without telling you. It's like you're stumbling blind and then getting hit on the side of the head with a log."

Orion blinked, utterly frustrated. It was one thing to keep potentially dangerous secrets about himself, versus not coordinating a plan involving their sister. "Call it what you want, but you had no reason to toss out our plan the moment Selleth walked in."

"Oh, don't throw a tantrum. I knew she would never willingly grovel, even to a queen," Rime said. "Especially if I suggested that's what the Summer expected. And I couldn't have her thinking I wanted to go. She would have fought me. Now she thinks I'm her compliant little kitchen brownie."

"That's not exactly what I had in mind when I said you should stand up to her." Orion frowned, though he had to admit that Rime's ploy worked.

"Why brave a fight when I can relax and quietly manipulate? It's less deadly that way. Besides, I'm not the one who will be tricking our family into getting what I want, will I? No, you're the only one in any real danger."

Orion turned his back on Rime, not wanting his brother to know how much his words unnerved him. He was risking everything for an elf who could never be by his side in the fair realm. Yet, he'd do it all again in a heartbeat ... hence Rime's warning. How blind was Orion when it came to Ivy? How much would he live to regret?

35

SUMMER DOLDRUMS

Emmyth lingered in the Summer Court gardens, already bored. With the queen leaving for the Accords, Emmyth had little to do. Left with her thoughts, she imagined what was happening at home.

Kolvar had dreaded putting Ivy in prison, but surely he understood that the Tides needed that meddling elf out of the way until the war began. After the fighting started, the fair folk would care far less about the use of the seeds, especially if they helped the orcs more easily take down their targets.

Emmyth paced, hating that she had no idea what was happening in Nylenn'or. She paused next to a hedge of flowers and reminded herself that her son needed time to get things back in order. She gripped a stem, ripped out a flower, and began plucking its petals. Each moment infernally stretched, and she kept glancing for a servant, hoping for news.

At her feet, petals littered the ground. She took a breath, chastising her impatience. Of course Kolvar couldn't contact her until after the Accords, well after the danger had passed; the council's window of opportunity to approach the queen must be closed before he messaged her.

Throwing the stem down next to the torn petals, Emmyth marched back toward the castle. At the very least, she could prepare her belongings in case Kolvar sent word for her today. No guards walked beside her or guarded her rooms, nor did formal and informal meetings take up her every waking moment. She wasn't quite sure what creatures did with themselves if they weren't running a city. Before she entered the castle, a servant rushed to intercept her.

"Emmyth Phiro," she said, a slight question in her voice as if she wasn't completely sure who the elf was standing in front of her. Emmyth nodded and the servant continued, "This arrived for you."

The Tides seal stared up at her before the servant flipped her wrist, revealing Emmyth's name inked across the front. But the script wasn't by Kolvar's hand, it was in Mormaris's.

She held the letter, expecting a threat or promise of retribution. Perhaps she needed a guard at her door. Finding an empty section of the garden with a "message station" for visitors, she ripped open the letter and found a warning.

Emmyth,

> *Nylenn'or is not as you left it. Lial and Nym, with the help of a glamour, sit on our councilor seats. Bellas betrayed us and helped free the five traitors from the dungeon, including your daughter.*
>
> *Kolvar is as resourceful as you'd hoped and has secretly tricked everyone and secured my councilor seat.*
>
> *I have lost my authority, and you are to blame. But for now, our fates are intertwined.*
>
> *Lial and Nym are preparing to replace our two most loyal supporters: the adviser of trade and the adviser of philosophy.*

You know what this means. The usurpers will have enough support to keep them in power indefinitely.

You must return before we are outnumbered.

—Mormaris

Emmyth read the letter again, her anger mounting. She'd planned for every possibility, every contingency. Yet, Ivy had ruined everything. Mormaris hadn't mentioned her, but this mess had "Balrel" written all over it. Ivy must've convinced Bellas to enforce the outdated law.

She threw the letter onto a metal tray, tipping a vial until a single drop hit the parchment and set it aflame. Staring at the parchment as it was consumed by heat and burning embers, Emmyth reminded herself that the queen's goals were aligned with the council. She'd already given Emmyth permission to stay in Summer. The new Elven Council would never be realized as long as Emmyth hunkered down in the fair realm.

Stifled by the humidity and the rising sun, Emmyth stormed through the gardens. Between the heat and imagining all the ways Nylenn'or could be dismantled in her absence, she blindly fumed as she looked for a shady reprieve. Turning a corner, she slammed into a satyr. Stepping back, she readied to teach him a lesson.

"Excuse me," the satyr interrupted with a grin. "I wasn't paying enough attention."

Emmyth blinked, and she realized she'd stumbled into an entire group of fair folk who were practically dancing through the gardens. A stone structure and tall hedges blocked her view of their destination, but the creatures were clearly lining up to enter the Accords. Some played wind instruments and others told loud stories as the group slowly moved forward. All the vapid Summer creatures seemed giddy at the thought of exploring the temporary realm for the day. Emmyth spun around without a word, headed for her temperature-controlled room, annoyed by the festive mood so at odds with her writhing fury.

A few paces away, Emmyth stopped short and stared at the castle entrance. Though masterful paintings with gilded edges covered the walls and servants attended her every wish, Emmyth dreaded staying cooped up in this place. The situation in Nylenn'or was spinning out of her control. They were all standing on a pivot-point in time; a wrong move could send the elves down a path of no return. Could she leave their fates in the hands of inexperienced Kolvar and impotent Mormaris?

If she stayed, the advisers would be switched out, loyal to Nym and that boot-licking Lial. But if she returned, she had a chance to wrestle back Nylenn'or and guide the Tides down the difficult, but better, path.

If threats wouldn't work to win back Bellas, a reward would work on Daecyne. He'd always wanted more authority for his family, which Emmyth still held the power to grant. And if Omasys wanted Lial to have the second councilor seat, she'd allow that concession. For a short time.

Eventually, she and Kolvar would govern, as planned. She could sway her son far more easily than a slew of selfish advisers.

Emmyth started for a dryad portal. Crossing the meadow of wildflowers, she neared the forest. Realizing that the boisterous fair folk had quieted, she paused. Turning, the manicured gardens still in sight, Emmyth pushed her sight back to the crowd.

The Summer Queen had emerged from the palace, and everyone bowed in deference. Even from a distance, Emmyth felt a discomforting wave of warmth roll across the grounds. The queen promenaded through her subjects, stopping frequently to allow them to kiss her hands. Emmyth shook her head at the pomp. Still, Emmyth knew to look beyond the ruler's shallow displays of beauty and frivolity, and at the deceptively clever manipulations beyond.

No, Emmyth couldn't stay here—the recesses deep in her mind warned that this wasn't her domain. She didn't control this land, and the queen could alter everything with a flick of her wrist or a single word. Emmyth turned toward the dryad portal again. But then, she stopped and took a breath. Why run headlong into trouble? Rushing was a recipe for disaster.

Clutching the medallion at her neck, Emmyth verified that it still glowed. She held Alysatraee's power. As long as she stayed in Summer, she would not be unseated.

Another thought, one that had never left but that she refused to examine: seeds. Here in the fair realm, they wouldn't work. Elves' natural lives in the fair realm were far shorter, a mere hundred years, give or take a decade. But in the human realm, with the seeds, Alysatraee extended elven lives tenfold. Would she rather live another thirty years in the fair realm, or three hundred in Trinth?

Emmyth's hands curled at her sides, her nails digging into the flesh. She never expected anyone to fight her battles. Such thoughts always led to disappointment. She always looked after herself. She had to protect the Tides. She had to help the fair creatures take back what belonged to them. Their lands, that the humans had taken, were just out of reach.

But she couldn't do anything from a distance.

If she returned home, she had to be clever. Only she and Mormaris knew the dryad portal location. But, had Ivy's meddling dryad rescuer discovered it? Would guards be waiting to capture her on the other side?

Emmyth chewed her lip, and in her periphery, the Summer creatures gushed over their queen. She felt more distant than ever from the fair court and their ways, an outsider. Her instincts urged her not to stay. But she wouldn't charge home, either. Could she find passage with another dryad portal to the mainland, and ride a wyvern home?

No, that wouldn't work. Once she portaled to Trinth, she'd have little time. She might have less than an hour to gather her advisers, turn that whining Daecyne to her side, and steal back the bowl. She itched for her staff, her favorite fighting tool. But she left the instrument at home, avoiding any hint at aggression when she entered Summer.

Emmyth lifted her gaze, taking a breath. From this angle, Emmyth watched the fair creatures exit the other side of the stone structure and enter a hedge maze, too tall for Emmyth to see beyond. The curious portal to the Accords swallowed up more and more visiting Summer.

She faced the forest again, and another idea began to form.

36

BAIT FOR A SUMMER QUEEN

After sunrise, Orion used his magic to raise a staircase of snow out of the smooth marble floor, elevating him up three stories to the Spring attendings' cell. A long row of cells lined the upper wall, plus another level much higher. As he neared, the bars, made of iron and ice, vanished.

As a thank you for his release, Alion threw a punch at Orion. Orion dodged, grabbed the fae's arm, and used his momentum to send him flying. Before Alion plummeted, Orion leapt out, unfurling his wings, and plucked his sorry, dimwitted carcass from the air. On the floor below, the Winter guards pulled their swords from their sheaths, a warning. Rime, a few steps away, brushed the front of his already perfectly-pressed coat.

"I'm escorting you home," Orion snapped to Alion. Though he knew the attending's short-sighted insult was more a projection of his frustration than an attack on him.

The Winter guards stepped forward, their shadows gathering, but Alion lifted his hands in subjection. Most of the royal guards shadow traveled; the gift was practically a requirement to protect the king's children. Above on the steps, Alyssum allowed another fae to escort her down. Though, her compliance may not have been by choice; she needed the support of her Winter escort. As the ice under her feet stayed slick, for the Winter, the frosty surface melted to a rough, stone stair, easily navigated.

Even though the Spring acted submissive, when he and Alion landed, Orion shoved the Spring forward, indicating he wasn't a weakling to control.

"Restrain them," Rime said, spinning on his heel. "Let's go."

Two guards marched behind Rime as he led the procession out of the dungeon while two others tied both Springs' hands behind their backs and blindfolded them. Once secured, they followed the procession through an ice-covered door. Orion and a Winter guard, the second attending, took up the rear, the nine of them heading for the Accords.

As they exited the dungeon, Orion grabbed a nondescript sack just outside the door and threw it over his shoulder. No one would notice the missing sapling until too late. And with it "lost" in the Accords, no one would know who'd taken it nor where. The king would be furious, but he wouldn't make a public example of Orion as the tree was never supposed to have entered the fair realm. And when the private confrontation came, Orion was prepared to point out the records Wirenth had shown him.

Orion tapped the bag, confirming the stiff leather scroll cases were still there, along with Ivy's satchel. Perhaps bringing her things was a fool's errand with no guarantee that he'd see her; still he longed to be near her, wanting her reassuring presence. The only thing he couldn't bring were her bow and arrows, which he lamented, but they drew too much attention. He might have tried except Rime's comment rankled. Orion had to admit that he'd acted rashly on multiple occasions, usually for reasons tied to protecting Ivy. But Ivy would want him to be strategic, not ruining his life unnecessarily.

Rime did have reason to worry. Since Orion met Ivy, he'd changed. He had walked a fine line between his fae father's expectations and protecting the humans he'd started to care for after serving them for so decades. Helping to destroy the orchard, leaving Winter without permission, and now stealing a sapling ... his actions helped humanity, not the fae.

Orion felt right about all his efforts, but he'd never dared irritate his father before, let alone go against him like this. And now, he was poised to lose everything if their plan unraveled at the Accords.

The guards guided them past interrogation rooms, storage closets, an infirmary, and barracks. The slippery, ice-coated floors made prisoner escape almost impossible. Of course, the ice melted before Winters' feet hit the floor, as long as they had the king's permission to be on that lower level. As they climbed the stairs, the ice disappeared completely. On the main floor of the citadel, they made their way to a small ballroom, only used for small affairs—which was rare.

Outside the ballroom, an astronomer silently signaled to Orion and Rime to wait and then she pointed to the hourglass. They needed to go through the portal in a quarter hour, no earlier. Besides, the two Winter servants and a specialized centaur guard hadn't yet arrived. Unfortunately, Orion had to leave Ash behind; if he glamoured, the dragon's attention would signal his identity.

"What's going on?" Alyssum asked. The twins were still restrained and blindfolded, which the king had insisted upon; there was no good reason to reveal the access point to the Accords in the Winter realm. Other courts didn't hide their portals, but Winter had their own rules.

"I'll get you home safely," Orion assured her.

She didn't relax, but at least she didn't put up a fight.

Rime pulled Orion off to the other side of the corridor,

leaving the Spring in the hands of the other guards. Even so, Orion didn't take his attention off of them.

"Are you sure you want to lead this little rebellion," Rime asked quietly. If Orion didn't know better, he'd say his brother sounded a bit pained, perhaps genuinely worried. "There's still time to change your mind."

Orion's mind slipped to Ivy, and he knew he'd do anything to support her. He put a hand on his brother's shoulder, his resolve firm. "If our trickery works, we will save thousands of humans, orcs, and fair creatures' lives. I have to try."

Rime dropped his gaze for just a moment before lifting his chin, grinning. "Well, then, here's to really pissing off our father."

Orion glanced at the Spring attendings—Winter's two invitations to gain proximity to the Summer Queen. For the first time, he actually felt like this plan might work. He just wished he knew if Ivy had been able to secure the Elven Council.

37

STARLESS OBSERVATORY

From the observatory, the forest rolled out like a green blanket in every direction, running into the cliffs and the sea to the south. Dark clouds rolled in, blocking the rising sun, promising a cleansing rain. Ivy kept watch, as she had since the predawn. The trusted guard, one of Lial's long-time sources, emerged from the tree line again and gave a signal. Ivy's heart sank, but she signaled back, and he disappeared again. They hadn't known the dryad portal location until one of the guards had spotted Mormaris six days ago, bolting into the forest. If he'd waited until dark, he might've slipped by unnoticed.

Ivy turned to the four advisers and Omasys. The six of them stood in the Celestial Observatory, located atop the palace's tallest tower. The open-air platform housed intricate, ancient telescopes and astrological instruments, including a gold and brass astrolabe atop a three-stair platform. As the sun had risen, the mathematical projections from the astrolabe against the night sky had faded, as they did each morning.

Only, today, as the images faded, both moons darkened—as the astronomers had predicted—and the portal opened. The astrolabe vanished and alabaster stairs appeared in its place, ascending into a mist in the sky. Frighteningly, the stairs extended out beyond the observatory structure, so if the stairs disappeared, one would plummet from above the tallest Nylen-n'or tower down to the unforgiving forest floor. Ivy shuddered at the thought.

Lyra caught Ivy's gaze, expectant, but she gave the adviser a brief shake of her head. Lyra's face fell, crestfallen, and the advisers' conversation quickly shifted.

"We cannot wait much longer for Emmyth to appear," Keyyarus said to the group.

"Lial and the others might have no other choice than to approach the queen with a partial council. Perhaps she'll still take your recommendation," Lyra said, though doubt dulled her words.

Mormaris had disappeared along with Ivy's wyvern, which had been a half-day walk from the dryad portal. His finding the creature was either a lucky coincidence or someone had told him. Either way, the loss of her wyvern was nothing compared to the gain of locating the dryad portal. Now they knew where to wait and watch for Emmyth's return. As soon as she portaled through, the guard would give Ivy a signal. The plan didn't even require anyone to approach or subdue Emmyth; the advisers just needed enough time to vote in another elf. A simple plan. But, of course, Emmyth never made anything easy.

The Summer Queen would arrive in the Accords at her leisure, but Ivy was certain that Orion had kept his word; he'd promised to arrive exactly two hours after the Trinth moons darkened, so less than a quarter hour after the portal appeared in his realm. She envisioned him in the Accords, waiting with the two Spring attendings. Would he still be there when Ivy finally arrived?

The longer Emmyth stayed away, the less likely Ivy was to

see him at all. She chewed her lip, tamping her short temper and sharp words. Now that the window for her to potentially see Orion grew near, so did her impatience.

Orcs entered the observatory, a unit of fifty, with Magdud at their lead. Her sullen group had arrived by boat yesterday and had stayed, along with two other units, crammed into guest rooms and tents near the greenhouse. Entering the observatory, Magdud acknowledged Ivy, speaking with her quietly.

"You did everything you could. I know you did." The orc's words were hollow comfort. "The queen will expect us to be waiting when she arrives, and then go where directed. I hope our paths cross again, Ivy Balrel."

With only two portal locations in Trinth, the orcs would be pouring back through Nylenn'or and Yllalen'al before dispersing to their positions throughout the kingdom. Ivy suspected the orcs would march to their wartime assignments without time for further goodbyes.

"Don't lose faith just yet," Ivy said. "I won't give up, even if this plan fails."

Magdud gave her a sad, strained smile. They both knew once the orcs were deployed and the Accords closed, the fae thrones would not call them back.

"On up!" Magdud shouted to her unit. They followed her, the alabaster stairs expanding to fit each row of warriors.

As they disappeared, Ivy's heart beat harder. With Magdud's every step, it felt like their chances were slipping away. Glancing at the advisers who were testing the bowl, she reminded herself that they had a plan. It would be played out. And they would come out victorious.

Behind Magdud's unit, Zel appeared. Ivy had talked with the gnome at length the day before, and his cure was almost ready. He just needed the last ingredient—the sapling; then he could concoct enough antidote for hundreds of Seekers. If he needed more, Ivy would bring bark from the Centennial the next spring.

"I must go, too," Zel said, his eyes glittering. "Orion promised to leave the sapling for me at the base of the tree inside the Accords castle. But I don't want any satyrs finding it. Who knows what silly game they might come up with, damaging the tree in the process."

"Be safe. I'll see you back here in Nylenn'or," Ivy promised.

Zel lumbered up the stairs, ready to find the last, living part of his old experiments.

Two more orc units followed Magdud, all headed to the Accords. Far more were entering through the Minerals land in the south, the location much closer to the orc's home. Magdud had warned that hundreds of orcs might congregate in the heart of the Accords, awaiting instruction.

Ivy kept watch on the forest, the guard returning periodically, repeating the signal that Emmyth hadn't been spotted. Ivy signed back, her heart sinking more each time. The advisers continued testing the water in the bowl, hoping it would work. It never did.

One of the Nylenn'or guards rushed down the alabaster steps, returning from the Accords. "The Summer Queen just arrived."

Tension rippled through the room, and Ivy tensed along with it. They needed all five councilors but they were woefully short. They needed Emmyth's seat.

"Send for Nym and Lial," Ivy said.

"No need," Nym-Emmyth entered the open-air observatory, running her finger down her amulet and dropping her glamour. "We're here."

Right behind her, Lial and Kolvar entered, their faces solemn. Kolvar was nearly always at Lial's side, which increasingly discomforted Ivy. Not completely confident in his allegiance, Ivy had asked Lial and Nym to keep the knowledge of the portal a secret. The advisers were only informed of its location hours earlier. Not that it mattered now. Emmyth hadn't returned.

"We must try to convince the queen," Lyra pleaded. "We cannot simply quit."

"She's right." Keyyarus gripped the bowl's edge.

"We need someone to wait here and send word if Emmyth appears," Daecyne said, his attention moving to Ivy.

Ivy hesitated. She missed Orion so terribly that her insides threatened to cave in. If she could only glance at him, she'd gladly take it. Still, the advisers didn't actually *need* her in the Accords. Not yet. "I'll stay."

Bellas emptied the bowl over the side of the observatory. While she stowed the vessel in a pack on her back, the other three checked the water flasks at their hips. Ivy watched their movements as if the tower were shifting, feeling sick about remaining behind.

"Meet in the castle on the second floor," Nym said, reminding everyone of their ultimate destination. When they arrived, petitioning an audience with the queen was the first priority. Queen Elowyn wouldn't receive the elves right away, of course, but even without all five of the council present, she would speak with the official representatives.

"I will join you soon," Ivy said, reassuring herself more than them.

Lyra's brows furrowed, and she spun to Omasys. "The advisers should enter the fae realm."

Daecyne huffed and crossed his arms over his chest. They'd had this discussion before, and it always devolved into arguments. Though the eldest advisers had traveled to the Accords, they only knew of one portal to the fae realm. They assumed the ley line entered the Summer Court, but none of them knew for certain.

"Guards from any court could be waiting for trespassers," Daecyne shot. "Or we could end up in Yllalen'al for all we know."

"The only real complication is if Emmyth decides to portal home after we ascend these stairs and leave Trinth," Lyra said.

"At this point, going to the fair realm is our best chance," Keyyarus admitted, frowning. "Ivy, give us an hour to get to the fae realm, vote in Nym, and return to the Accords castle. Meet us there."

Omasys nodded. "The castle is quite large, so I'll join you at the entrance and save you aimless wandering. When you meet with the rest of the Elven Council, they can vote you in, in the presence of the queen. We won't be denied."

Ivy looked from Omasys to the advisers, uneasy with the shifting, increasingly complicated plan.

"This can still work," Lyra assured them all.

"It is our only option," Daecyne grumbled.

Kolvar stepped forward. "I'll join you in case of trouble,"

Ivy's heart twisted, knowing her chances of seeing Orion were slipping further and further away. But she reminded herself that tracking down Emmyth was more important than glimpsing the half-dryad she had fallen for.

Nym gently squeezed Ivy's arm as the others moved to the stairs. "If I see your grumpy pixie, is there a message you want me to give him?"

Ivy paused, unsure of what to say. "Tell him that I miss him. And that I hope his dragon doesn't ruin his rooms with her smoke-breath."

Nym snorted. "Consider it done."

Omasys took the lead, hurrying up the stairs with Kolvar, Bellas, and Lial in the rear. Lial and Bellas gave Ivy a knowing look as Nym joined them. But, as usual, Kolvar didn't address Ivy, acting as if she was a piece of furniture. She'd hoped that he'd forgive her and include her once again, but she understood why he didn't. They'd chosen different paths. Still, it saddened her that things between them would never be the same.

Moments later, Ivy stood alone. Leaning with the half-wall against her hip, she didn't take her eyes off the forest. Could their plan possibly still work?

Emmyth had no way to know when the advisers would leave Trinth. So, she gambled everything on the timing of her return. Fearing that Emmyth would simply wait until after the Accords, they'd come up with a strategy to lure her out.

Lial arranged to vote in the new advisers tonight in an extravagant ceremony. Surely Emmyth would storm in before the public, decisive event. Obviously, their ruse hadn't worked. So, odds were, if Emmyth wasn't in Trinth, she was still in the fair realm. If the advisers hurried, they'd unseat her.

Heavy footsteps sounded on the spiral staircase leading to the observatory. Ivy glanced up, expecting to see servants or perhaps an astronomer. Instead, her mouth dried and her stomach dropped at the sight of the two intruders. The two orcs who'd hunted her through Unaria stepped into the observatory, both the statuesque female and the lean, deadly looking male. All hints of his injured hand and leg had vanished. Ivy's heart thrummed as her trembling hand reached for her knife. While she couldn't leave her post, she also knew she couldn't win against an orc.

She feinted to the left, hoping to throw them off, but then pivoted on her heel and sprinted to the alabaster steps.

~

Ivy barely approached the base of the stairs before the male orc lunged, cutting off her escape. He was fast—too fast—and she skidded to a halt, sliding slightly on the marble. His heavy boot stomped down right in front of her, blocking her path. Ivy's stomach twisted with dread. Her eyes darted for an opening, any way to escape, but the female orc had already circled around, trapping Ivy between them.

"I've been looking forward to this," the male orc snarled, his voice filled with bitter satisfaction. "I owe you for that little trick back at the tower."

"Remember," the female orc snapped, "we need her alive."

Ivy's heart pounded in her chest. She backed away, her knife drawn, a futile gesture. She was fast, but these orcs were relentless—and stronger. She quickly calculated her options, but the confined space of the observatory left her with little room to maneuver.

Just as the male orc raised his arm, preparing to strike, a powerful voice rang out. "Not so fast."

Magdud's presence filled the space as she strode down the spiral staircase, her footsteps purposeful and steady. Ivy's breath hitched, unsure whether to feel relief or dread. Was Magdud here to assist her, or had she come to help take her prisoner? The orcs hesitated for a brief second, just long enough for Magdud to insert herself between Ivy and the male orc.

"You're awfully far from your units," Magdud said coolly. "Care to explain why you stayed behind, hiding in Nylenn'or?"

The male orc sneered, his gaze flickering between Ivy and Magdud. "Our orders are none of your concern."

"You claim to follow orders." Magdud's eyes narrowed, but she remained calm. "Looks to me like you're taking a little too much initiative."

Ivy, still trying to catch her breath, felt a flicker of hope. Magdud hadn't turned on her—yet. But Magdud would sacrifice anything for her unit, including hiding any affiliation she had with a hunted elf.

"You're crossing the channel on behalf of a Minerals elf." Magdud glanced at the female orc, who shifted uncomfortably under Magdud's gaze. "Yes, I know why you're here. But did you know the Mineral elf you're bending the rules for is no longer in power? Lonsdaleite has been replaced by a Feldspar."

The male orc, growing impatient, lashed out, his arm sweeping toward Ivy. Magdud moved faster than Ivy thought possible, intercepting his strike with her forearm and shoving him back. The male orc stumbled, clearly not expecting such resistance from his own kind.

Rain began falling, turning the smooth, stone floor slick. Ivy took her chance. Darting to the side, she rolled behind one of the marble pillars, keeping low.

The female orc cautiously stepped forward, her eyes locked on Magdud. "We're not here to fight you, commander," she said, her voice steady but tense. "We just want the elf."

"It's 'captain,' now." Magdud stood her ground, her body a wall of protection between Ivy and the two intruders. "Ivy isn't your enemy. Trust me."

The male orc, undeterred, roared and charged again. This time, Magdud met him head-on, their bodies colliding with a thunderous impact. Magdud grabbed the male orc by the collar and twisted, throwing him into a nearby table. Celestial instruments scattered, crashing to the floor as the orc skidded across the wet marble, his boots slipping on the slick surface.

Ivy didn't waste any time. Using the rain to her advantage, she rushed across the slick floor, narrowly avoiding a strike from the female orc, who had turned her attention to her prey. Ivy ducked behind another pillar, her knife gripped tightly in her hand.

Crashing sounded from behind her as Magdud shouted,

accusing them of hitching a ride with another unit across the channel. But Ivy focused on the female orc. She watched Ivy's movements carefully, but didn't attack.

It dawned on Ivy that orcs trained in the desert, the one place in Trinth that rarely saw rain. Ivy waited for the right moment, then dashed forward, using the water to slide past the female orc's legs, slashing at the back of the orc's knee. She grunted in pain, stumbling forward, but didn't go down.

Lightning flashed in the distance, casting eerie shadows across the observatory. The male orc, finding his footing, lunged at Magdud again, but she disarmed him with a swift, calculated move, twisting his arm and sending his sword clattering to the floor. With one powerful punch, she sent him crashing into a marble pillar, leaving him dazed.

"Don't get up on my account," Magdud said, sarcasm lacing her words. "Looks like you need a moment. Or two."

The female orc's attention flickered to her companion. Seeing her chance, Ivy attacked, this time aiming for the orc's other leg. Ivy struck true, and the orc buckled, falling to one knee. But before Ivy could land another blow, the female orc raised her hand in surrender.

"I yield," she said, her voice low but resolute. She pressed her lips together as if she had more to say, but controlled her tongue.

Ivy's chest heaved as she took a step back, her heart still racing from the fight. Together, she and Magdud started tying up both orcs with ropes stored near the observatory entrance. Magdud, breathing heavily but still composed, put an extra restraint on the male orc, who groaned in defeat. Footsteps echoed up the spiral staircase, indicating that the Nylenn'or guards, alerted by the commotion, had finally arrived.

"Secure these two," Ivy ordered, and the guards moved swiftly, taking the orcs into custody.

"Dungeon now. Trial later," Magdud added.

"How did you know I was in trouble?" Ivy asked softly, gratitude flooding her.

"Is that a 'thank you?'" Magdud smirked, but continued. "While we were sitting around, waiting for the queen, I watched the portal entrance. When I saw the elven advisers and Nym hurrying by, I knew there was trouble."

"Well, I'm glad you were paying attention and returned to check on me."

Magdud simply grunted in acknowledgment. "I must go," she said, already making her way back toward the alabaster staircase. "As much as I enjoy kicking some arse and saving the day, I can't miss my appointment with the Summer Queen."

Ivy watched as Magdud disappeared into the mist, leaving her alone with the Nylenn'or guards and the subdued orcs. After gathering reinforcements, the guards escorted the intruders from the observatory. Ivy glanced out at the forest where the guard was waiting. Seeing her, he signaled that Emmyth hadn't appeared. Before Ivy could begin to gather her thoughts, scurrying footsteps on the portal stairs, caught her attention. Ivy pivoted, her hand on her knife.

Zel appeared, sweat beading his brow and no sapling in hand.

"What's wrong?" Ivy said, rushing to meet him.

"It's Emmyth," Zel panted, wide eyed. "I know what she looks like thanks to Ialant's glamour. I saw her in the Accords."

"It must have been Nym. She has the glamour," Ivy said, hoping he was wrong. "She might be wearing it."

He shook his head. "No, this Emmyth wore a cloak, the cowl pulled over her head. An elf or orc would not see her ... my height has its advantages. I walked right past her. She had no idea who I was—just another reveler. But when I saw her—" He smacked his forehead. "Oh, no. I forgot the sapling!"

Ivy darted to the ledge, but how could she alert the guard below that the spies were searching the wrong area? Emmyth wasn't coming through the dryad portal as they'd planned. She was hiding in the Accords.

"I must find Nym and Lial before Emmyth finds them," Ivy said.

"Go!" Zel gestured to the stairs. "You must find Emmyth, and I'll find the tree!"

Ivy nodded and sprinted up the stairs, headed straight for the mist beyond.

38

THE REALM OF THE ACCORDS

In a second-floor receiving room in the castle of the Accords, Orion and Rime waited, along with their guards and the Spring attendings. The air was cool, almost damp, with the faint scent of aged stone and decaying leaves carried in from the courtyard below. A servant had been commissioned to request an audience with the queen, but how long that would take in a place like the Accords was anyone's guess.

The castle's nickname, Labyrinth, suited it perfectly—walls and rooms shifted, creating a sense of disorientation. Every now and then, the soft groan of ancient stone echoed through the corridors as shifting occurred, a reminder to stay alert. The longer they waited, the more it felt as if the castle itself was watching them, anticipating.

From their shadowed position beneath the stone archway, Orion glanced over at Rime, his brother's face unreadable. Leaning against the doorway, the cold seeped through Orion's uniform, and a low draft from the hallway carried with it the smell of rain, though none had fallen. The anticipation weighed on them both, hanging as thickly as the stone itself.

Just steps from the balcony that ran the length of the castle, Orion could gaze out over the courtyard, a mixture of anxiety and determination swirling inside him. The circular castle, grand yet decaying, formed a protective ring around the heart of The Realm of the Accords. The courtyard below pulsed with a kind of heavy, worn energy. His eyes lingered on the tree at its center, a towering sentinel that dominated the space. Its branches hung low, like the arms of a weary giant.

An elder Winter guard spoke up, "I can't believe how much the tree has changed. Before the war, the leaves were a vibrant orange, and the bark was black. Not a rotting black, but vibrant and deep. When the sunlight hit the bark, it reflected a golden shimmer."

Now, the leaves looked sickly and discolored, like dying embers turning a lifeless grey, blending with the dull bark of the trunk. The breeze barely stirred the limp foliage; the whole tree appeared more like a statue than a living being.

"Realms change. Trees die. It's the cycle of life," Rime said.

Orion frowned, noting the time line. He suspected the change was directly related to the war or perhaps the way the Gathering Tree had been mistreated. He dropped his attention to the burlap bag he had brought. It still sat at the base of the tree, waiting for Zel. Had the gnome not received his message? Zel needed the sapling inside the bag, so Orion figured the gnome would be one of the first creatures through the Nylen-n'or portal.

The expansive courtyard circled the ancient tree, paved with weathered cobblestones that had seen countless generations. Cracks ran through the stones like veins, hinting at the creeping decay that mirrored the state of the castle walls. Moss and lichen had claimed the cracks, and ivy took the rest.

Other fair creatures wandered about the courtyard, divided into two groups. Most from the fair realm skipped about without a care, laughing and smiling as they rushed about, before spilling into the meadows and forests beyond. The orcs bore expressions of worry and resolve. On the higher floors, they gathered to make war plans, the air thick with a sense of urgency.

A familiar figure caught Orion's attention; Ivy skulked through the courtyard. His breath caught in his throat, and for a moment, the world narrowed to just her. It had been three weeks—three long weeks—without knowing whether she was safe or if she'd accomplished her mission of unseating the Council. Now, she was right there, moving through the courtyard. His chest tightened painfully. His heart surged, an unstoppable ache spreading through him. Why was she alone?

She moved with an unnatural tension, the furtiveness of her steps gnawing at him. Something was wrong. His mind raced, pulling him deeper into a spiral of panic. Had she failed in Nylenn'or? Was she in danger? She looked smaller than he remembered, more fragile, and the sight of her prowling the grounds alone sent his heart hammering. All of these thoughts flashed through his mind in a moment, and before he could react, his spy, a Winter centaur, clipped forward, stopping in front of him.

"Lord Orion, elves have been spotted entering the Summer portal," she said, her eyes somber with the cold wisdom of her kind. Her sleek, white coat and silver mane shimmered in the afternoon light, blending seamlessly with her light armor. "Nym and her brother, Kolvar, stayed here in the Accords."

Before he could ask for more detail, a Summer fae servant with yellow wings approached Rime. His vibrant attire of greens and golds reflected the splendor of the Summer Court. He bowed slightly to both brothers, "Queen Elowyn Seral'Az of the Summer Court is prepared to see you now."

Rime nodded, but Orion's attention slid back to the courtyard, searching for Ivy. Had the elves succeeded in unseating Emmyth? Orion had a sinking sensation. If events had gone smoothly in Trinth, Ivy would be looking for him, readying to address the queen together. So, something had gone wrong.

Rime followed his brother's gaze and sucked in a sharp breath. "We can't delay," he said, barely subdued urgency in his voice. "The queen awaits, and our presence is required."

"Honor requires us to ensure the whole Elven Council can approach the queen," Orion said.

"Maybe Ivy isn't the elven choice for the council seat. Have you considered that?"

Orion shook his head. "We can't risk it. We've staked too much on this for us to stand back and watch it fall apart."

"I've done my part, too." Rime shuddered, and Orion thought of Wirenth.

"We've all done hard things," Orion said as Ivy disappeared through an archway into the labyrinth. He shot off instructions to his spy and the guards before turning to his brother. "You take our Spring charges to greet the queen. Don't rush. I'll join you as soon as I can."

Rime grabbed his brother's arm, "Ivy is perfectly capable of taking care of herself. I tricked Selleth into giving up her position as representative, giving us the opportunity *you* desired. Tell me I haven't made a mistake."

Movement by the tree grabbed both their attention. Zel had finally arrived, barely keeping from under hoof. A group of satyrs was practically running him over ... as they were being pursued by a vicious cluster of pixies.

"Do all your friends have impeccable timing?" Rime asked sarcastically.

"We still need him," Orion said, shaking his arm free of his brother's grip. "I'll be there, at the queen's door. I promise."

With that, Orion jumped onto the stone railing. Then, lifting his wings, he dove for the tree.

39
CLASH OF STEEL

Ivy moved silently through the main floor of the Accords castle, her eyes scanning the dimly lit hallways. The vast, echoing spaces were eerily quiet, except for the sounds of orcs stomping up and down the upper stairwells. Besides the occasional open chest, dusty table, or spider's web, the derelict stone rooms were empty.

The other fair folk had vacated this lower level, opting to explore the hillsides beyond, away from the tense affairs of the queen and the orcs. Ivy held her knife at the ready, every sense on high alert. Suddenly, she caught sight of a cloaked figure slipping through a doorway. The figure moved with a familiar fluidity, and Ivy's heart skipped a beat. Emmyth.

She quickened her pace, closing the distance with a few graceful leaps. The last time Ivy had encountered Emmyth had been right after the councilor had literally stabbed her in the back. As she rounded the corner, Ivy called out, "Councilor!"

The figure paused, then turned to face her, pulling back the cowl to reveal a sharp, calculating smile.

"Ah, Ivy. I wondered when you'd catch up," Emmyth's voice

dripped with condescension. The medallion around her neck glowed against her skin, a menacing reminder of her authority.

Ivy tightened her grip on the knife, her muscles coiling. "I didn't want to attack you from behind. Only a truly insecure fighter would stoop so low."

With a sudden burst of speed, Ivy lunged. Emmyth sprung to meet her, their knives clashing in a flurry of sparks. The two elves danced around each other with incredible speed, their movements a blur of silver and light. Emmyth's experience showed in every calculated strike, but Ivy's determination wasn't easily cowed.

Ivy managed to land a shallow cut on Emmyth's arm, but the councilor responded with a swift kick that sent Ivy stumbling back.

"You're outmatched, Ivy," Emmyth taunted, her eyes gleaming with a predatory light. "Just give up."

Breathing hard, Ivy shook her head, her resolve only hardening. She only needed to keep Emmyth in one place until the advisers figured out the councilor wasn't in the fair realm.

Ivy aimed a swift slash at Emmyth's midsection, but the councilor parried with a fluid motion, redirecting Ivy's blade harmlessly to the side. Emmyth countered with a sharp thrust towards Ivy's chest, forcing Ivy to twist and deflect the blow with her forearm, feeling the sting of the near miss. Ivy danced back two steps, out of reach, reminding herself that she just needed to sidetrack Emmyth in this realm long enough for Omasys to find the advisers.

Lunging forward, Emmyth's knife grazed Ivy's shoulder, drawing a thin line of blood. Ignoring the pain, Ivy spun and aimed a slash at Emmyth's side. The councilor shifted just in time and the blade caught Emmyth's cloak. The councilor twisted out of the away, Ivy's knife shredding through the fine material.

Emmyth unhooked her cowl, letting it drop. "I've been a step ahead of you, even before the Gathering."

"I admit, fleeing to the fair realm was a clever move," Ivy replied, keeping out of Emmyth's reach. "Even so, we were able to swap out Mormaris."

"I knew you'd go after the voting bowl." Emmyth's lip curled into a wicked smile. "So, I let you steal it by assigning weak guards."

"You laid a trap," Ivy said. "You let me win, but didn't make it too easy. Otherwise I would've been suspicious. Still, I did wonder why you left Mormaris behind. It was almost like you *wanted* him out of the way. But, he wouldn't be your first betrayal, would he?"

Emmyth blinked, a flash of concern, before she snarled, baring her teeth.

"Mormaris was a fool to trust you," Ivy spat, "especially after you betrayed your own daughter."

Emmyth leapt, springing to an impressive height as she spun mid-air, her face twisted with rage. She raised her elbow, ready to deliver a punch to Ivy's face. Before the blow could land, the door behind Ivy burst open. Between Ivy shifting aside and the distraction, Emmyth landed next to Ivy, her punch impotent.

Nym, Lial, and Kolvar stormed in, their expressions a mix of shock and horror. For a moment, everything seemed to freeze, the tension crackling in the air.

Then Kolvar jerked forward, shoving Lial aside, the force sending him sprawling to the floor. Kolvar followed up with a swift kick to his old friend's ribs, barking a command, "Stay down!"

Nym clutched at her chest just as the room erupted into chaos. The walls of the castle screeched a warning before they *moved,* forcing them all to pivot and face off against each other at the same time, while Lial gasped and crawled just far enough to avoid being crushed. Ivy found herself facing Kolvar, trying to push aside her rising emotion as easily as he'd tossed aside his friendships.

"I don't want to hurt you," Ivy said, her knife slick with sweat in her hand.

"Then surrender," Kolvar said as pulled a short sword and lunged. Their blades flashed as they circled each other, Ivy struggling to defend herself against his longer reach. Emmyth and Nym fought nearby, their weapons striking with deadly precision as they argued. In her periphery, Lial struggled to find his feet.

"Kolvar, check your medallion!" Emmyth shouted, her voice tinged with panic.

Kolvar shoved Ivy back as he pivoted away, Ivy's chest heaving with more heartbreak than physical distress. She'd given Kol every opportunity to show his true allegiance. Which he had—to Emmyth and her corruption. His choices tore at her, especially knowing how much he'd soon regret them. Kolvar grabbed a Tides medallion from his pocket. In his hand, it glowed. But dimly.

"What's happening?" he gasped.

"No, it can't be ..." Emmyth's shock was palpable.

Seizing the distraction, Ivy darted forward, her knife glinting as she closed the distance between herself and Kolvar. With his attention still on the fading glow of the medallion, Ivy aimed a quick slash at Kolvar's wrist, disarming him. He reacted too slowly, the knife slipping from his grasp as he flinched in pain. Ivy didn't hesitate. She followed up with a sharp kick to his knee, forcing him to stumble backward.

Kolvar endeavored to regain his footing, but Ivy dropped and swept his legs. Losing what little balance he'd gained, Kolvar crashed to the ground. From behind, Lial pounced, pinning his old friend with his knee pressed firmly against his chest. Ivy grabbed Kolvar's arms and forced them above his head, securing them, as she tossed Kolvar's knife to Lial. Lial pressed the blade against Kolvar's throat in a warning. Kolvar struggled, but Lial's grip was unyielding.

"Take your own advice and stay down," Lial said, his voice low and fierce as Nym continued the fight with her mother.

"We found the rune, Kol," Ivy hissed.

Kolvar froze, his thrashing stopped. Still clutched in his hand, the medallion's ethereal glow vanished.

"When the advisers voted for Lial in the dungeon, Bellas suspected something was wrong with the ripples in the bowl," Nym said, her breathing fast as her knife clashed with her mother's. "She discovered the rune on the bottom of the bowl within hours. That night, she explained the rune to Lial and me, and we agreed to keep Kolvar seated as the councilor, letting him believe we had no idea he was using Lial as his puppet. We even kept it a secret from the advisers until last night."

"You lied to me. To your sister. To the advisers," Lial said to Kolvar, pressing the knife a fraction closer to his skin. "But, once we'd figured out you'd taken your mother's side, we realized we could use your duplicity to our advantage."

"We left you for hours in your rooms, hoping Mormaris would approach you," Ivy said, keeping Kolvar's hands pressed against the stone floor. She had hated the lies, but they had to know for certain how far Kolvar would go. Every step he took closer to the old council broke her heart a little more. Fighting him today had ripped away the last vestiges of their innocent youth, replacing it with a something dark and oily. "We needed you or Mormaris to send a letter to Emmyth, tempting her back. We simply had to provide a plausible threat in Nylenn'or. New advisers did the trick."

"Predictable to the end," Lial said, disgusted.

The medallion sat lifeless in Kolvar's hand, his body limp, defeated. Ivy wrestled it away, and tossed it to Lial. At his touch, it immediately glowed brightly. Just as much as Emmyth's still did against her chest.

With a strangled cry, Emmyth leapt, moving in for the kill, her knife aimed at her daughter's throat. For a terrifying moment, Nym froze. Finally, she threw herself to the side, but the blade grazed her flesh. Though Emmyth missed taking a fatal strike, she had bought herself space. And a direct path to the door.

Emmyth bolted, mere steps from escaping. Nym rolled to her feet, blood trickling from the shallow wound, starting after her. But was barred at the doorway; a figure appeared, blocking her exit. Ivy gasped, recognizing the form. Her heart thumped in response, immediately drawn to him.

Orion stepped forward, wearing an official Winter uniform and his wings flared, just as Emmyth attempted to skid to a stop. She spun, ready to dart away, but Orion was faster. With a fluid, almost effortless motion, he gathered the shadows from the room to him, disappearing.

Emmyth's jaw dropped, her attention flicking about the room. He could've closed the distance between them and restrained Emmyth, but he simply reappeared, blocking the side door along with her escape. Ivy quickly took in his broad shoulders and confident stance. He didn't even need to fight. His presence was lightning in a bottle.

"Lord Orion," her eyes narrowed as she scanned the royal crest splayed across his chest to his face, "is the Unarian guard from the Gathering." She stepped back, grinding her jaw.

The knife twitched in Emmyth's hand. Ivy jumped and grabbed the councilor's wrist, twisting it until her knife clattered to the ground. She slammed Emmyth against the wall, pinning her there with one arm. "It's over, Emmyth."

Behind her, Nym closed the distance. Ivy's heart pounded, not just from the fight, but from seeing Orion after weeks apart. The stern determination, his impeccable timing, the fact that he'd found her at all; his appearance reminded her why she had fallen for him.

Emmyth struggled, but Ivy's grip was ironclad. She couldn't help how her heart swelled at his arrival. Even in the chaos, he exuded calm. A warmth spread through her chest, a reassurance at his presence. Emmyth glared at him, but her words were for them all.

"A war with the humans is inevitable, and your decisions today will end fair folk lives tomorrow. You're naive to believe anything else."

Orion leaned in, his expression cold. "You have bought your own lies with false gold." He turned to Nym and Lial, "According to ancient records in the Winter archives, Trinth belongs to the humans. I can prove it."

The room buzzed with a tense but victorious energy. Orion looked at Ivy, his eyes softening. She nodded, letting him know that she was fine.

Emmyth's defiance faltered as she realized the futility of her situation. Ivy tightened her grip slightly, ensuring the councilor understood the seriousness of her predicament. With Emmyth secured, Ivy looked back at Nym. "Are you all right?"

"Don't worry about me." Nym wiped away the blood with the back of her hand. She strode over to her mother and snapped the medallion's chain from Emmyth's neck.

For a breath, nothing happened. Then the medallion began to glow.

Emmyth jerked forward, but Ivy held firm. Then, pained, pinched her eyes closed, her body tense.

"You can't be surprised," Ivy said, letting her sarcasm help her cope. She wondered if Nym and Lial knew where the advisers had tucked themselves away in the Accords while they voted. "You watched Kolvar's medallion dim. Of course they'd swap you out next. Or are you surprised at their new choice? I personally think Nym will do wonders for the Tides."

"What do you mean *I will do*? Faux-Emmyth got a lot done in a couple of weeks." Nym smirked. "By the way, Orion. Ivy told me to tell you that she *misses you*." She emphasized the last words and heat rushed up Ivy's neck. "And she hopes that Ash doesn't ruin your rooms with her smoke-breath."

Ivy internally groaned and wished she could slither away. Thankfully, before Nym could continue, a centaur clopped into the room, her eyes widening as she spotted Orion situated next to two restrained elves.

"My lord," she gave a slight bow. "Rime is waiting at the queen's door. And he's not pleased."

"Not pleased?" a familiar voice boomed. "He's fuming!" Magdud pushed past Orion and into the room. "I can't leave you for a moment." Magdud threw her arms into the air. "My unit received orders, and I emerge to find Rime mad enough to turn this entire place into a cyclone. And Lord Orion missing."

Ivy started to explain when Magdud stopped her. "We're headed back through Nylenn'or. I'll have my unit *deposit* Emmyth and check the orc 'visitors,' before we ship off. Will we be required to ship off?" She shot Ivy and Orion a serious look.

"Go," Ivy said to Orion. Although her heart longed to follow at his side, and she could barely take her eyes off him, he still had his part to play. If they had more time, he could tell her his exact plans and strategy. Assure her that his father was, indeed, tricked into coming to the Accords. For now, she just had to trust Orion.

40

QUEEN ELOWYN SERAL'AZ

Orion flew toward the massive receiving room where the queen awaited. In the distance, Rime stood, speaking with a Summer fae official in his stuffy green and golden uniform. Flying harder, Orion landed at his brother's side.

Rime fumed. "You convince me to take over, to be assertive. To stand up to Selleth. Yet you bend to Ivy's every need and leave me dangling like the last leaf in autumn."

"I'm here, brother," Orion assured him. "I told you I'd return, and I did."

"Cutting it *very* close," Alion mocked from behind them.

Ignoring the comment, Orion and Rime entered the queen's temporary receiving room together. Inside, the queen stood on a small dais, allowing the entire room to observe and hear her every instruction. Prince Devain stood at her side, along with a handful of Summer fae guards and two orc captains.

Behind the queen, massive open windows overlooked the rolling mountains of the Accords. The derelict stone walls were webbed with cracks, but the castle had existed since ancient times and would endure long after Orion died. The only other exit was a small side door with a brass latch. After Winter bowed to the queen, Orion signaled to the guards to usher the Spring fae forward.

"Queen Elowyn Seral'Az," Orion said, "We are returning your attendings after their attack on a witness under our protection in the Winter Court."

The queen bristled, hearing their accusations spoken aloud.

"King Eldrin judged them to be misdirected and, in hopes of gaining future favor with the queen, has delivered them unharmed," Orion continued.

Alion and his sister, Alyssum, approached the queen. Discreetly, she asked them questions, too quietly for Orion to overhear. The Summer Queen was not talented with spotting glamours, so perhaps she was verifying their identities. Hearing the familiar clip clop of hooves, Orion turned to see the centaur with Lial, Nym, and two other elves speaking with the Summer official at the door.

Glancing up, the queen gestured to allow the elves to enter. With a flick of her hand, the queen signaled for the Winter delegation to stand to the side.

"Rude," Rime muttered to Orion. "Apparently, she requires an audience to showcase her conversation with the elves. She must think she can humiliate the new council. This should be entertaining."

Despite Rime's teasing, the back of Orion's neck pricked a warning. While the queen exuded calm, Eldrin's children knew better. No one gained a crown except by great sacrifice—usually not their own. The council was ready for a confrontation, and if all went well, the queen would be furious. Orion surveyed his exit routes.

"We are here to present a unanimous decision by the full Elven Council," Nym said, speaking for the group of four elves, "We recommend that the fair folk sign an armistice, officially ending the war. The humans believe a truce has already been authorized, a misrepresentation on our part."

"But you are *not* a complete Council since Ialant died," the queen said, "I cannot take the recommendation without a full Council."

"We have already endorsed a new Seeds Councilor." As Nym spoke, Ivy entered the room.

Though he'd just seen her, Orion could hardly breathe. He could fly to her in a heartbeat. Could take her in his arms. Could brush the wayward hair from her face. Kiss her freckles. Whisk her away.

He reigned in his thoughts. They'd agreed to see this plan through. For now, Orion rooted himself to the floor, though his attention never left Ivy. Once she was voted in, the queen couldn't deny the council's demand to end the war. After that, they only needed the approval of the Winter king—or his official representative. Orion grinned, envisioning Ivy achieving her goal, gaining respect for herself, and saving two realms from bloodshed.

"We will vote her in right now, if it pleases the queen." Without waiting for actual permission, Nym continued. "Who votes for Ivy Balrel?"

Prince Devain stepped forward, his face stern. "Your vote will not work. Councilors do not have the authority to vote in a fellow councilor. Just as advisers vote in the Tides and the Minerals representatives, ambassadors are meant to vote in a new Seeds representative."

Gneiss spoke up. "In the case that no Seeds Ambassadors are alive, the councilors are next in line to conclude the vote."

Devain continued, his voice calm. "But one Seeds Ambassador still lives."

The elves looked at each other in confusion. Ivy's attention flicked to Orion, as if looking for assurance that she'd heard

Devain correctly. Orion caught her eye, his heart twisting, wishing he could explain.

Prince Devain strode to the side door and opened the brass latch. Through the door appeared Ambassador Wirenth, holding the sapling, with Zel right on his heels. Of course the gnome wouldn't let that tree out of his sight, and Orion was grateful for his vigilance.

Without explanation, Wirenth wrapped his wrinkled hand around the small trunk and spoke Ivy's name. Several of the elves let out sighs of relief, and Nym clasped Ivy on the shoulder, grinning.

Ivy lifted her chin and addressed the queen again. "The full Elven Council recommends the war be officially ended."

The Summer fair folk gasped and the orcs near the queen looked dumbfounded. Whispers began, but before they grew into shouts, Orion stepped closer to Ivy, and spoke up.

"I have records from the ancient scribes reflecting that Trinth belongs to the humans. Alysatraee only intended for elves and dryads to ever reside in the human realm, no other fair folk."

The Summer Queen frowned, but quickly hid her expression behind a mask of calm. "But there is no proof that Ivy holds the true power of the medallion. The Seeds have only one, unfortunately. Where is it?"

Nym paled, and she exchanged a look with Ivy before they glanced at Orion. He fought to keep a neutral expression, though his heart leapt.

"It's too bad Ivy doesn't have the Seeds Medallion to show her authority," Rime said as he inspected his nails.

Orion had noticed the extra weight in Ivy's bag, but only when he'd washed it had he discover a treasure sewn into the side. From his pocket, Orion drew Ialant's medallion. He tossed it in the air, the metal glinting as it turned end over end. Ivy caught it with one hand, lifting it high, the metal glowing at her touch.

Orion couldn't help the wide grin on his face, his heart soaring. He hardly believed the plan had come together to select a new, unified Council. Everything Ivy had worked for—hoped for—it was real.

Nym gripped Ivy's hand, a fierce grin on her face. Lial wiped his eyes, and the Minerals hugged. The mood of the room shifted, like a wave, favoring the elves. A wind blew through the windows, carrying leaves from the tree fluttering through the room, as if Alysatraee herself were celebrating.

Now all they needed was for the queen to agree and then, as the highest authority, allow the elves to address the Winter representative.

"Everyone," The queen said, this time not hiding her anger, "get out. I'll finish this discussion with the elves, alone."

The voices immediately hushed, and several servants fled out the doors. Prince Devain stepped to his mother's side, arguing, too low for Orion to hear.

"You have no idea how painful it was to ask Devain for a favor," Rime muttered under his breath. "You owe me."

Devain wouldn't be the worst person in which to be indebted, but Rime had elevated his brother and the elves above of his own desires. He'd sought out Devain and requested that the prince not only protect Wirenth, but to sneak him into the Accords. And, surprisingly, he'd agreed.

Summer guards marched toward anyone lingering. Zel scampered off with the tree, giving Orion a brief nod with the Seeds ambassador right behind him. Wirenth paused and spoke quickly to Ivy, his face assuring, before he left as well. The queen glowered at her son, flipping her wrist, dismissing him.

"Wait," Devain shouted at the Summer guards closing in on Winter. He stomped away from his mother, rushing to stop another skirmish. "I will escort our Winter guests to the portal. It's the least we can do."

Ivy's eyes fixed on Orion, and his entire being shattered. His bones seemed to crack, leaving him helpless. How could he be so close and not be at her side. Not touch her. Not console her. His entire body ached with regret. She blinked, almost frozen in indecision. If she called to him, he would rush to her, whatever the consequences. But she gave him only the slightest nod.

This was not over. They'd devise a different plan to enable the new council to gain an audience with Winter authority. Ivy had done her part; he had to do his. Orion straightened, pretending he wasn't broken inside.

The Spring warriors shot Rime and Orion smug expressions, but before they could leave, Devain stopped them. "You'll join with me and ensure we get Winter safely from this realm."

Alyssum dropped her chin, a wicked grin forming. "Nothing would delight me more."

The Winter guards quickly marched out, anxious to put distance between themselves and Spring, who were sauntering behind.

Outside the queen's receiving area, Orion, Devain, and Rime marched side by side. Behind them, arguing voices arose between the queen and the elves.

"I was afraid this might happen. And with your permission, we'd like to move on to 'plan B,'" Orion said to Devain.

"At this point, I'd say it's at least plan C. Maybe F," Rime said.

"Bringing Wirenth was one thing. He had every right to be there, and the ruling queen had not commanded I *not* bring him," Devain said. "But what you're asking ..."

Orion watched the Spring fae move down the steps. They'd all be to the portal just outside the castle in no time. Alion glanced back at Orion, giving him a withering glare.

"The queen didn't command you to do anything with us," Orion pressed. "You offered to take us to the portal. She didn't ban us from returning."

Devain grinned. "You make a decent point."

Rime sighed. "So, I guess you're going for round two with the queen?"

"I mean, what do I have to lose?" Orion asked. "My position. My title. My court's respect."

"I was thinking more along the lines of your *life*," Rime muttered. "I really don't want to take you home in the form of burned up ashes today."

41

A WINTER REPRESENTATIVE

The chamber in the Accords castle felt heavy with tension. Ivy could hardly believe they'd overcome every obstacle, only to have the queen order Winter away, including their representative. The queen would be forced to agree to end the war, but without Winter's swift approval, how many years of battle would unfold in Trinth? Only the new elven councilors remained, their expressions reflecting a shared sense of frustration.

Lial, his blond hair still a little mussed from his scuffle with Kolvar, continued their planned presentation. His voice, usually so confident, now carried a note of resignation. "Both our realms and the human world will suffer if we continue down this path."

Nym's blue eyes flashed. "There is no reason for a war. And as we've unanimously presented our plan, you are required to sign a peace treaty."

The door opened, and Prince Devain entered, followed by a Spring warrior. Ivy's heart sank, recognizing Alion. Her discomfort was immediate, a tight knot forming in her stomach. She remembered all too well his unprovoked attack at the Aequus.

Without Winter guards, what would stop him from further violence?

Devain's presence brought little relief, knowing he'd waited far too long to stop his own attendings from lashing out. Ivy couldn't shake her unease as she watched Alion. Though the Spring scowled at the other elves, he avoided looking at Ivy completely, as if she wasn't worthy of even a drop of attention.

Lial continued, "We urge the Summer Queen to follow the law and recognize our recommendation."

Queen Elowyn sighed, though even that was regal and imposing. "I recognize and honor the Elven Council's recommendation."

Gneiss grinned at the queen's words. The Summer ruler had officially acquiesced, agreeing to stop the war.

The queen continued, "Both courts must agree to end the war. Unfortunately, the Winter king never appeared. I will visit him myself and present our information."

Ivy's gaze shifted to the prince and Alion, who still refused to meet her eyes. Instead of agreement with his queen, his expression shifted to contempt before a mask slid into place, hiding his reactions.

Ivy's frustration boiled over. "Rime acted as the representative. He can speak for the king. Surely, we can call him back."

The queen's response was measured. "Summer will comply with the elven request for peace. But I cannot shift the law on behalf of both courts. While you might not appreciate it now, there are good reasons that Winter and Summer are afforded the opportunity to deliberate separately. I recognize your authority, but the recent elven upset and other questionable actions in Trinth deserve inspection before ensnaring Winter to do your bidding."

Nym's jaw dropped, mirroring Ivy's shock at the queen's absurd response. Her snobbish reply was nothing more than a thin excuse for fair folk greed. For a brief moment, Alion's attention flitted to Ivy, and his expression softened. The change was so unexpected that Ivy nearly faltered. What game was he playing now?

Gneiss stood and shouted, her voice filled with righteous anger, "Alysatree would never approve of this. The fae courts are completely corrupt. With a wave of your hand, your guards could fetch the Winter representative and have him back in this room in a snap. Don't think we don't know you're avoiding your duties."

The queen sighed, as if she were dealing with annoying younglings. "Unfortunately, I'm sure the Winter contingency is back in their realm. To send guards storming into King Eldrin's land, demanding his son, would be quite inappropriate."

Prince Devain interjected, his tone supportive of his mother's words. "But if the Winter representative were here, our queen would allow him to join her on the dais, I am sure."

"Of course," the queen said with a demure nod.

Suddenly, Alion's figure shifted, as dark shadows swirled around him. Ivy's eyes widened as the glamour fell away, revealing Orion. Gasps echoed through the room as he stepped to the queen's side.

"Orion," Ivy whispered, her heart pounding.

His gaze met hers briefly, the corner of his lip quirking upward before he turned to the queen. "How very fortunate that I remained behind. I am the official representative for the Winter Court."

The Summer Queen's eyes narrowed, displeasure clear on her face. "Prince Rime was assigned as the representative. Only he can speak for the king. This deception will not stand."

Orion remained calm. "I was the representative, with my brother, as my attendant by my side. Devain can confirm this."

Prince Devain put a hand on his chest, in mock surprise.

"What an outrageous trick." His voice was painfully flat, as if he had memorized this response, word for word. "I cannot believe you dared deceive the queen. You let everyone presume your brother was the representative, using assumptions to get you to this point. Very dastardly."

The queen's jaw tightened, her gaze settling on her once-golden child. Devain gave every indication that he didn't rebel against his mother in any way. Like Bellas, he was a rule-follower to his very core. But he'd clearly turned a blind eye to Orion infiltrating the meeting while glamoured.

"Where are my Spring attendings?" the queen asked, her voice tight.

"They are safe, though a bit tied up at the moment," Orion replied.

"But they did confirm that Orion is the official representative," Devain said, relaxing a bit. "Moreover, Mother, remember that Orion is a recognized son of King Eldrin. He has every right to represent the Winter Court."

The queen's expression hardened, but she couldn't deny the truth. She turned to Orion, "Your father will be furious. Are you sure this is the path you wish to take?"

Orion strode from the queen's side down to Ivy. He took her hands in his and kissed her fingertips. A shiver ran down her spine at the warmth and familiarity of his touch. Then he turned to the queen, his voice resolved.

"As the representative of the Winter Court, I concur with the Elven Council and with the Summer Queen," Orion said. "The war is officially ended."

The air shifted, and Ivy's ears nearly popped when a scroll appeared between Orion and Elowyn, hovering in the air. No hands touched it, but the parchment unfurled, gold filigree writing appearing, glinting in the light. Quills appeared, waiting, drifting toward the queen and Orion. Orion quickly walked to the scroll. Plucking the quill from the air, he winced.

"We sign in blood," Elowyn remarked, her voice cold as she stood next to Orion. She, too, grabbed a quill, her face frighteningly calm. She signed her name, and Orion signed next to her, crimson signatures at the bottom of the scroll. The tension that had hung in the air dissipated, replaced by a surreal assurance.

Outside, thunder sounded, yet no clouds marred the sky. A few distant cheers arose from the fields at the spectacle in the sky, even the creatures playing in realm recognized something significant had happened. The scroll rolled itself up and disappeared with a *pop,* the quills vanishing from Orion's and the queen's hands.

A wave of relief and joy washed over the room. Lial's face broke into his old, familiar smile, and the elder Mineral's eyes sparkled with tears of happiness. Gneiss let out a triumphant cheer, her earlier anger now jubilation. The elves embraced one another, a palpable sense of victory encircling them.

Orion's gaze never left Ivy's as he returned to her side and grasped her hands. The connection between them stronger than ever, Ivy's heart swelled. How much he'd risked, Ivy could only guess; she never would have asked this of him, but he'd given it freely. And because of him—because of everyone's sacrifices—they would have peace.

Amidst the celebration, the Summer Queen's face twisted, her lips pursing. She turned abruptly, her robes swishing as she stormed out of the room. Her departure barely registered with the councilors, who were caught up in their moment of triumph.

Devain clapped Orion on the shoulder, a look of respect in his eyes. "Well done, Orion. But, if you'll excuse me, I must go and smooth things over."

"The queen is right," Ivy said as Devain disappeared

through the doorway. "Your situation could be difficult in Winter for a while."

A soft smile played on Orion's lips. "Eldrin just needs time to cool off. Besides, with the Trials coming up, his attention will soon be elsewhere," he said, his voice filled with tenderness. He ran his fingertips across her cheek, and Ivy leaned into his touch, feeling a warmth and comfort she hadn't experienced in weeks. "Until the king calms, I plan on spending all my time in the human realm."

Ivy reached up and wrapped her arms around him, an even bigger smile forming on her lips. But her celebration was cut short as a centaur rushed into the room.

"We must go," she said, pointing to the large window.

In the distance, parts of the mountains began crumbling away to dust. The double new moons were emerging from their shadows in the human realm. The Accords would, once again, disappear.

Omasys burst into the room. "The portal to Nylenn'or is crowded with creatures. Everyone is in a jovial mood, especially the orcs. But anyone who doesn't leave soon will die when the realm collapses."

The councilors grabbed their things, their earlier joy tempered by the realization that their time was running out. Orion grasped Ivy's hand tightly as he rushed to the room where Wirenth had been waiting. There, she found her old satchel. Hastily, he guided her out to the center balcony surrounding the ancient tree.

He wrapped her in his arms and launched them both into the air. They flew above the aging tree and ruinous circular castle. She glanced down, taking it all in. Deep down, she knew one day she'd return. Now that Seekers were not hunting her and the war had ended, she'd be able to live her life.

Orion flew her to the Nylenn'or portal, and a sense of calm

settled over her. They had achieved a great victory, and she had hope for a bright future. Ivy wrapped her arms tighter around Orion, watching as fair folk rushed from the outer portions of the realm and closer to the castle. Others disappeared through the portals, back to their respective courts.

"In upcoming Accords, many of the orcs will be moving back to the fair realm, their true home," Orion said. "Will the elves assist in overseeing the migration of fair folk out of Trinth?"

"We'll set it right, exactly as Alysatraee's records indicate," Ivy said.

"I trust the new Elven Council," Orion said, pulling her in closer.

The distant meadow began to crumble, and Orion dove down to the portal to Nylenn'or. Their feet landed on solid ground before they both rushed through the archway.

42

SIMPLE JOYS

Orion stood near the base of the Stormbringer Mountains, the snow-capped peaks towering above. The crisp spring air carried the faint scent of pine and the distant roar of waterfalls. The sun bathed the landscape in a golden light; the snow glistened like diamonds, though lower on the mountains, trees and plants budded with green life.

He had waited for four days, knowing Ivy was somewhere in the mountains at the eleven Centennial. Each day was an eternity, the anticipation building with every passing hour. Ash, his little dragon companion, had been his only solace. She fluttered around him in lazy circles, her scales shimmering in the sunlight. Occasionally, she would land on his shoulder, her tiny claws gripping gently as she nuzzled his cheek affectionately.

Ivy and Orion had spent almost every day together since the Accords. They both had apartments in Carrus, and Orion was the new Captain of the Guard, appointed by the very grateful and relieved magistrate. Magdud allowed Orion and Ivy to travel extensively without complaint. Besides, if anyone could keep peace and order in the captain's absence, it was an orc in a human glamour. Magdud had requested permission from King Eldrin before extending the offer to Orion, of course, because she refused to risk gargoyles invading her town.

The king had agreed to the appointment, which Orion appreciated. Even though his father was angry, Orion knew he was impressed with what his son had accomplished. He'd allowed Orion to keep his title, but he'd revoked his position. With that act, his father signaled that Orion wasn't welcome home, at least not yet.

Rime had promised to send a note as soon as their father's boiling anger had simmered. Then, Orion would return and make amends. The dismissal of his father stung, more than he wanted to admit, but Orion had already decided that he couldn't depend on fickle love. He wanted to build a life in the human realm with Ivy. She'd never dangled her affection as a prize he had to earn, and he loved her for it.

Still, he anticipated a future visit to the fair realm. He desired a relationship with his father, if he would allow it. And he wouldn't abandon Rime.

Orion chuckled as Ash darted off, rapidly flapping her wings. She flew toward the trail that wound down the mountain, her keen eyes catching something that Orion had not yet seen. He felt a surge of hope, his heart pounding in his chest.

Straining his eyes, Orion spotted a figure in the distance, moving swiftly down the trail. His breath caught in his throat as the figure came into focus. Ivy was running toward him, her long brown hair streaming behind her like a banner. The sight of her filled him with a wave of joy so intense it almost brought tears to his eyes.

"Ivy!" he shouted, his voice echoing off the mountains. He broke into a sprint, closing the distance between them. Every step felt like a release, each stride bringing him to the elf he loved.

As they neared each other, he could see the joy and relief on Ivy's face, mirroring his own emotions. Ash darted in circles above them, reflecting his excitement. Orion's heart pounded seeing the huge smile on her freckled face.

When Ivy was still several feet away, she leapt into his arms. Orion caught her and spun her around. He buried his face in her hair, breathing in her familiar scent of linden trees and rain.

"Ivy," he murmured, his voice choked with emotion. "I missed you."

Ivy replied by tightening her arms around his neck. She lifted a hand, running her fingers through his hair, finding the willow twigs.

Ivy leaned back, taking his face in both of her hands and kissed him squarely on the lips. He relished the familiarity, that she knew everything about him and, amazingly, still sought him out.

Orion set her down gently, his hands still holding her close as he kissed the freckles on her cheeks. She ran her hands across his rough forearms before looking up at him with her big brown eyes, her expression bright. For a moment, they just took in the sight of each other, the mountains around them a perfect backdrop to their reunion.

"Tell me everything," Orion said, taking her hand and meandering along a trail that led to a vista he'd discovered earlier.

She lifted two vials tucked into her tunic, seeds resting inside. "Fifty seeds. Plenty to last me until the next Centennial." Her smile grew larger, and she pulled a new, blue box from her satchel. She held it up, pulling Orion close, to capture their images for the future. "I want to remember this moment. Returning to you."

Orion leaned down, and Ivy kissed his cheek. Nym had already unearthed and returned the blue box Emmyth had stolen; Ivy had tucked it away months ago. Clearly, now she was ready for a fresh start, making new memories.

"What was the mood like, knowing that all the old councilors and their conspirators are all serving sentences for disobeying Alysatraee's laws?"

The offenders would eventually be transferred to the fair realm to serve out their sentences. The councilors, including Mormaris, would live out their natural elven lifespans, no longer extended by the gifts of the seeds. Though some the lesser involved elves, like Kolvar, would be allowed to return to Trinth eventually.

"Initially, many were confused. Maybe a little angry," Ivy said. "But Wirenth spoke on the first day, before guiding us in receiving our seeds. He was such a calm, steady hand, explaining Alysatraee's deeper laws. She allows all her children to exercise agency, even our leaders. Elves could have demanded a change, like Brecc had urged. But we'd blindly supported the council and the Mother honored the elves' choices. Many tears were shed and difficult conversations shared, but in the end it was cathartic. I'm looking forward to the next Centennial."

"When will we visit Nym and Lial?" Orion asked.

"Nym gave me extensive notes with the safest times to cross to Nylenn'or," Ivy grinned. "She really doesn't want me 'making myself sick' by riding a wyvern. All the Houses agreed to work far more cooperatively going forward."

Ivy had relished recent opportunities to travel in peace, on her own schedule. She and many other elves had been assigned to comb Trinth in search of Seekers, and many had been found and healed of their corruption. Each week they'd encountered fewer and fewer Seekers, and Zel felt confident in a lasting cure. Their original ailments returned, but whatever the humans' future's held, it was better than the corrupted lives they'd been living.

"I want to take you to Neidrei on our way back to Carrus," Orion said, squeezing her hand. He'd hired the best craftsman in Trinth to make Ivy a proper bow and arrow, one fit for a councilor.

"I guess a stop by The Tree House is in order," Ivy said.

The new Elven Council had explained to all the fair workers in Neidrei that they'd all been deceived, but only Ivy had remained with them for nearly a month; the one stretch that she and Orion had spent apart. Ivy and the workers had formulated a plan for the future, one that didn't include poisoning humans.

Orion guided her into a cluster of trees. Just steps beyond, the mountainside gave way to a gorgeous view of the land below and the sea in the far distance.

The landscape drew her attention as she contemplated. "The Council will be quite busy making adjustments. Not only are we assisting with the many fair creatures in Yllalen'al as they move back to the fair realm, but the elves' lifestyles will change as well."

Ivy had already visited the southern elven city, at Gneiss's request, to help announce the relocation to the fair realm. The process would span several decades. For the four days that Ivy spent helping Gneiss, Orion had visited his dryad sister, revealing everything that had happened.

"Elves will no longer be separated from each other," Ivy continued. "Many will move to the woods in central Trinth. All the elves must spend time among humans—we must understand and have compassion for those we protect."

Then Ivy blinked and turned back to Orion, a smile spreading. "But, do you know what I look forward to most?"

"Building a sprawling, interconnected city of tree houses in the deep woods?" he teased. Orion wrapped his arms around her, pressing his palm against her back.

Ivy laughed, but it caught, emotion in her voice. "I've realized I love sunrise strolls in the Carrus woods, piles of pancakes with strawberries, evenings at the tavern while surrounded by friends, and a really comfortable chair for reading." Ivy nestled closer. "It's been so long since I've been able to stay in one place without fear. These last few months ... I think my nerves are finally settling." She paused. "Small joys are underrated. I want more sweet moments."

She gazed up through her dark lashes, tears lining her eyes. "I want them with you."

Orion kissed her forehead, pulling her closer again. With one hand, he reached into his pocket, but didn't find what he was looking for. Glancing up at the sky, he scowled.

Ash swooped down, landing on his shoulder, her chin lifted as if she hadn't done anything wrong. Orion cleared his throat, narrowing his eyes at the dragon. Finally, she tipped her nostril into her pocket and pulled out a ring.

Noticing what Ash held, Ivy's eyes widened. The ring was fashioned from petrified wood with a ribbon of inlaid amber. Dryads, including his sister, had actually crafted it using a secret method.

Orion plucked it from Ash's jaw. "Magdud stated that she's only tolerated our 'ridiculousness' because she is expecting a 'fabulous' wedding in the main park near the forest next summer. She's already planning."

"She knew you would propose?" Ivy laughed.

"She assumes a lot."

A tear escaped, streaming down her cheek, yet she giggled and stepped back, holding out her hand. He slipped the ring on Ivy's finger, and it magically shifted to fit her finger.

"When I lived in Unaria," Ivy said, admiring the ring, "I

never would've guessed I'd be standing here, completely in love with the frightening captain of the guard." She gazed up at him, smiling.

Orion wiped the tear and then kissed her cheek. "I'm looking forward to living a million, underrated moments with you, Ivy."

He wrapped his arms around her again, and she did the same, knowing what was next. He spun and leapt, soaring off the mountainside. They fell together, weightless, before his wings unfurled, catching a draft, pulling them upward.

Beholding the forest and Neidrei, a dot in the distance, Orion let his heart fill with every happy emotion. And he burned the moment into his memory, as only a Winter could do, never to forget.

EPILOGUE
THE ROYAL VISITOR

Rime trudged through the streets of Carrus, the light from the double moons enough to help him navigate through the quiet streets. At the wide doors of the massive municipal building, four guards kept watch. From a distance, Rime gave the signal, a double tap to his shoulder. One guard stepped forward and dropped her hood, Magdud. Though anyone who didn't know her glamour would observe just the human magistrate.

She pushed open the doors, leading him inside. Lit sconces sent shadows dancing along the stone carvings set on both sides of the room, twisting their faces in grotesque expressions. During the day, several humans worked here, but in the night, only two guards stood watch on the opposite end of the massive room, next to the shiny black doors.

"Timing between realms is always such a bother," Rime said.

"You could've asked one of your astronomers for assistance," Magdud said. But by her smirk, she knew he couldn't ask for help without revealing he was sneaking off to Trinth.

"Your message was vague," Rime said, hoping his assumption was correct and that Magdud had found a potential champion to represent him at the Trials.

"Per you request, I've kept my ear to the ground, seeking one strong enough to make a good showing. And not die."

Rime had planned on asking a Winter fae to fight for him. Someone who would see it as an honor and not demand a favor in return. But once Selleth had announced her champion, the few who'd hinted at their interest soon changed their minds. Rime figured it was for the better. Most fae would rather stab him in the back at the first opportunity for gain rather than show any real loyalty.

As they approached the guards, Magdud signaled, and they opened the heavy doors with low grunts. The magistrate fell silent as they advanced through the stone chamber. The walls shone black like obsidian, but with a band of a phosphorescent mineral that threaded overhead, casting the entire space in an eerie, green hue. They passed several doors constructed of wood, their occupants muffled, until the doors turned to iron. Rime's stomach churned. He expected Magdud to find him someone with fair blood and by her meeting location, he assumed her selection was not an upstanding citizen. But observing the metal doors was a stark reminder that Magdud had unearthed a criminal to be his champion. Someone dangerous.

Rime straightened, reminding himself that he didn't care as long as this fair creature was loyal to him and could fight. Magdud stopped at one of the doors and pivoted to Rime.

"Once we're in the cell, we can talk freely," Magdud said.

"Who is this creature you've found?"

"A half-elf. A recently healed Seeker who cannot seem to stay out of trouble." Magdud paused. "Even with her mind cured, she's reckless. You should know, she was one of the

Seekers who hunted Ivy last year, right here in Carrus. Ivy's friend released dozens of seeds, but not nearly enough for all the Seekers. This one is scrappy; she got a seed and lived. She might not look like much, but she's a survivor."

"But will she be loyal?"

Magdud shrugged. "Ask her."

"Can I trust her response?" Orion was always good at spotting liars, but where was he? He'd abandoned Rime, his own blood, for some elf who'd aligned herself with Selleth. Rime frowned, but stopped himself from complaining. It was a waste of breath.

"Find out for yourself." Magdud pressed her hand in the middle of the door four times, triggering it to slide open.

The pair walked in, and the half-elf bolted up from her mat on the floor. The room reeked of sweat and sewage, but Rime didn't bother commenting on the obviously disgusting state of the cell. The elf backed up against the wall, her legs bent as if she were ready to leap. Her limp hair stuck on one side of her face, her scrawny arms and legs visible in the short, sleeveless shift she wore.

"Are you sure we have the right cell?" Rime asked. Even if this half-elf pounced, he could easily defeat her.

"Elfling, tell our guest about yourself," Magdud said.

The half-elf scanned from the open door back to the magistrate. "I don't know why I'm in here. I told your judge already that the vendor obviously wanted to gift me the necklace because they placed it in my hand."

"For you to try on, as you'd requested," Magdud said. "Besides, jewelry has gone missing regularly from the vendors, stemming from the time you were healed. If you tell us where the pilfered items are, we'll release you."

She's like a hoarding little dragon.

"You're trying to pawn off a little troublemaker, not a champion," Rime said, spinning on his heel to leave.

"She's fast and intelligent," Magdud snapped back, stopping him. "If you use the next two years in Trinth, you can train her. Transform her. She won't win, but she won't lose, either."

"Win what?" the elf-girl asked.

With his back to the elf, he rapped his fingers against the cave wall. Wasn't Magdud offering him exactly what he'd requested? Sure, Magdud was getting rid of a pesky criminal in the process, but maybe this deal could be good for both of them.

"Have you heard of the fair realm and the Winter Court?" Rime inquired.

She gave him a slow nod, her lips tugging into a frown. "The Trials for the crown are already here?"

"In two human years, yes," Rime said, impressed that she'd heard of the contest. Then again, the prestigious event would be known across both realms. "I'm looking for a champion to represent me."

She stepped closer, scrutinizing his face. Her breathing quickened, and she rasped a response. "I will never represent a fae, especially not in some sham of a competition for the crown." She reached out and brushed his cloak, probably a finer material than she'd ever touched before. "I'm not a pawn for your kind and never will be."

"See what I mean?" Magdud asked. "She is not fae, but she's far more straightforward."

Rime sighed, the back of his throat growling in annoyance. He'd wanted to know if the elf could be loyal, and he'd gotten his answer. Shaking his head, Rime exited the cell. Even if she agreed, he wasn't sure he was inclined to train her as a champion anyway.

"Give it back, elfling," Magdud said from behind him.

"He won't miss it," the elf said.

"Very funny."

Rime turned in time to see Magdud smirk and something small and shiny flying through the air toward him. Reacting, he caught the object, the metal *thunking* into his palm. Opening his fist, he realized he was holding his ring—and this one was his signet with the family crest. Did she know its importance?

"I was going to give it back," the elf insisted. "It was just for fun. Obviously, I don't want him returning for it later. I never want to see his smug face again."

Magdud groaned and followed Rime into the cavernous hallway. "Selleth must be pleased about your situation. No champion. I'm sure she'll torment you when—"

"Princess Selleth?" the elf bounded forward, pressing her hand to the invisible barrier trapping her inside her cell. "You're not aligned with the princess?"

The very opposite, in fact.

He slid his ring back on his finger, perplexed at how he hadn't even noticed that she'd lifted it. "The princess and I have a complicated relationship."

"They're not aligned," Magdud interjected. "It could even be said that for the duration of the Trials, they will be enemies."

"Wait!" The elf chewed the side of her nail, the other hand still pressed against the barrier. How she knew about the princess, Rime didn't know. But then again, Selleth was a Winter royal. If her elven parent knew anything of the fair realm, she could've heard stories about Selleth. Maybe she knew enough of the princess to stay away. She was the most openly vicious royal in all the courts.

"If I fight for you, I could humiliate the princess?" the elf asked.

"Potentially," Rime responded, but his sister had already signed a contract with a capable, very ambitious orc. All bets were on Selleth. Chances were, no one would make a fool of her. But then again, anything was possible.

The elf slowly dropped both her hands to her sides and lifted her chin. "I'll be your champion."

"And you'll be loyal to me?"

"As long as I can humiliate Selleth, we're aligned."

Magdud gave Rime a sidelong glance, then turned back to the cell. The elf should learn his identity before she puzzled it out on her own. He couldn't afford to screw up his choice of champion, so he might as well be honest before they struck a bargain.

"Princess Selleth is my sister," Rime admitted, wondering how she'd react to the news.

"Family is complicated. I understand that well." Her expression darkened. "As long as you won't stop me from mortifying your sister, I'll fight for you."

"What is your name, elfling?" Rime asked.

"Callium," she said. "But you can call me Calla."

Ivy and Orion are getting their happily ever after, but if you want more in the Alysatraee realms, be sure to find out what happens to Calla and Rime in the Winter Crown Trials in "Winter Throne and Trials," coming January 2026!

Follow Kristin J. Dawson to receive book announcements >>
Amazon
Bookbub
Subscribe to her newsletter for insider news and exclusive giveaways!

Acknowledgments

I had my biggest "behind the scenes" team of helpers for this duology, and I'm so grateful to each and every one of them. Abby J. Reed was the phenomenal developmental editor; not only did she help refine the overall story, she was also wonderfully specific about where to add more emotion. Paul Tallman came to the rescue (again) when I wanted to elevate the story—his creative, magical insights always add sparkle to any writer's plot. Thank you to my persnickety copy editor, Kathleen Gooch, who attacked the story with her red pen.

Big thank you to my brilliant beta reader, Jessica, who has been with me on every story after my debut novel. And to my sister, Kimber, for her eagle eye on the final manuscript. And thank you to my BBQ writing besties for your encouragement!

The Deranged Doctor team created another incredible cover for this series.

And, finally, thank you to my team at Oliver Heber Books, including my editor S. E. Welfonder and proofreader Dan Hilton!

ABOUT THE AUTHOR

Kristin loves chocolate(*quality* chocolate, because ... life is short!), research (I know, I know, who loves research ... *raises hand*), English movies (especially with my mom or my sisters), and reading fantasy novels (by Jeff Wheeler, Melissa Caruso, J.K. Rowling, and ... a thousand other great stories with fun characters and lots of tension!).

I was born in L.A., grew up in Utah, spent a short stint in Bristol, England, then ended up in the Pacific Northwest. I've been here ever since!

Note: When Oregonians say, "I live in the country," they're not talking about living near cornfields or cows. They're talking about the woods. The woods! (I know, it's not like the farmer stories I grew up with, either.)

Also by K. J. Dawson

Epic Fantasy Adventure

The Unchosen Omnibus

-female protagonist with a massive character arc

-cunning female mentor

-kingdom-ending stakes

-magical linguistics

-sweet romance

Unravel the mysteries, secure the smartest alliance, win the crown